First And Only

Tim Paul

CHAPTER 1

"Wake up, baby."

Thomas touched its shoulder. It was still warm from being inside its mother, though the pink skin was becoming whiter.

Baby Lady had cleaned off most of the fluid from the baby's face and body. Some of it lingered in the thin black hair on its head. Spots of puffy redness decorated one cheek. Its eyes were sealed shut.

"Time to wake up." Thomas was using his sweet and quiet baby voice, the one he used around Joy's little brother who was born only months ago.

He knew it was his sister. Baby Lady had made the gender announcement moments ago. Thomas had been peeping through the bedroom door. There were enough bodies in the room that obscured his view of his mother during the moment of birth. And then there was another commotion immediately afterward, though Thomas had not understood the cause of the crying. He was oblivious to it, attention instead directed at the sister.

Joy had Ricky and played with him more often than Thomas. Newfound jealousy spat at her in rejecting their normal playtime. Now he was happy to have his own sibling.

"Wake up," Thomas said more loudly, though his voice was still small compared to the chaos next to him on his parent's bed.

Baby Lady needs to clean the eyes better so she can open them.

He stood at the side of the bed and watched the baby girl lay still on a white towel with other towels covering most of its body. The Baby Lady turned her head briefly and hissed at him to move away.

Thomas did not obey. He touched the shoulder again, moved it slightly. He was confused. The skin was soft, but the baby moved with the stiffness of a doll.

"Why doesn't she wake up?"

There came more hisses for him not to touch the child.

Too busy to intervene herself, the Baby Lady yelled some naughty words in Ilocano at Thomas' father.

1

Ted came from the other side of the bed and lifted Thomas into his arms. It wasn't until Thomas saw that his father was crying that the frantic postpartum work of Auntie Rowena and Auntie Annie assumed some significance. From over his father's shoulder, he could see the two women sopping up blood and discarding a purplish colored glob with a long tube that lead to his sister. Their clothes were painted in red smears. He couldn't see his mother's face, but he could hear her crying too.

They were outside in a matter of strides

"Daddy, the baby is out, but she don't cry. Why don't she wake up and cry? Auntie Annie needs to turn her upside down and spank her butt to make her wake up and cry."

"Hush, Tommy."

"But I want to play with her now. She is out."

"Babies aren't toys, Tommy."

"Can I show her to Joy?"

"No."

"It isn't fair. Joy plays with Ricky all the time."

Thomas' father kept walking and brought him to the river. He saw the worry on the man's face. Ted chanted to himself a mantra of no more babies, it isn't worth her life, no more babies.

"Daddy?"

Ted turned his face, jaw quivering. He reached into his shirt pocket and produced a pack of cigarettes. With a flick of his wrist, one slid out of the packaging and into his mouth.

"Are we going to put her in the ground by the tree like the other ones?"

Ted hid his face in his hands, smearing dark red on his cheek, ears and hair.

"That's what we do to babies that don't wake up. Right, Daddy? We put them in the ground near the tree."

"Tommy, hush. Please, hush. Be quiet for awhile."

A little flash of a lighter and Thomas could smell the cigarette. Between puffs, Ted continued to mumble that there would be no more babies.

Thomas was quiet, but not still. He dug a bare heel into the dirt, making little mounds, eyes darting across the river. That's where Joy was and he missed her. With no babies and no Joy, he would be all alone.

CHAPTER 2

DUA

"Get it."

"No, you get it."

It sat on a stem, not nearly as tired from the pursuit as its pursuers. Decorated with green and yellow and tiger stripes, the dragonfly clung sideways onto the plant with its tiny hairy legs. It casually fanned its four long wings.

If Thomas had not seen it land, the insect could have easily escaped, invisible amidst the hectares of flooded rice paddies with evenly spaced green sprouts poking their heads above the surface of the murk. Thomas knew its eyes were fixed on him, waiting for him to pounce again so that it could dance away from his swiping hand.

"Get it for me," Joy urged again. She seemed to have much less murk on her than he did.

"No, I'm tired of this." Thomas panted, kneeling several paces from the insect. The dragonfly stopped moving its wings. It was baiting Thomas again.

"Can't you do anything for yourself? I've caught enough of them for you."

"You don't catch them right," she complained. "You're supposed to catch a dragonfly with your hand while it's flying, not smack it dead with your hat."

Thomas groaned. There wasn't time for this. There were a dozen paddies yet to be planted. He was behind schedule and he didn't want mother to hire Aris and his crew to finish the work. That drunkard didn't deserve any more pesos than he was already getting from Joy's father to manage the small Lapez mango grove.

"But if I catch it, then how is that good luck for you?"

He regretted asking the question, even before the answer came. There was a convoluted rationalization of a superstition coming.

"Wait… I can transfer the good luck to you by handing it over."

Joy turned her head from watching the dragonfly and smiled. "That's right."

Thomas rolled his eyes. "I'm starting to think like you now. It's not even the right superstition. Catching a dragonfly isn't good luck."

3

Before the superstition could be corrected, Joy leapt from her crouch in the tall grass and followed the dragonfly.

Twisting.

Stepping.

Jog.

Stop.

Turn.

Like a jerky waltz. All the while she managed to avoid stepping in the paddy, tepid pools of mud and manure

These were Papa Justo's fields near the river, flanked by Wagner lands and Botalico kin on the other. Stripped trees acted as crooked posts to note the property lines. This was the best land for rice near Calamba.

Joy clawed futilely in the air.

"We're already halfway to Pingaping. Let it go. We'll find a different one."

"No," she protested. "This is the first one I saw today. That's extra luck."

"You're just making things up again. I don't know where you get these notions. I just got you to stop pinching your nose in the wind to keep it from becoming flat. Now this."

Thomas stopped trying to chase the dragonfly, simply trotting to keep up with Joy instead. Even in the cooler temperatures of the Cordillera Mountains, the sun broiled those in its sight. The peaks were brown in the distance. Calamba and its *barangays* were settled in one of the flat valleys that dotted Abra Province and made it more amenable to agriculture than some of its neighboring mountain provinces.

Sweat, heat from the tropical sun and repeated washings in the river had eroded Clay Aiken's face from the front of Joy's pink T-shirt, which now clung to her back.

Thomas paused his pursuit to remove his sweat-soaked shirt, leaving it hang inside out by the collar around his forehead.

"Put your shirt back on. Why do you insist to walk around without a shirt and keep your skin dark?"

Joy instantly regretted issuing the complaint because she lost sight of the flying insect. Funny that she should complain since her hat flew off long ago.

"I'm in no danger of being elected president of Kenya," Thomas retorted.

The color of his arms contrasted dramatically to that of his chest. Thomas had never seen his skin become its lightest. The Philippine sun kept his skin as dark as everyone else around him. Only baby pictures—in black and white, though—and stories from his mother held confirmation that his skin could even be lighter than it was.

He had a Filipino's body, thin with well-toned muscles. Brown hair, not black, that seemed to lighten in the sunlight topped his circular face. Almond eyes sparkled when he laughed. His nose was perfect, not as flat and wide as his Filipina mother's and not as long and narrow as his American father's.

Westerners would notice him as Asian.

Asians would think him as Western.

"I'll put my shirt back on if you take your's off," he said with a sparkle of amusement in those almond eyes.

"You'd like to see that wouldn't you."

"I have seen that."

"I was a kid then, that doesn't count."

"You're still a kid," Thomas said, gesturing in the direction of the dragonfly.

"It is over there? Come on."

Pink shirt, pink shorts and pink flip-flops trotted anew, in the direction of the Abra River, which flowed through the northern Luzon province of the same name.

Joy's body was still very childlike. She lacked the shapely figure of town princess Nina Justo. The straight black hair stretched to her lower back so it could hide the flaws of narrow hips and small bottom. There was nothing Joy could do about the flat chest and the flat nose. She could only be thankful that her nose wasn't as wide—and ugly—as Amelie Valera or mouth as big—and ugly—as Marites Galope.

"Don't you dare try to put that skin lightening cream on me when we get back," he warned.

"You're more handsome when it is whiter."

"You don't want me to be more handsome. Remember the fit you threw last week when Jon-Jon and Ronaldo were discussing the pretty college girls in Baguio?"

Joy cries over anything, but never prolonged unless something was disturbing her. She'd stared at Thomas tearfully for days with worried lip-biting pouts over the possibility of someone else turning his eye. Then she scolded him for transgressions he'd not committed, and could not possibly commit for another week.

It was disheartening to Thomas that she thought she was replaceable. Joy Lapez was aptly named. She was his joy. They met at birth, laid together in the same bassinet while their mothers gossiped. They were playmates as toddlers, sweethearts in school, not yet lovers, though there had been prior ill-timed advances on one another's virginity.

Joy was standing near a narra tree, gesturing for Thomas to quicken his pace.

They really were halfway to Pingaping. Thomas could see the river and the signature bend that led to the ruins of the old church over the next hill.

"Hurry up. It's on this leaf."

"Then grab it."

"I can't. It's too high. You can see I'm the shorty one."

Another subject that would send her into fits. Say nothing about height. Don't mention the nose. Notice not the lack of curves. Thomas had a quip in his head about her calling on Clay Aiken to help because he's taller, but kept it unspoken.

Thomas saw the dragonfly perched on a low hanging branch. He was tall enough to reach it with a small leap. It crawled off the leaf and onto the branch, turned and seemed to stare at him.

"See. It's just trying to make a fool of me again. The moment I take a step toward it … gone." Thomas removed his shirt and twisted the damp fabric. He intended to use it as a weapon to smash the bug. "I've had enough of you."

Joy grabbed his arm. "Please, this is important, *ayat*."

Ayat was love in Ilocano, the regional dialect. Thomas pursed his lips at her obvious attempt to bend him to her will through the use of his most intimate nickname.

He stared into her eyes and could see that it really was important. He knew her well enough to see that there was something else going on inside her head, a notion that went beyond possessing some good luck charm. But there wasn't time to unravel the mystery.

He regarded the insect and came up with a quick plan of attack. He knew he couldn't net the thing with his shirt, though that would be easier, because that would somehow negate the luck and that was the entire point of the exercise. But the shirt could come in handy for a distraction.

Thomas coiled, wiggling the shirt in his left hand. He jumped with both hands in the air, the shirt landing behind the fly and the other acted as a cup to block its escape. It worked. The dragonfly was in his grasp as soon as it launched itself from the branch.

Thomas smiled a hero's smile once he landed. The fly was buzzing its protest in his hand.

"There. Got it. Now I'm going to squish it. No, throw it against the tree. Make me run all the way out here…"

"No, don't kill it. You have to give it to me now."

Joy had an eager face, left hand palm up. Thomas grabbed the wrist to steady it, turned his hand down and released the insect to her possession.

"I got it," she cried in exhilaration. Her demeanor changed quickly to surprise. "Oh, yuck! It's buzzing in my hand."

She let it go.

Thomas howled.

She wiped away the offending bug cooties on her shirt.

"You're right. This is good luck. That's the funniest thing I've seen in a week."

Joy slapped Thomas on the arm to curtail his laughter.

He pointed at the green insect flailing on the dirt. Now only one wing was working.

"What happens if you maim the insect after capturing it?"

Joy shrugged. "We caught it, that's the important part."

"We?" Thomas crossed his arms.

"Yes ... *we* ... I'm the one that chased it to the tree while you were walking so slow and moaning about going back to work."

"Of course I was moaning about it. There's work to get done. It has to get done in the daytime. I can't plant at night."

"You don't like to spend time with me?"

"I can spend all night with you..."

"Fine. I'll help you catch up."

"You don't even plant rice in your own fields. It'll take longer just to show how to do it right."

"Just because father has me busy in the house cleaning everything and cooking for everyone doesn't mean I don't know how to plant rice. I even remember the song—*planting rice is never fun, cannot stand, cannot sit, cannot rest for a little bit.*"

Joy's sing-song sent Thomas back into a chuckle.

"You haven't planted rice since the snake bit you. You'll be too paranoid to get anything done."

"I won't," she proclaimed. "I'm not scared of snakes anymore."

"You can't fool me. You're scared of everything. You can't even hold a bug in your hand for more than a second."

Joy crossed her arms and stuck out her tongue. "You never let me win an argument."

"Let you? What kind of victory is it if I let you? Victory is earned, not given."

Joy narrowed her eyes and produced her best bratty little sister face.

"Stay just like that. You should have snappy comeback by tomorrow."

Thomas darted through the tall grass, across the uneven terrain and dove into the brown river. It was a relief to be cool. As it was not the rainy season, he was able to find the bottom and stand on the smooth rocks. The pace of the water was slow, but refreshing.

Joy moved closer to the river, but did not join him. Thomas sent a splash in her direction at the water's edge as an invitation.

She stuck out her jaw. "I thought you had work to do."

"I thought *we* had work to do," he countered.

"See." Joy picked up a rock and lobbed it. "I can't win an argument and you never let me have the last word. You've always got a comeback."

She tossed a rock and it plunked into the water to join its brethren, but nowhere near Thomas.

"Who am I going to talk to while you're gone?"

"Reggie and Car-Car."

"That's gossipy stuff. I can't really be myself around them, they don't tolerate me like you do." She looked dejected. "We've only got a few more days together."

"I'm only going to college. Stop acting like I'm never going to see you again. It is only Baguio. That's a few hours by jeepney and Jon-Jon will always take you. And I'm coming home every second weekend to check on mother and the farm."

Thomas waded out of the river. He mistakenly anticipated that this scene would happen closer to his departure. And she wasn't going to be placated by words.

He'd still not had enough time to unravel the notion behind catching the dragonfly. It had nothing to do with good luck, that was obvious. He combed the water out of his hair and padded his way toward her.

Joy wrapped her arms around his waist and buried her face into his wet chest. She was the perfect height for this embrace. The top of her head came to the tip of his chin.

"*Ayat*, what will I do without you?"

Her hair smelled of Cream Silk. Pulled back into its typical pony tail, Thomas ran his fingers through the long lengths. She melted into him further.

"I can't help but act this way. It is hard enough living here. How am I going to do it without you? They've already turned me into the maid, the cook, Ricky's *ya-ya*. There'll be a constant droning of Mr. NBA basketball star in one ear and criticism of my *pancit* and adobo in the other. At least having you here makes this place tolerable."

Before Thomas could say anything, they heard a "Hoy, Toe-mas!" from the other side of the river. Their brief solace was interrupted by farmers. Dark brown men under tan thatched hats walked along the trail there. Thomas waved back. He knew them all. He knew everyone in the valley because the Wagner farm had the only plow tractor in proximity.

Joy dislodged herself from Thomas. "Let's go somewhere else," she suggested, annoyed by the interruption. "Come on. The hideout."

Joy started her stroll along the rock bed toward the old church.

The farm hands smiled wide at what they were watching. It wasn't proper to have affection displayed in public, even though it was Joy and Thomas together, which was like seeing blue with sky and green with trees.

"If I catch you doing something disgraceful, I will cripple you and stick you in a corner for the rest of your life," Emma Wagner once threatened her son upon discovering the youngsters kissing. Since then, they resorted to more remote areas for their private moments. The most frequented was the abandoned Catholic church.

The replacement church in Calamba was much less attractive than its predecessor in the countryside. It lacked the Spanish architecture. Instead it was cinder block and mortar like most of the houses in the poblacion—the municipal center—sturdy enough to withstand the typhoons that marched occasionally across the Philippines. Yet, the old one never seemed to have a problem with the storms, other than the two old trees that had toppled into its side. Thomas never knew the old church in its heyday; it had been abandoned long before his birth. The cemetery remained, however, full of nuns and priests and townspeople who'd passed away decades to a hundred years ago.

Joy ducked inside. The sun at mid-morning height illuminated a wide swath of the inside, shining through the gouge in the side and ceiling. Thomas stuck to the shade. Joy was circling the walls, no doubt searching for reptilian residents.

The insides were unrecognizable as a church. It was devoid of any religious symbols. The stained glass windows followed the church's relocation into the center of Calamba town. Looters long ago raided the structure for its doors and wooden flooring. It was a dirt floor under a vaulted ceiling.

It was secluded. It was cooler. It was their most treasured hideaway and playground.

"Some of our things are still here," Joy said from the far corner. "Cups, a plate, those old towels."

Thomas and Joy were technically on Botalico land now. Members of that family owned land intermittently spaced from the church to the edge of Pingaping. Most people avoided crossing the Botalicos, partly for reverence, partly for fear. They had such strong ties to the rebels that defended these mountains, first from the Spanish, then the Americans, then the Japanese. With Thomas' mother being Emma Botalico Wagner, it made his presence barely acceptable if discovered.

Thomas was a mistake, the result of an indiscretion 17 years ago. Employed on the American base at Subic Bay as a clerk, Emma met a tall, blond medic at the twilight of his military career. Like so many Filipinas there, she fell for the G.I. Joe in uniform. But unlike so many of his peers, Staff Sergeant Ted Wagner married his Filipina when he found out about the pregnancy. To the amazement of many, he chose to settle in the Philippines in his retirement, buying one of the Botalico households and setting up a home near Calamba. But he died seven years ago of lung cancer.

Most of Emma's family remained unhappy that she chose to marry the American. What became lacking in the companionship of her family, she found in Rowena Lapez. Joy and Thomas met as sleeping infants through Rowena and Emma's constant commiserating.

"Come here," Joy said.

Thomas was enjoying the shade. "I don't need to see those things. I remember carving those bowls out of husks after we ate the coconut."

"Not that. Come here."

There was something different about her voice. Thomas wondered what she was planning now. "If you want me to eat a Toko lizard while standing on my head, forget it."

Joy was sitting where the shade was darkest.

"I can't see anything."

"That's okay. I have nothing really to show. I don't have a chest, just big *tingy-tingy* sticking out from tiny bumps."

"Joy …?"

"You asked me to take it off," she said, nervously.

Thomas' eyes adjusted to the limited light. She was situated on one hip with her legs tucked around her. He saw her gently cast aside her T-shirt, landing on top of her *sapatos* and a pile of clothing. She was only wearing three pieces of clothing in the first place…

"Sit beside me." Joy's voice was simultaneously scared and soft. Her hands went up and escorted him down in front of her.

His heart raced. The last time Joy was naked in his presence was swimming in the river as children.

"Kiss me before I lose my nerve to do this."

The sun was at a different place in the sky before Thomas regained his interest in going back to the fields. The sun was at its highest point now and had stopped making shadows with the trees. Joy slept on his chest with half of her body draped over his. The exploration before and after lasted longer than the experience itself. But at least it lasted long enough to require a nap.

Joy's invitation to meet Thomas at the old church had irrevocably escalated in its meaning. No longer was it simply a chance for private conversation or daydreams. Before, in the days when their relationship was simply brotherly and sisterly, it was a hideaway from stern parents seeking the pair who had pilfered some mangoes or orange soda without permission. It had also been a hideaway from one particular parent's physical abuse even after he defeated his alcoholism.

The half day absence would earn him a scolding from his mother. Luckily, any explanation that started with "Joy and I…" was quickly dismissed as not needing any further details. Thomas had no intention of providing details of this morning, although they would stick with him for a lifetime.

"I only wish you had had this notion months ago, not one week before I leave," he muttered into a sleeping ear.

Thomas rolled his eyes. Of course, it was so obvious now. His own words triggered the unraveling of the notion. Ronaldo and Jon-Jon were talking about the college girls they always see in Bangued at Abra Valley. Joy imagined him drooling over the women he'll see at the university in Baguio, had a fit of jealousy, then came up with this notion about catching a dragonfly. Catching a dragonfly means the person will get married before one year is over. In Joy's mind, that meant marrying Thomas. And since they were getting married anyway, that made it acceptable to perform a sacred act.

"Now that we're lovers, I'm forever cured of wanting anyone other than you, so you can rest easily with me being out of your sight in Baguio." Thomas chuckled. "You still can't get one past me."

Joy stirred at the sound of his voice.

"*Ay-ayatenkita*," she breathed.

He loved her too.

"*Sika ti immuna ken siksikanto laeng*," she continued.

My first and only?

"You found a new name for me?" he whispered in English.

"It's true. You've always been my only. You've always been the first."

He got his look. Pure adoration. Whenever he wondered if they were together only because they knew no one else, that lovingly look answered the question.

"Joy, my joy, I will never be able to shake you. We talk of marriage and babies as though it were inevitable."

They shared their first kiss as lovers.

"At least you had the awareness to warn me before..." She hid her face and peeked back after assuming some composure. "It's not time for a baby yet. Although a baby would probably sweep away some of the ghosts you carry around with you."

There was an uncomfortable silence in response to the reminder of Thomas' dead siblings, to his now-dead father sitting next to the river and weeping that there would be no more attempts to have children.

"Sorry," Joy said. "This is a happy moment. Let's not ruin it with those memories. It is nice to kiss like this, I don't have to stand on my tip-toes to reach you."

Thomas followed on Joy's lead to find a new subject for conversation.

"Where did you get the idea to do that?" His hands made a side-to-side motion above his waist.

Joy again could not contain her embarrassed smile or suppress her giggle.

"I saw a drawing of it in a book that I read to get ready for this."

Thomas cocked his eyebrows.

"I liked the title. Joy of Sex," she emphasized her name and resumed her giggling.

"Where did you get that?"

"From Reggie."

"And where did Reggie get such a book?"

"She goes back and forth to Aunt Rosella's house in Manila. You can get anything in Manila."

"You seem to get interesting things from Reggie."

"Don't bring that up again." Her weak slap grazed his chin. "I haven't smoked any cigarettes in a long time."

Thomas' tirade over Joy's experimentation with smoking caused the only separation in their relationship. He didn't want to be around the cause of his father's cancer. The coming separation would be more stinging now that a new barrier of intimacy had been crossed.

"Maybe I should think of a way to take you with me to keep you out of trouble."

She had another round of giggles. "Are you sure that's the real reason?"

She kissed him passionately for a minute before lifting herself off him and dressing.

"Now is not the time to tease me and get my hopes up," she said.

"No joke. I'll ask Uncle Lopito to bring you over as a maid."

Joy shook her head. "It won't work. I'm suddenly too valuable to father's household to send me to his brother's house."

Valuable as a slave.

Joy still had her father, but Thomas was acutely aware that she was sometimes just as fatherless as he was. Politics, money, Ricky, anything else was more important to Marino Lapez than his daughter.

"I wish I could go to Baguio with you, but I'm not smart enough for college."

"You're smart enough," Thomas protested. "That is Marino talking. You should stand up to him when he talks down to you like that."

"You tutored me through high school."

"Just math, but that doesn't mean you're dumb. Just pick something that isn't accounting."

Joy shrugged. "It's all wishful thinking anyway. I'm not going to college this year. Father won't pay for it and I missed all of the deadlines."

"It's not right, a father should want the best for his children. Marino is being stingy."

Joy was right. It was wishful thinking. She had not been permitted to take the entrance exams in high school. Without them, she would not be admitted anywhere. She was a year behind Thomas even if Marino found a change of heart. His godfather had him fuming again.

As mayor of Calamba, Thomas thought Marino would enjoy the political boasting of being able to say he sent his daughter to college. But the reverse was true. It was the crab mentality of Calamba. Fill a bucket full of crabs and they will all try to climb out. Once one reaches the top and is ready to escape the bucket, the rest will drag it back inside. So long as everyone was equal, there was no jealousy. The Lapez family hovered at the top of the bucket and Marino worried about being dragged to the bottom. Yet other townspeople pushed their children to attain higher education, especially those with rich aunties in Manila or siblings working overseas in order to pay the tuition.

"If he won't send you, then I will after I graduate. We can get married then and I can work as a doctor in Bangued. I should be able to afford Abra Valley for you once I get a job. Or, God willing, we can stay in Baguio and you can attend Saint Louis also."

Joy kissed the hand that cupped her cheek. "That is a sweet gesture, but it still means I'm going to be stuck here without you. For four years. Wait, medical school is six years." Joy frowned. The emotions of the day were as steep and shallow as the mountains around her.

Joy sought the sun's position in the sky and determined they'd been in the church for more than a few hours. She had her own chores to do at home. She cursed, said a quick prayer for saying the Lord's name in vain and waited for Thomas to dress before leaving the structure.

Joy washed away the morning's activities in the river while fully dressed. In this heat, she and Clay Aiken's face would be dry by the time their walk home ended.

CHAPTER 3
TALLO

Mother Emma carried more weight than a woman her age ought to, yet fat feet in dirty flip-flops ambled nimbly and quickly down the narrow mound of dirt between flooded rice paddies. She gathered her dress close to her in order to see where she was stepping. The distance between the back of the Wagner house to the furthest away fields was even greater than her voice could carry. She was exasperated when she reached the pair crouched over ankle-high brown water jamming germinated rice seed into the loose earth.

The dog barked and jumped as Emma approached. "Dirty dog! Dirty dog! Shoo!"

The light brown unnamed mutt was a danger to nothing but chickens and itself. It was a friendly dog, but too stupid to guard anything. At least it was good enough to spot snakes, which kept Joy productive.

Joy said good afternoon to Emma, calling her *nanang*, mother, just the same as Thomas.

"Joy Flora Lapez, your mother was searching for you all morning."

"She's been busy here with me," Thomas explained. He was shirtless again, but she insisted he wear the well-seasoned woven thatch hat.

"She's always busy with you," Emma retorted, all the while surveying the progress. "You haven't gotten very far. Maybe I need to send her home. You've been squabbling all day instead of working, I'm sure."

"We weren't arguing," Joy insisted. "We were just having a conversation about San Francisco being more interesting than Manila."

"Hoy, not that again! If Ted were still alive I'd force him to send you both to America so I wouldn't have to hear Joy ramble about the States ever again."

"Why didn't you ever go back there, *nanang*?" Joy asked.

Emma twisted her face and said it was too cold the first time. Everyone could remember the sergeant complaining of the long, cold and snowy winters of his native Wisconsin.

Thomas once laughed for days when he caught Joy sitting inside a half-closed refrigerator. Her notion behind the experiment was to see if she could bear the winter in America. It was 30-something degrees in the refrigerator, she reasoned, the same temperature needed for snow.

"It's only in some places. Miami is nice and warm," Joy said to her godmother.

"Miami? You hate being hot," Thomas interjected. "We all know you like the cold."

Joy knew the smile on his face and was ready to rail on him for thinking of the refrigerator incident again. She knew what was going to follow, he was going to bring up her daydreamed American house with running water and reliable electricity—and air conditioning. Her own car—with air conditioning. An office job—with air conditioning.

Emma dismissed the commentary with a "blah" and a wave of her hand. "I'm not letting you drag me into this never-ending argument. Seeing you two squabble makes me glad to be a widow sometimes."

Emma told Thomas there was *adobo manok* and rice sitting untouched in the kitchen and scolded him that he was too old to need reminding to eat lunch. Adobo, with chicken simmered in vinegar and soy sauce, was a staple of the Wagner household.

"I have a chore for you. You need to hitch a ride with Jon-Jon to go to Bangued and pay the electric bill. While I was visiting Rowena, I saw a group pile out of Jon-Jon's jeepney, so he'll be parked in the square for an hour."

"Why don't I just hand the money to him and let him pay it for us like he always does?"

"I don't trust him with it anymore."

"Jon-Jon is not a thief," Thomas said in defense of his closest male friend.

"No, he doesn't steal, but he holds onto the money for a few days before paying the bill. I'm not going to allow another late charge because he wants to have a stack of pesos to impress people at the cockfights."

Thomas removed his hat and sent it sailing toward the tractor, parked near the fields heaped full of plastic crates of rice seedlings. Ted Wagner was entrepreneurial in getting the tractor, the only one near Calamba, frequently rented out to the farmers near Calamba. The four-wheel drive tractor was in good shape, just a little cranky when it came to turns. It was an old tractor now, purchased used from Camp John Hay when it was still an American military installation. The deceased Marine gunny sergeant knew many people there, most of them expats like him.

Thomas gingerly stepped over the rows he'd just planted in order to exit the paddy. The dog chased after the hat, darting past Emma and nearly upsetting her balance.

"I don't know why you insist to treat this thing like a pet. You got that from your father, I know. I wish you could take it with you to Baguio to get it out of my way, but I'm sure Lopito would not put up with it. Maybe there will be an accident in your absence."

Thomas feigned a painful expression. "I love my dog."

Joy doused the side of his leg with a splash of paddy mud.

"Not as much as my mother and my Joy, though." Thomas' faux smile gleamed at them.

"And you're not going to waste time playing with it today," Emma continued. "You've already spent enough of it visiting with Joy."

Joy giggled and started making up a song about how much fun it was to chase dragonflies.

"You're eating too," Emma told Joy, "and then I'm sending you across the river. There's food to be prepared for tonight for mahjong night and Rowena doesn't want to do it by herself."

Joy was accustomed to the fact Thomas' mother scolded her as effortlessly as her own son. There were a seemingly endless number of Aunties and grandmothers in Calamba who weren't shy to correct a youngster.

Thomas and his reddening back were walking toward the house at a quicker pace than Joy and Emma. He was brooding about the additional chore placed upon him. It would waste the rest of the afternoon, pushing the field work to the next morning.

The wooden Wagner house stood obscured by trees and a collection of small huts for the animals. Another trail winded through a different screen of trees led to a walking bridge over the Abra River and into Calamba.

Thomas went under the wooden awning of the porch. There was nothing ornate about the house. It was a simple square. The trees shaded most of the tin roof that had a slight pitch over the one story structure. The windows were single pane with black trim. The only thing unique to the house was a spot on the front porch, a painted yellow square framing a white "G" outlined in green. Joy knew it was the symbol of a sports team in Wisconsin, but had forgotten the sport. She also remembered there being green grass around the compound. Emma saw to its demise when Ted died since it was such an oddity to have a lawn in Abra—or anywhere else in the provinces.

There was plenty of space in the house for the both of them since Thomas' siblings all died in the womb. Emma's string of miscarriages and stillbirths physically weakened her. The last one, a girl, nearly claimed her life in labor. Emma's asthma got worse with each passing rainy season, when the mountain climate produced colder temperatures than in other parts of the tropical nation. Emma's coughing often dredged up memories of Ted's last days alive, when the years of smoking caught up to him.

There was a shrine to Ted on one wall, lined with pictures, the flag draped over his coffin and his military decorations. For the longest time, no one knew Ted Wagner by his real first name. Here he was Joe—as in G.I. Joe, a common Filipino term for most Americans they see.

Ted's legacy, the college fund, barely had enough money left in it to pay for all of Thomas' college studies. It had been tapped over the years to make ends meet, paying for Emma's asthma medications, food during the drought years, parts for the tractor. Other than the money Thomas made driving the machine and what crops they were able to trade or sell, there was no other income. There were no Wagners left alive in Wisconsin, save for some cousins whose names Thomas did not even know. There were no rich aunts or uncles to ask for help. And Emma was too proud to ask for help from her Botalico kin, whom Thomas doubted would be able to help even if she were to ask them. They were no better off as farmers than he and his mother.

Living with Marino's cousin, Lopito, in Baguio instead of paying for a boarding house was the only way Thomas was going to stretch the pesos enough to obtain his college education and fulfill his father's wish that his son would become more than a rice farmer.

Joy left her *sapatos* on the mat on the porch entering the house barefoot, which was the custom before entering any house.

Inside, she grabbed him by the hand. "I'm sorry, Thomas," she whispered. "Our first time was supposed to be special, not a crazy jealous ambush. I know we agreed to make it sacred with our first time on our honeymoon..."

Thomas gripped her arm and quieted her apology. They locked eyes. She wasn't the source of anger. His eyes darted to his mother's progress toward the animals.

"I want everything done before I go so that she doesn't have to worry about it. Who is going to help her? *Nanang* Rowena will send Lazy Velasquez out here, or worse, Aris."

Aris Lucero was the youngest of ten Luceros. It took that many children for a son to be born. Whenever there was Lapez work to be done—mangoes to be picked or rice to be bagged—there was Aris in charge of it. Because Ted was G.I. Joe, it was only natural that Thomas came to be known as Little Joe to the bullies. Chief among those bullies was Aris.

"Aris doesn't do anything for free. Mother needs the money more than him. He's only going to spend it on gin."

Thomas made a line for the kitchen counter, where the food sat atop the two small kerosene-fueled burners. He scooped steam warmed white rice into a bowl for himself and another for Joy. The adobo went on top. Plenty of the vinegar and soy broth for Thomas and not so much for Joy, the way she liked it. He served Joy and received a smile for a thank you. Sitting across from her, he pinched rice between three fingers and brought it up to his mouth.

"Cheer up, you can still see me tonight. That's what you said earlier," Joy said. "It's mahjong night. How long do they usually stay out?"

Thomas coughed, choking on food, the effect of the implication of Joy's statement.

"I might be tempted to haul you over my shoulder and back to the hideout right now if you don't stop teasing."

"With your mother around, not likely. She might take a bolo to you."

"Good. Maybe she can chop it off and you can't have any more fun with me."

"If you're maimed, I might have to marry a different man."

"Fine, you can take Ronaldo and put a bag over his head when you make your babies."

She stuck her tongue out at him and ended the verbal sparing there so that they could finish eating. She would have her chance to get the last word.

"I need some more rice. Can you get it?" Thomas asked, politely.

"No. You get it."

< <> >

Ricky Lapez followed Thomas down Calamba's main road, bouncing a basketball as he walked. The street had no name. None of them did. The houses had no numbers. It wasn't necessary in a town of 3,000 people. The mailman knew every family. He was related to most of them himself. Rarely did a person have to think past a second cousin to find a link to someone else in living in Calamba.

"Please, *manong*," Ricky begged. "Just one game. You're going away."

In all practicality, Ricky was Thomas' 11-year-old brother. He always called Thomas *manong*, the term for an older brother. A lack of blood connection, even past second cousins, did not deter him from using the phrase. Marino and Rowena were Thomas' godparents, true, but Ricky grew up seeing Thomas in his house nearly every day.

"No, Ricky, I've got to go to Bangued right now."

"But I've been practicing. And one day I'll be tall like Shaq and you won't have a chance."

Thomas chuckled and waved to Amelie Valera in the sari-sari store, the convenience store that was a small room behind a metal grated window.

Every family was its own small industry. The Paculdars, including his friend Jon-Jon, were transportation, taxiing people in their jeepneys. The mother of his friend Maricar was the traveling beauty parlor. Auntie Betty cut hair and painted nails. The Floras had their food stand in the town square, selling goodies from their small grill to those waiting in line to use the municipal phone or sitting in a gazebo for the next jeepney.

Thomas knew were to go for a new piece of rattan furniture, to have some rice ground into flour, to mend a shirt. Most every family had land outside of Calamba to grow rice or vegetables or sugar cane.

The Lapez family was once synonymous with carpentry until Marino turned to politics. It was luck that his marriage to Rowena Flora garnered him a mango grove at the southern edge of the poblacion. Marino was a terrible carpenter through incompetence and alcoholism.

The jolly patriarch that people saw now was the clean and sober version of Marino Lapez. Thomas' memory was filled with the testy and abusive Marino. The man's thick hand had once or twice graced Thomas' cheek as a child, and not for disciplinary matters.

"You are done with school. Why would you want to go back for more? I don't like school that much," Ricky said in English.

Whereas Joy shied away from speaking English because she was acutely self-conscious, Ricky used it more than his own native tongue, testament that the second of the mayor's children was as overtly fascinated with America as the first.

"I need more schooling to become a doctor."

"But why? I don't like doctors. They always give me shots or make me take yucky medicines."

Thomas tousled the boy's hair. "I promise to give you tasty medicine. How's that?"

"I'm going to play basketball when I grow up," Ricky said as though he had not said the exact same phrase hundreds of time per week.

Ricky filled the rest of the walk illustrating moments of the game with mock shots and sound-effect rebounds. Thomas paid little attention to it, instead reflecting on the new level of intimacy with Joy. He didn't think it was possible to become any closer to Joy than he had been, but it had happened. Sex was the only door closed off to him and now that it was open, Thomas felt as though he finally had all of Joy's life essence revealed to him. After all these years, his stomach still did spins when he saw her waiting for him in the darkness in front of Valera's sari-sari so that they could kiss goodnight on the busy days when there was no other chance to spend time together.

How did she still manage to surprise him? There were times he could finish her sentences. He knew her thoughts and feelings so well that he found himself arguing her side of an issue along with his own. Joy would retort "And you are going to say..." That was the point where attending adults usually threw their hands in the air and proclaimed Joy and Thomas insane for arguing each other's point of view instead of their own—just to see the Thomas and Joy start fighting that they were fighting backwards. The pair laughed about it later. Squabbling was their affirmation that they cared.

Thomas was glad her notions were harmless, if not recently life altering. When Joy got an idea in her head, there was no containing it, even if it defied common sense. Catching a dragonfly was no measure of wedding inevitability or timing, but somehow the completion of that idea gave her a peace of mind. Thomas had no reservations about making Joy his wife, but it shouldn't happen until he was able to support her, which meant after medical school.

Ricky had run ahead and was taking some wild practice shots. The presence of a ball attracted a herd of boys. The community basketball court was a series of cracked concrete slabs next to the yellow cinderblock building that served as the Calamba municipal hall and jail.

"Aren't you going to play with the little boys, Little Joe?" Aris said from a distance. The devil's lieutenant emerged from the town hall, negotiating through the queue of people waiting to use the landline telephone. "I hear you've been playing all morning. Why not make a whole day of it?"

Those who knew Aris would swear the smoke came out of his horns, not his cigarettes. It was hard to understand why the mayor paid him to supervise his lands. He was too menacing to be a good leader, too lazy to be a hard worker, too drunk to be a decent human being.

Macho and arrogant, Aris was among that group of men who thought a woman should lay down and spread her legs for him simply because he smiled at her. Though always a bully, Aris didn't become the current drunk and mean version of himself until his Elnora Justo went to work in Hong Kong, met an American penpal and became Elnora Everson of Las Vegas, USA. It heightened his hatred of America and Americans—*kanos*.

It was a hatred long in the making.

Two of his oldest sisters had slipped off to Olongapo to work when the American naval base at Subic Bay was still open. There was plenty of work at the base until the Philippine government closed it. Whoring themselves for years, they never found American husbands. One caught a venereal disease, didn't seek treatment in time and died from it. The other eventually gave up a life of prostitution in the Philippines and started one in Japan, dancing in its clubs in front of rich businessmen. She was never heard from again and presumed dead from drugs. A third Lucero sister danced in a go-go bar in Angeles City now, one of the last havens in the country where bargirl prostitution was tolerated. There was even a governmental term for it now, GRO, guest relations official, with licensing.

The six other Lucero daughters had better lives. One was a midwife like her mother. Another ran a restaurant in the provincial capital Bangued. The remaining four had seemingly happy marriages in other parts of Luzon.

Aris' feelings didn't stop with *kanos*. It washed over all white people, and it didn't matter that they were from somewhere other than America. Even the Dutch priest who pastored the Catholic church in Calamba wasn't immune to hate-filled racist mutterings from Aris. Thomas wasn't the only half-breed of Filipino and American blood in Calamba, but he was the only one close to Aris' age. And he was the only male, which made him a constant target.

"Some men in this town are hard at work," Aris continued, closing the distance with Thomas, "but you're running around the countryside without a care in the world."

Word travels fast. What else did those men on the other side of the river have to say?

Sweat glistened in Aris' buzz cut hair. He finished his cigarette and tossed it at Thomas' feet. Thomas remained emotionless.

"... So we all come out of the grove expecting our lunch, but there's nothing there. Auntie Rowena cannot find Joy. Nothing to worry about, though, because there's a little bit of cold rice left from yesterday. That's enough to hold over a group of hungry working men."

So his stomach is what agitated him. Was it enough food to cure the hangover?

"So what did you eat today, Little Joe? It must have been delicious. You were running around with my chef all morning."

"Joy was helping me plant rice," Thomas explained. His legs and feet still bore proof of that.

And stop calling Joy your chef like she belongs to you, he wanted to add. And stop acting like eating old rice is such a travesty. Up until Joy graduated high school and went to work in the kitchen, the workers ate whatever Rowena had left over, or they fended for themselves.

"So you've been working so hard today ... walking with Ricky to the basketball hoop."

Thomas kept his breathing steady. Aris was just being himself and would only be satisfied if he succeeded in getting under Thomas skin. He set his jaw and went with the non-confrontational high road, taking a step in the direction of the Paculdar residence. He didn't want to disobey his mother, but he planned on handing over the pesos for the bill with an admonishment to Jon-Jon not to hold it, and then return to the fields.

Thomas felt a shove in the middle of his back.

"No answer? You disrespecting me by not giving me an answer?"

Thomas stopped and returned his attention to Aris. The high road just got blocked off. Aris took a few cocky steps to get into Thomas' face.

"I get it." Aris smirked. "You think you're better than me. College man better than the working man."

Thomas did not understand why Aris was picking the fight now, but it was apparent he was intent on some final showdown. Opportunity plus motive. Was he making up for the inability to taunt Thomas in the future?

"No. No half-*kano* is better than me," he said to the sky, as of he were having this conversation to himself, saving his own face. "It must be something else. You are scared. That is it. Little Joe is scared of me."

This tactic wasn't going to work either. Aris was blatantly goading him into a fight. There was no one of authority around to stop him. He only witnesses were children and the onlookers in front of the town hall, who were not going to cross the mayor's number one man.

"I don't have time to listen to you play with your ego, Aris..."

"*Manong* Aris, to you. I'm your elder. You need to be more respectful."

Thomas smelled it on his breath. Drunk already.

"That's okay, Little Joe, doctor Joe." He smirked again. "You go back to your hard work of watching kids play basketball and hugging girls near the river. I'm strong. I can take it. Climbing trees and managing carabao teams with only a little bit of rice in my stomach. I can take it."

Drinking gin without Rowena noticing was the only difficult thing Aris did today, Thomas thought. Lazy Velasquez managed the animals. Fernando Cabasan was the only person Thomas ever saw climbing a mango or coconut tree.

"My hard work will be rewarded," Aris continued. "Once you're gone, I might be asked to take on more responsibility. Mayor Lapez has been very generous with his support of Auntie Emma. I might have to take care of all this extra land. I'll be so impressive that the mayor will reward me with other responsibilities."

Aris laughed.

"Her cooking is good. I wonder if there are other things that taste good."

Aris reached a topic that worked.

"If you think you're going to terrorize my Joy while I'm gone..."

"Wow, a threat from Little Joe," Aris said, feigning fear, overacting to the point where he even took a step backward. "What are you going to do? Want to fight me?"

Thomas had no chance to answer. He even saw the sucker punch coming. Unfortunately, Aris was too quick in the swing for Thomas to move out of the way. The jab hit him in the nose.

Aris assumed a boxing pose, holding his fists out in front of his face. Thomas was aware of his own face and the blood that was draining from his nose down across his lips.

"*Manong* Thomas!"

"Ricky, stay away!"

With Thomas distracted by the boy, Aris tried another jab. This one missed.

They traded blows, landing few of them with impacts only in the chest or stomach. Aris kicked Thomas in the shin, then using the pain as distraction enough for another punch to the face. The blow knocked Thomas off balance. He didn't like the feeling of his face's impact with the hard dirt road. Thomas squirmed in pain.

"You are nothing to me, Little Joe. I will always be more of a man than you. *Kanos* cannot fight."

Ricky ran up to Thomas, placing himself between the combatants. The boy bleated for Aris to leave his brother alone. That he was going to tell his father what happened.

Aris laughed that Thomas needed the help of a little boy to end the fight. He told Ricky and his friends to get out of the way, that he was busy teaching Thomas a lesson in respect.

Thomas kept his forehead pressed to the road.

Play dead.

He could see Aris approaching in his peripheral vision.

Play dead.

He heard the laugh of a man who thought he'd won and was simply contemplating how to put a suffering animal out of its misery.

Play dead.

Aris was a step away when Thomas lunged. He put a shoulder square into the right knee. The pop was audible. Hyper extended or broken, Thomas didn't care.

With a roar, Aris fell to the road. Thomas leapt to his feet and dragged Ricky away from Aris, who was writhing on the ground.

"Get back out of the way, Ricky," Thomas ordered, dust clouding his vision and blood warming his lips.

"This isn't over, Thomas," said the knee-clutching Aris.

"Yes, it is. It wouldn't be fair to beat up a one-legged man," Thomas replied.

Aris tried to put weight on the leg, but tumbled back to the ground.

"This is not over, Thomas," Aris chanted.

By the time Thomas turned his back on the scene to get to the Lapez residence to wash away the bleeding, police chief Albio was racing out to break up the crowd that had gathered around the fighters.

"Aris is *bagtit*! Crazy! He has nothing to do but get drunk every night," said Ronaldo Farinas, dealing a hand of cards.

"Oh, he's an important person, don't forget," Jon-Jon Paculdar chimed. "A supervisor."

"Do you think Aris will be back for more?" Ronaldo asked Thomas.

Thomas admitted silently that is was worth enduring his mother's tirade over being bloodied in a fist fight to have seen Aris roiling in pain on the ground. Aris had to be escorted away from the scene by officer Albio, over to his mother's house so that the town's midwife and general nurse could examine the knee.

No one ever beat Aris in a fight, but the consensus was Thomas had won the noon showdown in the town square.

The trio sat in the jeepney lot on the west side of Bangued, Abra's provincial capital of 35,000 people. The floor in the back of Jon-Jon's jeepney was a makeshift poker table.

Thomas decided it was better to fulfill his mother's wishes, which made him scarce in town for the next few hours. The bill was paid, but the jeepney route took them to Bangued before returning to the road that lead back to Calamba.

"Next time you fight him, Thomas, let me know. I can sell tickets," Jon-Jon said.

Thomas regarded his friend with skepticism that his plan for riches would get past conception.

"You're lucky that Aris didn't have his knife. He probably would have tried to kill you," Ronaldo said.

Thomas used his own knife to slice green apples and slide them into open gin bottles for flavoring. And then unripe mangos, perfect for dipping into *bagoong*. They preferred the pink condiment of salted and fermented shrimp.

"Aris deserved it. I wish I could have punched him too," Jon-Jon said.

Ronaldo laughed. "You never fought Aris in your life. At least Thomas stood up to him sometimes in school."

If not for Aris' bullying, the trio may have had more friends in school. The commonality of being social outcasts drew them together as companions.

Thomas had few real friends. Only into manhood did Thomas begin to attract the interest of girls in the town. It was a different life as a youth. He was *puraw*. White. Treated cruelly by some of the other children, but nowhere near the extent of Aris. The same was true of Ronaldo and Jon-Jon.

Jon-Jon had the stigma attached to his obesity. Outside of his circle of friends, he was *taba*. Fatso.

Ronaldo had a deformed upper lip, a birth defect. He was l*aad*. Ugly.

"Look everyone," Aris would say, "*laad* and *taba* and *puraw*, the three amigos."

There were few toys for the trio to play with as they grew up. The kids games with stones and sticks turned into adolescent games of cards and watching cock fights. Thomas was less fond of cock fights than the other two. Jon-Jon took the competitions seriously. When he wasn't watching the fights, Jon-Jon's nose was under the hood of his father's old jeepney. The Paculdar father and son team made money by taking fares, toting people to and from Bangued each day.

Ronaldo's passion was girls. An irony since the focus of his face was the deformity. Ronaldo paid it little mind, frequently hitching a free ride with Jon-Jon and enjoying his walk around Bangued to go girl shopping. Ronaldo's delusions of being handsome provided amusement for his friends whenever his advances to an unsuspecting girl were refused. The thin mustache Ronaldo had recently grown did little to age his baby face.

"Can you imagine losing your girlfriend to a 40-year-old American guy?" Jon-Jon asked, keeping up the talk on Aris.

"Aris was never really nice to Elnora anyway," Ronaldo said. "He kept getting spotted with all those other girls in Danglas and La Paz. I think he even hit Elnora a couple of times too."

"Or maybe you're just jealous of him, Ronaldo," Jon-Jon prodded. "You keep pining over those girls you see in the market even though they will not give you a second look."

"Arlyn does too like me!"

"You are just making that up. It's probably not even her real name," Jon-Jon continued.

"She is real!"

"Go get her then since we're in Bangued."

Thomas piped up to stop the brewing argument. "I am trying to concentrate on my cards," he said. Two nines, a deuce, an eight and a ten. No chance of a flush, but enough of a straight to make Thomas wonder about tossing one of the nines with the deuce.

"Thomas doesn't have to worry about losing Joy to an American guy. He is the American guy," Jon-Jon laughed.

"American only on a piece of paper at the embassy," Thomas said. The only time he'd been to America was as an infant. Grandma and Grandpa Wagner were dead now. If there were any Wagner kin still alive, he didn't know them.

He kept the nines.

"And if Ronaldo behaves himself while I'm at college, I don't think I'll ever have to worry about losing Joy to another man," Thomas said.

Ronaldo groaned at being teased by Thomas too.

"With you leaving so soon, I thought Joy would be here." Ronaldo fluttered his eyes. "She cannot bare to have you out of her sight."

Thomas ignored the mockery.

"The girls hate it when we gamble," Jon-Jon said.

"No, Joy hates it when I drink," Thomas interjected.

Ronaldo made a noise of agreement. Joy could never take watching the hours of gin drinking, man talk and the eventual argument over who was cheating at the cards. When the girls were present, they got tired of the scene quickly and began to nag.

"She's going to cry a lot, Thomas, so I might have to give her a lot of comforting hugs," Ronaldo said.

Thomas chuckled. "That would be amusing. Joy would probably knock that mustache off your face." It was one thing for Ronaldo to tease about making a grab for Joy, Aris was a different matter.

Ronaldo groaned again, he wasn't winning the verbal jibes. He threw down his cards. He wasn't winning any hands of poker either.

"Are we going to wager something?" Ronaldo reached for his own bottle. "I don't have much money."

"Me neither. I used most of my money paying the electric bill for mother. How can electricity cost so much? It is never on in the first place."

"Keep track of the hands. Loser after the first hour eats *balut*," Jon-Jon suggested.

Thomas feigned nausea. He had never been fond of *balut*, the soft-boiled eggs containing partially developed duck embryos.

"Okay, but we keep track starting now," Ronaldo said between swigs of gin. "You're already up two hands."

Before Thomas could protest the bet, Jon-Jon had dealt the next hand of cards.

Thomas was of two minds. Drink enough now to be able to actually eat *balut* when the hour ended, or drink little in the hopes of keeping his mind clear to win enough card games to stay out of last place.

As Thomas was contemplating a strategy, he won the first hand with a pair of tens. He decided to go with Plan B. It was a good plan for another reason. He thought he could get away with telling Joy he was drinking alcohol to lessen the pain from his fight with Aris, but it would still make her angry enough to prohibit intimate relations later.

"Papa Justo may have been just as influential as Aris in Elnora leaving. There was no way he was going to allow his daughter to marry a man who works for Mayor Lapez," Thomas said.

The Justo-Lapez feud was legendary. It was more of a quiet hatred now, but it had been a violent battle in past generations.

The pair of tens put Thomas up one hand.

"College next week," Ronaldo said. "You're lucky Thomas. Imagine being surrounded by so many girls."

Jon-Jon shook his head in disbelief.

"And they're all *laad* and *taba*. Right, Ronaldo? Ugly and fat," Thomas said in a way to suggest to his friend that he not return to prodding Joy on that subject.

The living arrangements were another matter that thankfully hadn't reared its head yet. Uncle Lopito's daughter, Grace, was a sophomore at Saint Louis University. Joy knew her cousin Grace well. She had a good disposition. Hopefully, that would dispel any wild swings of jealousy for Thomas boarding in the next room.

"Don't worry, Thomas, I'm only teasing you," Ronaldo said. He uttered a curse, having lost another hand to Thomas. Jon-Jon was faring no better.

"Where is Shadow anyway?"

Shadow was Joy. Thomas' shadow, always a step behind him wherever he went as a child. They called her that. It was hard to get rid of her whenever the boys wanted to go off and do boy things, like smack snakes with a stick or play basketball. It wasn't a nickname used very often in her presence.

"She went to the market."

Eye shopping for clothes moreso that buying fresh fish, Thomas surmised.

The conversation turned to planning an activity for Thomas' first weekend visit. The debate wrapped up with a movie in Bangued.

"Man, that means I'm stuck with Reggie again," Ronaldo complained.

With Joy and Thomas coupled, as were Jon-Jon and Maricar, that usually paired the remainder of their clique to one another. Ronaldo and Regina Flora never became sweethearts, but quite the opposite.

"You always bellyache about Reggie. There is nothing wrong with Reggie. She's cute," Jon-Jon said.

"She has that mole," Ronaldo said.

It was on her nose and was frequently the source of ridicule throughout the school years, and even now in the brief period they've all been adults. Regina also had some freckles, but was generally attractive nonetheless. She was technically Joy's aunt, being her mother's youngest sister. However, what banded Regina to their clique of outcasts was the unproven belief that she was a Tom Boy, a lesbian. She never sprouted in the right places and insisted on short hair. It didn't help that Regina's oldest brother was openly homosexual—he was the best barber in town. Regina wasn't even around to be stuck with Ronaldo. She left to live in Metro Manila soon after graduation.

"Besides, no one watches the movie. All you do is sit in the dark and kiss," Ronaldo said.

"Then bring Arlyn," Jon-Jon dared.

That hushed Ronaldo.

"I think I should mention that we've only got a few minutes left in the hour." Thomas paused to look at the tally. "And Jon-Jon is behind."

That brought out an ironic laugh from Ronaldo.

Jon-Jon won the next hand, but it wasn't enough. Jon-Jon hid his face in his hands in disbelief.

"Caught by your own bet," Ronaldo said, smiling. "Now we have to get some *balut*."

The market was only a few blocks away. There would be some there for sure. Thomas gestured to Ricky, who left his makeshift soccer match in the jeepney pit to attend to his hero big brother. Thomas placed a few pesos in the boy's hand with an order for one *balut*. He was met with a barrage of yucks and faces, but the boy ran off with his companions to comply.

Joy emerged from the arched walkway into the area shaded by awnings where hundreds of people sat in wait for a jeepney headed to their town. Maricar lumbered behind her. They had a frown for the men when they saw the cards laid out in the back of the vehicle. Jon-Jon, though, had smartly discarded the empty gin bottles.

Joy had softer eyes for Thomas, whose nose marked the duel for her honor. As soon as she'd heard of the fist fight between he and Aris, she chided him nearly as much as his mother had. Thomas told her he wouldn't allow Aris to get comfortable with the idea that he could continue to harass her in his absence. "I can stick up for myself," she had said. "You never do, though!" he had replied.

She had a present for Thomas, *bibingka* wrapped in tin foil. He could feel the sweet sticky rice with coconut was still warm. He wanted to thank her with a kiss, but there were too many people around and it wouldn't be a proper sight for a public place.

Ricky returned with an egg, holding it like it was a grenade ready to explode in his hand.

"You and Car-Car going to be busy tonight," Thomas teased. *Balut* was regarded by some to be an aphrodisiac.

It earned him a punch in the arm from Jon-Jon as he bit through the white of the egg and into the mostly formed duckling inside. Thomas averted his eyes before Jon-Jon tried to show him the duck parts inside the half he hadn't swallowed yet.

Jon-Jon made kissy lips to Maricar. She backed away from his advance. "I don't kiss *balut* mouths no matter how handsome the face."

Fulfilling the terms of the wager, and not vomiting in the process, Jon-Jon did a quick bow. Thomas gathered the cards and stepped up into the back of the lackluster chrome machine. Most jeepneys had names. Mr. Paculdar's was named Big Man, but Jon-Jon wasn't about to put on a placard declaring the older jeepney as Little Man. It wasn't his style to delve into ironic nicknames like fat men named Tiny.

Jon-Jon started the engine and did a wave to those sitting in the shadows who were waiting for the hour-long return to Calamba, or La Paz, Danglas and Ba-i since there were along the way.

Maricar sat in the front passenger seat. Joy sat on Thomas' lap for the journey. Ronaldo's lap became Ricky's seat. The two metal benches in the back filled quickly, and the aisle filled with bags of vegetables, fish and rice. An older man had bought a rooster, whose cage occupied the space in front of Thomas' feet. An umbrella stroller was folded and slid under the legs of the mother, the child sleeping on her shoulder. Late arrivals climbed up the side of the jeepney and sat on the roof, the dangling legs obscured the view out the long thin windows.

Jon-Jon counted his passenger, asked destinations and slid into the driver's seat. He touched the cross hanging over the dash board on a chain and said a quick prayer for God's blessing to reach home.

The sun was beginning to set as the jeepney crossed the Abra River over the wooden bridge. The overloaded vehicle began to bump and toss on the uneven dirt road. One of the men on top complained that there was only one working headlight.

"Don't worry. We have Thomas to protect us if someone tries to raid the jeepney," someone called out. Thomas swore it was Ronaldo.

CHAPTER 4

UPPAT

Lino Justo for most of his adult life was known in Calamba as *tatang*, father, papa. The Justo house was always open to those in need of rice when times were tough, a place to stay in times of personal tragedy, a place for a job at his two grinding mills.

Papa Justo's days as a benefactor ended the day after he became Calamba's vice mayor. He still gave to the church, but anyone else received favors with strings attached. In the years since he entered local politics, he had his eyes on a grander prize, but Marino Lapez was sitting in that chair.

The change in attitude came with a change in his family's life—when the riches came from afar and not simply grafted from the town's coffers.

As vice mayor, his salary was good. Combined with the money he made running his two grinding mills, he was able to get a better house, more land, nice appliances, his own small Korean-made car, albeit a used one. Then eldest daughter Elnora became married to an American and moved to Las Vegas.

That was why Aris hated Papa Justo, allowing the only woman he loved to be sent away. Elnora had been a brat, coddled, high maintenance, told so often that she was perfect that she believed it. His lust for her was so powerful that he overlooked her faults as much as he could. Unfortunately, she needed to be brought down from the clouds from time to time. The younger sister, Nina, was becoming the same way. The moment Nina Justo became Miss Abra, there was no turning her back around.

Aris crouched under an open window, the only window for the back room of Justo's grinding mill office. The sill was slightly cracked open, held that way by a piece of wood. Elnora had sneaked him into the room many times through the window. It was perfectly located, so close to the metal fence that it only took a step to reach it—or escape from it. He knew the room in his mind's eye. It was rectangular, poorly lit and had a large wooden table in the middle of it. The centerpiece of the room was an old plush chair in the

29

opposite corner from the window. Aris and Elnora had done many memorable things in that chair.

Aris wanted a cigarette, but he dared not light one now and draw attention to himself. His back touched the fence, he ear tilted to the conversation inside. Mayor Marino had a bad feeling when he saw some members of the Calamba council discretely gathering at Justo's mill. He dispatched Aris to spy.

"I don't feel comfortable with this, vice mayor."

Aris knew the voice to be Marlon Arroyo, the newest councilor. Arroyo did not come from Calamba's poblacion, but one of its barangay's, Pingaping.

"But you are also not comfortable with the way Calamba has been managed over the last eight years either. Right?" Papa Justo said. Aris could hear him the best, he must be standing close to the window.

"Right. But why all of this secrecy?" It was the voice of the third chair councilor, Augusto Galope. Old and high pitched.

"Politics, Galope. Mayoral politics. I need help from you and Arroyo."

"If we're here to discuss the mayor, then where is Ramirez? The first councilor should be here too," Arroyo asked.

"His children are too close to Marino's children," Justo replied. It was true, Maricar and Joy were close friends.

"That doesn't mean he dislikes Marino any less than we do..."

"Maybe I will include him in another meeting, Arroyo, but not yet," Justo conceded.

Aris heard other voices inside the room, but there were too far away to discern what they said or who was saying it.

"Okay, to the point," Justo began. "I had a meeting with the governor recently. Right after the mayors meetings. We all remember Mayor Marino's report from his talk with the governor? There is no help for Calamba for a water system. No new bridges are in the budget. The governor cannot help us with our brownouts."

Someone said it was depressing.

"And false," Justo replied, causing a brief ruckus.

When it quieted, Aris heard Papa Justo describe the governor's concerns that the money he has been setting aside for Calamba seems to get spent, but the projects never get done.

"We have been led to believe—through Marino—that the governor cares only about Bangued, not any of the mountain towns. The truth is that we are supposed to have some paved streets by now. The pipes for the water system should have been dug into place last year. The governor has money next year to give us a pump station, but he's not going to release it when there are no pipes in the ground yet," Justo said.

"What happened to the money?"

There was silence.

The same person who asked the question then cursed.

"My brother Bennie took those pictures. The woman is obviously not Rowena Lapez. I recognize her. She's a bank teller. The house looks very close to the style of Marino's here in Calamba ..."

"That is his red Jeep parked out in front of it," Galope said. "But that still doesn't answer Arroyo's question. Certainly he cannot spend that much money on a house and a mistress in Bangued. The fact that he has a secret house in Bangued only puts him on par with just about every other mayor in the province. It does not look like she is wearing expensive Italian clothing and I do not see a Rolls Royce in the garage."

"I don't know where the rest of the money went," Papa Justo said. "But the governor suspects it is being hoarded for a political run at him."

"By Mayor Lapez?" Arroyo was laughing. "Who is going to vote for him? Or any of us for that matter? The only practical way to become governor is by being Abra's congressman or mayor of Bangued."

"Or a movie actor," one of the unknown voices said.

"Bangued's mayor is the governor's wife. This picture establishes Marino's residence in Bangued..." Justo trailed off, not needing to explain the implication.

"So what?" Galope said. "We now have a greater suspicion that Mayor Lapez is corrupt. It may be true that he has been keeping much of the town's money for some political run for Bangued mayor. The Bersamins are popular. It will be a terrible feeling watching him waste Calamba's money to humiliate himself. So far, vice mayor, this meeting has only been enlightening gossip."

"Yes, and if the governor wants to get Marino for corruption, he has the power to do that himself," Arroyo said.

Justo cleared his throat.

"Congressman Baronas will be retiring in a few years. Mr. Bersamin, the governor, will certainly move up to congress. Mrs. Bersamin, the mayor, does not want to become governor, so she will move to Metro Manila to be with her husband. Baronas wants his youngest son to run for governor, but that still leaves open the post of Bangued mayor for someone to slip in and capture it. That is Marino's window of opportunity, but it is five years away."

"So this is about keeping Marino out of Bangued?" Arroyo asked. "I say good riddance. Let's help him run and get him out of *here*. If he is that corrupt, he would be out of our hair and we would be able to use the town money for water and roads."

"The governor doesn't like Marino Lapez," Justo explained, "and does not want him in a prestigious position of running the capital city, nor be within a stone's throw of running the province. Lapez was a nobody, a drunkard carpenter with no education, who has been a mediocre mayor..."

"Which makes him no real threat," Galope interrupted. "I think governor Bersamin is becoming paranoid over a flea."

"Nevertheless, he asked me to run for mayor of Calamba next year and put an end to it now."

There was a silence in the room again.

Aris shifted his position outside the window, cursing under his breath that the pain in his right knee made him so uncomfortable.

"I want your opinions, but more importantly, I want some support among the council."

Galope chuckled this time. "I think you give Marino far too much credit also. The only reason he became mayor is because you didn't run to succeed your father after his death in office. So it was him and me. Marino made outrageous promises and still needed friends and family campaigning on his behalf to defeat me. And the only reason I was running at all is because your father wouldn't have wanted a Lapez sitting at the head of the table."

"Oh, don't bring up the feud again," Arroyo snapped.

"Then call it a rivalry," Justo said. "It is a political rivalry now, anyway. There has not been any real bloodshed in decades. The massacre I am thinking about is on election day that brings Calamba back to some favorability with the governor."

Provided the governor was being honest, Galope commented.

"I am beginning to lean with Galope," Arroyo said. "How much money has Marino hoarded for politics? The pictures show a house in Bangued. His mango grove got bigger, but the new trees died. He wastes money on all those workers who don't do very much work. We know what police officer Albio officially makes. His secret payroll got him a nice looking house." Arroyo made a noise of disbelief. "I even saw Marino's own daughter planting rice at the Wagner farm. I think the man is broke."

One of the unknown voices said not to forget Rowena's habit of losing money on mahjong. And doesn't Marino take care of the Wagner widow too? Someone heard that Marino's supervisor was going to take over running the Wagner farm when the half-breed boy went to college.

"That G.I. Joe helped get Marino elected in the first place. Honestly, I would rather have him for mayor than Marino. At least that Joe was hard working and hospitable."

"Oh, come on, Arroyo," Galope protested. "An American mayor?"

Papa Justo called the meeting back to order. Even if money wasn't going to be a problem, he still wanted verbal support. He said he had resources in America and even in the governor's office if he needed more money to run against Marino.

"Marino was unopposed last time. He positioned himself as the caring mayor, trying so hard to make things better, but being denied by the governor because the governor does not care about the small towns in the mountains. We all collectively gave him a pass. It will not work this time," Justo said, confidently.

The occupants of the room, one at a time, told Justo to proceed.

< <> >

"Painting me as corrupt and incompetent, eh?" Marino huffed heavily in anger between words. "Hypocrites."

The dim light of the cigarette fire marked the location of the sole person listening to the mayor's rant. In the darkness, Aris leaned against a mango tree near the work area of the Lapez grove. Aris left the Justo compound when he heard the rustling of someone walking around. He felt as though he had heard enough of the secret meeting to have gotten all of the important information to report to Mayor Lapez.

"He had them eating out of his hand, eh?"

"Galope seemed to think this was all an overreaction."

Marino chuckled. "Galope on my side?"

"Not really. He seemed to think you were such a small fry that it wasn't worth the effort to worry about you."

Marino chuckled again. "Beaten by a small fry. How does he live with himself? Money was the real reason Galope wanted to be mayor when Francisco Justo died. He was an opportunist just like I was."

Marino railed against the old rebel grandfather Justo, the king of graft that lined his pockets with the tax money of the town and then funneled it to the anti-Marcos militia combing the mountains.

"You were just a teenager at the time and probably paid no attention to politics. Everyone around was scared shitless. Every day we looked up into the mountains and wondered when the New People's Army was going to ride into town. Francisco Justo was a member. It was a double edged sword having him as mayor. On the one hand, the NPA wasn't going to burn the town down. But when they came by to see their friend mayor, they scared everyone with their guns. People were tired of being scared. That is why they elected me. Marcos was gone anyway and the NPA was wearing out its welcome."

Marino paced as he talked. Aris could only see the expression on the man's face when he passed the small lantern that he used to find his way in the dark.

"This garbage from Papa Justo about the governor asking him to run against me is just that ... garbage. I will tell you what this is really about. It goes back to the feud between our great-grandfathers. The Justos were damned Japanese sympathizers. There was bloodshed and the Justos lost a lot of family. And now, he can no longer stand it that a Lapez is sitting in the same seat that his father held. All these years of regret that he didn't even try to keep the mayor's chair in his family have finally gotten to him. The governor hates me? I am too corrupt? It is all a smoke screen to hide his animosity toward me."

Aris finished three cigarettes while watching Marino think aloud, vacillating between what was the catalyst for Justo's entry into mayoral politics. Was it the feud? Maybe it was the governor because Bersamins were NPA too, until they legitimized with the Cordillera movement.

Aris had brought up the pictures, but Marino did not delve into whether he actually had a mistress holed up in the house. Instead, Marino admitted it was a savvy and correct observation about the upcoming opening for Bangued mayor.

"No matter the cause, the situation is different than I anticipated," Marino said after a long silence. "Papa Justo is no longer just an annoying man. He has always talked against me behind my back, but he has never tried to turn other town leaders against me. Sniveling back biter. That American money has affected his mind."

Aris sneered, still intimate with the sorrow and hate that accompanied reminders of Elnora.

"I will call Lopito in the morning. We have to plan for the worse case scenario, which is campaigning against Justo, his American money and perhaps even the governor's blessing. How will I win in the midst of all of that?"

Marino grabbed a machete and savagely drove it into the nearest tree.

"It is too soon. I do not have the money for this!"

The mayor approached Aris, standing close to him now. "I will need more than spies now. I will need security. Papa Justo may try something to depose me—or dispose of me—before we get close to the election. You have been a long time employee of mine. A trusted one. You are good with weapons?"

Aris nodded, knowing Marino was asking him to become a bodyguard.

"I could be your bodyguard. But why me? You have other members of your family working for you as advisors. Lopito helped with going door to door. Thomas' father helped you get elected in the first place. Why not pick Thomas for this?"

"Thomas is too pure," Marino said matter-of-factly. "Politics is messy business. Sometimes very messy. I trust Thomas with other affairs, but not with my political interests. Thomas is a healer, like his father. Thomas won't kill for me. He won't injure for me. Step in front of a bullet, maybe, shoot back, certainly not."

"And me?"

"I think you would step in front of that bullet and shoot back at the same time if the reward is large enough," Marino said, searching Aris' face for confirmation.

Marino nodded when he got it.

"I will pay you double your salary now. More when things get a little exciting."

Aris gripped Marino's hand in acceptance.

"Do you have any cousins, friends, other people you trust?"

Aris nodded.

"Are they good with guns and will they follow your orders? My orders?"

"For the right amount of money, yes."

Marino said he didn't need them now, only if Justo began to amass too many guards.

"Justo can have this damn town once I am in place in Bangued," Marino muttered. "He had the five years right. It will be perfect. Ricky will be college age. I will have the money and influence to get him enrolled anywhere he wants."

As he fetched the machete from the tree, the mayor laughed, not because something was funny, but because he had an idea. He cleared his throat. "Unfortunately, that would damn my soul to hell." From that comment Aris was able to determine that Marino had just decided against knocking off Papa Justo early. Correction: having Aris kill Papa Justo.

Marino pulled out the machete and wished pesos grew on the trees instead of mangoes. It wasn't easy to gather millions of pesos from such a poor town, he lamented.

"You can go home, Aris. Papa Justo took away your future. Now he is trying to take away mine. We will be a good duo fighting him."

Aris said nothing. After a long drag on another cigarette, he discarded it and walked slowly out of the grove.

"Prestige. Power. Money. I can relax and enjoy my grandchildren." Marino sighed. "Nice house. Nice cars. Maybe a second or third young mistress. Most of all, I can thumb my nose at everyone here who once looked down on me."

He glanced back in the direction of Calamba.

"These are about to become dangerous times."

< <> >

Aris went home, but he did not sleep. Marino's reminders of Elnora weighed on him.

"What did a goddamed white dick have that mine does not," he said to himself in a haze of nicotine and gin.

Armed and drunk, Aris wandered the town, sometimes losing his balance in a pothole on the concrete roads. At the outskirts of the town, the concrete turned to dirt and stone. Along that road, uphill, Aris reached the town spring. Water bubbled up from the aquifer underneath the stoned-in pool. Hot water in the morning and cool in the afternoon.

Townspeople bathed in it. Washed clothes in it. The children played in it.

It was the place Aris had taken Elnora's virginity. At a night like this, not so humid. He recalled little of the quality of their first sex, they were both too drunk at the time.

Aris was alone at the spring. No one dared to come here in the night because of a superstition of a mermaid haunting the waters.

Aris stumbled down the steep stone steps, laying on his back near the statue of Mother Mary. The sound of his beating heart filled one ear, the sound of the water rushing out of the pool and down the overflow waterfall in the other. The water filled a trench at the bottom of the hill, irrigated some of the rice fields nearby and then emptied into the Abra River.

Aris emptied his stomach of some of its alcohol.

The orange light of the pre-dawn told Aris he had been laying on the steps for hours, passed out from the booze.

A scraping sound drew Aris' attention to the spring. Someone was descending the other set of steps.

Aris blinked. It was female.

Aris blinked again. It was Gloria Casao.

Gloria, who was Elnora's cousin and friend. Yes, of course, the Casao family lived on the spiraling mountain road out of Calamba, several minutes walk from the school ahead. Gloria had come back to the Philippines after Elnora got married to the *kano*. She had been with Elnora in Hong Kong during that time. Yes, she was probably in on it all, Aris seethed. She was a Justo relative after all. Gloria's grandmother was Lino's aunt.

Aris kept still and Gloria did not see him watching her from behind the statue. He watched her undress and step into the water. She unwrapped soap and a shampoo bottle hidden in her towel.

So early? Yes, she was a teacher at the school. She had to be ready by the time the children arrived. It was Lino Justo that got her the teaching job once she'd returned from a career as a Chinese's housemaid.

Aris could make out no more than her shape in the water. It was a nice shape, he thought.

Aris spit out the left over vomit pooled in his cheeks. In the roar of the waterfall, Gloria heard nothing. She also didn't hear Aris creep down the remaining steps and crouch at the other end of the spring's pool to watch her.

Gloria had lathered her arms and chest and was working the shampoo through her long straight hair. Aris sprinted and pounced on her, driving her head beneath the water surface. He could hear her bubbling scream. When the flailing and struggling ceased, Aris pulled Gloria's head out of the water and dragged her by the hair out onto the edge.

Aris saw that she had no pubic hair.

"You are a whore," Aris said. "A shaven whore."

Aris forced himself upon her, all the while muffling her complaints with his hand.

And it felt good.
When it was over, he took his knife and slit her throat.
And it felt good.
"Give my regards to Papa Justo."
Aris left her for the mermaid, floating face down in the water.

CHAPTER 5
LIMA

Joy didn't know the name of the typhoon raging outside, but she had some unflattering ones of her own for it.

A week ago, the first typhoon of the season had blown through southern Luzon, hit the ocean and was now a tropical storm on its way to Taiwan. It barely affected the northern section of the Philippines' largest island.

The second one was on its heels. This one descended upon northern Luzon. It was barely a typhoon, but strong enough to keep people indoors until it passed later tonight. There was no threat of being carried away by it winds, but there was a danger in getting hit by debris while outside. The rain bit into the faces of people trying to race from house to house. They were soaked in an instant. Trees tilted slightly. Palm leaves waved like little banners.

The battery-powered radio was playing in the kitchen for musical distraction and typhoon updates. The radio announcer, probably a student at Abra Valley in Bangued, began her banter with others in the studio. The exchange was Taglish—Tagalog and English words mixed together—along with some Ilocano. Typhoon Banyan was holding steady in Category 2 with the eye to reach the Cordillera Mountains later in the day. Coming up, Sharon Cuneta and Toni Gonzaga. But now, here is a song from an American Idol winner.

Mayor Marino always opened his home to townsfolk during typhoons. Hundreds gathered, disbursed throughout the den, hallways and kitchen. For a time, there was singing. If the storm lasted long enough, the oil lanterns would be lit in the evening and there would be bingo.

Because of the fun, Joy always enjoyed typhoons in the past. There was no fun in her new role.

The smell of *pinakbet* wafted from the kitchen. Joy observed the simmering stew of eggplant, bitter melon and okra. On the other burner fueled by a small butane tank was a pot of rice. Preparing lunch was sure to exhaust the tank, forcing dinner to be prepared using the old wood burning stove, which was obscured in its corner by an old yellow sheet.

To cook for this many people required the dirty kitchen and its wide wood fire cooking surface. That was outside. It was usable in rain storms because of the overhang. It was usable on windy days because of the courtyard wall. The protection from the elements was useless against a typhoon.

The inside kitchen wasn't big enough to efficiently cook for an entire neighborhood. She was sure she'd need to light it just to have another cooking area for lunch. Ricky ignored her request to bring in the wood and start the fire. Joy was occupied with slicing vegetables for *pancit*. There were long beans to ready for the *sinagang*.

"Luis! I told you to stay away from the door," admonished Maricar's older sister, Lara, catching her son again trying to sneak out to play in the puddles.

"Luis can't walk," the toddler wailed.

"Yes, you can. Walk back here and get away from the door."

"Luis can't walk," the tantrum continued.

"Pouting again. You are lucky you are over there and my hand cannot reach your butt."

"Luis can't walk."

"Joy, get him so he quits," Lara ordered.

Lara, stuck in a marriage with a cheating husband, was perpetually sour. There was no way to divorce the man, since divorce wasn't legally recognized in the Philippines. Annulment was an option if Lara wanted to pay for it. Since she could not afford it, estranged separation was the best Lara was getting out of the situation. The husband had fathered another child with the other woman and seemed to be apt to care for the bastard than his own legitimate son.

Privately, Joy didn't blame the man. It was hard enough to be around the surly woman for a few minutes, she could not imagine enduring the brunt of Lara's negativity all day, every day. No one knew where she got it. Lara took after her father in body shape, but little else. Auntie Betty was as fat as Maricar, yet both of them carried good demeanors.

The *chika chika*, gossipy girl talk, had centered most of the morning on Lara's deadbeat husband and condescending names for a bastard child. Joy paid little attention to it, focused internally on her own sufferings.

Even if there wasn't a 150 kmh wind blowing outside, there was no force of will that got Joy out of the house. Rowena was sickened by the constant moping. "It is so hard to be separated," Joy had cried. "Hoy! Girl, I wish I were away from your father for a few weeks," Rowena had said. "There is too much stress all of the sudden from that damn politics. Whatever is going on with your father is making him crazy."

The rainy season from July to November always made the Abra River high enough to flood out the bridge leading from Bangued. Even though it was

July and early in the season, adding the high winds to rising water made the river waves unmanageable now. It kept Thomas from coming home last weekend, and now this weekend, and maybe next weekend. Three weeks without her *ayat*!

Jon-Jon had driven Thomas to Baguio. Joy hung on him the entire trip in the jeepney and lingered in Lopito's house while he unpacked. Maricar and Jon-Jon had to peel her off him to get home before it became dark. Come on, Joy, only one headlight works. He's not leaving forever, Jon-Jon had said.

No, not forever, but the last three weeks had felt like it.

Joy left her lunch preparation long enough to pull the legitimate child, the perpetually pouting Luis, away from the kitchen door that led out into the Lapez compound. The boy went limp as soon as her hand touched him, so she had to drag him for a second before lifting the expert of nonviolent resistance into her arms in order to deposit him next to his mother.

Too busy talking to help, Joy noticed. As were the rest.

Amelie Valera's feet were propped up in front of Auntie Betty, Maricar and Lara's mother, who was one of the people sought out in town for manicures and pedicures. There was no salon shop in Calamba. Betty and a few others with knowledge made a small living out of going to people's homes to cut hair and paint nails.

Marites Galope was waiting her turn. She had the biggest mouth, thus she was the loudest voice. "There are fewer people here than normal," she noticed.

"There are a lot of people at the Justo house this time. He has electric generators," Amelie explained. "I'd be over there watching television, but I need my toes cleaned out."

Joy wished Maricar had accompanied her mother and sister so that she could have her own companion. But since her engagement with Jon-Jon became official, she spent less time with Joy. Understandable, she supposed.

The neighbor Merly Legadi drifted into the kitchen. The woman noticed Joy's vegetable cutting technique and couldn't resist the urge to correct it.

Joy tried to be attentive, dropping her arms to her side. "Yes, Auntie," Joy answered. "Thank you, Auntie."

Merly had a satisfied smile on her face as she left Joy's side, as though she'd actually parted with some useful knowledge. Joy mumbled to herself that she wasn't stupid, she didn't need instruction.

"What is that awful coughing?" Merly asked.

"That's Emma. Her asthma is bad again," Betty said.

"I'll go see her." And off Merly was to the main room.

To teach her the correct way to cough, Joy wondered.

Joy internally cursed Ricky's absence. The boy needed to go get some fire wood for the other stove. The fish *sinagang* could simmer there while she used the burners for *pancit*, which was faster cooking.

"Jon-Jon named his jeepney after my Maricar after she said yes," Betty said.

There were some fascinating innuendos in that.

Auntie Betty was leaving out the best gossip, the fact that Jon-Jon proposed because he thought Maricar was pregnant. But Joy wasn't about to offer that to the conversation.

"Shout outs going to Bong Bong, Arlen, Tess and Mary Rose stuck at home from the typhoon from your dorm friends ... Lovely says hi to Sammo ... And a happy 18th birthday today for Joy in Calamba. Thomas is thinking of you. Romantic, *na*? Be back with some Britney Spears on Hot FM 105.5."

There was a small roar in the room.

"Oh, *ayat*," Joy said. A smile disturbed the path of the joyful tears descended her cheek.

"Joy, you cry for everything," Lara said, rolling her eyes. "Overacting. It is only a radio message."

And you complain for everything, Joy thought.

"He may even be swimming up the river now just to get a glimpse of you," Betty teased.

"You two were like brother and sister," Lara snarled. "Isn't it weird kissing him?"

Joy got flushed in the cheeks. To even suggest such a thing meant Lara thought she and Thomas had... But of course, they assumed. Small town talk started the moment anyone saw a boy and girl together. Even if there was no sex, the assumption was to the contrary.

"Oh, come on Joy! What else are you two doing at his farm?" Lara said. "Or in front of Valera's sari-sari every night?"

Amelie Valera concurred from her chair near the radio. There was some laughter in the room, except for Lara, who was naturally immune from smiling.

Ricky finally crashed into the kitchen. "Did you hear that? Thomas called into the radio station from wherever he is."

Joy was thankful for the interruption allowing her to shift the conversation away from delving into her intimate relationship with Thomas.

"Ricky, fetch me some wood from the dirty kitchen."

"I'm not going out there," he protested.

"It is safe, Ricky, the wind is hitting the front of the house, it isn't going to blow you away."

"I'll get wet."

"Come on, you went swimming in your clothes yesterday."

Ricky shook his head and bolted back the way he came. Joy closed her eyes and seethed. It was bad enough there was a typhoon blowing on her birthday, which she'd celebrated with Thomas in the American tradition where Filipinos tended to ignore the day. Bad enough Thomas wasn't here. Bad enough she was the only one charged with cooking for 50 people.

She was fooling herself. When did Ricky ever help? When was he ever forced to do so?

Joy stood in the back doorway. The only water dripped from the sill, making a puddle where the welcome mat once laid. The wind gusted, creating a quick vacuum that stole Joy's breath.

"Luis, don't you even try it," Lara warned.

She held back Luis in the child's next chance to bolt the boredom of being inside. The boy went back to wailing. This time Lara bothered to get out of her chair to get Luis.

Joy didn't really want to wander out into 150 kmh winds either, but the consequences were less dire than her father walking into the kitchen demanding to know why his guests are starving. She used her hand as blinders to stop the wind from cutting her eyes with the rain and then sprinted into the storm. As soon as she was far enough into the courtyard that the wind was able to work its way around the house, she knew her back was instantly soaked. Her front would be also soon as she turned to face the typhoon with an arm full of chopped branches and logs.

A wet shirt wasn't her chief concern. It was the wind smashing her nose. The habit was too strong to resist and before she started gathering the wood, she pinched her nose for good measure. Thomas always said it looked the same after she pinched it as before she did so. It was irrational to think it would be flattened by the wind and stay that way. But she made sure.

Everything was drenched by the time she got inside with an armful of wood that was dry enough to burn. She felt embarrassed, even though it was a kitchen filled with women. Thankfully, Aris wasn't hanging about. He always stared at Joy. And it wasn't in the same manner that he watched the men working in the grove.

She pulled open the old metal cover and piled some of the wood on the bottom. Ash from the last time it was used dusted the sides. Efforts to light the sticks with matches failed. Perhaps some charcoal lighting gas was needed. She thought of igniting one of the sticks by placing the end in the blue flame of the burner.

"That old wood stove should have been lit a long time ago," Rowena said.

Her mother was standing behind her and it startled Joy.

"It will be well past time to eat before it is hot enough to cook."

"Sorry, mother, I was waiting for help to get the wood."

"Get the wood? The wood should have been brought in last night. The typhoon wasn't a secret." Rowena examined the pile. "This is too wet to even light. Even after it dries a bit, there will be a lot of smoke because of the water in it now."

"Sorry, mother."

"You're in charge of the kitchen now, Joy. You're responsible for making sure it operates properly. You need to think ahead. If this was organized properly, you'd have everything done by now."

Joy didn't get out another apology. Rowena's slap across the back of her head was more quick than hard. It wasn't painful. Not in that way.

"Stop moping about Thomas and start taking your job seriously."

Rowena threw her hands in the air and declared it all a disaster. How were the people going to eat on time?

She told Joy to stop chit-chatting with everyone, even though she really wasn't, get the rice in a serving bowl, start the *pancit* over one burner, heat the leftover fish on the other before starting the *sinagang*. At least the most hungry would have something to eat now. Even though Rowena complimented the *pinakbet*, the humiliation of being scolded in front of her peers was too stinging.

She wanted Rowena to take over so that she could escape to her bedroom and kick out whomever was hiding out in there. Her mother didn't.

It was silent when Rowena left. The *chika chika* crowd was relishing the moment, Joy knew. They were enjoying her incompetence and failure.

It wasn't fair. It was her birthday. Thomas always got a party on his birthday. A sweet cake with lots of sugar and butter spread on it. As a child there were candles to blow. She never got that. Until last year, when Thomas bought her a small cake so that she could experience an American-style birthday once. If the storm hadn't prevented Thomas from returning to the province, there'd be another such party today.

Joy told herself to stop moping over Thomas, as her mother had ordered, and stop moping about having a miserable typhoon-ruined birthday. She put the rice and *pinakbet* in large bowls. She retrieved some smoked fish from the stores and warmed it in a pan. She didn't care if the smell was initially pungent and oppressive. As a matter of fact, she wished it was terrible enough to clear the kitchen. The leftover fish was still cold in the refrigerator, though the appliance had not been running since the electricity had died the night before when Typhoon Banyan was just starting to whip its winds.

While the fish was cooking, she finished chopping the vegetables for *pancit* and *sinagang*. The fish went onto different plates. She took the bucket of clean cooking water and poured it into another to soak the *pancit* noodles.

The *chika chika* resumed. Auntie Betty finished Amelie's pedicure and moved onto Marites. Luis was content for the moment sitting on the concrete floor and banging an iron skillet with a stick.

"I heard Elnora sent some movies in her last *balikbayan* box," Amelie said. "Taped them off HBO in America. I'll bet they're watching them now over at the Justo house."

"Well, I'm not running over there now," Marites retorted. "Auntie Dina's roof already flew off."

Joy started boiling water. The wood stove would surely be needed for another meal. Rowena will probably blame her for not having any extra butane tanks stored in the compound. It was Aris' fault they were empty. He always raided them to fill his cigarette lighter. Occasionally, he was too drunk to realize that he needed to re-seal the tank after he was done.

"I heard Elnora sent a bold movie once," Amelie gossiped.

"Nina probably studied it," Marites said.

"Em-Tess!" Auntie Betty looked up. "I can't believe you just said that."

"Ever since she won Miss Abra, Nina Justo has been so stuck up to everyone and the boys won't leave her alone."

So boys have been ignoring you, Marites, Joy thought, as if that was any different than before.

"She must be doing something," Marites continued, "because they're certainly not chasing after her because of that crown."

Joy sighed. "Nina is not a *puta*. She never had as many boyfriends as you think. She only wants you to think that so she can get what she wants. Men think they can get something if they do her a favor. Papa Justo is not going to let his daughter be so fast and easy with men."

The jaws were more slack in reaction to Joy's comment than in the gossip that Nina could be watching dirty movies.

"Did your mother knock your head too hard?" Lara asked. "Since when did you start sticking up for Nina Justo? You two stopped being friends in high school. Justo and Lapez are a feud."

Nina didn't stop being friendly to Joy because of the Justo-Lapez feud that was only political bickering between their fathers anyway. Being prissy and stuck up was as natural to Nina as jaded condescension was to Lara.

No, Nina hated Joy because of Thomas. He was the only boy who dared to ever break up with her.

Joy recalled many fights with Thomas when they were small children. Hair pulling. Throwing stones. Smashing well constructed dirt houses. She recalled only one fight since their relationship matured to dating, when she took up smoking. From his father's death, it was natural for Thomas to have very strong feelings against smoking. It became the only break up in their dating lives. It was only for two weeks. Sophomore year in school. When Thomas ventured to Nina.

He was mad enough that Joy had taken up cigarettes, but then she started sneaking to the church so that she could smoke without her parents knowing. When she offered one to Thomas, he snapped.

"Hell no! Goddamn it, what are you thinking?"

"Stop cursing. Say a prayer for God's forgiveness or you will end up in hell."

"Hell no, I am not going to say a prayer! And hell no, I am not going to put one of those things in my mouth!" He slapped the pack out of her hand.

"What?" she asked, indignantly. "Car-Car and Reggie tried them…"

"Where did you get them anyway? You're too young to be buying them."

"Reggie," Joy answered, picking up the pack. "She got Amelie Valera to take some out of her dad's sari-sari."

"Stealing?"

"No, stupid. Reggie paid. And then I gave Reggie some pesos…"

"You should know better!" Thomas kept raging.

"What is the problem? I'm just trying them. I like it. My head gets fuzzy for a little bit."

"If you're going to smoke, I don't want to be around you!"

"What?"

Thomas stormed out of the Hideout. She called his name.

"Leave me alone. Stay away from me."

Joy played it cool for a few days, staying away from Thomas, thinking it would blow over and things would return to normal. He smelled smoke on her clothes when she tried to talk to him again. An hour later he asked Nina Justo if she wanted to accompany him to Bangued. He was seen holding her hand before school the next Monday.

When Joy saw Thomas holding hands with Nina Justo, she was devastated. She went into insane fits of crying. Thomas was her *ayat* and no one else was to have him. Emma and Rowena talked, tried to intervene and were unsuccessful. Thomas did not tattle on Joy's newfound habit. He kept his answers short and ambiguous. Crying was Joy's weapon on Thomas. He couldn't stand to see her cry, to see her hurt. Joy gave herself credit for not abusing the knowledge, but she used it to get Thomas back that time. After two weeks, Thomas had reached his tolerance of seeing Joy's puffy red eyes and tolerance of dealing with Nina's starvation for attention. He was sorry for using Nina to hurt Joy. Joy apologized for being insensitive to his father's death from smoking. "I don't want you to die like him," he had told her. In a few weeks, their relationship was back to normal.

Nina turned spiteful in the aftermath of Thomas spurning her growing affections. He was not surprised that she was the cause of him being taunted as Little Joe again—at least among the classmates who sought popularity with Nina.

Joy wished she had the guts to stand up to Thomas the same way when he wanted to drink alcohol. She carried just as strong feelings against it as he did for smoking. If there was a chink in their relationship, that was it.

With Marino's sudden presence in the kitchen, talk of Nina Justo came to a halt.

"There are guests waiting for food," Marino said. It was hard to discern whether he was simply making an order clouded in an observation, or was angry about the situation and concealing it because of the guests.

Rowena floated into the kitchen as Marino said some pleasantries to Betty. He inquired as to where the First Councilor was holed up for the typhoon. Oh, the Paculdar residence with Maricar. It made sense since Ramirez and Paculdar were friends, the same batch in school too.

"What do you want, dear?" Rowena asked her husband dutifully.

Marino stopped smiling at Betty and scanned the kitchen.

"No coffee?"

Of course not. Without electricity, there was no coffeemaker.

Marino did as much talking with his eyes as most people did with their mouths. Uncertainty began transforming into disappointment. Disappointment easily became anger.

And Marino's blows to the head actually hurt.

Rowena's concerned glance reached Joy.

Joy had an immediate thought. There was hot water on the burner. Instant coffee. She gathered the essentials and poured the hot water into a clean mug.

Rowena then took over. Marino waited until Rowena had stirred in the sugar and powdered creamer before reaching for the mug. He tested the liquid. Nodded. Took a swig. Without any thanks, he turned to leave the kitchen.

The tension inside Joy left as well.

"Make one for Auntie Emma, too. She needs to drink something warm," Rowena said. "And then get these plates out there. Finish cooking the rest. I'll think about what's to be for dinner. We'll get that old stove running soon."

With new orders, Joy went back to her slaving. Activity in the kitchen went back to normal.

"Luis, get away from that door."

Emma Wagner laid in state in the front room of her house for two days before Thomas had the chance to return from the university. Marino had phoned Lopito with the news of Emma's death. Lopito relayed the message when Thomas returned from classes. Information was sparse, he only knew that Emma died in the hospital in La Paz.

The Abra River was high and the bridges submerged. The water was too rough for the ferry. Boatmen declined to take anyone either, watching their colleague's boats flip for the sake of the small fare. A desperate Thomas played on one of their consciences and offered to pay double for a short trip across, who took pity on him and transported him for the extra money. Thomas walked several kilometers to La Paz. There he was able to talk his way into a motor trike ride to Calamba. He was met in the middle of town with an onslaught of condolences, but all he wanted to do was get home to see his mother. He had to see her with his own eyes.

The river was less fierce, but still high, as it wound around Calamba. The driving bridge was submerged. Thomas saw that his own kayak was beached on the wrong side. Tied at its highest point, the rope bridge was not completely submerged. Thomas became soaked to the shin when he reached the sag in the middle where his weight was enough to dip himself into the river's current. Stepping one foot in front of the other, and clinging tightly to the guide ropes, he was able to navigate the waves.

He sprinted up the path through the small woods and into the clearing of dirt and wild grasses that constituted the front of his house. He did not get his customary greeting. The dog was tied to one of the trees. Ricky was sitting on his basketball in the courtyard and had only the chance to get "*manong*" past his tongue before the running Thomas was inside.

Marino was standing in the living room with a weeping Rowena kneeling in front of a white coffin. It was tradition for the dead family member to lay in the coffin in the house for a week before entombment. Blue and red flowers and pictures were already piled around Emma's body. A lifeless face stared up at Thomas.

Rowena was keeping vigil, recounting the good deeds done by Emma throughout her life. "She always played fair at mahjong ... She made the best *lumpia* in Calamba ... She gave rice to the Masakayan family in the drought ..." When Thomas arrived, she ceased the vigil, but did not rise from her knees. Her godson dripped water over the hardwood floor.

Thomas released his dammed up sorrow. The cries brought Joy out of Thomas' bedroom. She bounded through the house and crashed into Thomas, arms wrapped tightly around him. He dislodged Joy to be able to reach for his mother. He shoveled the gifts and flowers out of the coffin so that there was room to fit his arms around her and lift the body into his chest. "*Nanang! Nanang!*" He shook the body with his heaves of grief.

The feel of her was alien to him. She had always been soft and warm. As a child, his face disappeared into her belly when she hugged him, bombarded with the smells of Tide and whatever she was cooking. Now her skin was cold and hardened.

"*Nanang!* Wake up, '*nang.*"

Mother wasn't waking up. He kissed her cheek. She always smiled when he kissed her cheek. Despite being an adult, she would smile and slap him on the arm and call him *ubing*. Child. Baby. Her first child. Her only child.

Thomas examined her face again. It looked like her, but he found nothing else of her essence. She smelled like the coffin and whatever spray they had used to keep her hair in place.

Marino begged Thomas to put Emma back down. Rowena finally came to her feet to help Marino prevent Thomas from destroying the coffin and disheveling his mother further.

Thomas settled himself and returned his mother's body into a prone position within the coffin. He wiped his eyes on his T-shirt sleeve.

"How can she be dead? Lopito said she was in the hospital. Why? No one told me she was in the hospital. Why?"

Joy grabbed him again, this time to move him away from the coffin. While Marino recovered the items on the floor, Rowena tried to explain Emma's hospitalization. Her asthma had gotten worse from the last typhoon through the weeks of constant rain. When Rowena felt it had gotten worse and couldn't stand it, she took Emma to La Paz. She had actually contracted pneumonia. Because she was always coughing from asthma, it wasn't caught until too late.

"How? I was home only a few weeks ago and she wasn't bad."

"It was sudden, Thomas," Rowena tried to console. "Emma didn't want to tell you she went to the hospital or you'd worry and not be able to concentrate on your class work. Her death was sudden. She was responding to the medicine. We were playing mahjong by her bed. I went home. When I came back, the doctors said she died in the night. In her sleep. It was sudden."

Thomas was inconsolable for awhile, but found himself sitting in a chair, silently watching Rowena resume her prayers for Emma. Joy brought him drinks and food and dry clothing. Marino left the house to supervise Ricky, who wanted to feed the water buffaloes, chickens and pigs.

In the afternoon, visitors started to arrive to pay their respects to Emma and the orphan *puraw*. The wailing women got on Thomas' nerves after awhile. He was thankful Joy kept her composure, standing at his side to meet the mourning visitors. Then she sat quietly with him when the people left.

Marlon and Lorena Arroyo had flowers for Emma's coffin. Auntie Betty brought a replica of the hat Emma wore in sun. Even Aris seemed sympathetic when the Luceros officially visited the house. Merly Legadi brought barbecue pork skewers for Thomas from her daughter's small food stand. Regina Flora came back from Quezon City to be with Jon-Jon and Maricar and Ronaldo, who hung around the house for most of three days.

It was instantly tense when Papa Justo arrived.

Marino watched intently from his perch in the kitchen, away from the procession. Aris was not in the house, but was nearby just in case there was a ruckus. It would be unwise for Justo to do anything now. The time of mourning over one of the town's beloved Aunties was not to be trifled with, so Marino expected nothing but a respectful visit from his rival.

Justo did not even acknowledge Marino's presence when he entered, trailed by his wife Imelda, and then Nina and then their bodyguard, Ringor Fillion. Strapped to Ringor's belt was a black baton, a painted metal night stick that he used often in his dirty work. At least that was what the reputation told of the nearly 6-foot Penarubbia man. Ringor wore his hair short, the product of military service or prison time – either reason fit.

Ringor stood behind Papa Justo as the family looked down onto Emma's face, presenting some trinket—a gift from the past perhaps—to leave with Emma forever. After the solemn moment, Justo turned to the head of the casket and offered to shake Thomas' hand. Thomas accepted the gesture of condolence and the kind words that followed.

Nina was bawling worse than he had ever seen her cry. She had the looks of a Barbie doll and was just as plastic. Thomas thought the weight of the moment was probably overpowering her more than any real remorse over Emma.

"It must be difficult to finish your college and run the farm. I can help you, Thomas. I have some extra people at the mill who are good farm hands. They can keep an eye on things here while you are in Baguio," Justo offered.

"*Salamat, po,*" Thomas replied respectfully. "Thank you, Papa Justo, that is kind of you, but I haven't had a chance to decide what I'm going to do."

It was an honest answer.

"If you need help, just let me know," Justo replied with a hint of disappointment.

When the Justo family had left, Marino stood and approached Thomas. "You handled that well," he said with a pat on the back for his godson. Thomas would note later that it was one of the few times he'd ever been praised by the man.

Marino may have been pleased about that, but leaving Joy in the house at night to watch over Thomas didn't. He was unhappy enough to have a loud conversation in the hallway, awakening Thomas from a late afternoon nap.

"Someone needs to watch Thomas. You know the traditions, he is not supposed to do any chores or else he's the next to die, so he needs someone to attend to his needs."

Auntie Ro's persuasion garnered a disbelieving "bah" from Marino. "That is just old superstition."

"He's not going to leave here to stay with us. And he cannot be left here alone with Emma's corpse. Ricky is scared of ghosts and wouldn't let Thomas get any rest. It has to be Joy."

"But staying the night..." Marino started.

"Do you want her crossing the high river in the dark? The bridges are flooded. Even the walking bridge was stretched higher to miss the water, but people still show up with damp shoes. The only other way across is by kayak. I don't want someone down the river in Pingaping to find her washed up dead. Not to mention, young ladies don't walk around without an escort in the night. Not after Gloria Casao was murdered at the water spring."

Marino's frown was so pronounced, Thomas could hear it. "You know what people will think if she stays the night. I don't want them to infer... They will talk up a storm that the mayor's daughter is... They're not married..."

"Not yet," Rowena retorted, "and you know what I'm talking about. I know how it would look to the rest of the town, but how do you think you're going to keep them apart? I already taught her cooking and cleaning to be a decent wife to Thomas when they finally get married. I cannot take care of two households and arrange a funeral dinner at the same time. I cannot do everything. Joy has to help me. So she helps me over here."

Marino was steadfast. "She can stay until dark. An escort can bring her home. Maybe Aris."

"She hates Aris."

"Then Albio, or some of the grove workers, like Cabasan or Velasquez."

Rowena reluctantly agreed to the terms.

But Lazy Velasquez never showed up the first night to escort Joy across the river. Nor the second. So she had to stay in the Wagner house. When the next mornings arrived, no one asked how Joy watched over Thomas in the night. Sleeping beside him in the same bed, she watched him very well.

Thomas had been sleeping until he felt Joy's hand run through his hair. With the curtains drawn, it was completely dark inside the house. The only sound was that of the electric fan moving the air. There was electricity in the night. Brownouts were only commonplace in the day. Outside the house was the normal din of the roosters with vague answers in the distance from the town.

"You're awake?" he mumbled, reaching out to find Joy.

His hands found her. She wasn't dressed either.

"I cannot sleep. I'm thinking about you. About us," she whispered. Joy rolled on top of him to lay her head on his chest. "The funeral is tomorrow and then you're free from being the grieving son."

"I'm going to be the grieving son for a long time."

Thomas had thought a lot about his father in recent days, recalling the man's death as vividly as his mother's was unfolding now. There were times Ted couldn't breathe if he laid down, so it was not uncommon to find him sleeping in his chair in the living room—a chair now relegated to a barn to avoid invoking the memory of his death. Then one morning he didn't wake up.

"I didn't get to say goodbye to either of them."

Joy exhaled a sound of sympathy and squeezed him.

Thomas had to grow up faster than his peers. Ronaldo and Jon-Jon even now were able to laugh and play and live with little responsibility. Thomas assumed the man-of-the-house role since the day Ted died. Health always kept Emma from being able to do anything burdensome. Despite Aris doing a decent job of running the tractor, Emma still had to watch the crops and tend the animals while Thomas was away. It weakened Emma to the point of sickness. Then death.

"If I had not gone away, she would still be alive."

"It is not your fault your mother died."

"It is."

"No, Thomas, don't try to blame yourself for this."

"Medicine is expensive. College is expensive. She sacrificed the one for the other."

"Stop it. She had the money for both."

"She coughs a lot in the rainy season, but she never got so sick while I was around that she needed the hospital. She wouldn't have worked too hard if I was here. She wouldn't have let herself slip so far if I had been here."

"What would Father Herman tell you right now? Everyone has a time on this earth. God took your mother. Her time was up. God is going to take her up to be with your father. Where you were and what you were doing at the time didn't matter. When God wants you, that is it, He is going to take you up also."

Yes, Father Herman would say exactly that.

"Did you ever notice her staring at us sometimes? I know she was piecing together our features to make up images of our children," Thomas said. "She

51

could hardly wait for her grandchildren. She wanted babies all over the house because she couldn't have enough of her own. I must have been some kind of miracle to be born alive. She isn't going to get to play with our children, Joy. We even named them. Remember that? Joel for a boy. Josephine for a girl."

Thomas was trying so hard to keep himself in check.

"How old were we then? I can hardly remember it except that all of our friends laughed so hard that Little Joe was going to have a little Joe-sephine." Joy tried to laugh also, but it came out weak. "We can name the first one Emma in honor of your mother. Or Ted in honor of your father."

"No, I still like Josephine."

"Okay. Josephine Emma or Joel Theodore."

Thomas wanted to make Joy his family. In reality, not just perception. He wanted to propose marriage, but the timing wasn't right. Even if it weren't the night before a funeral, the timing wasn't right. It was the tradition that the groom and the groom's family paid for weddings. They were large affairs involving the entire town. Everyone ate—and ate well—at weddings. Thomas did not have the means yet for such an event.

"Oh, Joy my joy, I don't have a family anymore. I have only you now."

Joy tried to shush his tears. Thomas hadn't cried since his father died. She would not retain her own composure if he was crying. Thomas hiccupped a few times and breathed deeply to ward off the another onset of weeping.

"When the time is right, *ayat*, it will be a happy day," Joy whispered.

"Reading my mind again?" He kissed the top of her head, threading her hair in his whiskers. "What can I do now? Stay here or go back to Baguio? I feel like I cannot leave. I feel that I should not stay. I cannot decide anything now. There is too much happening. It is hard to think clearly."

"Take your time. Your mother just died, no one is going to force you to choose a path."

There were tears welling in his eyes again, but this time for a different feeling. "My God, how could I take this if I didn't have you? Everything else is irrelevant. It is not a life without you."

It was too dark to see her face, but he knew the look he was getting. It was that pure adoration that showed through her eyes when her heart was the warmest. She lowered her head and kissed his chest instead of burying her face there. She whispered her pet names for him and told him that she loved him.

Joy pulled the sheet atop them. While Thomas enjoyed the fan blowing directly on his body, Joy got cold in the night. She settled her head on his chest to be used as a pillow, nestled close to use his body for warmth. He had the emotions to make love to her again, but not the physical strength. Instead, he stroked her hair until she fell asleep. Not long after that, he did also.

The next morning's funeral followed the Ilocano traditions.

Thomas kissed his mother's hand and paid his last respects before the coffin closed. Joy and Rowena then lowered black veils across their faces. On cue, Marino beheaded a hen and threw the carcass in the courtyard in front of the door.

Thomas threw rice atop the coffin for good luck. Pallbearers lifted Emma's coffin and quickly walked it out of the house, making sure it didn't touch any part of the house.

One of the Botalico cousins lost grip and allowed the coffin to dip and touch the doorframe on the way out. Another cousin hissed at him about it being bad luck, another death will occur in the family, if the coffin touched any part of the house now.

When the coffin left the house, all the doors and windows were closed to prevent Emma's soul from going back inside and haunting those that lived there. The house would not be reopened until after Emma had been laid to rest.

Father Herman conducted the funeral Mass under the largest narra tree on the Wagner farm. It was where Emma buried Ted.

When Emma was in the ground, most of the townspeople left for the after-funeral meal at the mayor's house.

Thomas talked to them both, quietly, for several more minutes before becoming aware of someone watching him. He expected it to be Joy, but saw Father Herman De Vries standing at a respectable distance.

Father Herman spoke flawless Ilocano in his rich Dutch accent. He was the only non-Filipino priest in the province. Calamba, Danglas and La Paz made up his parish. He was no longer wearing his priestly robe and sash, dressed instead in blue slacks and a white T-shirt, as if he were no different than the Filipinos around him. His hair was whiter than his skin. No one really knew how old he was. He was fit, though, from the amount of walking he did. It took an hour to walk to Danglas, but he made the trek on foot a few times a week if it wasn't raining. Herman was accustomed to country life before arriving in the Philippines on assignment four decades ago. His family in Holland were dairy farmers. Herman was tall, long armed, but wide in the shoulder. His feet were too big for Philippine-made flip-flops, so he had special sandals.

Kidnappings for money or political reasons were common throughout the nation, but Westerners were fairly safe in Abra so long as they paid attention to their surrounding and didn't insult the wrong people. Herman was safe anywhere and with anyone, however. With the leaders of the NPA going into self-imposed exile in Holland, it was granted favored nation status among the Communist rebels and Dutch citizens like Herman became untouchable.

Father Herman gave Thomas a bear hug and a hard pat on the back. The priest was Thomas' baptizer, presided over his first communion, tapped him from time to time to assist around the church with odd jobs. Herman offered words of sympathy and encouragement. Thomas expected the priest to mimic Joy's words from last night and tell him it was God's will that Emma died. He came close, saying there was a reason for everything and it was up to him to make the best of the situation given to him.

"Ah, no smile for me today? I understand. I was in the Philippines when my mother died. I was low for many months, but it helped just to be back here and working in my routine. Eventually, the sadness went away and I smiled when the memories of her came to me."

"Thank you, Father."

Herman's warmth and jocularity was infectious. The aged man could find a silver lining in every cloud. People smiled when they were near him. Genuine smiles, not polite ones to hide their feelings. Thomas could not find his genuine smile this time.

"This will be harder on you than most. I can see that. There is so much family around everyone else here. Big families. Lots of aunts and uncles and cousins. Not you. Half of your kin is not even here because of an ocean. And the rest... Well, I was happy to see some Botalicos remembered that your mother was one of them. Death has a tendency to break loose misplaced animosity. Perhaps something happened today and your extended family is finally open to you."

Thomas sighed. He had as much use for them as they did for him. He did not believe a gap created over the course of his lifespan had closed because a few Botalicos came to a funeral. He wouldn't be surprised to see that none of them stayed for the feast.

"Come. Let's eat. I can smell the pig."

Herman gripped Thomas by the shoulder. Thomas glanced back to the Wagner graves. There were more than two. Next to Emma and Theodore were the stones of two others, stillborn siblings who could have been leaning on him now as the oldest. Joel Wagner would have been three years younger than him and as energetic and playful as Ricky. His sister Josephine Wagner would have been nine years younger. Others never lived long enough in his mother's womb to be named. How many? He remembered three of them.

Instead of six Wagners walking across the river to the wake, there was only Thomas.

It was the first time in his life he truly felt alone.

< <> >

Joy continued to pull Thomas by the arm down the street. The declining sun illuminated his face, which was both quizzical and exasperated.

"Please, tell me where we are going. I'm tired and I don't have the mind right now to unravel one of your mysteries," Thomas said.

Joy shot him a stare that he could only interpret one way. Whatever was happening was important.

She had pulled him out of Ricky's bed, where he was napping to recover from the emotional turmoil of the morning. Now she pulled him toward the Catholic church.

Unlike other churches throughout northern Luzon, there was nothing architecturally marvelous about Calamba's. In Vigan, they were relics of the Spanish Empire. Calamba's church was concrete with wooden columns.

"We were just here a few hours ago, praying for *nanang*," Thomas said.

"That is how I got the idea," Joy blurted.

So it was another convoluted notion.

Thomas was still dressed in his barong, the traditional embroidered—and nearly translucent—shirt. Joy wore a white dress, the one she donned for special occasions, first communion, receptions, junior prom. Her tiny frame still fit inside the dress. Why she was wearing that dress and not the one from the funeral added to the suspense.

"And while I'm thinking of it, remember to say goodbye to the light. Your mother's spirit will visit you when you go to sleep."

"I *was* just asleep."

"You'll see the light in your head. It will linger. Talk to it, tell her you love her and miss her and ask her to watch over you."

"What? How could possibly know this?"

"Auntie Cita said so a long time ago that the spirit of her husband visited her on the night he was buried. It was a light and she felt it was him and talked to him."

"Nonsense. There wasn't any magical light visiting me when dad died."

Thomas saw no one inside. The angle of the sun sent the stained glass pattern across the wall. Oddly, two candles were already burning near the altar.

Joy genuflected to the cross when they reached the steps of the altar. She knelt neat the candles and drew Thomas to follow.

"I couldn't find everything I needed," she said.

"Everything for what?"

Joy didn't answer. From under her dress, she produced a folded piece of white cloth. Undone, Thomas could see that it was a wedding veil. Joy slipped it onto her head, the sequined net shielding her face.

His winsome face started to loosen. She took back his hands, her's now trembling, and took some deep breaths.

"I, Joy Flora Lapez, take you, Thomas Botalico Wagner, to be my wedded husband. To have and to hold..."

Thomas' eyes grew wide as she continued, reciting each part of the wedding vows. For richer or poorer. In sickness and in health. Through the good times and the bad.

"... until death do us part," Joy finished.

Stunned, Thomas stared into her eyes.

"This is oh so romantic, but there is no one else here. There is no priest. You get these ideas ..."

Joy shushed him.

"I didn't want anyone else here," she said softly. "This is for us and only us. There is time for the normal wedding. I can wait for my dress and my party. I cannot wait another day to bind myself to you. I leaned on you for so many years of my life. My mother spent so much energy battling Marino's demons. There were times I felt like I didn't have a mother or a father. You're leaning on me now. I didn't want you to have that same empty feeling."

His heart came alive again, springing from the malaise of the past weeks. He wanted to kiss her as hard and as passionately as he ever had. He waited, however, finding his own notion. He slid closer, so close they nearly touched lips. And then he started his vows, in the same order as Joy, kissing her through the veil between each part. The longest kiss came after "until death do us part" and he lifted the veil.

Still kneeling, Joy buried her face into Thomas' shirt.

"No rings?"

"I didn't have time to find those, but it doesn't matter. We are married in the way that counts the most and God heard us vow it," Joy said, using the shirt to wipe away tears of happiness. "You are part Lapez now, Thomas. You have a family again, a mother Rowena, a father Marino, a brother Ricky, and a wife, Joy. What is important is that you know you are never going to be alone again."

CHAPTER 7

A man with a green towel wrapped around his head fled from the small nipa hut. Knife wounds decorated his chest. He looked back in fear to the hut, a resting place from the sun in the middle of Mayor Marino's easternmost rice fields.

"*Bagti! Bagti!*" There was no one to hear his cries of crazy in Ilocano.

Halfway through the paddy, blood erupted from his right arm. In the blink of an eye, a second bullet ripped through his right shoulder.

The gun made no sound. No boom to announce its presence. The man's blood and cries were the only evidence he'd been shot.

The shooter in the hut lowered his handgun with a silencer when the fleeing man lost his balance and fell into the flooded paddy.

Aris removed the pair of bandannas he used to conceal his face and apathetically watched the man perform a one-arm swim and crawl through the water to the paddy's edge. Aris cleaned his knife on a grimy pillow and then put it back into its sheath.

He would have cared more if Xavier Velasquez was a better worker. He had always wanted to harm Velasquez for being lazy. Sure enough, the short, pudgy man was caught sleeping in the nipa hut instead of working.

Why Marino ordered such a deed wasn't clear to Aris. It had nothing to do with Velasquez' work habits. Part two of his instructions made no sense either.

From a saddle bag, Aris removed a coke bottle filled with petrol. The cap came off easily and he poured it on the pillow. With his lighter, Aris lit a cigarette between his first two fingers and a petrol soaked bamboo stick between the last two fingers. He laid the fiery stick on the pillow, igniting the rest of the fuel there.

Aris placed the gun the bag, slung it over a shoulder and slinked out of the hut. The fire had engulfed the pillow and was creeping down webbing of the rope hammock by the time the exit was complete.

Aris walked in the opposite direction of the wounded man, who trying to hide in ankle high water and greens, which was pointless since the water around Velasquez was turning pink.

There was no chance of Velasquez identifying his assailant. Black smoke obscured Aris' nonchalant escape from the scene.

Aris was willing to harass Papa Justo with random acts of violence, but it made no sense to attack his own people. Perhaps Marino was trying to frame some of Justo's bodyguards. Police Chief Albio was in Marino's back pocket after all. If three or four of Justo's men lounged in jail, the odds would start to even.

But that didn't explain part three. Aris jogged the long way around Marino's lands, eventually crossing into Wagner land. He had to "check" on Thomas. He wasn't asked to double back to "help" Velasquez and complete the impression that it was a Justo attack. No, he had to comfort that damn *puraw*.

Aris continued his jog until he reached the line of trees between the river and Wagner's land. He went through the screen of trees, past the lean-to and up to the back of the house.

Joy was there drying her hair with a towel. Aris felt disappointed that she was already fully dressed. She jumped when she saw him starting at her.

"Are you blind? You notice it?" Aris pointed to the cloud of smoke in the distance.

Joy shot him a querying glance.

"Someone shot lazy Velasquez and set fire to a nipa hut. Mr. Lapez sent me here to make sure everyone is safe. Maybe the attackers ran through here on their way back to Justo lands," Aris replied, gesturing to the north, where Justo had some property.

Joy stammered that she didn't see anyone.

"Where is Little Joe anyway?"

Aris heard the squeal of a pig being slaughtered and ascertained Thomas' whereabouts.

"Getting some meat for our lunch and dinner," Joy said.

Aris spat. "*Our* dinner? What ... you are living here now? Out of wedlock? That is a sin."

"Since when did Aris Lucero start caring about sin? Besides, I'm not living here ... I'm just helping Thomas."

"I know better. I spend a lot of time at the Lapez house and you're never around. Still helping? Hah! Auntie Emma was buried weeks ago," he said, pointing vaguely in the direction of the gravestone.

Joy began to move toward the front of house and called for Thomas. He was busy in the dirty kitchen and didn't hear.

"Nice bruise. Thomas beating you up?"

Joy covered the spot with her hand and then lifted the towel higher on chest to conceal it. "You know where I got this."

Aris averted his eyes and smirked.

"You can tell Thomas about the attack. I don't really feel like talking to Little Joe," Aris said, fumbling in the bag for cigarettes. He felt the need for a smoke now that his running was over. "Little Joe is going to have to guard you, I need to keep checking for the attackers. I wish we had some more helpers. If Papa Justo is going to act on the feud like this, nothing is safe."

Joy's loathing changed into concern.

Aris turned and walked away, back in the direction he had just ran. Watching the smoke billow into the horizon, his smile grew wider. The punch bruise from yesterday. Frightening Joy this morning with news of an attack on her family's land.

He understood Marino now.

He knew what had really happened.

< <> >

"Oh, *ayat*," Joy purred, stretching out his pet name until he had fully entered her.

Sex immediately after they awoke was as common as sex before they went to sleep. She wrapped her arms around his neck and drew his lips down to hers. Thomas continued to thrust.

"Careful, *ayat*, not inside. Not yet," Joy reminded.

"I know," Thomas said, followed by a grunt. He withdrew and released onto her thigh.

"I wish we could just start having our children now," she whispered during their intimate after-sex petting.

Playfully, Thomas pressed his thumb on her nose.

"Don't flatten my nose," she protested. "It will stay that way."

She pinched it back into place as though that would somehow cancel out the flattening.

She was glad to see him in a better mood. They did not make love last night. They went to sleep angry. Simple arguments between them were common enough to be swept aside. Emotionally-charged fights were not.

Since the funeral, they had been sleeping in bedroom once occupied by Thomas' parents. It had more room. It was Thomas' bed, however. Emma's bed was fine, and large, but it felt uncomfortable sleeping on a dead person's mattress. Thomas' mattress was smaller, but perfectly cozy for the young couple.

As the sun rose, more light came into the house. Eventually, there was enough for Thomas to see the bruise on her chest above her breasts.

"Where did you get that?"

Joy's insides did a leap. The bruise. She immediately brought her hand up to conceal it.

"Carabao bumped into me," she stammered. "I didn't think it left a mark. It must have been harder than I thought."

"Whose carabao?"

"The one *tatang* has penned up out at the fields ..."

"When?"

"The other day."

"Which day?"

"Stop interrogating me."

Thomas examined it closer. It didn't look water buffalo sized. He knew she had worked with her father two days ago, but hadn't known it was out in the fields. Joy had been wearing T-shirts lately, so Thomas didn't have a chance to this until now. With Joy being self-conscious of her naked body, even in front of him, it was always dark when they had sex.

"Is Marino hitting you because you're living out here with me?" Thomas probed.

"No one hit me," she replied defensively. "It got mad at ... getting hitched and then slammed its head into me."

Thomas did not move, his eyes piercing. She could tell that he wasn't convinced.

"You know that carabao is wild. He nearly gored Fernando Cabasan last year," she continued.

"That is why you are scared of that bull. You don't go near it. You make Fernando handle it."

It was true. She had always been scared of that bull. It had a habit of thrashing its head and hitting people with its horns whenever it had reached its tolerance for daily toil.

"I'm not a little girl anymore. It isn't so easy to frighten me." She removed her hand and said the spot didn't even hurt. "My leg is so sticky now, I have to wash," Joy said, using the distraction to rise from the bed and leave the bedroom.

She washed herself with a cloth in the kitchen, dampened in the water pail near the sink. She planned her bath for later, using the old tub in the bathroom by hauling in some water from the river and then adding some boiling water to make it warm. Aris' sudden appearance yesterday morning after Joy's shower had spooked her into discretion.

Thomas dressed in some shorts and a dirty T-shirt and hastily slipped his feet into dusty *sapatos* at the front door.

"Where are you going?"

"I might be going outside to cut a branch off the narra tree so I can use it to bat Marino's head."

"Thomas!"

"You've never been a good liar, Joy. That is a fist-shaped bruise on your chest. A big knuckle, fat hand, Marino-sized punch mark. He has been edgy and nervous ever since you have been staying out here. Someone probably said something to him about noticing Thomas and Joy living together. Then the next time he saw you, his temper went off and he slugged you in the chest. Am I right?"

She circled the kitchen looking for a nearby towel to dry herself in haste.

He had threatened under his breath for years to get even with Marino for the years of physically abusing Joy. It was all talk from an adolescent boy whose relationship with Joy had suddenly shifted from brotherly playmate to protector. Thomas was now a man, not an angry teenager, and was capable of acting on his threat of retaliation.

In the old days, Marino easily found excuses to strike Joy whenever there was enough alcohol inside of him. Joy ran to the old church to hide and to nurse her wounds. Thomas would find her there most times that she ran there to hide. He cleaned her face with water, fetched ice from the house refrigerator to lessen the swelling and sat with her to make sure Marino did not coming searching for another round of boxing. Her self-esteem suffered more than her face sometimes. Joy was still amazed that a teenage boy also understood that her sense of worth also needed mending.

"Thomas, stay here!" she called out the front windows and then raced for the bedroom.

"Wait for me!" She went for her shorts without putting on her panties first.

"*Tatang* did not hurt me!" she called out the window after her shirt went over her head.

Joy nearly plowed into him bounding out the front door without slipping on her own sandals.

He was standing, arms crossed, jaw set, on top of the Green Bay Packers G. The dog was doing everything in its power to get its master's attention, but he was focused on her.

"Have you gone crazy too? I don't need some macho man going off to pick a fight to defend my honor."

"It has been a long time coming."

"No, Thomas, not this time. You are right, I'm not a good liar and I'm not lying now." She grabbed him by his shirt to pull him back inside the house. "You are jumping to a wrong conclusion. Calm down and come back inside the house. I will make some coffee. You are still mad from yesterday."

"Oh, bringing that up will certainly calm me down."

Yesterday had not been a good day for Thomas. First, the fervent search for Papa Justo's men on his property produced a tense hour of fruitless labor. He made a search of the area around the house to be sure Aris was not hanging around either. Then after lunch, Joy broached her idea of becoming an overseas worker, applying to become a maid in Singapore.

Thomas removed himself from her grasp and began to make his way toward the gate. Joy shadowed him and was about to reiterate Marino's innocence when Thomas said he was only going to make sure there were no interlopers.

"No, you're going to brood again. I let you brood last night. I even let you drink last night."

Thomas stopped. Yes, letting him drink in her presence had been a real concession. Her stance against alcohol was as staunch as his against smoking. She saw alcohol as the root of Marino's abusive behavior toward her. Thomas knew alcohol was not the cause, only the fire that had ignited the violence.

Joy's newly proposed profession had sparked the tension between Joy and Thomas. She hoped round two would be less emotionally-charged. Yesterday's argument sent Thomas out to the front porch with gin for most of the night. It was late when he finally crawled into bed beside her.

"What makes you think living without you for two years is a good thing?" Thomas asked, turning to face her.

"We survived separation when you were in Baguio," Joy started. "We can survive this."

Joy clapped her hand once to calm the dog and it complied.

"We're not getting anywhere here. We have no money. We're just waiting for the harvest. All I do is cook and clean and I can do that in Singapore and make money," Joy reiterated her point from yesterday.

A Filipina going to Singapore or Hong Kong, even the Middle East, as a contracted maid was commonplace. Many families survived off of the money sent home from a mother or daughter working overseas. The land provided food, but little money for everything else in life. Half of the "placement fee" was paid up front. The rest was worked off in the first few months of her contract. Since Singapore paid well for Filipina housemaids, the fee was hefty.

"Your first three months over there is just getting the fee paid off," he complained.

"And the rest helps us. I get paid more because I'm educated and speak English. It is good money, 10,000 pesos in a month with the exchange rates right now."

Thomas knew she was serious. It would only be childish to argue the notion was a product of boredom. And it wasn't a disparagement of his status as an orphaned rice farmer in the middle of nowhere. It was frustration at their situation and he shared it. Without familial support, young couples always struggled with nothing for the first years of their lives. Their situation was stagnant.

This notion of Joy's was different. There was some common sense behind it, which made Thomas wonder if it was her's at all. The idea surfaced suddenly yesterday afternoon. Joy had never hinted about a desire to be an overseas maid. Going to Singapore? The only other place on earth she'd ever dreamed of living was America.

Joy chided him several times for the stubbornness of his Botalico blood for sticking to his decision to not allow Marino to manage the land so that he could return to the university. There was no such thing as free management, even from godfathers. Papa Justo would be no better. They would occupy his home and use its proceeds to line their pocket with more blood money. He envisioned them hiding guns in the house and using his land as their front line. He was not going to let feud blood spill from his home.

His mind had mulled the possibility of returning to school and leaving Joy to run the farm. She was a hard worker and could possibly do it all herself. That scenario led Thomas to thoughts of her safety while trying to do so. She would require the services of Aris or Fernando to guard her, which was no different than turning over the farm to Marino anyway.

He briefly entertained his own wild notion of selling the farm in pieces to his friends or to good neighbors like Mr. Masakayan. His emotional attachment to his home was too strong, though. It was all that was left to remind him of his parents. Their smiling faces were on the walls. He had moved his father's chair back into the house. His memories were in Calamba. Joy was in Calamba. His friends were in Calamba. No, he was going to keep his home and protect it and make it prosper.

A part of him wanted to spend the remainder of his college fund on a real wedding and start the rest of his life with Joy now, make her a permanent part of the Wagner house and fill the other room with children. A heightened sense of mortality had shaken Thomas. There should be more life in this house. The only way that was going to happen now was through he and Joy.

Joy ran her hands through Thomas' hair to bring his attention back to her.

"I don't like the idea of being separated from you for so long either," she said. "What is two years when we have the rest of our lives to benefit from it?"

She hugged him, burying her face in his shirt. So soon after making love, his emotions made its next climb on the rollercoaster.

"Use the money to finish college. I will not be here to distract your studies. You can then get a good job. I get a vacation after one year, with a free ticket home and back, so I can visit you."

"You make it sound so simple, Joy," Thomas replied.

"I can help everybody by doing this. I can take the weight on my shoulders. This is my contribution to our new family."

They stood in one another's embrace before Joy released him to make his rounds. She went inside to start breakfast and coffee before the electricity went out.

Thomas walked around the house, looking into the sky for evidence of further Justo harassment. He also scanned the trees for anyone who had taken a perch to watch Joy shower outside.

From the day after his mother's burial, he found himself following her daily routine. Thomas lifted a staff with an empty water pail on each end and walked down the trail to the edge of the high river. With the pails filled, Thomas balanced the staff on his shoulders and poured it for the large livestock to drink. Another trip filled the tin basin in the tree. The sun would eventually warm the tin and the water inside. He dropped the pails near the gate, allowing the dog to lap up what was left inside. He fed the animals and checked their health. He made a cursory look at the crops from the edge of the fields.

Joy's words followed him the entire time he did his morning chores. He could smell the coffee and bacon when he returned to the house. His coffee was cooling on the kitchen table, she knew he was fond of lukewarm drinks. Joy was sitting and already drinking her steaming instant with cream and too much sugar.

Thomas reported everything to be clear outside, there were no peepers or signs that Justo assassins were on the loose like yesterday morning.

"Did you mention this idea to Marino or Ro before talking to me about it?"

"Yes."

"And?"

"Father is supportive of the idea. Ricky does not want me to go away. Mother was not sure what to think. She does not want me to go away, but she sees how helpful it would be for the family."

If Marino liked the idea so much, then why didn't he offer to pay the placement fee? Thomas didn't need to ask the question. He knew the answer.

"This is not about them, though," Joy continued. "This is our life. This is our decision."

"At this point, you mean my decision."

Joy nodded and stared into her coffee clouds. Even if she didn't need Thomas' money for the placement fee, she would have deferred to his judgment.

Thomas ate his breakfast. Scrambled eggs, bacon, warmed up leftover *pancit*. Joy had never been a good cook, but learned quickly and had become quite good. He said so and received a patient smile. She knew he was still wrestling with the idea.

After breakfast, Joy joined her mother and the other women at the edge of the river to do laundry. Thomas walked to the church and climbed atop a ladder, hammering nails to secure a new window casement. The old one went with the wind in the last typhoon. Thomas washed off the paint and sawdust in the water spring. It was not a quick bath. A group of boys fresh from school asked him to toss them into the water.

It was mid-afternoon when Thomas returned to his house. He was examining the chicken coop when he heard Joy shouting his name. It was coming from the fields. He pried the hatchet from the chopping block. His flip-flops flew off his feet as he scrambled around the trees.

Joy was running along the edge of the rice paddy and then suddenly stopped, crouched and stared into the distance. She put a finger to her mouth to quiet Thomas when he reached her side.

"What is it? Someone with a gun?" he asked, concern written on his face.

Before she had a chance to answer, she crawled on her hands and knees, stalking something like a cat. She lunged, flew into the green rice stalks and cursed. It was then that Thomas saw the prey, a tiny flying insect with a long tail.

"A dragonfly?" His hands dangled at his side in dismay.

"Help me get it, Thomas." Joy had her tongue sticking out the corner of her mouth. "Come on. Have some fun."

"I thought you were being attacked," he called after her.

"There. I see it going that way." Joy ignored the comment and jogged barefoot in pursuit, oblivious to the weapon in Thomas' hand.

"You're not going to catch it. It is too fast for you."

"Then help me get it." Hand locked in a claw, Joy stalked the insect as it hovered. Some fruitless wild grabs for the air and the fly was racing away from her.

Thomas dropped the bolo and raced after Joy. The contest to catch the dragonfly disintegrated into Thomas trying to catch Joy. She shrieked and tried to twist away from him as his hands dug into her ribs.

Their play ended at the front of the house. She napped on his lap after a few minutes of arriving at the rattan bench.

He was content. Sitting in the breeze. Watching the mountain peeks in the distance. Holding Joy. The dog ran with other wild dogs in the fields. Even though it took tragedy to reach this spot in his life, this was life as he imagined it.

Joy stirred next to him. "Sorry, I fell asleep," she mumbled. "We turn in late and get up early." She sat up and cleared her eyes before sliding upright back into his arms.

"No, old habits die hard, sleeping in the afternoon."

"Well, at least I'm not doing that because I'm terrified to sleep in the night." She waggled a finger at his nose. "And don't you start about that bruise again. You can keep trying to trap me into admitting Marino did that, but it won't work because he didn't."

He didn't bat an eye. She followed his stare out into the distance. She saw the noses of the three pigs protrude from their pen. Chickens strutted freely around them. Drying clothes swayed on the clothes line. He saw none of it. The stare was focused on a series of small stones in front of a narra tree.

Her tears drew his attention back to her.

"I know I'm all you have left, *ayat*. I would never ask to leave you here alone unless it was so important."

"I know." He pet her hair. "I don't want you to leave, but I can't think of any other reason for you not to go."

It would take more than a month for Joy to obtain her passport, file her fee with the agency and go through its brief training. Her presence in Manila was required to accomplish the tasks. In that absence, Thomas returned to Baguio to finish his first semester since it had already been paid for. It was hard to catch up after missing so much time, but the university and his professors were understanding and helpful. Thomas begrudgingly let Marino's men tend to the farm during his absence.

Joy needed permission to leave the job agency's compound while her paperwork was being processed and they were finding her an employer. She needed to be readily accessible if they found one who would take her contract. When she wasn't doing odd jobs or running errands for the agency, she was permitted a few hours to herself to wander around Paranaque City, one of the 16 municipalities comprising Metro Manila.

It was a world vastly different than the one she'd grown accustomed to, with millions of people and streets choked with traffic. The agency was in the shadow of Ninoy Aquino International Airport, serving as a constant reminder the day was coming she would be boarding one of those jets.

Thomas spent his Friday nights riding the bus to visit her and then returning Sunday morning so that he would be in Baguio in time for Monday classes. It was time consuming and the bus fare was expensive as it added up over the passing weeks. Sometimes the other women in the compound would all leave together, giving them enough time and privacy to make love. When a new girl arrived, she would always ask about the *guapo* man visiting Joy.

"Who is the handsome one?"

"*Asawa ko*," Joy answered. My spouse.

"Oh, you are the lucky one," the girl would always reply.

Regina occasionally kept Joy company during the week. She was working as a maid for her aunt in Cubao, the commercial center of Quezon City, itself most populous part of Metro Manila. Once the work was done, Regina was free to make the hour-long taxi trip through the congested streets.

Once Maricar came to Manila and three of them shopped for wedding items and clothes for themselves, eating spicy crispy chicken at KFC.

One the second level of the American restaurant, Joy asked the pair for a favor.

"Take care of Thomas if something happens to me."

Regina stopped chewing, facial expression asking why.

"My God, Joy, what are you nervous about?" Maricar asked. "What is going to happen to you?"

"Singapore is safer than Manila," Regina said. "Come visit some of squatter areas in Quezon City if you want danger."

"Serious. I'm serious. Can you promise me?"

"She's nervous about the jet, Car-Car. She thinks she's going to fall into the ocean."

"No. This has nothing to do with being mugged or crashing. I'm going to a different country, I can't just rush back to help him if something happens. At least when he was in Baguio and I was in Calamba, I was close enough..."

"He's a grown man, Joy," Regina said, wiping some of the chicken grease from her fingers with a napkin before reaching for her coke. "And what can happen to him now? There's no one left to die on him except you."

Joy seemed even more concerned as Regina kept talking. Maricar nudged Regina to stop.

"Don't talk about death, Reggie, something might happen."

Regina scoffed at Maricar's superstitions. "Now you're talking like her. You going to start pinching your nose to stop it from going flat too?"

"God, Joy, why do I need to promise something like that? He's always been our friend and we'd help him no matter what, same as you. I don't need to make a promise for that. Besides, your mother is practically his mother too."

With that Maricar broke into her third chicken breast.

"You really are pregnant," Regina said.

Joy kept up her insistence. "I'm just scared for him. I would do that for Jon-Jon."

"You always bring up Jon-Jon whenever you want Car-Car to do something for you," Regina jabbed.

Maricar promised between bites.

"Oh, you always let her manipulate you."

"Quit, Reggie. I'm not promising anything I wouldn't do anyway. At least Joy will feel better and we can go back to shopping without her bugging us all day."

"I'd do the same for you, Reggie," Joy said.

"Don't make me pull status," Regina warned.

"I'm older though," Joy replied.

"A month? I'm still your aunt." Regina was the baby of the family. Rowena Flora Lapez was her eldest sister.

"Think about it, Reggie," Maricar interjected, "if your sister is Thomas' mother now, then that would make him your nephew."

"Don't help her, Car-Car," Regina scoffed.

"That's right. That makes Thomas practically family."

Regina shook her head and rolled her eyes before relenting. "*Sige, sige*, if it makes you feel better, I'll promise to take care of Thomas if something happens to you."

"See, now we can finish eating in peace and find me a bathing suit for the honeymoon."

"That's impossible. You're just guessing your size."

"I won't be that much bigger by that time, Reggie. My mother said she didn't gain a kilogram before giving birth to me. I'm just as *taba* as she was, so I'm probably going to stay the same."

"What if you have twins?" Joy queried.

"God, no!"

"What do you need a bathing suit for anyway? Aren't you and Jon-Jon going to spend the whole honeymoon in your hotel room?" Regina snickered, but Maricar was unfazed.

With reassurances that her friends would care for Thomas if something unforeseen occurred, Joy was able to enjoy the rest of the day with them, testing clothes and teasing each other. It would be the last of such friendship for awhile.

Maricar was able to find a swim suit for her size, with a little room left over just in case she was carrying twins.

Joy was saddened and elated the afternoon she was called into the madam's office to be informed that an older couple in Singapore had hired her. Their former maid had gotten married to an Australian man and left the country when her contract expired.

Airline arrangements only took a few days. Joy was thankful the jet was leaving Saturday as Thomas would already be in Manila.

Singapore Airlines flight 71 would put Joy in the air a little more than three hours, arriving just before lunchtime in the city-nation that would become her new home for the next year. It was leaving in 90 minutes.

The bustle of travelers at Ninoy Aquino International went by at a pace conscious of the passing of time. Bags checked and tickets in hand, Joy had only to pass through the metal detectors with her purse to enter the bowels of the airport and eventually board the Airbus that would take her to a life without Thomas.

Joy sat on Thomas lap, eyes closed and head resting on his shoulder with his arms wrapped around her. They sat in the most secluded spot they could find, on a waiting bench with the discolored padding that was torn in several spots.

Joy's handler from the agency—a Filipina waiting for her own placement in Singapore—had already left the airport, feeling embarrassed to watch the pair say their goodbye. It had begun to rain too, peppering the window behind Thomas with streaks of water.

"It is almost time to go," Joy said, voice raw with grief.

Thomas combed his fingers through her hair, unusually free from the bands that kept it back in a ponytail.

"I will be heart sick too. I want my last minutes with you to be happy ones. Can you smile for me?"

She tried, briefly, to turn up the edges of her lips, but they too soon went back into their pout.

Thomas answered her half-hearted smile with a wry one.

"What are you up to?"

"Nothing," he teased.

"Nothing. Nothing. You are no good at secrets. I always know my Christmas gift a week before because you cannot—"

He handed her a tiny box from behind his back.

She regarded the square box with a little bow on top. She gasped. Inside were two shiny gold bands. Nothing fancy. No stones. No inscriptions.

"Since you insisted to marry me, I got these with the rest of my money."

"With the rest of your money? How are you going…"

"I'm joking. Not all of the rest of my college money. Just a semester's worth."

"That is still a lot"

"I can make it up later." Thomas reached around her body and pulled out the smaller of the two rings. "Give me your hand."

He slipped the ring on the finger where wedding rings belonged. She stared at her hand. Her breathing increased and she swallowed hard. She buried her face in his shirt.

"I don't want to get on that jet, *ayat*. I don't. Let's go home instead. Let's tell everyone we're already husband and wife."

"It is a little late for that. The agency has all that money for your placement fee."

Joy grabbed the larger ring and placed it on Thomas' ring finger.

"I should have thought of this myself," she said, smiling now.

"I love you, Joy."

She played with the ring with her thumb. "In all of our years together, didn't you once just want to be alone, to be rid of me?"

"No."

"You tolerate me, don't you?"

"Huh?"

"All the crazy stuff I do."

"You're not crazy, Joy."

"Defending me to the last. There are so many people in Calamba who think I can do nothing right, but you see no wrong. You're unconditional. When it comes to loving me, you've always been unconditional."

"I took that vow with you. No matter what, I'm yours." He ran his fingers along her cheeks, disturbing the path of tears. "And where else will I find a face with eyes that look at me like that?"

Their lips met. She did not let her lips let go of his for more than a minute.

"You are my first and only too," Thomas said. "I don't want some Chinese guy trying to steal you away from me."

"I'm scared, Thomas," she admitted. "You joke about losing me, but I am scared of losing you."

"Losing me to who?"

There was no answer, just a wistful face.

"You haven't lost me yet. You were scared of the college girls and none of them even turn my eye."

"But I may be gone a long time. You may not wait for me."

Thomas drew her close. "Stop fretting. You are making yourself crazy thinking about this too much. I married you in all the ways that mattered. I will still be here when you get back. I will still be your husband. I will always be your husband, Joy my joy."

It was time to leave, the crowd was getting larger at the metal detectors.

There was one more kiss before she left his side. She stared at him while waiting in line at the metal detectors. She watched him watch her and she strolled slowly toward the opening that led to the hallway where there was another line for the exit tax. Being an overseas worker, though, she was exempt and could bypass further lines on the way to the exit gate.

She waved and blew a kiss at Thomas before lowering her head and disappearing from sight.

The departure left Thomas drained and empty. The taxi ride to EDSA bus station and the bus ride to Baguio was a haze of passing cars and trees and roadside stands. It was the kind of malaise that made a person want to sleep all day.

A letter from Singapore arrived in the mail at Lopito's house by the end of the week. She wrote it on the jet and mailed it when she got settled into her new home and job. It was filled with love, apprehension and hope. She was excited and made the trip feel like the opening of an adventure movie. Her employers were nice old people with grown children and several businesses.

"There is nothing I wouldn't sacrifice for you, *ayat*. No matter what happens, always remember you are my first and only love," Joy wrote in the conclusion.

And that warning went off in the part of Thomas' mind that he used to unravel her notions.

CHAPTER 8

WALO

Thomas was disinterested in the mauling taking place in front of him. Two angry birds collided recklessly. They exchanged midair kicks with the curved, razor-sharp spikes fastened to their legs. Feathers floated upward from the pit and hung in the air above their melee. Jon-Jon shook Thomas' arm and cheered with the rest of the men. They sat on a set of wooden bleachers that circled a mesh wire dirt pit. Those not lucky enough to have seats stood atop fences or sat on the roof of their jeeps and jeepneys to view the Sunday matinee *sabong*, cockfights. Frail toothless men in slacks commiserated with shirtless teenagers in shorts. The *sabong* connected the generations.

It was an unsanctioned event, but with Pingaping's barangay captain as the pit's owner, it was unlikely to be shut down by the authorities.

Pingaping was a smaller version of Calamba, though it had better ground for tobacco and sugar cane. More of its residences resembled the old traditions of the Igorot peoples, the Itneg speakers, the mountain tribes. Elevated bamboo framed nipa huts dotted the side of the dirt roads. Other houses were made of corrugated tin for its walls and roof. A few were lucky enough to have cinderblock houses on concrete slabs with metal fences. For the most part, the church and school were the sturdiest structures in the village.

Thomas wanted to take Jon-Jon to a better *sabong* to celebrate his pending marriage, perhaps in Bangued or the regional capital in San Fernando that had stadium style seating and derby-quality roosters. Jon-Jon wanted Pingaping because he knew the rooster owners and had been studying the birds.

In the pit, the gamecock on the left ducked under a flurry from the one on the right. As they turned to face each other again, they leapt into the air and clawed toward one another. One went down and flailed there. The arbiter stepped in and stopped the advancing bird by grabbing its tail. The downed gamecock still had some fight left in it. The arbiter handed the birds back to their owners, who swung the birds' faces toward one another, nearly beak to beak. When their neck feathers stood, they back up and dropped them again to the dirt, backing away from the explosion. Both gamecocks were

71

Roundheads, tall and white legged, known as the ring generals, good flyers and athletic fighters.

One of the gamecocks re-established its advantage. Red marks began appearing on the disadvantaged bird at a faster clip and it went down again. There was no flailing this time. The winner had been found. The carcass of the loser would become dinner tonight for the winner's owner. The arbiter held the winner's tail until its owner came into the ring to retrieve it.

As one of the *kristos* came by and Jon-Jon palmed over 50 pesos to the bet taker. He had bet the underdog and lost. Thomas wondered what he had been studying.

"You are going to have money after this to enjoy your honeymoon, right?"

Jon-Jon groaned. "I thought... Well, that one had a longer leg reach. They were both Roundheads..." He hung his head.

"There was a reason that the odds were that far apart. 1-to-4 when most of the odds today have been 2-to-3 or 5-to-8?"

The *kristos* held up their hands for the next bout. Three fingers on one hand and two on the other. Some of the spectators held up five fingers, 50 pesos bets. Five fingers sideways meant 500. Five fingers pointing downwards was 5,000. There weren't many bets at the highest amount here in Pingaping. For that kind of action, people went to the registered cockfighting arenas for a derby.

Jon-Jon did not bet this time. A new pair was at it. Each flurry, each peck, each slash brought a reaction from the crowd.

There was a fight, a human one, behind one of the sets of seats. Someone had reneged on a bet, Thomas surmised.

"Have you thought about what I asked you?" Jon-Jon asked, drawing Thomas' attention away from both arenas of violence.

"What? You have asked me a lot of things."

"About raising my own gamecocks at your farm."

Thomas laughed. "You were serious?" He gestured to the *sabong* pit. "You cannot even win betting on them from the stands. How are you going to do down there fighting them?"

"Stop razzing me. Just like Ronaldo, laughing. Well, this is no joke. I have connections here and in Danglas who are willing to see me some chicks and pullets. One has Greys, the other Roundheads."

"My farm? Is this to keep it a secret from Car-Car?"

"No. I don't have anywhere to raise them. Am I going to put them in the garage with the jeepneys? The exhaust will kill them. And you have lots of space for pens and practice pits. And feed. I can pay you for the feed."

Thomas could tell Jon-Jon was serious. His friend's immediate family didn't have any farm ground. Jon-Jon's uncle, the younger brother to his father, inherited the land upon his grandparents' deaths, as was the custom. It was thought the eldest children had the means to support themselves better than the youngest, so the younger sons ended up with inheritances. The eldest drove jeepney for fares to support himself.

"Put them on your uncle's farm."

"He doesn't have chickens. He's never raised them."

"Neither have you," Thomas observed.

"That is why I have you. You can judge growth, tell if they get sick."

"Yes, but I've never trained roosters for that," Thomas replied, gesturing to the pit, where another winner was quickly found. "And what if that is yours? The dead one there. After months of feeding and training?"

Thomas wondered how deep Jon-Jon's delusions were becoming.

"I have seen your face when you lose 50 pesos, I can imagine what it will look like when your first self-proclaimed derby champion winds up in someone else's stew pot."

"Please, Thomas. You are my best pal. You should be supportive of this. You should want to help me."

He rolled his eyes. "I am honored to be your best man. I am willing to take you to the cockfights instead of setting up a bachelor party..."

A stocky man sat beside Jon-Jon. "You are getting married, Paculdar?"

Jon-Jon greeted the man, called him Gary, and seemed annoyed at the interruption. Thomas knew Graciano—"Gary"—Palangchao to be one of Jon-Jon's betting buddies, a forest ranger out of Vigan who spent much of his time hunting illegal loggers in the forest reserves of Cordillera.

Jon-Jon nodded and offered a sheepish smile to go along with explanation of the blessed event. November 25, one month before Christmas. That way Jon-Jon would never be able to forget his anniversary.

"A jeepney driver marrying a councilor's daughter?" Gary laughed. "How did you manage that?"

Jon-Jon feigned insult. "I'm not that bad looking!"

"Sure, sure, you also are not bad at eating." Gary could get away with such a comment because he shared the same stomach size. "Hey, Thomas, are you winning?"

He replied that he wasn't betting on the roosters. "I'm only here for moral support."

"Maybe you should do the betting. Paculdar is terrible."

"Terrible? That time I won 15,000..."

"...was because I told you to bet a lot on that one," Gary finished. "How do you think I'm so rich, Paculdar? I always pay attention to what you're betting and go the other way."

They traded more barbs and Thomas could tell Jon-Jon was getting flustered.

"If you won a few, he wouldn't be able to get on you like that," Thomas said.

"I know," Jon-Jon whispered. "Bet one for me."

Thomas stared at him.

"I know I'm unlucky. You know I'm unlucky. He knows I'm unlucky. So you bet one for me. Gary is right, you should do the betting."

"I don't have money for this."

"My money."

Thomas agreed. At least it would keep Jon-Jon from bringing up the transformation of the farm into his rooster boot camp.

"How about this bout? I see that Juan has a Sweater."

Through osmosis, Thomas had become unwillingly knowledgeable about gamecock breeds. Sweaters were the fashionable breed and the sudden trend to possess and train them was because in back-to-back years the national derby champion had been that breed.

Thomas eyed the birds that were in the pit. He didn't know Juan, but he recognized the other owner as Armando Botalico, a first cousin. He was holding a fowl with gray feet and dark feathered body, a white feathered neck. Regular Greys were known for power. Armando had outfitted the bird with short spurs. The Sweater had one of the longer knives. Confidence on Armando's part, Thomas thought.

"Bet the Grey," Thomas said.

"The odds are against him," Jon-Jon protested. "Just now you were on me about betting the underdog."

"The Grey isn't the underdog. People are betting the Sweater because they are hot for them."

"Are you sure about this?"

"You wanted me to bet one for you, right? Well, that is my pick."

When the bet taker came by, Jon-Jon held up five fingers—sideways—and pumped it twice.

"1,000 pesos, are you nuts?" And Gary was getting another good chuckle out of Jon-Jon.

Thomas himself was a little dismayed at the size of the bet.

"Don't worry," Jon-Jon told Thomas. "I had myself budgeted for 1,500 pesos anyway. I can make that back within a week."

Thomas saw Gary bet against Jon-Jon. The *kristos* was shaking his head in surprise. Suddenly, an innocuous bout was becoming a big money draw. He smiled as some of the others got in the action, betting with the favorite, a few hedging themselves with the underdog.

Armando saw Thomas in the stands close to the pit. They exchanged polite waves. Most of Thomas' Botalico kin treated him with the same warmth they would give a tax collector. Armando had become more amenable, at least agreeing to act as a pall bearer for his Aunt Emma.

"Hey, *puraw*. I noticed that you're living at the farm again. I thought you were a college boy."

Thomas found it incredible that someone who spent most of his day in an office in Bangued, with whiter skin than his farmer's tan, was calling him *puraw*, white. To them, he was simply the son of Ted, the white guy American. Ted was white skinned, therefore Thomas was too. Even if it wasn't true. Botalicos had called him *puraw* for so long that it was only his name to them. He let the comment go.

"I dropped out for now. No money for that."

"Why don't you plant some tobacco? It is getting a good price," Armando said, advice-like.

"Not interested in tobacco."

"Price is better," Armando repeated before retreating into the pit with his Grey tucked under his arm like a ball.

Armando didn't understand that it had nothing to do with price.

The arbiter raised his hands and drew attention back to the pit. Juan and Armando faced each other from behind lines etched in the dirt. They placed their birds on the ground, controlled them by their tails. The handlers allowed the roosters to inch closer to one another. Their neck feathers stood in anger. The birds were pulled back to the line and their owners released them.

The melee was more of a marathon than some of the other matches. The birds flew, sidestepped, stalked, lured. In the end, it was Armando's Grey declared the winner. Armando did not make any champion's bow, he took the bird and walked over to the chicken doctor, who would mend as many wounds as possible for the bird to fight another day, though recovery from this bout would take longer than two weeks.

The *kristos* handed Jon-Jon two blue notes. 2,000 pesos. His eyes had the wonder of a child that had just been given a jar of candy. He jabbed Thomas in the ribs and mouthed his appreciation.

Jon-Jon started gloating to Gary. Thomas smiled. Jon-Jon's last hurrah as a bachelor was becoming a good one. He started to think about how to diplomatically wean him from the idea of becoming a breeder and cockfighter.

Jon-Jon's cellular phone rang, breaking up the banter between he and Gary. The phone was a gift from Maricar. To keep track of him? On Sunday, it wasn't a matter of what Jon-Jon was doing, she knew, it was simply a matter of which *sabong* in which town and when was it going to be done. Jon-Jon answered the call without checking the incoming number. Maricar had a similar phone for herself, recharging their SIM cards and buying minutes as they went. Thomas was amazed there was enough signal strength in Pingaping to have a conversation.

Jon-Jon handed the phone to Thomas. "Car-Car wants to talk to me?" he asked.

"Not her. It is Joy."

Thomas could not grab the phone fast enough.

"It is so loud there. What are you doing?" her voice crackled.

"*Sabong* in Pingaping with Jon-Jon. You have a day off today?"

Joy only got two days off per month, alternating Sundays. It was the typical arrangement for Filipina maids in Singapore.

"Yes. Too bad I cannot fly home for the wedding next weekend and then come back. Mr. Song frowned at me and shook his head. Too expensive, la," Joy said, mimicking the man's Chinese accent. "Maybe you don't come back, la. You good worker, you stay here, la."

"Well, at least he thinks you are a good worker," Thomas said, walking toward the back of the stands and away from the ruckus of the *sabong* pit.

"He is the nice one. Mrs. Song is different. I think she is jealous. I am young and I am cute and her husband is nice to me. Of course, she turns mean. They are older than my parents. They have children older than me. Every day I get a letter from you. But somehow she thinks I am going to steal her old man husband? I talked back to her a few times already, when she was being unreasonable."

Thomas blinked. He wasn't sure he heard her correctly. "You did what?"

"I was busy washing their cars and she came out to complain I had not started cleaning the extra bedrooms. This place is huge. They have more rooms now than they need. Anyway, I told her as politely as I could that I have two hands and I cannot clean bedrooms and cars at the same time. She kept complaining. I didn't catch it all because we have to communicate in English and their English is as bad as mine, so we are always missing words. I finally snapped at her and said if she did not like my work, there were plenty of Thai girls in the neighborhood she could hire. That made her stop. Thai and Malay are cheaper maids, but they are worthless, that is why they hire Filipinas."

"You defended yourself? You stood up to her?"

"Of course, I got tired of it. For a few days, she left me alone then she was back to herself again."

"I'm proud of you," Thomas said.

"What? What? The signal there is weak…" And the call was dropped.

His heart was bursting. Joy fought back. Off on her own, now needing to rely on herself, she was learning to do just that. Thomas did not have to defend her.

Joy was changing and he was missing it. Though she had included him by describing the events, he was sad that he wasn't a part of it. It was like a father missing the first steps of a child and then watching it on video tape afterward.

"You're in a good mood now," Jon-Jon said when Thomas returned the phone and took his seat.

Jon-Jon made a few hundred more pesos driving home with some Calamba folks coming back. Thomas reluctantly agreed during the drive to let

Jon-Jon raise his gamecocks at his farm. He looked at it positively, he wasn't going to feel so lonely out there with friends visiting daily. Joy called back during the ride and Thomas was able to talk to her a few minutes longer before the signal cut. It had been three months since she had left. Her pay at the end of the month would be hers to spend, or send home. With luck, Thomas would only have to skip one semester, which meant waiting until next June to resume his quest for a medical degree. Despite his mother's death and his Joy's departure, the emotional distractions had not affected his marks. His exam scores were high.

The jeepney stopped in front of the Paculdar residence. It was a short walk to Joy's house. He joined Auntie Rowena and Ricky for dinner. Marino was absent in Bangued on unrevealed mayoral duties. Judging by Rowena's demeanor, the duties were suspected to be a "whom" and not a "what."

Thomas shared information from Joy's phone call. He roughhoused with Ricky. And he left before Marino got home. It was fine that he didn't see Marino. Though he had a lot of complaints of the way his people managed the farm, it would fall on deaf ears. When the semester ended, Thomas came home to fewer animals in messy pens, wild grasses growing throughout the compound, weeds in the paddies as high as the rice. At least the inside of the house was clean, a testament to Rowena's manner. There were long days of pulling weeds and making holes in his work gloves. Thomas had not bothered to hoist water into the shower, it was easier to jump into the river.

The Abra River had receded from its August high at the height of the rainy season. Some of the rocky river bed was visible now. It was getting dark and only a few teens were near the river bed. No one paid any notice to the underwear clad *puraw* sitting on the rocks and soaping his extremities. Fully lathered and with a head full of shampoo, Thomas dove into the water to rinse.

At the house, he sought the small box on top of his dresser that held his wedding ring. He slipped it into place and felt the tickle there of a finger not accustomed to wearing a ring. He wore it only in private.

With two kerosene lamps illuminating the porch, he sat there and stared at his ring and drank beer. It did not fill the pang of loss, but numbed it for awhile. The night was worse than any other time of the day because his mind wasn't occupied with chores. He thought for a minute about sleeping in the old church. The effort to tack up enough mosquito netting to insure a night without insect assault changed his mind.

In the middle of the beer, he fetched paper and pen to write his daily epistle to Joy. He described the day, his feelings of her growing without him.

A truck with headlights approached the house from the opposite direction of Calamba, along the mountain trail that lead to the hamlet of Masakayan family houses and then to one of the distant barangays. In this part of the Philippines, everything was distant.

The truck parked near the barn and three men exited. With little light illuminating that far, he could only tell that they were tall and skinny.

"*Puraw*? Is that you on the porch?"

It was Armando.

"Hoy," Thomas called back.

Armando strolled through the gate and stood in front of Thomas. The other two remained at the edge of the shadows. They were dressed differently than Armando, more like farm hands in torn pants and grimy shirts. Armando was better dressed, clean jeans and plain long sleeved button shirt. Thomas guessed the other two were Abel and Pedro, Armando's older brothers, and that guess was made only through their likeness. Even then, he didn't know which was which. He could not remember the last time he'd seen them, they did not come to Emma's funeral.

"We were here earlier and you were gone," Armando said, clasping Thomas hand in greeting.

"I was in town all day after the *sabong*."

"Tell me, honestly, there was no way that Paculdar made that bet and won that money."

Thomas grinned.

"I knew it. I saw the way he was eyeing Juan's Sweater. And then he plunks down money on me instead? It didn't seem right."

"Jon-Jon needs all the help he can get. He's getting married soon. All that he has to support his family is that old jeepney."

"He needs help that is for sure. He contacted me after the *sabong*. He bought that winning rooster from me. The down payment was the money he won. I think he is crazy. That Grey is getting to the end. It got carved up good in that bout with Juan today. He will be lucky to get two more fights out of it."

Thomas would have something to say to Jon-Jon when he next saw him. There was a baby to support. There was a house to buy. Though it was unfortunate that Auntie Dina died of old age, the old woman's family lived in Danglas and were happy to part with Dina's roofless Calamba fixer-upper. He didn't have disposable income to be wasting it on overrated champion cockfighting roosters.

"It looks like you're doing well out here, *puraw*," Armando said.

"Thanks. Really? My land manager left the place a shambles."

One of the brothers mumbled something in disgust about the White One having a land manager.

"Easy, Pedro," Armando said.

Thomas regarded Pedro, standing two paces back from Armando's left. He was staring at the Packer's symbol and had made no effort to look at Thomas since arriving.

"Tell him," Pedro said impatiently to his brother.

"You tell him," Armando snapped. "He is your cousin too."

"You know him," Pedro retorted.

Abel remained silent during the exchange. Thomas didn't know whom to be more wary of, the one that couldn't bear to look at him or the one that was staring with the disgusted look on his face.

"You want some beer?" Thomas offered, seeing that there was tension mounting.

Armando declined with a wave of his hand. "It is a long drive in the dark back to Pingaping."

Not having a drink with him spoke volumes about the purpose of their visit. It wasn't a social call.

Even if the two older brothers would not, Thomas suspected Armando should at least drink with him. Armando sat down next to Thomas and cleared his throat.

"This was the part of Botalico land that was the best for rice, right next to the river for irrigation. There is a section of mango and coconut groves over near Langinilang. Sugar cane and tobacco are in Pingaping."

"Two cavan of rice are supposed to be left at the old church every month!" Abel exploded. A small family could eat a 50-kilogram cavan every month.

"Aunt Emma used to give us rice. Making amends, you know…" Armando trailed off. "Since she is gone, we have to deal with you."

"Amends for what?" Thomas inquired, incredulously. For marrying an American and bearing a half-breed? Ted bought the ground and the house from them, the Botalicos had no right to be demanding any reciprocity.

"What is this? A shake down?"

"Hold on, *puraw*," Armando said, holding up his hands. "I understand your mother probably never told you any of this, but it is true. She used to have some rice sent to the abandoned church and Abel picked it up and took it to *Lolo* Botalico."

How was that done under his nose for so long? Someone else had to tote the rice all that distance, Emma certainly was incapable of it.

"This is my house and my land now…" Thomas set his jaw, making it obvious to them that he wasn't going to be making any peace offering, especially since years of offering had apparently done little good judging by the behavior of Armando's brothers.

"It is not a shake down," Armando said. "I am just telling you what your mother once did and to make you aware that this place is still an important part of the family's economics."

"So you want me to be part of the family? If I give you rice, does that mean I get to come over to *lolo's* house and eat some of it with him? In the 19 years of my life, I've never seen the man, so it might be nice to finally meet my grandfather. Or am I giving you the rice so that the great anti-Marcos rebel doesn't call up the troops and order them to overrun me?"

"Emma was his favorite child and she betrayed him by going to work at the American base and then finding an American husband," Pedro said.

"Love is not a betrayal. My father was a good man. He was honorable. He gave up the chance to run a family business in America to stay here. He loved my mother, he loved me. And what is wrong with him being American? Half the girls in this town dream of finding an American penpal so they can get out of here. Pingaping too. How many daughters of Pingaping are living in America or Canada right now? You're not going to treat me like I am some shameful waste of skin. I am Ilocano, the same as you."

Then in Itneg, Thomas told them that he even knows the language of the mountains.

Pedro averted his eyes again.

Abel shuffled uncomfortably on his feet.

Armando started chuckling. Thomas flashed a glare at him.

"Hey, *puraw*, you bark just like *lolo*. He never backs down from a good argument," Armando explained, unable to wash away the smile. "We don't see him very much either. He can hardly get out of his chair now. He still hits us with his walking stick like when we were naughty little kids stealing mangoes from his tree."

Armando's jocularity eased the dander on the back of Thomas' neck, but it seemed to do little to change the attitude of Abel and Pedro. The brothers turned and started walking back to the truck.

"Don't mind them. They don't know you, so their judgment falls back on what they've heard about Emma from our father," Armando said. "And they are a little embarrassed to ask for help. Abel's family always collected the rice and ate it. He has too many kids and not enough work. They are starting to miss the kindness of Aunt Emma."

"Kindness? He acted as though it were a tax to the king."

"Yes, that is the way he thinks about it," he said, candidly. Before Thomas launched into another protest, Armando held up his hands as a gesture of peace. "The way they think will take some time to change."

"What about your thinking? You brought them here."

"For all of their barking, they're intimidated by you. You're going to be a doctor. They need me to talk to you because I'm college educated and they're not. All the better for me to defuse the situation before they did something rash without you having a clue as to why."

"I'm not feeling very generous with my rice right now." Thomas stood to walk inside the house.

"I'll have that drink," Armando said, turning Thomas around in the doorway. He met Thomas' anger with a stare of sincerity.

The beer he found for Armando was still cold though the electricity had been off most of the day.

"You're the only one interested in more than my rice." It was a question more than a statement.

"While I was getting my education in business, I also got some education in life." Armando opened the bottle and sipped at the lip. "I was the smartest grandchild and *lolo* didn't want an entire family of farmers and freedom fighters. He was able to get me into college in Vigan. With a business degree, I was able to get a management position with Forex to oversee all the *balikbayan* box delivery around Bangued, Benguet and Kalinga. Delivery is pretty safe from robbers and bandits when your last name is Botalico," he smiled.

President Ferdinand Marcos lost three Army majors and half a colonel to grandfather Botalico.

"More importantly to your question," Armando continued, "I went on a church mission trip during a college break and worked side by side with some Americans in the Peace Corps. We were fixing a town in Cebu that had been blown away by a typhoon. I realized my perception had been formed by the family and it was based on stereotypes."

Armando got a far away gleam in his eye that only a woman causes. He was reputed to be no stranger to the fairer sex. Perhaps one of the beautiful members of the Peace Corps had given a personalized educational experience.

Thomas was feeling less confrontational. He saw the chance of establishing ties to a family that had been lost to him, though it was only Armando at the moment.

"About the rice. How about a trade?"

The idea surprised Armando.

"I want to make my own *basi*, but I don't have any sugar cane. I never grew it. I can spare a few cavan of rice."

"A trade sounds good." Armando scratched his chin. "Pedro has extra cane. A trade of equal weight, price for price?"

"How about for starters, we make the deal for whatever you need to eat well for a few months in exchange for enough cane to keep me occupied perfecting the recipe for a few months."

Armando's lips broke into a grin. "You are not so bad, *puraw.*"

"See you at the old church tomorrow?"

Thomas and Armando finished their beer while talking about the terms of the deal, then he joined his brothers in the truck. When the headlights were no longer visible, he glanced over to the sealed envelope addressed to Joy. He tore it open to add to the letter. What had just happened was too good to wait another day.

CHAPTER 9
SIAM

It was probably the only time Maricar Ramirez was ever called beautiful. Her mother Betty had worked hard to get her ready for the wedding. Hair up. White gown. Long train. Makeup in the right places.

There were two video cameras set up to capture the event. Instant cameras flashed in the church and under the reception tent. Maricar was the attraction, the star, for the first and only time in her life.

Her natural obesity hid the fact she was pregnant.

She wasn't Maricar Jumao-as Ramirez for very long. By the end of the afternoon, she was Maricar Ramirez Paculdar.

It was the first councilor's daughter. It was an important day. It meant a lot of food would be prepared. It meant the 3,000 people in Calamba and hundreds more from nearby barangays would gather for the reception. No one was going home hungry today.

In the church, Jon-Jon stood in his black pants and barong. The bride held a bouquet of orange blossoms, the same flower that decorated every crevice of the church. Thomas stood near them in his own barong, the best man to Jon-Jon. Behind Maricar was Regina, standing as maid of honor in Joy's absence. Maricar was not happy that her first choice for maid of honor left for Singapore two months before the wedding.

The rearranging of the wedding party meant Ronaldo didn't have to be stuck again with Regina. It gave Thomas great pleasure, though, to see Ronaldo escort Nina Justo down the aisle instead. Nina's expression was one of complete annoyance with the situation, though she flashed odd twinkle eyes and smiles at Thomas whenever she noticed him gazing at her.

There was a time Nina had been a childhood friend to Maricar. Her inclusion in the wedding party, however, had more to do with the first councilor trying to keep the festivities feud-neutral than acknowledgement of the prior friendship. It could also be reasoned that Nina was family, since Betty Ramirez and Imelda Justo were cousins, though such a connection could be reasoned for just about every family in or around Calamba.

Watching Ronaldo and sitting alongside the Farinas clan in the front row of the church pews was a girl his friend claimed was Arlyn from Bangued.

Thomas was certain the trickster Ronaldo had hired her to pose as his girlfriend. It didn't seem to fit that such a pretty and well-natured girl would be paired with *laad*. He made a mental note to steal some time with the girl later to ascertain the truth.

Jon-Jon shuffled from one foot to the other. Getting married was only part of the reason for Jon-Jon's nerves. Papa Justo and Marino Lapez entering the church created some tension. Though both feuding parties were present, they sat in different areas of the church, the mayor in the back and Justo in the third row. Ringor and Aris were in the church too, though dressed up and seemingly unarmed.

Thomas was sure everyone intended to be on their best behavior, but getting Marino and Papa in the same room was throwing dynamite on a bonfire, there was always an argument. Several of the councilors had already threatened to boycott their regular meetings because of the raucous shouting matches. Townspeople gathered outside the municipal hall just to listen to the verbal assaults, finding them to be entertaining. They would blame one another for the weather if they could determine a way to make it stick.

Father Herman performed the Catholic wedding Mass. The man spoke the regional dialect flawlessly, reading the scripture, asking for the exchange of vows and then the wedding rings.

As the ceremony progressed, Thomas could feel the weight of Auntie Rowena's stare upon him, sending the sight of him from her eyes up to heaven to his mother, who would never see her son wear a barong at an altar. Since Emma's death, Rowena did as much as she could to act as a surrogate. Food for lunch and dinner came to the Wagner house periodically, whenever Thomas was knowingly too busy to prepare his own meals—a task he progressively got better at doing, though had not mastered. Rowena's cooking was vastly superior to his own and was appreciated. He always chuckled when the meal waiting on his own kitchen table was adobo without enough sauce. Thomas always liked to spread around the soy and vinegar so that every rice kernel was properly covered with the brown liquid.

On occasion, Rowena herself accompanied the meal, though Ricky was most frequently at his doorstep to taunt the dog or play basketball in the back using the shower basin as a makeshift basket. Thomas suspected silently that Rowena came out to make sure the house wasn't becoming part of the pigsty. Thomas tried to wash his own clothes in the river—to the amusement of most of the older women in town—until Rowena once a week added his pile to that of the rest of her household.

Thomas suggested she hire of one of the local teenaged girls to be a maid, common enough for the more well-to-do in the cities, even Bangued. Rowena was becoming frazzled trying to run her own household without Joy's help in cooking and cleaning—and then adding Thomas' along the way. It wasn't an expensive proposition, the pay was practically nothing compared to what

Regina was probably making with her aunt in Quezon City—and was insignificant to what Chinese paid Filipina maids in Hong Kong and Singapore. Marino, though, never seemed to make it happen.

Just prior to the ceremony, Rowena met him outside the church to fiddle with his clothes. Satisfied everything was in order, she pecked him on the cheek as she would do to her own children and sent him on his way with a half-hearted smile.

There were awkward moments when the woman would cry in his presence, but only during discussions about Joy. Any other topic produced the normal range of emotions. She was mad at the dog, exasperated with Ricky's energy, annoyed with Marino's schedule, happy to finally beat Auntie Betty in a game of mahjong. There were no tears when she discussed Emma. But a hint from Thomas that he missed Joy and was looking forward to being with her again produced swollen red eyes and an effort to hold back tears. A mother missed her daughter, true, but there was something about it that gave Thomas an itch on the back of his neck.

The ceremony turned to the Philippines traditions. Godparents acted as the first witnesses, pinning Maricar's veil to Jon-Jon's shoulder, the symbol that they are clothed as one. Next the witnesses hung a white cord around each of their necks, representing the eternal bond between the young couple.

The Paculdar and Ramirez parents then lit two tall white candles on either side of the unity candle. Maricar and Jon-Jon in turn then lifted the lit candles and used the combined flame to light the middle one. The smiling old priest gave the couple the arras, blessed coins asking for wealth and fidelity.

Several times during the ceremony Thomas scratched the spot on his left hand where he wore his own wedding ring when no one was around. It helped and hurt at the same time to think of Joy as his wife. It was only a silly notion if he let it be one. He often recalled the secret ceremony in the spot he was standing now. Recollection of that moment was unavoidable today with Maricar and Jon-Jon making their vows.

It was time for the kiss, the applause and the evacuation of the back of the church over to the large tent city at the first councilor's house, which has supplied the town with wafts of pleasant smells all the morning.

Regina took his arm and they exited the church to mug for the camera even more than they had already. The groom gathered with his men of honor. The bride stood with her maids of honor. They smiled as couples, as groups, with parents, without parents, some even with Father Herman. Thomas was certain the photographer was getting some outtakes too—of Maricar slapping Jon-Jon's head for complaining she weighed too much and was crushing his leg instead of sitting on it.

A small boy running down the street broke up the photo session. He had Maricar's cell phone in his hand. A call from Joy. She had good timing, Thomas had grown tired of the sun beating down on him. It was a chore in of itself to keep the sweat off Jon-Jon's and Maricar's plump faces. In perspective, it was better than a rain storm rolling off from the South China Sea.

Joy spent time with both the bride and the groom, though the congratulations talk went on longer with Maricar than with Jon-Jon.

"No, I won't need to make Jon-Jon eat balut. Ha, ha. We will have fun honeymooning in Baguio and Laoag. Thanks again. Yes, he is standing right here."

Maricar handed the phone to Thomas. Joy cried a lot and kissed the phone, adding that she was hugging to death a pillow while imagining it was him. They had spoken only a few days ago, but she reiterated that she wanted a letter detailing every aspect of the wedding day. In the background, Thomas heard an older woman yelling something in Chinese. Joy said she had to hang up and told him she loved him. It sickened him that she was across a sea on a day like today.

Thomas rejoined the group in time to loudly announce the newlyweds to those gathered at the reception.

The area was under eight green tents, arranged into a square pattern. They were borrowed from the municipal storage, left behinds from the military's occupation of the town long ago during the separatist National People's Army's more active era.

High spirits were abound inside. And not all of it had to do with the wedding. The townspeople had been happier since the string of violence ended at about the same time as Joy left for Singapore in September.

Thomas escorted Regina passed Lazy Velasquez, one of Marino's men who had been shot during a raid. He was seated and eating and apparently none the worse for wear from the ordeal.

The lines were long at the buffet. It didn't matter to the honored guests, as food would be brought to them after they sat down. Thomas saw several pits behind the serving area. A few of them still had entire pigs rotating over the fire. *Lechon baboy*. Meat had already been trimmed of two of the pigs and filled serving trays. Other spits had large pieces of meat, probably carabao. The last one seemed to be a goat. There were trays and more trays of food with small Bunsen burners under them. Different kinds of *pancit*. An army of women must have been needed to roll all of the *lumpia*, the Philippine egg roll.

Thomas asked for a plate filled with different kinds of *pancit*, a few pieces of *lumpia* on top and a separate plate with the barbecued pork on a stick.

Idle chit chat with Regina centered on the ceremony. She had spent the last few months in Quezon City with an aunt, serving as the woman's maid. She said Joy was probably happier being a maid in Singapore, at least she would be paid more for the same ordeal.

"Of course, the reason a girl goes to be a maid has nothing to do with learning how to clean clothes and cook food..." Regina unleashed her peculiar laugh, which could only be described as a hiccupping mouse. The normally reserved Regina didn't produce it very often.

"A boyfriend for Reggie?"

She answered with her eyebrows. Thomas was unsure whether it was a yes, no or maybe.

"You can't date here in Calamba, you know that. Parents are always sending a sibling to tag along to make sure you and the boy can't..." Regina bowed her head, slightly embarrassed of the topic.

That narrowed the answer down to yes or maybe. The fact she said boy started to dissuade some rumors of her orientation.

"There is no freedom here. Noah was always around ... not that I wanted to do anything with Ronaldo." Her tongue protruded at the thought. "At least I have unsupervised time to myself in Quezon City when Aunt Rosella goes to work. My cousins will not tell on me if I so much as talk to a boy."

She hit his arm to quiet his smile.

"You were an only child, it was harder for your mother to send spies after you."

"Oh, but we had Ricky," Thomas replied, "even if we were just going to the market. We bribed him with pesos and told him to go find some ice cream when we wanted to have a few moments alone."

"I cannot imagine how you and Joy got away with living together," she said, openly jealous. "*Tatang* would beat me silly if he thought I was sleeping over at a man's house without being married to him."

The comment brought back the memory of Joy's bruise. Thomas still didn't believe Joy's story that it was caused by a disgruntled carabao. The only cause that made sense was Marino punching her in the chest in a fit of rage.

"You're either staring at me because I am stunning," Regina said, "or you're so deep in thought you do not see me at all."

Thomas blinked, not realizing he had been staring at her.

"Well, you are beautiful today," he said off-handedly. It earned him a slap on the arm and then a shy smile.

The food arrived and Regina threw her pork skewers on Thomas' plate. "I know you, Mr. Barbecue." Yes, she would know that well since it was the Flora family that barbecued in the town center every day.

"Complimenting women pays off," he said before lifting one to his maw.

He was expecting another slug in the arm, but got received a cry of disgust instead.

"Whose idea was it to make adobo with monitor lizard?"

Handwriting on the side of the bowl said that's what it was. Thomas looked inside the bowl and couldn't tell if it was indeed alligator, or if it was chicken and they were the butt of a joke. It looked like Ronaldo's handwriting.

Thomas peered to the other side of Jon-Jon and Maricar and spotted Ronaldo. Nina had vacated her space at the table of honor next to Ronaldo, giving it up to the girl with odd eyes. Thomas still had not had the chance to ask the girl if her name was really Arlyn. It would have to come later since Ronaldo was eating and talking to her.

Thomas was sure Nina didn't give up her seat at the head table to be nice to Arlyn. She was snubbing Ronaldo and didn't want to be photographed or seen with him any more than she had.

"Whatever it is, it tastes like chicken," Regina said.

Thomas found Nina sitting with her parents—and Ringor and Bennie. He kept scanning the crowd for an unfamiliar face, finding many.

"So is he here?"

"Who?"

"Him…"

Regina furled her brows. That answer was clearly no, with a hint of displeasure with the idea. Boyfriend was evidently past tense.

"Well, I had to ask," he said, apologetically. "We haven't seen much of you since graduation."

"You are not missing much. It is Quezon City."

"Shopping malls and dancing at clubs?"

"Cooking breakfast, lunch and dinner, force feeding it to cousins who want to be difficult, cleaning clothes, dusting already clean shelves."

"There are some days I wish I could have a maid," Thomas said, recalling Auntie Rowena's constant reminders of how difficult it was to manage two households.

"Hire me," she pleaded. "Aunt Rosella sometimes makes me iron Uncle Jose's underwear to give me work to do."

When their shared chuckle was finished, he suggested working overseas like Joy.

"No. I would rather stay in my own country. I heard too many bad stories about the way Chinese treat their maids. It is less money, but at least I work for my own relatives. Rosella can be mean, but she won't beat me or lock me in the house like a slave."

Joy's employers were difficult sometimes, but were kind people. She was lucky in that regard. Stories surfaced annually of Filipinas and Filipinos being abused overseas, locked in houses while Chinese families took vacations in order to keep their maids from running away in the absence.

"Maybe I would make you iron my underwear too."

"Stop it. How can I eat with you teasing me?"

Thomas wished for the sun to hurry and descend, taking the heat with it. Papa Justo donated his power generators to run enough electricity to power some fans, but it was as effective as digging with a spoon. One oscillated behind Jon-Jon and Maricar, but Thomas could hardly feel its presence.

Thomas did his best to eat and greet people at the same time. Well wishers who'd already finished eating gathered in a line in front of the newlyweds, stretching past Thomas and Regina and parents of the bride and groom. While they were waiting to talk to Jon-Jon and Maricar, many of them took a moment to speak to Thomas. Shouldn't you be getting married soon? After college, good idea. Shame about your mother and father being dead now. Your rice crop looking better than mine? Too much flooding this time, had to replant. Wish I had triple crop land with river irrigation like you.

"That Nina is such a snob," Regina whispered, leaning into Thomas' ear. "She barely wants to be seen with us all day. But now that everyone is filing past the table, she kicks Arlyn out of her seat so she can be greeted by the masses."

Thomas rolled his eyes when he saw it was true. All hail the queen. Ex-queen now that her reign as Miss Abra ended. She had plastic grins for her subjects. It was too bad she didn't have a pen for autographs.

With so many people around, Thomas kept his mouth shut. There was the possibility of Justo supporters within ear shot. Thomas didn't want to be involved in the Justo-Lapez feud any more than he was.

Thomas lifted his glass in toast. "To Jon-Jon and Car-Car, who have been in love as high school sweethearts ... no ... elementary sweethearts. May you have lots of little Cars and Jons and a long, loving, fulfilling life together."

The newlyweds cut the wedding cake and were, to the dismay of many, respectful and did not mess one another's faces with smashed cake. Nina, to the dismay of many, caught the bouquet. Ronaldo, to the humor of many, caught the garter.

Bellies full, the newlyweds moved to an open area for dancing. Guests pinned money to the clothing of Jon-Jon and Car-Car Paculdar during their marriage celebration dance, the pandango. The money would go to paying off their honeymoon. With a baby pin, Thomas attached a 5,000 peso note to Jon-Jon's sleeve. They smiled at him.

He went back to his seat and drank a second glass of sparkling wine until the end of the song. Regina came up from behind and wrapped her arms around Thomas' stomach, planting her chin on his shoulder. It startled Thomas, such an intimate posture was unusual for Regina. "You look so sad. Cheer up, you will have your wedding some day."

Thomas downed the remainder of his glass. Little did she know.

"It is time to dance," Regina said, clutching at his elbow until he stood.

Thomas spent the next song dancing with Regina, who seemed overly happy about it. He got his chance to dance with Maricar, then mother of the bride Auntie Betty before returning to Regina.

The floor filled with people. Ronaldo danced by and mouthed, "ha, you stuck with Reggie now." He smirked and danced away with "Arlyn." The girl was stiff as a board. There was daylight between them, but she seemed to grasp his arm more in terror than to be lead in the dance step.

Thomas was stuck with Regina only until Marites Galope cut in, brandishing a very wide perpetual smile. The women were lining up to dance with him, not the other way around. Songs came and went. Dance partners came and went. It felt odd to dance with Lovelyn Lucero, who decided not to dress down from her usual Angeles City attire and heavy face makeup. She had a pleasant demeanor and danced respectfully, despite being a beacon of sexual overtones.

Such overtones were not lost on Thomas. It had been a shock to go from frequent loving to a dead stop. He thought celibacy would be easy. It was easy at college. Living at Lopito's house in the evening and staying home in Calamba over the weekends allowed Thomas to avoid social situations with most of the university girls. In Calamba, it was tougher. Every doe-eyed teenaged girl knew Joy was in Singapore and tried in any way imaginable to get Thomas to notice her. It seemed even the decade-older Lovelyn was wiggling her nose his way.

He took his leave of the dance floor to get something to drink. He was thankful that Maricar's father had brought a cooler with San Miguel beer. He opened the squat bottle and was drinking and walking back to his seat at the honor table when he spotted Ronaldo's dance partner sitting alone. Ronaldo was trying to impress his mother with his dancing and moustache.

"Hello, I'm Thomas, Ronaldo's friend."

Arlyn was staring into nothingness with an ear turned to the speakers. She acted as if she didn't notice his protruding hand. Unblinking, she tilted her head in Thomas' direction.

"Excuse me. Are you speaking to me?"

"Yes," Thomas sat next to her. "I'm Thomas. Ronaldo and I are friends..."

"Oh, yes. Nice to meet you. He has talked about you a lot. I'm Arlyn."

This time, she protruded her hand. It hung in front of her until Thomas grasped it. It was obvious then that Arlyn was blind or almost blind.

Thomas grinned on the inside. Arlyn was real. Ronaldo was a sly one, finding a girlfriend who couldn't see the deformity on his face.

"You're the one that is going to be a doctor. Your parents must be so proud."

"Yes, they will be very proud of me when I become a doctor." Ronaldo must not have told her that his parents were dead.

Arlyn Gertos spent a lot of time with her mother in the market in Bangued, Thomas discovered through their conversation, which is where she met Ronaldo. Arlyn was a good looking young woman, so Ronaldo undoubtedly found her while girl watching in the square. She lived in Bangued and attended the school there for the deaf and blind.

Thomas found a new side to Ronaldo, who so frequently hid behind his nonchalant behavior. Arlyn was telling him more, no doubt, than Ronaldo would admit if Thomas cornered him later on the topic. She had met the Farinas family, he ascertained from remembering her sitting with them in the church. Meeting the family was an important step in a relationship. Blind or not, Mr. and Mrs. Farinas were probably doubly as happy Ronaldo found a girl as Thomas was.

"You farm?"

Arlyn nodded. "Vegetables. Eggplant, bitter melon and long beans. I cannot see well, but I am good at finding weeds."

"How well can you see?" he asked as though it wasn't that forward to do so.

"Mmm. How to explain? My right eye, I still have some sight. I can tell light and dark enough to know if it is day or night. Big shapes, like the mountains, I can see the outline if the light is right."

She smiled at the end of her explanation. Thomas could sense an inner joy. Her disability didn't define her.

A wedding party-colored dress appeared in Thomas' peripheral vision. Their brief talk was rudely interrupted by Nina.

"Does a maid of honor get a chance to dance with the best man?" she asked much too sweetly to be taken that way.

"Go ahead," Arlyn said. "I will be fine here, resting, until Ronaldo comes back."

Thomas sighed and swallowed what was left of his beer. Nina had him right where she wanted him. He couldn't refuse because she was entitled to a dance. He excused himself from Arlyn.

"Has anyone told you that you are very handsome in a barong?" The gleam in Nina's eye was easy to interpret.

"Yes. As many times as you've been told you are beautiful in that dress."

She tilted her head so that her long black hair did a flip, all the while trying to peer straight into his eyes. Nina was a tall girl, able to stand eye-to-eye with Thomas. She plastered a plastic charmed look on her face. The look she got in return was one of immunity. It wasn't two steps into their song that she made her intentions obvious.

"So, got yourself a girlfriend?"

"Yes, I've had one for a long time," he said, trying to be cool through the brazen question.

"I don't mean Joy. She's in Singapore anyway."

Thomas bit his tongue.

"I've been to Baguio, there are girls everywhere. No one catch you yet?"

"Shameless flirting and personal questions? What are you fishing for, Nina?"

His answer was a not-so-innocent smile.

"Just because Joy is in Singapore doesn't mean I'm free to play around behind her back. I'm not that kind of person."

Thomas wanted to get his dance with Nina over as soon as possible. He searched for Regina, hoping eye contact with her would prompt her to come save him by cutting in. He felt doomed when he saw his escape dancing with an older gentleman.

"Relax, Thomas. Lighten up. You can't take being teased? I'm not going to kidnap you and hold you for ransom. We're just dancing."

A tease? That was a great analogy. He kept his face neutral.

"Don't you miss college? When are you going back to Baguio?"

"With some luck, I'll be back there in June."

"Six months of watching weeds grow? That's a lot of time to sit in Calamba and be bored. I don't understand why you dropped out. You're smart. I thought you weren't going to suffer the syndrome of everyone else around here."

The drop out syndrome. Go to school for a year or less and then leave. Money problems. Family emergencies needing another hand on the farm. Disinterest in really going, but attending in the first place because it was a parent's wish.

"Not everyone has a sister in Vegas to pay for it."

Nina had stiffened with Thomas' comment. "You have a girlfriend in Singapore to pay for St. Louis, so both of us are lucky to have overseas sponsors," she retorted. "Peace treaty. Okay? Peace? We used to be friends as kids. Car-Car pushed the past aside and let me be in her wedding. At least we can be friendly. What happened between us was years ago. I'm sorry. It was high school. We were young. You're the only person who ever dumped me. I'm sorry that I didn't take it well. Okay?"

They lost eye contact. She shifted her eyes to look beyond his shoulder.

It came out so fast that it took Thomas a few moments to digest it all. Nina apologized, admitted fault and wanted peace.

Thomas cleared his throat. "I'll go back when my ... sponsor has had a chance to save enough for me to return to Baguio," he answered less antagonistically.

She smiled hesitantly. "See, we can be friends."

They floated politely across the dance floor for another minute and then the song ended. With its conclusion, so came the end of the dancing. As Thomas escorted Nina from the floor, someone came on the microphone to announce karaoke would be starting. Thomas groaned. The crowd was thinning, but not for the same reason that Thomas now wanted to leave. He understood that part of a normal Asian's genetic makeup made them disposed to enjoying karaoke. From Japan to China to Malaysia, the love of singing embarrassingly out of tune was enjoyed by all. The gene seemed to miss him.

The first on the stage were Jon-Jon and Maricar, a duet of "Islands in the Stream." Every nerve burst along Thomas' spine when the newlyweds reached the chorus. Thomas assessed proper etiquette. He had to dance with Nina because he was the best man. Would he have to sing too?

Nina shifted uncomfortably in her chair, turning her back to the singers. Her eyes beamed with annoyance. In the interest of peace, Thomas didn't chastise her for being so childishly stuck up that she couldn't politely watch Jon-Jon and Maricar. He hated it too, but at least he was watching and smiling.

"Can you walk me home?"

"Why?"

"Can't you see it?"

"See what?"

"Aris," Nina said, using her lips to point out where the devil's lieutenant was sitting in a corner. "He keeps staring at me. I noticed it when I was sitting at the head table for dinner. It was disturbing, so I moved. He hasn't stopped. How many hours have we been here? And he hasn't stopped. I can't take it anymore. Please, walk me home."

Thomas didn't need to ask if she was scared. Apprehensive, probably. Scared, no, despite the fact it was Aris staring a hole in her head—and probably imagining a real hole based on his not-to-secret hatred for the Justo family.

Thomas nodded and gentlemanly offered his hand for Nina to get out of the plastic chair. There was a silver lining. It gave him an excuse to vacate the karaoke torture grounds.

Neither of them acknowledged Aris as they walked passed his table. Nina was stiff and quick footed. Out of the corner of his eye, Thomas could see Aris was sitting alone, and judging by the number of bottles standing on the tabletop, he had nursed several beers.

Thomas did not realize how hot it was under the tent until he emerged into the clear night. The sound of insects was more pronounced now that there wasn't a sound system pumping music into his head.

It wasn't a long walk to the Justo residence. They strolled past the ornately decorated protective wall. Thomas thought back to how many years it had been since he'd seen the inside of the house. It had always been a two-story with a real staircase, not a ladder into a loft. Year by year there were improvements. A new roof made of shingles, not tin. The exterior received a more attractive brick. Greater amounts of concrete covered the plain ground. Landscaping appeared around the trees. Petroleum-based emergency generators powered the visible window air conditioners.

Papa Justo and Bennie were sitting on the porch. Their conversation abruptly ended with the approach of Nina and Thomas. She brought the hand of her father to her forehead, a sign of greeting and respect.

"Sir," Thomas said, nodding at Papa Justo.

Nina's father bent his perplexed expression into a crooked smile.

"Thank you, Thomas," Nina said with a flourish. Smiling widely, she spun so that her dress did a flourish, and she went inside the house.

As Thomas was walking away, he began feeling uncomfortable with the way Papa Justo greeted them. It was as if he thought...

He didn't want to return to the heat of the reception tents. To wash out the corny singing, he sought to the comfort of a cold beer. Someone had brought some *lambanog*, essentially coconut vodka, as a gift to Jon-Jon and Maricar. She wasn't drinking because of the pregnancy. And Jon-Jon wasn't drinking because she wasn't drinking. And he had to drive later tonight. The groom was sharing the bottles instead.

The world felt off its axis. It was a feeling that had nothing to do with the glass after glass of 80 proof. Two of his childhood friends were now married and off on their honeymoon. A third friend was dating a blind girl. Regina and Joy had careers as houseworkers. Had he misjudged Nina all these years?

After the tents had emptied, Thomas fumbled his way across the rope bridge. Muscle memory got him to the front door. He flicked away some small lizards.

The *lambanog* made Thomas forget that he needed to chronicle the day—in nauseating detail—in a letter to Joy. He fell into bed instead.

Reaching under the bed frame, he fetched a small box and put his own wedding ring in its rightful place.

CHAPTER 10
SANGAPULO

Thomas quietly stood near the doorway. The bead curtain did little for maintaining privacy in the bedroom. Baby Lady, Annie Lucero, knelt at the edge of Maricar's bed. The room was filled with the noises of childbirth.

Thomas felt the familiar tickle in his gut. Old memories returned. He had buried the scenes of stillborn and miscarried siblings, but those mind movies resurfaced whenever he encountered a newborn or heard the painful wailing of a mother in the throes of labor. What most men were abashed to witness, he watched in morbid fascination.

"Get used to it," Auntie Annie said. "When you become Doctor Wagner, you'll be a lot closer than the doorway."

Thomas' presence in the doorway was required, however, to keep Jon-Jon out of the bedroom. Auntie Annie banished the father-to-be from the room because he was making Maricar more nervous by jumping at every sound she made.

Thomas didn't understand why they chose to have the baby in Calamba. Most women were starting to give birth in the small hospital in La Paz. It cost more that way, Thomas understood, but it cut down on infant mortality. Even Auntie Annie was surprised at Maricar's decision. Only the mountain people in the barangays were still interested in midwives these days.

Auntie Betty passed through the door. It brought Jon-Jon out of the chair.

"Not yet," Thomas called out behind him.

Jon-Jon sat down. Auntie Betty went back inside the bedroom, shooting a look to Thomas to stop peeking.

"Or it is time," he corrected himself.

Jon-Jon paced. He had never been around this event. He was nervous for his wife and emerging child. Thomas envied that Jon-Jon didn't really taste the fear of it. He also envied that Jon-Jon was getting something he had wanted for years. Fatherhood. The Paculdars were growing. The Wagners had been shrinking. He knew his time was coming, though. Joy would return home in a few months for the week-long visit that was guaranteed in her contract. They would touch, then separate for another year, but be able to marry public ally and have their own children once she returned again.

94

Thomas turned his back on the curtain and watched Jon-Jon fret.

"The last time you looked like this was just before that Grey of yours won in Bangued."

Jon-Jon acted as though he wanted to smile. "Yes, that worked out well. I needed the money from the winnings."

Maricar, the old jeepney, unofficially still known as Little Man, was falling apart. Oil leaks. Flat tires. Broken suspension. Thomas didn't understand it. The roads had gotten better. The town's money was burning Marino's hands. He couldn't spend it fast enough. Of course, Thomas understood the sudden desire to improve the town when he hadn't done anything for years. Papa Justo did some behind the scenes negotiating and was able to locate a new cellular phone tower on a hill between La Paz and Calamba and another near Pingaping. With Papa Justo taking credit for clear cell phone service for the northwest corner of Abra—though it was rumored the governor actually fostered the deal—Marino felt obligated to start matching the accomplishments. The town hall got a fresh coat of paint and newly paved roads sprung up in weeks. A metal bridge over the river was proposed. Pipes for a supposed water system were trucked into Calamba and stacked beside the town hall, for show for now. Thomas suspected Marino would only make good on using those pipes if Papa Justo racked up another accomplishment that could be used politically.

Jon-Jon had won a sizeable amount, more than enough to repair the jeepney that was his living. There was enough left over to make up for the delinquent payments on their house, the typhoon ravaged structure that once belonged to Auntie Dina, who had died earlier in the year from old age.

"If you keep winning like that, I'm going to have to increase the rent on your chicken coop."

"I wish he didn't die so soon after winning, I would like to have entered him in some more *sabong* derbies," Jon-Jon continued.

"*Sabong* again," came Lara's complaint from the front door. Luis flew around her and went straight to his uncle "Jah Jah" when he saw him. Then it seemed Lara's sour antics ceased without an audience.

The cell phone beeped at Jon-Jon's hip. Luis pointed at the beep beep. It was a text message.

"Joy wants us to call when the baby is born," Jon-Jon relayed.

Joy was using her employers' computer and Internet connection to send a text message to the cell phone. It was cheaper than making calls, and more discrete, not giving Mrs. Song cause to scold her for talking instead of working.

Thomas had wagered pesos on Jon-Jon's gamecock out of friendship. Many in the audience knew Paculdar and eagerly wagered against him, increasing the odds. Thomas walked away with decent winnings of his own. He wanted to use the money for a cell phone, that way Joy could call him directly instead of using Jon-Jon's or the very non-private municipal landline phone. Joy was against it. She had become overly sensitive on the issue of money. Her efforts had already paid back the placement fee as well as Thomas' front money. Her toils now were becoming their nest egg.

Joy's behavior had become erratic over the course of her stay in Singapore. Hysterical crying during a phone call on a Sunday was replaced by the next Sunday's call of tearing into him for transgressions he hadn't committed.

"Father told me you were dancing with Nina Justo," she had said with an edge to her voice.

Thomas sighed in disgust. "It couldn't be avoided."

"You couldn't avoid leaving the reception with her though?"

"I only walked her home because Aris was making her nervous," Thomas had explained. Joy replied with a rude noise. "No. Really. He was drinking heavy and stared at us like he was going to pull a knife."

"Or maybe you're renewing your relationship now that I'm gone."

Joy's jealousy raged for a few more minutes. She hung up on him even after he pointed out that he danced with Regina and Auntie Betty too, but she didn't seem jealous of that. Joy had called back two hours later and was apologetic.

With eyes watching him, Thomas made sure Nina's visits were discrete, even though they were innocent calls on his well-being. Nina had brought books for the current semester's class work. Even though he wasn't attending, Thomas kept up by reading them in the evenings. When it came time to actually return to the university, he would be ready.

There was a high pitched squeal, an infant's siren that it had entered the world. In time, Auntie Annie came out with the baby tucked in a swaddling cloth. "Hoy, look at this nose," she said, handing over the newborn to her father. She had to adjust the way Jon-Jon held the baby.

"It's not a rooster, you know," Lara declared, peering over Jon-Jon's shoulder to look into the baby's face.

Thomas kept Luis occupied in the corner of the room as the family moved in and out of Maricar's bedroom. Mr. Ramirez, now a grandfather, came jogging to the house when word finally reached him. It was reaching other parts of the town, neighbors peeked inside and took great joy in telling someone that the baby was out. The infant's gender and measurements were spread by word of mouth, as well as the name. Tammy. Immediately, the nickname became Tam-Tam to follow Car-Car and Jon-Jon.

Thomas retrieved Jon-Jon's cell phone and sent a text message with the news back to Joy's Internet ID.

Thomas took his turn holding Tammy, but refrained from making silly faces and noises to his future goddaughter. By the time she reached him, her eyes were closed and she was wrapped in a white swaddling cloth. The sight made his gut tingle. After an appropriate amount of Thomas' smiling stare, the child went back inside the bedroom to her mother.

"Can you believe it? This was more exciting than *sabong*. Could you ever imagine me saying that?" Jon-Jon beamed.

"Don't stand out here talking to me. Get inside and kiss Car-Car," Thomas said, nearly shoving the larger man through the bead curtain.

Unlucky at cards, lucky in love. Thomas wondered how that translated to cockfights. However it was, Jon-Jon was on the lucky end today.

< <> >

The sun was barely poking over the horizon when Thomas waded into the river to retrieve his net. Empty last night when he submerged it into the slow moving river, it was now filled with small wiggling fish. They would make for a good Sunday lunch, fried in oil with garlic and ginger. They were small, but not so much as to make for a wasted effort to clean them. He wasn't fond of eating the eyes, but wouldn't let them go to waste.

Emptying the net into one of his water buckets, he saw Rowena's tiny frame cross the rope bridge.

"Auntie Ro," Thomas waved. He lifted one of her hands to his forehead. "*Mano po*," he said in the traditional asking of the blessing from one's parents.

He offered his godmother some of the fish to take home. She offered to cook the entire bucket. She reminded him that the Lapez family was the church sponsors today and he was to be with them. He was invited to the house afterward, where they could eat the fish along with some *pinakbet* and *sinagang*.

Rowena left with the bucket as Thomas jogged back to his house for coffee and a change of clothes.

At the church, Thomas greeted Marino with a polite *mano po*, only to be answered by a condescending grin. Thomas had never openly expressed his animosity to the shorter, more dense man, but sensed that Joy's father knew it. They spoke very little to one another in recent years. At the proper moment in the Mass, he walked at step behind Marino in taking the offerings to the church up to the father, along with the wine and bread.

Ronaldo was sitting inside the kitchen when Thomas returned home at midday.

"Jon-Jon was just here tending to his gamecocks," Ronaldo said.

"And what have you been tending to? I haven't seen you since the wedding."

"Sorry, I've been busy."

"I'm not surprised. Arlyn was nice."

"Yes, she told me that she talked to you at the reception," Ronaldo said, not dignifying the inference. "Miss me at the card games?"

"No. There haven't been any Saturday night games since Jon-Jon got married. We need to have one. Fish eyes for the loser. Or, better yet, some monitor adobo...?"

That got Ronaldo's laugh started.

"And she still ate it?"

"She said it tastes like chicken."

"Yes, that is what monitor lizard tastes like."

Thomas blinked. "It wasn't chicken?"

Ronaldo shook his head no.

"It was really monitor?"

Thomas sputtered along with Ronaldo after his affirmation.

"She ate it because she thought you were trying to trick her. If she thought it was really the alligator, she wouldn't have touched it."

"I know. That is what made it so funny."

He offered Ronaldo some leftovers from his lunch with Joy's family.

"They're really taking care of you?"

"More than I want sometimes. Auntie Ro is so busy without my mom or Joy to help her with the house and the work crews. Even though she is so busy, she cooks and cleans for me when she can. I am getting better at doing it all for myself, though it still looks like a bachelor pad."

"You are not going back to college yet? Right?"

Thomas nodded, discarding his shirt to hang it on the back of a chair. He opened a jug on the kitchen counter and offered a glass of milky liquid to Ronaldo.

"*Tuba*. Made it myself."

"Homemade *tuba*? Your own *basi* wasn't enough? You really are bored out here. When do you start erecting the *lambanog* distillery?"

Ronaldo sipped the brew of fermented coconut tree sap and gritted his teeth as it traveled down his throat.

"It'll become vinegar in about seven more weeks," Thomas explained.

Ronaldo nursed a few more sips and sat pensively staring into the glass.

"You've met Arlyn, so you know how nice she is..."

Ronaldo's face wore a more serious expression. Thomas sat down beside him at the kitchen table.

"She is beautiful. More lovely than I ever thought I would find. My face, you know..." He gestured to his malformed upper lip that seemed to drag down the corner of his nose. "I know she's mostly blind and cannot really see me, but I get the feeling from being around her that it might not matter even if she could see."

Thomas thought about teasing his friend over his newfound feelings. It was obvious that he harbored strong emotions for Arlyn.

"You and Jon-Jon have had someone your entire lives. This is the first time I have ever... though Reggie and I tried to once." Ronaldo grimaced.

"She was the neighbor girl. She didn't really like me that way and I knew it. Actually, I don't think Reggie liked me in any way."

"None of us ever expected you to marry Reggie and follow in our footsteps so we would all be two-by-two."

"Maybe not you all."

He knew what Ronaldo was saying. Ugly Ronaldo was only going to be paired with someone equally as ugly, and that was freckles and moles, no chest, boy body, we-think-she-really-likes-girls Regina Flora.

"Who cares what they think. Where are those people now? Our school batch is scattered to the wind. Some of them are stuck here working as farm hands for someone. When I come driving down the trail in the tractor to plow up a field for one of them, no one is calling me Little Joe any more." Thomas finished his first cup of tuba.

"That is because you look like Aga Muhlach," Ronaldo jibed. Aga Muhlach was the Brad Pitt of the Philippines and one of the country's most popular movie heart throbs.

Thomas nearly shot the *tuba* out of his nose. "You timed that on purpose."

When Thomas had finally composed himself, Ronaldo finally spit it out. "I want to ask Arlyn to marry me."

Thomas regarded his friend.

"Jon-Jon was the same way. Silent. Shocked."

"It's not that. I don't know what to say. You're the trail blazer. I have never had to date someone and then meet her parents and then ask. Joy and I are getting married when she gets back from Singapore and I graduate medical school. We just decided when and how to do it. There was no bending at the knee, pop the question. Little Tam-Tam made that decision for Jon-Jon and Car-Car."

It was true, Thomas and Joy had decided their fate long before the secret ceremony.

"I'm stumped for advice. I'm happy to hear it. I like Arlyn. She has a good disposition and probably laughs at everything you say."

Ronaldo dropped his head but could not hide his grin.

"Any worries about her saying no?"

"Not from her. It is her parents that I am worried about."

"You said they liked you."

"Yes, but they are rich and I am not."

Arlyn is blind. If not Ronaldo, who are they going to marry her to? Thomas kept the comment to himself, lest Ronaldo think he was disparaging her.

"I'm thinking of getting a nice engagement ring. Something that will impress them," Ronaldo said. "And I wanted to ask you for a loan, since you are not going to medical school right now."

"How nice is the price to impress them?"

"8,000."

Thomas choked. "If I spend that much money from the account, Joy is going to notice it and get mad."

"I will pay you back somehow."

"How? You don't have a job."

"I do now."

Thomas raised his brows.

"Her dad owns a building in Bangued, so he was able to convince the security company to give me a job. I'm a night watchman now."

"Stop kidding me."

"No joke. I walk around all night with a shotgun. I have to wear this body vest with armor plating in it. It is heavy. And the job is boring. Nothing ever happens. It is Bangued. There is no nightlife," Ronaldo said. "Come on. He even gave me a job. I have to impress her parents somehow."

Thomas sighed and regarded his lifelong friend. Jumpy. Pleading. Worried. Not the same Ronaldo that was fond of putting stones in peoples' rice or lizards down the back of girls' shirts.

"On one condition."

Ronaldo nodded without even hearing the condition.

"I have to be the best man and there is no karaoke at the reception."

Ronaldo chuckled and agreed again.

"You are lucky Jon-Jon was a winner at the *sabong*. I can lend you the money from the 10,000 pesos I won from wagering. Otherwise, I would have to sell one of my carabaos."

They were drinking and playing cards and planning a suitable Ronaldo-esque way of popping the question when they were interrupted by visitors.

The tight yellow top and a flowery white skirt at the front gate could only belong to Nina. Peering outward from the kitchen through the open house door, Thomas saw the completed package, including dangling earrings, leather sandals and a handbag that matched the top. He stood to meet her and the dog scrambled out in front of him. Thomas called it off before its greeting leap put a mess on Nina's outfit and infuriated her.

Thomas' smile turned into a frown when he saw Bennie Justo in tow. Of course, a bodyguard. There was a gun-sized bulge under his white T-shirt near the armpit. Bennie was Papa's youngest brother. Thomas knew him to be a reasonable person and a contrast to Ringor. He was thankful she didn't drag Ringor with her, although there was no way of knowing from his position on the porch whether there were other armed men down the trail.

Bennie waved to Thomas and stayed outside the gate. He ignored the dog's antics and looked about aimlessly: to the trees, to the tractor shack, out to the fields, the condition of the road at his feet.

"Oh, you have a visitor. I thought you were alone. Hello, Ronaldo," Nina said pleasantly.

Nina produced two books from her bag. Thomas handed her some money and thanked her for bringing them. Nina glanced at Ronaldo and the cards and said she would visit some other time. The corner of her eyes wrinkled with her smile and she left the house. Ronaldo was aghast during the entire exchange, eyes darting from Nina to Thomas.

"What was all that? Nina full of smiles. And she didn't call me *laad*. What happened to her?" Ronaldo blinked. "Is there something going on?"

"No," Thomas said, watching Nina and Bennie depart. "She was just bringing me the last couple of books I needed for this semester in Baguio. I thought I would do something productive while being stuck in Calamba until Joy gets back."

Thomas saw Ronaldo's expression, read his mind and slugged him in the arm. "Oh, sure, Nina and I are going to do that with Bennie standing outside with a gun! What are you thinking? You know me better."

Ronaldo shrugged. "I'm just surprised, I guess. She is one of the last people I ever expected to come out here. She's never been nice to us. You especially. You remember that time she convinced her sister into getting Aris to throw carabao dung at you?"

"She apologized for all of that history in high school. She's been nice to me since," Thomas said, gesturing to the books.

"Miss Abra is coming to your house and all you can say is that she is being nice to you. Joy would—"

"—spit knives, I know, which is why I am not broadcasting Nina's visits to the farm to her."

"How often?"

"About as often as you," Thomas said in the hopes of silencing Ronaldo's further attempts at innuendo.

Jon-Jon returned before dusk to check on his roosters. Thomas wrangled him into a round of cards. "We haven't done this for awhile. It may be a long time before we can do this again."

"I think I've already drunk enough that I'll need to stay here for the night," Ronaldo admitted.

"We can tell you the plan for Ronaldo asking Arlyn to marry him," Thomas told Jon-Jon while dealing the first hand.

"Before we get into that. What is the bet?" Jon-Jon slipping some cards into his hands.

"Fish eyes in the frig," Ronaldo said.

CHAPTER 11
SANGAPULO KET MAYSA

Thomas went back to St. Louis University in March. With the money that Joy had sent, he paid the tuition for the semester he missed, bribed the clerk into overlooking his months of absence, paid the fee to take his final exams and surprised all of his professors by passing them. Thomas was pleased that he was able to get credit for the time he missed, though it was an overly expensive way to attend college and he didn't want to repeat the procedure.

In the aftermath, he was surprised that it had worked. Nina was the source of the idea. Thomas originally had planned to retake the classes and be a step up for reading the textbooks. Nina suggested that he knew enough to take the exams anyway and knew whom he had to bride—as well as how much to pay—to have the records suddenly reflect his daily presence at the university.

"I would rather pay 420 pesos for the class tuition than 3,000 pesos to bribe the department clerk," Thomas had said.

"Stop being so honorable," Nina had replied. "You know how things get done. 'Peso, say so.' You never paid an extra 20 pesos to get some government form processed faster? From what I heard, you paid more than you needed for Joy's agent. She got faster placement because you threw in those extra couple thousand pesos."

Despite the success, Thomas did not celebrate his dishonesty. There was consolation that he at least learned something. Reading paid off.

Reading paid off for Ronaldo too, becoming engaged during a Bible reading session. Thomas wished he had been present for the event. In true Ronaldo fashion he had altered the Braille pages of Arlyn's Bible. Her fingers moved quickly and she was reading so fast that she stumbled into Ronaldo's alterations without stopping. "Ronaldo will you marry me," she had said. The trickster had been so scared of the prospect of asking that he got Arlyn to do it instead. In shock, Arlyn had brought her hands to her mouth. Ronaldo pried one of them away and placed the engagement ring on her finger.

Thomas was hoping that they would get married soon so that he could perform his duty as the best man before returning to Baguio in June to start his sophomore year. With a freshman year so full of life-altering events, he was hoping the sophomore year would be at the opposite end of the pendulum. There was only one interruption foreseen for the year and that was when Joy finally came home for two weeks. Planting and harvesting would be a pain, but Thomas decided he would only plant as much as he could handle on the weekends when he was able to go home. With Jon-Jon going to the farm twice a day to check on his next cockfighting champions, he felt secure that nothing bad would happen in his absence.

He knelt in the shade of the old narra tree. "Mom," he said, touching his mother's name on the grave marker. "Dad." He touched his father's name. "I miss you both. I wish you both were still here. It is hard, but it is working. I am fulfilling your dreams. Joy is helping me. Nina is helping me. It's a struggle. I have to be in two places at once it seems. It'll happen though. I can feel it. I will graduate with my bachelor's degree and then finish the medical school part. Auntie Ro will be at the graduation ceremony. Her eyes will send up the images of me walking on the stage."

Thomas wasn't remiss in saying goodbye to his siblings' stones before departing for the Lapez residence.

With all of his school clothes and uniforms still sitting in a drawer in Lopito's house, there was little he needed to take with him on the journey. It was a quiet hour in the mayor's jeep. Aris drove and Fernando sat beside Thomas in the back. Marino used them as a sounding board for some campaign ideas. They were little more than yes-men. Lopito was the smart one when it came to elections. He helped get Marino elected in the first place, as well as several other friends and cousins into minor positions in municipalities near Baguio.

The governor was campaigning on behalf of Papa Justo, Thomas learned. Disinterested in politics, Thomas had stayed away from the governor's swing through Calamba and its barangays.

"Justo has *kano* money. I'll be able to match that. But governor's money in addition? That will be a problem." Marino turned and faced Thomas. "If you were a doctor already, Thomas, you could be really useful to me right now."

Thomas smiled as though that were a compliment. The only time he wanted to be useful to this corrupt and violent man was to be his coroner and pronounce death following a wasteful disease. Ted Wagner was a good man and died early of lung cancer, yet Marino thrived strong and healthy. Thomas kept smiling, but it was because he was imaging Marino's liver failure.

Joy cried for the loss of Ted. Would Joy even cry over her own father's death?

While the three of them sat around the table with Lopito, Thomas snuck out to go downtown to the Internet café. He typed an email to Joy to let her know he had returned to Baguio.

Some of her messages sent weeks ago chronicled fun with her Filipina friends there in Singapore. Through them, she had been able to learn the nooks and crannies of the city nation. He knew enough from her letters and electronic messages to eat and shop if he were able to go there himself.

She wrote: *Thank you for my birthday present, Ayat. It is a nice cell phone. And you're right, now I can call you from my room at night and Mrs. Song can't scold me. You should not neglect yourself and spend money on me. I'm sorry that I get so emotional about it, but this is not an easy life in Singapore. Lucky that my neighbors are Filipina so we can chika chika to pass the time. I wonder how Auntie Dina's sisters ever managed to do this for 10 years in Lebanon. After the newness wears off, you start to miss everything back home.*

Thomas quipped in his reply about her sentimentality. She missed toting water from the river, no electricity and no flushing toilets?

After he loaned Ronaldo the money from his gambling winnings, he sold the carabao anyway. That was the money he used to buy Joy's cell phone. He would get one for himself when he had the money. Since everyone else around him had a cell phone, he was never far from borrowing one to send a text.

There was a tap on his shoulder just before he clicked to send Joy's reply.

"Reading my email?"

"Smile at me," Nina said.

Judging from her attire, she had just come from class. She was nervously glancing at a gaggle of similarly dressed girls on the other side of the Internet café. They were sitting at the bar. Thomas knew from sight that they were prissy, self-absorbed, money-soaked, clique-ish, bubble gum band Barbie girls.

"Play along," she said through her teeth. "Smile at me."

Thomas smiled.

Nina tossed her hair and urged him to stand. She wrapped her arms around his waist for a second and then grabbed his backpack for him. Nina led him away from the rental computer by the hand.

Beaming.

All show.

"Thomas, can you buy me a mango juice?" she asked loudly, in English, once reaching earshot of the gaggle.

She sat him at the bar a few chairs removed from the others.

There was something else off about Nina today.

"Are your eyes blue?"

She drew a hand to her face and fanned herself. "You noticed my eyes?"

"Stop acting silly. Your eyes have always been dark and now they're blue."

"Colored contact lenses."

Her eyes, however, lingered on the other girls for a moment.

"Perfect, we're face to face. Oh, the looks we're getting now."

Nina smiled wide and winked. The wink was meant for the gaggle. Thomas sat quietly until the mango juice arrived. Once the gaggle had their own beverages, they took their leave of the café. That's when Nina relaxed her fake smile and let up fawning Thomas.

"Who are you trying to impress?"

"I'm a beauty pageant queen at an expensive private college. I have to keep up appearances."

"Am I your friend or your trophy?" Thomas protested.

"No, you're a shield," Nina corrected. "The girl who was at the far end, I don't want to go out with her cousin. He likes me, but he's a dumb rock. I don't want to insult her because her other cousin was a candidate to be on Pinoy Dream Academy. She might introduce me so I can ask how to get on the show. But I won't be invited along to Manila next month if I insult her by turning down the cousin that likes me. It was easier to use you as a boyfriend so that I have an excuse to turn him down."

Thomas actually followed the logic.

"You've been telling people that I'm your boyfriend?"

"Don't look so disappointed."

"You lied to them. What are you going to try to do to keep up with this charade when they start inviting you to events?"

"Keep your voice down," Nina hissed. "Don't ruin this. This might be my chance for my dream to come true. I can get on that show and end up with my own recording contract."

Nina actually could sing well, but Thomas had his doubts that there was a superstar-in-waiting sitting next to him.

"If it gets too complicated," she continued explaining, "I'll tell them that we didn't work out. It will be fine because then I'll be too distraught to get involved with someone new. That also keeps the cousin away from me."

Nina sipped her juice. "I helped you a lot, you can help me a little."

"The day you came by the house, Ronaldo thought I had gone over to the enemy. I don't need boyfriend rumors compounding the situation."

"Relax, Thomas, none of those girls have a clue who you really are outside of studying to be a doctor. I'm barely at their level since I don't have a lot of money. If they found out we're a couple of farmers from the mountains, they'd never talk to me again. I have designer clothes from Nora's box from Las Vegas, so I can out dress them on the weekend. I've already shown them my Miss Abra crown. Because of that, I was able to pose in pictures with congressmen. I've got them thinking that I'm just as rich as they are."

"Wouldn't you rather have real friends that cared about you instead of status symbols?"

"I have you for that. I need them to like me enough to take me to Manila next month."

"Using people to cut corners. Using me…"

"Sorry, Thomas, it was easier to do it this way and get your forgiveness than to ask permission," Nina said, finishing her drink. "And as much as you're trying to work on improving my character, I'm going to work on loosening yours a little. You've had this sheltered, boring, pent-up life. You're in college now. You're supposed to get wild. Live it up. Experience new things. Come to Manila with me and watch a live TV show."

"I have to go home over the weekend."

"You shouldn't go to Calamba anymore. Lazy Velasquez got shot again."

"I heard that. I wonder who shot him."

"Obviously someone who wants to frame it on my father. Anyway, I've been forbidden to go home unless I have a bodyguard. My dad even forbid Elnora to come home. She wanted to bring her husband and spend Christmas with us. Too dangerous."

Thomas wanted to suggest that she use Ringor as one of her props to impress that gaggle of girls. That would frighten them away instead.

"How did hear about Lazy? Your nose is in a book all the time," she complained.

"I have my sources. By the way, why don't I ever see you with a nose in a book?"

"I'm very studious when I'm in class. I just don't bring the class with me wherever I go," she said, gesturing to Thomas' backpack full of books. "My degree isn't going to do me any good without knowing the right people. I'm not planning to get a job back in Abra, so I need some influence around here or in Manila. Influence like having some rich acquaintances … or like appearing on a television show."

"Like being superficial?"

"At least I know that I'm good looking and know how to use that to my advantage."

"What does that mean?"

"Do you look at yourself in the mirror every day? Do you even realize the power you have? You can have any girl in Calamba that you want. Here too," Nina pointed out the door to the girls. "Whatever motivates a girl, you have at least one thing she wants. You are handsome. Now that you're out of the fields, your skin tone is perfect. Straight hair, a bit brown, a bit long right now like a rock star. You don't have a wide, flat nose. A little taller than all the girls. Already a land owner. Smart. College student on his way to being a rich doctor…"

"This is all very flattering, but irrelevant," Thomas replied. After thinking about Nina's words for a moment, he muttered Aga Muhlach.

"What?"

"Nothing. Inside joke."

Nina sank into her bar chair and crossed her arms.

"You think I'm the only one to notice you? Tessie Galope wouldn't be able to get out of her panties fast enough if she thought she could catch you. Just a kiss and Amelie Valera would pee herself."

"Now this is becoming gross and irrelevant." Thomas wrinkled his nose in disgust.

Nina smiled at him. Not the fake one. But it was hard to discern whether the gleam in her eye was real or fake.

"Are you trying to seduce me now?"

"Crazy. You're immune to me. Besides, I'm saving myself."

"What?"

"I'm saving myself," she reiterated.

Thomas paused and searched her face. "Let me get this right. You're a ..."

"Don't say it in public," Nina warned. Her eyes darted to the girls to make sure they were still outside.

"You went to the junior prom with Bong Bong Masakayan. His reputation alone should have made you a ruined woman. You were spotted alone with that short guy from La Paz, a few guys from Danglas at the same time..."

"... they were brothers, and I never ..."

"Amelie's older brother was your escort for the party when your reign ended."

"He's a first cousin. Yuck."

"After him was..."

"Why are you keeping track, anyway?"

"... Angel Legadi ..."

"He was an angel, a gentleman."

"Dingdong Dantes."

Nina sputtered. "Right. And Heart Evangelista is standing behind you in a two piece. I wish a movie star would walk into my life."

"Who else?" Thomas tapped his chin.

"How about you. I've been spotted with you here and there for the last nine months. Doesn't that factor into this equation?" She was becoming displeased.

"Didn't you even date my cousin Armando for awhile too?"

"Not very long. I found out he was married."

"You are the most unlikely vir..."

"... don't say it ..."

"Virgin," he said anyway, though in a lower voice so no one around them could hear it, "that I've ever met."

"Why is it so unlikely? I can date guys and not... I dated you for two weeks and didn't." She slammed her drink and twisted her face into a frown. "Maybe you are too. You're actually studying to become a priest and your relationship with Joy was a hoax to hide your impotence."

Thomas chuckled. "I guess I won."

"Won what?"

"The argument. I pushed the right button. You insulted me. I won."

Nina's frown continued.

"What?"

She shoved away the juice. "This isn't a game to me. I don't like what you're implying. I'm not a *puta*."

"I didn't say you were a prostitute. I only find it hard to believe you've never had sex with anyone yet. You've worked very long and hard to give people the opposite impression. You just flung yourself at me five minutes ago."

"I had to go through a lot of men to find Mr. Right," Nina explained matter-of-factly.

The playfulness of the conversation was already dwindling, but that was the clincher, the implication that she'd found Mr. Right. They'd been dating all these months?

"I want to know that I'm loved before I have sex," Nina continued.

"Very noble." Thomas said.

"I'm not going to end up like Elnora," Nina blurted, hotly. "Sex and sex and more sex messed up my sister. I'm not saying that Bong Bong or Armando would have treated me the way Aris treated Nora, but it scared me enough that I wasn't going to give into them and find out. I found her once in the back room, the one in the mill office, naked in a chair, so high on something that she couldn't move, blood was all over her scalp where Aris was trying to rip her hair out. It wasn't love between them, it looked like rape."

The relationship between Elnora and Aris had always been ripe with wild stories. Juicy tales of trysts in the mountain caves where they stumbled upon areas where the NPA kept their hostages, using the restraints on each other.

"Makes me glad I popped his knee," Thomas finally said. "We all have our defining moments. When you put it that way, I guess it isn't so unlikely. Sorry for not believing you."

Nina was pensive and then scowled.

"I think you're studying to be the wrong kind of doctor. You should be a psychologist. You goaded me into revealing a secret after only one drink and it wasn't even alcohol."

Thomas credited himself for not standing in order to take a bow. "It's easier to develop a bedside manner than read people's minds." His career as a mind reader being extensive.

"Can I help you with the bedside manner?"

He grinned. "There's the Nina I know."

The short walk from the café to Nina's boarding house was clear of Barbie Girls.

"I think she's going to invite me," Nina said at the metal gate to the house. It was as far as Thomas was going to be allowed to travel. The lady of the house was very strict about visitation once it was dark.

Nina surprised Thomas with a kiss. It was on his cheek, but very close to his lips.

"Nina…?"

"Thanks for helping me today."

The walk to Uncle Lopito's house was full of reflection. He'd been kissed by Nina in the past. Sexual inexperience aside, Nina knew what she was doing. A man isn't kissed by the princess and not become tempted. It was obvious there was more than friendship and appreciation behind this one. Unraveling Joy sometimes took hard perceptive investigation, mulling over subtle clues, sending them into the realm of the impossible sometimes. Nina wasn't as complicated. It was probably true that she was using him as a shield just now. It was just as probable that her reference to him as a boyfriend wasn't a charade.

Thomas wondered where in a book of psychology he could find help in telling Nina that she still hasn't found her Mr. Right.

Aris had run out of cigarettes and patience.

He sat in the mayor's red jeep, well hidden off the road between Calamba and the barangay Pulot, one of the closer hamlets to the poblacion, town proper. A sweat soaked shirt sat in the back seat. He occupied the passenger seat with the door open. The fiberglass frame of the jeep radiated so much heat that the shade of its interior provided little relief.

Fernando Cabasan was relieving himself in the tall grasses, even though half of his bottled water he had dumped on his own head.

Papa Justo drove into Pulot in his new jeepney two hours ago. It was full of people, some of whom were hitching a ride to the barangay that was on the same road as the schools.

The more politically savvy eye saw that Papa Justo had screened himself with innocents to leave town safely for campaigning. The jeepney ride home would be the same way. Aris knew it was still possible to ambush the jeepney and shoot Papa Justo, but the consequences would be his own death at the hands of Ringor or Bennie. And blame for the ambush would fall back to Marino.

Shooting Lazy Velasquez didn't work the second time. People weren't becoming wary of Papa Justo because Mayor Marino's men were being "ambushed" in the countryside.

Shooting Lazy the first time worked perfectly. It got Joy on that jet to Singapore.

Three boys came jogging down the road and saw the jeep.

"Fernando," Aris called.

Staggered in height, the eldest came up to Aris' chest. He dangled the 50 peso note from his hand.

"What is Papa Justo doing?"

The eldest boy said the vice mayor was just talking to people at the gazebo where people sat out of the sun to wait for jeepneys and trikes.

"Did he go door to door?"

All three nodded.

"Did he spend a lot of time at each place?"

All three shrugged.

"Did you see him hand out money to people?"

They nodded.

The youngest boy held up 10 pesos. He said it came from his cousin who was walking with Papa Justo.

"Who is your cousin?"

He named Pedro Botalico.

Aris handed over his money to the boys and watched them scramble back down the road to their hamlet of houses.

Fernando cursed the fact that the Botalicos had joined Justo's cause.

"Quit being so worried, Fernando. Lopito and Marino always figure a way around the obstacles."

There was this obstacle. Money. Joy's money from Singapore was going to repay a damn college fund right now instead of helping Marino sustain his campaign. From overhearing Marino, that was going to be rectified in a few months.

As the sun was setting, the two men Aris was expecting finally came walking up the road from Calamba. His sister found them in some dark corner of Angeles City. She said they were professionals, but death wouldn't follow their hit tonight.

Aris made sure they spoke Ilocano. It would be more convincing if they spoke the tribal language of the mountains, but the fit the minimum requirement. The pistol hanging out from the waist band was the other.

Fernando stayed with the jeep at the edge of Pulot. Aris followed the anonymous men with his face concealed in case someone spotted him. The men followed their instruction and knocked on the first door. When Mr. Jasareno said something from within, they pushed their way inside. In a forceful voice, they claimed to be Papa Justo's cousins.

"What is this? You Justos give me money to help me and then take it back the same day?" Mr. Jasareno protested.

One of the men waved his gun on the way out of the simple hut to keep the old man from poking his head outside.

They went house to house. Quietly. Efficiently. The gun did wonders in prying Papa Justo's money from the people he tried to win over with it. The jeep took them back to Calamba. There Aris paid them the money his sister had promised.

One of the men asked what Aris was going to do with the rest of the money.

"Give it back to them in a few days," he answered.

They didn't understand and Aris didn't feel like explaining it to them. The men walked into the shack in the grove where they could hide and sleep until a morning jeepney could return them to Angeles City.

When the money was returned it would be as a new bribe by Marino Lapez.

"Lopito is a smart one," Aris told Fernando.

"What are we going to do when Papa Justo figures it out?"

"Always thinking negative, Fernando. Always worried."

Fernando found Lazy Velasquez nine days later near a cobra nest at the mouth of a cave several kilometers from Pulot. There were no snake bites. Lazy had been bludgeoned to death by a heavy instrument.

Thomas was threshing the October rice harvest when Ricky came running down the dirt road. The small diesel-powered thresher belched noise and fumes.

Alvin Masakayan, whose rice paddies touched the southern edge of Wagner land, had used his carabao-pulled cart to transport some of his rice harvest to Thomas for threshing. He did not have the means to cross the river with it, making Thomas' thresher very convenient. It was common to rent threshers from the neighbors that had them. Thomas charged Masakayan the normal rate of one cavan of rice for every ten he moved through the machine.

"Hard," the old man complained. "Not enough backs to help harvest. The same young men that I've hired for years and years are too scared to come here. Too many guns this time. Last month, that Pingaping barangay captain was shot dead in plain sight in front of his house. I can hear gunshots echoing through the mountains from my house."

Masakayan said he called in all of his relatives from other barangays to do the harvest. He held a hand level at his knees. "Even little ones this tall to help do some work. Still takes all day. I would be done by now if I could just hire 20 men."

Thomas politely nodded at the thin, white-haired man. Masakayan was maybe 70, yet still tough enough to tend his own farm. The man never stopped moving, perhaps that was the secret. No vices either. Ask his age and would jokingly talk about the Spanish colonial days. Anyone who paid attention in school knew he was born 30 years after the Americans took possession of the islands from the Spaniards.

"I want to grind some of it into rice powder, but that means going to Justo's mill." Masakayan sighed and shook his head.

"I work there now. Maybe I can grind some for you later and bring it out to you."

"I heard that you had a new job. You're a brave boy to be messing around in that pot. So close to the mayor, yet you work for the mayor's rival." The grizzled face carried concern.

113

"It is not like I'm part of Justo's campaign. I'm just working at the mill sometimes. I'm not worried. I'll be fine."

He didn't like working for Papa Justo, but it seemed to do more good than harm. The job opened because Justo had tapped so many of his employees into becoming guards at the mill and the house, counter moves to the growing number of Marino's men toting guns.

Nina arranged the job. Thomas didn't go out of his way to avoid Nina since the kiss, but he didn't seek her out as much either. The charade as her boyfriend ended after her invitation to Manila, so at least there was no temptation or opportunity for Nina to try to convert fake boyfriend Thomas into a real boyfriend Thomas. Because of the lack of contact, he had no idea whether she was succeeding in her quest to get on a television talent show. The last update he had was that she was still plodding away in Baguio at a computer science degree with no real interest in ever using it.

The new job made people confused initially. But it seemed to settle the townsfolk's nerves. They came whenever Thomas was working, and only then. They no longer felt as though it were picking sides just to get some rice flour made if it was done with the mayor's godson working the mill. It was a good move on Papa Justo's part.

He was a little worried, though, with shotguns and pistols turning up in nooks and crannies of the mill. It was happening in Joy's house too. Whenever he visited Ricky and Auntie Rowena, he noticed the increase of weapons in defensive positions around the compound, jarring one loose one time playing basketball with Ricky. The Lapez residence felt more like an army base now than the home away from home it once was.

Finally, Thomas decided to stay away, making Ricky's near-daily visits the sole means of communication with Joy's family. Working for Justo created more of a rift with Marino, but the man's acceptance and favor had long been irrelevant.

Thomas wore a smile for Ricky as the boy finally got within earshot.

"We're back," Ricky yelled over the noise.

Masakayan continued to load rice stalks into the thresher; the finished rice pouring into a bag held by one of his older grandnephews.

"That was a long trip just to go to Pangasinan to visit relatives," Thomas said.

Marino, Rowena and Ricky had been gone for four days. It was an unusual length of time to be away with the harvest underway. Work did get done, however. With no one to guard, Aris armed the men with scythes instead of shotguns.

"We just got home. *Manong*, look what I got!"

In his hand, Ricky held sea shells. Thomas gave an approving nod. All of them were small, though there was a myriad of shapes and colors.

"I collected them myself from the beach. It was hard because there were so many people there, but I found enough to fill up my pocket."

"So that is what took so long, you went to the beach."

"It is too bad *tatay* did not take you with us, you could have been at the beach with us ... and Joy was there too."

Thomas blinked in confusion. "But Joy isn't coming home until next month."

"No, she's already back. We got her at the airport ..."

"Joy is back already? Joy is here? No one told me she was coming home early!" Thomas beamed. "Oh, you sneaky girl."

His mind raced. Leave Masakayan here. He jogged toward the house, then decided he didn't care about the dirty shirt. There was no time for a river bath. She was in town, so just run to town.

"Masakayan! Joy is home. She surprised me."

The old man waved and smiled.

Joy had surprised him. Her trip home had been scheduled and rescheduled a few times because the Songs were dragging their feet about letting her go home.

"Come on, Thomas, look at my shells!"

"I'm sorry, Ricky, but I don't really care about the shells now. I want to see Joy. Is she following you out here?"

"But these are neat shells," Ricky humphed and let his arms fall to his sides in feigned disappointment.

Thomas decided there was time for a quick change of clothes. So Ricky had been sent to fetch him. There might be a party planned too and it would be better to change now than have to come back after offending a house full of people.

"Let me go inside for a minute, Ricky, then I'll follow you back to Calamba to see Joy."

"Joy is not even in Calamba," Ricky blurted.

Ricky's comments snapped Thomas' head around. Defeated, the boy put the shells back into his pocket.

"Where is she then?"

Ricky shrugged.

Thomas knelt down, apologized about the shells and coaxed the boy to talk to him.

"She didn't come home with us. She stayed in Manila. She is still on vacation with this strange guy. He is *puraw*, but more than you, a lot more, but then he got a red skin sunburn at the beach. *Tatay* told me he was Joy's—" He dug his flip-flop in the dirt and tried to remember the word. "But he was always holding her hand like you did. He said he was going to buy me a Shaq shirt when he got back to America with Joy."

Thomas found himself racing for town anyway. The mayor's red jeep was parked in front of the municipal hall. Aris was smoking out front, which meant Marino was inside. He jogged down the street and hunted for Rowena at the house. She wasn't home. He stood in the road and scanned the rows of houses for her.

A jeepney laden with people slowly approached. It was Big Man with Jon-Jon's father was at the wheel. He was certainly bound for Bangued. It was instinct, not logic, that propelled Thomas to grab onto the ladder on the back of the jeepney and hold on.

Ricky's continued explanation was brief, but armed Thomas with enough information to know Joy had not left for America yet.

America! Not Singapore?

She had said goodbye to her family this morning in Manila. Ricky also remembered them talking about visiting Corregidor before leaving. Thomas was not sure if that meant leaving for America later today or in subsequent days.

His wallet did not have much money left inside. There was enough for bus fare to Manila, but not much more. He walked into the Bangued branch of Philippine National Bank. It held the account Joy had been using to send him money.

"I'm sorry, sir, but the account has no balance," the bank teller said. "It is empty."

"How can it be empty?" Thomas demanded. "There were thousands of pesos in it a few weeks ago. I didn't take the money out."

"Hmmm. The record shows a legitimate withdrawal this morning," she said, looking up from her screen.

"That's not possible. This is my account and I haven't withdrawn money in weeks."

"I'm sorry, sir, but the account shows no balance. There is a record that 43,000 pesos was withdrawn this morning..."

"I wasn't here this morning!"

"...and I see a note here that a request to close the account is being processed."

"I requested no such thing! Where is my money?"

A supervisor arrived behind Thomas with the security guard that had been standing in front of the bank.

"Sir, please, you are making a scene... Sir, please lower your voice ... Sir, can we handle this in my office..."

Thomas had no luck with the supervisor. He merely backed up what the teller was saying. He seemed hesitant to investigate and scoffed at the idea that there had been a theft. The supervisor narrowed his eyes at Thomas and fired back questions that implied Thomas had withdrawn the money this morning and was trying to scam the bank. By the looks of him, he had just come from the fields. Money problems? The drought affected you? Suddenly, there was an interest in notifying the police, but not for the disappearance of Thomas' money, but for them to investigate an attempted scam.

Thomas ran out of time. The hour was up and the bus was leaving, with it his chance to catch Joy and find out if Ricky was telling the truth. He threatened the bank supervisor that he would be back once he got back from Manila.

The bus ride from Bangued to Metro Manila was eight hours, a long time to be confused. Thomas was uncertain he would locate Joy in the mass of people entering the airport, but waiting them out at the airport was the only plan he could develop with the information and time handed to him. Joy had an affair? She had been lying to him about when she was coming home? He had to see it for himself. He needed answers.

His wallet was as empty as the pit of his stomach. The only sustenance on the trip was a bottle of Coke poured into a plastic bag and consumed through a straw.

Arriving very early in the morning was nice, resulting in a smaller amount of traffic, but there was still enough congestion to make it a 90-minute taxi ride from the Cubao bus station to Ninoy Aquino International Airport.

Thomas immediately made a quick sweep of the airport's departures area as soon as he arrived, walking as fast as could to glance at every face. Nothing. But it was early. On the screens, he saw there were many flights leaving. Few of them for America, but that meant nothing since most of the flights there went to Japan or Korea first.

Thomas sat on a curb outside when he was satisfied that Joy was not in the airport. He realized he couldn't just hang out without arousing suspicion and attracting the attention of the security guards there. Many of the guards were in place to control the throngs of poor hanging out to carry passenger's bags for tips. Thomas regretted not changing his clothes before leaving. He was dressed no better than they were with a dirty shirt and jeans.

His mind was too frantic to think clearly. What happened in Singapore? Why was Joy holding hands with another man? He was her ... what? What was the word Ricky was digging for ... boyfriend?

It wasn't possible. Thomas' mind could not grasp the idea that Joy had left him for another man. She had dragged him into a church to marry him. She had jealous fits about him just dancing with other women at wedding receptions. In all the phone calls and letters there weren't even hints that she was displeased enough with him to seek an end to their relationship. Everything was to the contrary. She said she could hardly wait to see him again. She had planned an itinerary for her week back, putting in a letter her desire to go to Borocay and lounge on the beach. But with Thomas not this unknown man!

Thomas was expending just as much energy ducking the security in international departures as he was trying to find Joy standing with a tall American. Of course, he had no idea what this American looked like. He could only search for a tiny woman with a familiar face with long hair pulled back into a single pony tail dangling to her waist.

There were periods of intense boredom, hunger, weariness, punctuated by a rush of adrenaline whenever he saw a white man walking with a Filipina— only to find it wasn't Joy.

He was afraid to leave the airport. When all of the international flights for the day had left, Thomas stayed anyway. He huddled into a corner in the arrivals area, breathing the exhaust of taxis and jeepneys whisking away jet lagged travelers. It was the only area at the airport with people milling about. While they were waiting for loved ones to exit baggage claim, Thomas was holding up for the next day in a place where he wouldn't be harassed for loitering when it got to be the wee hours of the morning.

He slept in fitful cat naps, placing his forearms atop crossed legs and using them as a pillow. It was hard to sleep with the discomfort of concrete beneath him. It was hard to sleep because his mind fought the enormity of a life without Joy.

When the next day arrived, he washed his face and arm pits in the public bathroom. He used a healthy portion of hand soap and worked it into his dirty shirt under the tap, content to wear a wet shirt for an hour than continue to smell rotten all day. Breakfast was water from the tap and a bag of Chippys from a vending machine.

When he had reached the other side of the airport terminal, he saw the same throng of would-be baggage porters waiting for travelers. Pick up the bags. Tote it inside to the counter. Hand reached out for a few dollars or yen or Euros. A thanks and then go back outside and wait in line.

Thomas tried it once. His pockets were empty of money, consumed by the bus fare and few snacks he'd eaten. He helped a Chinese couple. He didn't understand a word they said, but the gentleman tipped him with the remaining pesos in his wallet.

"You got a good one," admired one of the porters when he returned to the line. "We will be okay today. These guards don't have to be bribed to let us work. Some guards want half at the end of the day to convince them not to toss us in jail."

It was going to be a sunny day. It wasn't even mid morning when Thomas' shirt had dried and then became damp again with sweat. It was a perfect position to see who was entering the terminal. Thanks mostly to the Chinese man, he had accumulated 400 some pesos. Other wallets had not been overflowing with change and the tips had been nominal, 5 or 10 peso bills. Hunger struck him again. Or was it sleep deprivation coupled with heat prostration?

Taking his tour of the check-in counters, Thomas ate from another bag of Chippys and wondered how many days of this he would be able to take. Weakened, he sat down in the area where he had spent his last moment with Joy before she went to Singapore. He toyed with his wedding ring and closed his eyes for a moment.

Two loud Australians sharing a joke awakened Thomas. He cursed at himself for falling asleep. Worried, he sought the nearest clock. More than half an hour had passed. He snaked his way outside the doors to the drop-off areas, then inside the doors to the ticket counters and then back outside the next set of doors. He double backed as quickly as his feet would take him. He scanned the queue of those waiting to pay their departure tax, a hurdle along the hallway that led to the immigration counters and then the security check points and ultimately to the gangways to the jets. There were hundreds of brown faces, dozens of white ones, occasionally there were black ones.

And there she was.

Already strolling down the hallway past the tax counter, she was walking with a tall white man, dragging a small suitcase on wheels behind them. If he hadn't fallen asleep, he might have caught them getting out of the taxi. He cursed his luck. There was no way through the check point unless he had 500 pesos, a ticket and a passport.

Thomas began to call her.

"Joy Lapez."

It drew stares from those around him, but she did not seem to hear him.

"Joy Flora Lapez." He cupped his hands around his mouth to megaphone his yells.

The tall, redheaded American turned to look. He said something to her, but she did not turn her head.

"Joy, my joy! Joy, my joy!"

The *kano* kept talking to her. She slapped his hand and started walking away. He followed, head turned behind him, eyes searching for the voice. They kept walking, hand-in-hand now, almost as though she were dragging him to the next destination point.

He wanted to jump the turnstiles and race after them. The money takers were watching him, however. His antics had already attracted the attention of several security guards in the vicinity, some of whom were also watching him, inching their way down the hallway.

The feeling hit him in the stomach—the nauseous tingling that a person gets while watching a wounded animal die. The love of his life was leaving with another man. She was holding his hand. She heard the calls, but did not acknowledge them.

In one last desperate plea, Thomas yelled the only thing that came to mind, "I will take you instead. Come back, Joy! Come back and I will take you to America instead!"

And they were out of sight. The queue of people waiting to have their passports checked swallowed them.

It wasn't going to end like this, he vowed. He had to know why. He had to stop her. She was just over there. It would take three or four minutes for them to clear the checkpoint. The turnstile was only waist high. He would be able to reach her before the guards caught him.

Thomas backpedaled to give himself a running start to hurdle the turnstile. But he was in a headlock before he had the chance to try it. A burly man in a blue uniform securely had him by the head and waist. Thomas tested the man's hold and was able to free himself long enough for a second guard to grab his arm and a third to bar his way toward Joy. One guard ordered him to calm himself and stop yelling. The first guard re-established his hold and demanded into Thomas' ear to know why he was acting crazy. Do you have a ticket? Who were you calling?

Thomas pointed down the hallway. "*Asawa ko! Asawa ko!*" He asked them to let him go. His wife was down there, leaving with another man.

A fourth and fifth guard arrived. One of them said he recognized Thomas from the line of baggage porters, and that Thomas had been sniffing around the airport all day yesterday. A beggar turned troublemaker, they concluded.

The burly guard squeezed his arm around Thomas' neck, nearly choking him and making it impossible to yell for Joy any longer. Whispers of her name still gurgled out. As they overpowered and dragged him away, Thomas found Joy's bob of hair in the distance.

She never turned around.

Thomas pressed his sweaty brow against the window pane on the old red and white, non air conditioned Philippine Rabbit bus. Two old women argued in the seat in front of him. The man beside him hummed along to the pop songs on the radio, his feet resting on a cage in the aisle with a hen inside it.

Thomas did not hear them.

He did not see them.

In the blur of mountains and trees, he only saw the back of Joy's head, her hand grabbing the American's arm to be led away, never looking back as she disappeared into the bowels of the airport where Thomas could not follow.

There had been hours of questioning by the airport security, and then the Manila police, and then the National Bureau of Investigation. In between questionings, he sat in an airport holding cell. After two days of hearing the same story, they let him go without charges. They gave him a stern warning to stay away from the airport. One of the officers even took pity on him for his situation and handed him enough pesos for bus fare and a meal.

Thomas wasn't interested in eating.

Joy was already in America. It was past midnight there. She had already walked into his house. She had already kissed him goodnight. She had already laid beside him in his bed.

Thomas coughed violently in the direction of the floor, but no vomit would come.

The bus driver protested about messes on the bus floor and threatened to make him clean up anything disgusting. Thomas only stared at the floor with his head between his knees and hands resting on the back of his head. The man with the chicken suggested that they stop the bus and let the kid vomit along the road. Two teenage boys in identical Tommy Hilfiger shirts asked the driver to stop so they could relieve themselves. The driver complied, himself walking off the bus to smoke a cigarette and fan himself in vain against the heat. Windows down and legal speeds were not enough to cool the bus to comfort.

Thomas remained on board and stewed in anger. It had been a well-timed family vacation without Thomas. So Marino and Rowena knew about Joy.

They must have all been working in concert to keep this affair with the American a secret. Rowena, who was supposed to be his surrogate mother, knew that her daughter had been cheating on him and had said nothing all those months. That's why Auntie Ro cried whenever Thomas brought up Joy in a future tense. It was all clear now.

During his release from jail, Thomas pondered asking Regina's help. She was already in Metro Manila. But she was Rowena's baby sister. And he had a sudden aversion to her. She was longer a childhood friend, but part of a family that had just betrayed him.

When the teens had finished watering the trees along the side of the road, the bus continued, stopping in darkness in the middle of Baguio. Thomas' feet were tired by the time he reached Nina's boarding house on the edge of campus. A girl was sitting on the front stair talking on her cell phone. He put his arms through the rails of the gate and waved at her. Knowing him, she waved back.

"Is Nina here?"

"Yes, but you're too late to get her for a date. The house mother has already called for curfew."

"This is not a date. Emergency. Can you get her for me?"

"*Sige, sige,* I will go upstairs and get her." Though she didn't seem to believe him that it was an emergency.

In a short time, Nina, dressed for sleep, trotted down the stairs to the gate.

"You look like hell. What is happening?"

"Let me borrow your phone."

Nina opened the gate, slowly, grimacing that it would not squeak. It opened enough for Thomas to slip inside sideways.

"My cell phone is upstairs. Are you hurt? Did you get robbed?"

"I can explain later. Please. Can I borrow your phone?"

"Stand here by the gate."

The other girls were fascinated by his anxious energy. One held her nose and backed up. There was no bathing in jail.

Nina returned with the silver device. "What's the emergency?"

"I need to call Joy's cell phone," he replied, reaching for the phone.

She made a clicking noise and whisked the phone behind her back. "Are you kidding? Call her from your boarding house."

"I can't go there, not after what they've just done to me. I'm desperate, Nina. Please, help me. Peace treaty, remember? I have to call Joy. She went to America. She left me."

Nina blinked a lot. The explanations came out of his mouth so fast that she wasn't sure she was getting it right. Reluctantly, she handed over the phone.

"Thank you, Nina. Now I can find out. Coming home from Singapore with another man. Ignoring me at the airport."

The number you have dialed is either unattended or out of service.

"Damn it. It was working fine last week."

"You're frantic. You're shaking. Sit down."

"No. I can't stop, I can't slow down, I can't waste any more time. Enough time was wasted sitting in that jail. I need to keep moving."

"Jail? Sit," she insisted. "Tell me again what happened."

Thomas shook his head. "I need to get back to the bus station. The bus to Bangued leaves at about 6. I need to go to the bank in the morning to clear up what happened to my money. I need the money for a ticket."

"I'm confused. Joy's gone. Jail. Missing money? What are you doing?"

"Chasing her, of course!"

"Chasing her to where?"

His gut got tight. He wanted to vomit again.

"I don't know," he shakily admitted. "I don't know where she went. I got arrested before I could check the departures board and find out where the flights were landing. All I know is that she went to the States and I have to go there too. I have to stop her. I have to know why this happened. Maybe I can get Ricky alone for a few minutes and he can find out where they went. Or Reggie. She can inquire of Rowena somehow and tell me."

A few of the other girls gathered around Nina and watched Thomas babble, brainstorming aloud on how to find out where Joy went, planning a schedule to fetch his passport from home.

"They warned me not to go back to the airport, but if I have a ticket they can't stop me."

Nina made him explain the events of the last few days.

"Why did she just ignore me? Was she mad? Were there gossips talking into her ear about us?" he said to Nina. "Did they twist our friendship into something else, she got insane with jealousy and grabbed the first white guy in front of her?"

"I doubt that it is revenge. Even the fastest visas to America don't happen that fast."

Nina was right. Joy wasn't a vengeful person.

Nina sat beside him and wrung her hands, on the verge of tears herself from watching Thomas disintegrate in front of her. The other girls poked her in the shoulder and gestured to Thomas, clamoring that it was after hours and he should leave.

"Kick him out now? Look at him," Nina said. "He just lost his girlfriend to a *kano*. The unthinkable happened. Thomas and Joy aren't together any more. The whole town will be slack jawed with bewilderment. The oddball Joy finally succumbed to her obsession with America."

Thomas slowly shook his head. No, it is not that simple. This is not about Joy and America.

"You said something about fast visas."

"Elnora's visa was pretty fast, especially since it was through Hong Kong, not Manila. It was a fiancée visa."

Thomas remembered now. No one had an inkling that Elnora had a new beau either. It was a sudden announcement one day that Elnora had a visa for America and had flown to Las Vegas.

"It still takes a couple months. But getting to a fiancée visa take a lot longer. When Elnora was a housekeeper in Hong Kong, she put an ad out through a penpal dating agency like the rest of her friends, received letters, some of the men flew to meet her in person, she got engaged to Everson, let him file immigration papers and then got a visa. Penpal ads take time. Letters take time," Nina explained. "For Joy to accomplish all that in just over a year means she started working on it the moment she landed in Singapore."

Thomas lamented that he once again lost someone without a goodbye.

But had he been warned? Joy's first letter home from Singapore. *No matter what happens…*

"Elnora's been helping your dad's campaign to become mayor, right?"

Nina hesitated and then nodded, adding "a little" onto the reply.

"Papa Justo has American money. Marino Lapez is now poised to get American money. Who else schemes as much as Joy? Who else has enough power over Ricky and Rowena to keep them silent to me? And who else can make fist shaped bruises on his daughter to get her to go along with it?"

Thomas' thoughts were drawn to the bank. That now made sense. Joy was the only other person to have access to that account. She must have taken back her money. She didn't want him having a lot of money.

Enough money for an airline ticket.

A ticket to America.

A way to stop her.

She didn't … or Marino didn't?

Wasn't one of Marino's mistresses working at a bank?

Thomas was astounded at the breadth of the betrayal.

There was so much more he didn't understand. A punch in the chest couldn't have been enough to convince her to do this. Maybe her obsession with America played into it. Maybe Thomas cavorting with Nina was enough to push her over the edge. This was Joy's mind here, nothing was impossible, no notion was too unreasonable.

"She still can't fool me," Thomas smiled. "Give me enough time and I can figure out any idea that pops into her head."

One of the girls said Thomas had gone crazy. Now he's smiling.

"What is that noise out there? It sounds like a man. Is there a man in the house at this hour?" It was the lady master of the boarding house. Thomas saw her face in the window. She knew him, but that would do nothing to curb the woman's wrath.

"Thanks for the phone, Nina. You want me to stay and take the heat?"

"No, you better leave. Wait. Where are you going? What are you going to do?"

"I'm going home. Lapez aren't the only schemers."

He was gone before explaining that to Nina. While walking away, he heard the sound of the girls sticking up for Nina.

It wasn't the homecoming moment Thomas had envisioned. Instead of carrying Joy across the threshold of the front door like two people on a honeymoon, he was greeted by sacks of rice left by Masakayan as the payment for using the thresher.

Thomas didn't need rice, he needed more information, he needed a plan, he needed cash.

He knew his land was worth at least 75,000 to 100,000 pesos. A sale that sizable could take time. Selling the pigs, carabao and chickens would not take much time, but the amount would pale in comparison to what he needed for an airline ticket.

He kicked the nearest sack of rice.

He cursed that he wasn't able to figure out something was wrong with her until it was too late.

"You really got me this time," he cried. "Okay, Joy? You finally got me. You finally fooled me good. I never saw it coming! Run out from in back of that tree and tell me 'got you.' We'll have a good laugh."

When his voice finished echoing, he collapsed to the dirt and hugged his knees. Figuring out Joy's scheme didn't stop his soul from shrinking. He had answers to whats, had some of the whys, but nothing on the how. How could he be *ayat* one day and ignored the next?

"You can pick on me for the rest of my life that you finally got a notion past me. Just come out of the trees and tell me this is all a joke. Tell me you're not really gone. Tell me you're not really going to marry another man."

The dog trotted up to its master. The panting, mud-covered mongrel sat on its hind legs. Its body smelled of something foul.

Thomas wasn't going to go back to work for Papa Justo, though it meant a salary of pesos at a time he needed money. Despite his friendship with Nina, he wasn't going to allow himself to assist one side of the feud that had now made him a casualty of political greed.

When he collected his senses again, he went inside and found the small blue book from the bottom shelf of his mother's dresser. The cover said Passport, United States of America. Inside was a picture of his younger self, nine years ago.

Thomas didn't know where in America to find her, but he knew he had to be there to start.

< <> >

Gary Palangchao was a nervous intermediary standing on the steps of the observation tower in the mountain forest. There were no illegal loggers before him, just Abel Botalico dismounting a jeep and walking toward Aris Lucero. Gary had tentatively offered his forest service lookout as neutral ground.

"Why?" Abel asked.

"Mayor Lapez has an offer."

"There are better ways to deliver terms to Papa Justo than making me drive up into the mountains."

"It is for you, not Papa Justo," Aris explained.

Abel was listening, though skeptical.

"The mayor would like you to change sides."

Abel laughed at the absurdity.

"Why should I do that? You're the losing side. The governor and congressman back Justo. And you have to pose as Papa's people to steal his money back from townspeople just to keep up. What offer can Lapez possibly make to convince me to stop helping Papa Justo?"

"He is in a position to do something for you that you've wanted for a long time."

"Going to kill Thomas so we can have our land back?" Abel said as a wild guess.

"Well, at least the second part," Aris replied.

Abel composed himself. "Listening."

"Mayor Lapez has a way to get the land. It seems Thomas is an American citizen. They're only allowed to own small pieces of Philippine land. Thomas is violating the law by possessing the farm. The mayor has no choice except to seize it."

Abel began to smirk.

"Who gets the land after that..." Aris shrugged, suggestively.

Gary was pleased that they left without a violent incident. It seemed everyone was happy with the arrangement.

< <> >

The sender's address on the large rectangular cardboard box bemused Thomas: 1720 Upper Changi Road West, Singapore. It arrived today. It came from Joy's address in Singapore, written in Joy's handwriting, sent just last week. It came by the same special courier as all of Joy's previous *balikbayan* boxes. It was packed the same kind of items that the boxes had always contained: toiletries, coffee, canned goods, a decoration to hang in the house.

And a letter.

Thomas scanned the letter feverishly for some explanation of her actions. Instead, he found a mundane epistle that cataloged a work week of cleaning up after Mr. and Mrs. Song, a neighboring Filipina's disastrous attempt to cook Peking duck. She wrote that she was coming home soon, as planned, but the Songs are talking about extending her contract. She wanted Thomas' opinion on that, but told him to use e-mail because her cell phone was suddenly having battery and reception problems. The letter began with My Dearest *Ayat* and ended with love to her First And Only.

It was dated last week.

He saw her leave the Philippines with an American man a month ago.

He stared at the box hoping his mind would come around to an explanation to solve this new mystery. How could a woman living in the USA send a box from a place that she no longer lived, pretending that their encounter in the airport didn't happen?

When his mother died, Thomas found that it helped his grief to follow her routine and surround himself with the things that she loved. And so he tried it to combat his depression about Joy. His hair smelled of Cream Silk, washing it every day in the woman's shampoo so that the pillow where he slept would smell like Joy and he could imagine her beside him. He frequently sat in the dark in front of the sari-sari store where he and Joy sometimes had to meet to kiss goodnight. He wasted hours staring down the road in the hopes he'd see a tiny woman in pink flip-flops race toward him.

But he could not bring himself to go near the old church, the hideout.

The anti-grief tricks didn't ease the loss and he constantly felt as though he was half of himself.

The events had not been so good since Thomas returned from chasing Joy to Manila.

He had an offer for the purchase of his land from Ronaldo's father-in-law, enough money to buy an airline ticket to the States. But Marino was waiting for him when he'd returned from Bangued. The paper was signed by a judge and Thomas had already lost without even knowing he'd been asked to come to court. Police Chief Albio physically removed him from the mayor's presence and delivered him to the second blow of the day. Abel and Pedro were waiting for him at his front door, holding the deed to his land. The only thing left to his possession was the house, which was on a small enough portion of property to be allowable for an American citizen to own.

Determined not to be thwarted, Thomas turned to a get-rich-quick alternate plan. He sold the rest of his animals. He took the money to a *sabong* derby in Bangued and lost it all. When it mattered most, Thomas' ability to pick a winner abandoned him.

Thomas had no money to chase her to America. He was also no closer to determining where in the States she'd gone.

In one of the few times he'd seen Ricky in the last month, he saw the lad wearing a Shaq shirt. He hadn't been lying about Joy leaving for America with the tall redheaded man. Then how was she sending boxes to Calamba from Singapore if she wasn't there?

Joy's only previous experience commanding a machine was the time Thomas allowed her to drive his tractor down the lane. It was a slow moving vehicle, yet she still managed to nearly crash it into the grove of trees. The scream of terror, the last-second swerve. Jon-Jon even rescinded his offer to let her sit behind the wheel of his jeepney.

And now Bill was asking her to steer something going 45 mph down a four-lane street with a highway designation. The fact it was 1 a.m. and there were few cars on the roadway wasn't reassuring. Never mind that she wasn't legally allowed to do so. Adding to her stress was the film of salt and melted ice. The concrete wall dividing the highway was a snow bank.

"Just us and the drunks, dear," Bill quipped. "You'll be fine."

It wasn't illegal for a husband to teach a wife how to drive, but Joy discovered quickly why it wasn't a good idea. Bill lost his cool several times, ordering "slow down" and "stop" and "no, get in the other lane to pass that guy." Joy on some of those occasions contemplated stopping the car and forcing Bill to drive them home.

"I feel like I'm not driving straight. I'm weaving in the lane," Joy said.

"No one will notice. This is Chicago. Everyone drives like a nut," Bill replied.

She wanted to slap him for not helping. This was important. She had to learn to drive so that she could take herself to work. One of their first acts as husband and wife was to go to the federal immigration office downtown and get Joy's employment authorization document. Until she was able to get her green card, that was the only thing she could show to prove she could work in America.

Bill wanted to hire Joy for a position at his architectural firm office, but she did not have any skills to be useful. At least that's what she said. It was one of the aspects of their relationship that made her uncomfortable: he was a college-educated professional and she was a high school educated houseworker. The newness of having machines that washed the clothes and dishes wore off in Singapore. She was thankful for that experience so that she couldn't be embarrassed now by ignorance.

Not being able to work with Bill meant they couldn't car pool to work. It meant Joy would have to learn to drive and use Bill's older Chevy. He worried of being out of town on a project meeting when Joy needed to get somewhere. Bill's brother had volunteered to be her chauffeur on those occasions.

A slight sideways slide on black ice caused a sharp rise in adrenaline and an audible breath. Joy corrected and the tires seemed to hold firm once the car zipped past the icy stretch.

Joy found work at one of the city's many Filipino grocery stores. There were dozens of them scattered around the Windy City and its suburbs. The only one with an opening was the one in the northwestern suburbs in Hoffman Estates, 30 minutes on the road from their home in Des Plaines.

"How much longer, Bill?" Joy asked, shaking one hand and then the other to put feeling back in her fingers from gripping the wheel too tightly. "I have to work tomorrow—I mean today."

She didn't want to surrender the experience despite the treacherous moments. She never felt more freedom in her life. She was willing to go into work a little tired for a chance to master driving before taking a test. She flip-flopped on how ready she was. Bill thought she was. Times like now, she thought she was. When the time arrived to go to the motor vehicles office to take the leap, she became unsure and found excuses not to go.

Bill directed Joy to make a series of turns and they were back on their street. She still had trouble discerning her location in the daytime. It was worse at night. Worry number two about her getting a license. One wrong turn and she'd be on her way to Milwaukee.

Joy kept her foot off the accelerator and let the car slow on its own before making the right hand turn into the driveway. It was a nice neighborhood. Close to the airport for travel when Bill needed to meet out-of-state clients or fly to them. There was a park with swings and slides two blocks away.

"You did it," he said, encouragingly.

"Except that it is so hard to see at night. Those headlights hurt my eyes. I weave around."

"Stop that. You did fine. You're ready."

Joy smiled at Bill instead of continuing her critical self-assessment.

Once the keys were out of the ignition, Joy darted from the car, which had its heat vents blowing on full for the entire jaunt. Bill's grin followed her inside the single-story house. The street lights turned its white brick facade into shades of gray.

Bill's first house on the South Side was occupied by his ex-wife Monica, a woman whom Joy hadn't the pleasure of meeting yet. Bill himself hadn't seen the woman in three years.

It was no wild bachelor pad, but it certainly wasn't set up for a female resident when she arrived. There were no flowers to be found. Other than the shrubs that came with the house, no other green either. After a few frowns and trips to a few stores, there were some fake fronds inside the house, a hanging plant and decorations on the walls that had nothing to do with professional football.

Joy didn't remove her winter coat until she was down the hallway, into their bedroom and into the master bath.

A naked body scrambling for a fresh set of underthings, Joy noticed the answering machine was blinking on the night stand. She didn't bother to play it. She knew it was a call from home, most likely Rowena asking for money on Marino's behalf. Once, Ricky left a message that was four minutes of basketball and send money as a last-second afterthought. She was already sending them every other paycheck, using the remittance center at her Fil-Mart.

Joy was happy to have her own job and not have to ask Bill anymore for his help. He was certainly able to be generous on his salary as partner of the firm. And he was a dear about it, never complaining once, or even blinking to send of few hundred dollars to the other side of the planet—to mom and dad and brother who pretended to be waifs when they met him.

Joy was more comfortable sending her own earnings. In her mind, it eased the shame of why she married Bill in the first place, turning the black and white of right and wrong a little more gray.

With her own bank account, separate from Bill's—his idea to foster his wife's independence—he had no idea how much of her work money was going home to Calamba and how much she was saving. She wasn't saving much, fighting off the desire to indulge her newfound pleasure of mall shopping in order to send some money to Thomas' account. Sending money to him would never make up for her shocking deception, but she felt better—and a little more gray on the right and wrong scale—assisting him to stay in college and find a life beyond the rice fields of northern Abra.

Joy fought hard not to think of Thomas. Time alone with him on her mind ultimately ended up in sessions of paralyzing guilt. The ride on the jet after Thomas found her at the airport was the worst, hours of shaking and weeping that Bill dismissed as nerves about going to a new place.

Thomas' voice had struck a raw nerve. She remembered moments where Thomas had been scared, moments of profound sadness. She'd never heard them together, desperately shouting promises to her in the crowded airport.

Having other things on her mind was the only way to prevent the temptation of wondering about Thomas' well being. She turned herself into a workaholic, a clean-the-house-aholic, a cookaholic. A shadow sometimes to the point that it made Bill edgy that she followed him to every room in the house, even to the bathroom.

In the first call home from Chicago to tell them that she'd gotten married, Rowena told her that Thomas had been shaken by the news. With mother's counseling and insistence, and help from Father Herman, Thomas went back to Baguio. She said he was living with Lopito again and was on the path to finishing the semester. In every subsequent call home, she said everything was as fine with him as it could be.

"Come on, time for sleep," she told herself. "He's fine, just like *nanang* said. He's doing the same thing I am. Concentrating on something else."

Pep talking Thomas out of her thoughts, she finished getting dressed. The floor heater in the master bath was always set to high so that she could tolerate the cold. Sitting in the refrigerator to test her tolerance for winter was one thing. Stepping out of the shower to freezing linoleum was different. She left on her socks to change into the pink sweats that were her most comfortable, and warmest, sleeping attire. Bill snickered for an hour after she told him she'd found them at Kids R Us. There were no clothes in her size anywhere else but petite shops.

There was something about this Bill Vandemark that touched her heart. From all of the letters and emails from interested suitors, Bill stood out at the beginning. After three months of writing and online chatting, Bill took her up on the offer to visit Singapore. Two months later he came back and proposed. Sweet talk and lots of sex moved the process faster.

Gradually, another voice started to speak inside of her heart. Bill was in many ways an older version of Thomas, which was both a blessing and a curse. There was the familiar comfort coupled with the acute realization that it wasn't the man she loved for so long. Bill was gentle and fun. He had a strong sense of honor and pride in his work. When the Songs met Bill and heard the news, they were so giddy for her that they let her out of her contract early so that she could go to Chicago.

"Sweats and socks and three layers of blankets," Bill said from his pillow next to hers.

"It's too cold."

"The heater is already jacked up to 74."

"Yes, cold."

It brought on a laugh and a set of hands tickling her stomach. She swatted shoulder blades in retaliation.

"If you are going to make fun of my first experience with winter, then I am going to go get the pictures of your sunburn in Borocay." She grabbed him by the middle and slid closer to his body. "Cuddle me, you are a chicken."

"What?"

"Your skin is so hot to the touch, just like a chicken. When we were kids, we would hug chickens to keep warm."

"You say the silliest things." That brought on another round of tickles. When the wrestling match was over, she was smothered in arms and blankets. Cozy. Warm.

Drifting off to sleep, he asked if she was going to listen to the message.

"No. I don't want to fill my mind with problems from home right now. I need sleep. If I listen to that I'm going to be awake all night worrying."

"I could always wear you out," he said salaciously.

"Then my body is twice as tired and I can't sleep because of the worry, which makes me twice as cranky in the morning," she threatened.

Bill kissed her goodnight and said they'd make up for it tomorrow night.

Well, it turned out to be the next morning.

Doing what a husband ought, teach her about pleasures, her relationship with Bill had opened new chapters on sex. She discovered cunnilingus during their first night together and became an instant addict. It was the first time that she felt sex's overwhelming and explosive conclusion.

A good night's sleep despite late night driving, morning sex and a cup of coffee, Joy was wide awake for work when Bill deposited her at Fil-Mart.

Her spirits were low, however. The message had been as expected, Rowena's voice updating her on the situation in Calamba, the political campaign, Lopito's troubles in bending people to Marino's cause, even after double bribes were being handed out. Of course, they weren't called bribes, referred instead as *regalo*, gifts, an offer of friendship. Joy thought her father was spreading her hard earned money around Calamba like a thick rain.

Joy spent most of her work day stocking shelves, cashing out customers, filling in as needed as the remittance clerk. She cleaned up after the cookers in the kitchen when they finished making the Philippine dishes they sold all day long. She even had to help mop the floor and clean the counter for the fresh fish. It was only natural they would turn her into the cleaning lady since she had told them she was a housemaid in Singapore.

"*Mabuhay*," Runilla greeted, dressed in her blue smock with the Fil-Mart logo over the pocket.

Runilla was a fellow provincial and latched onto Joy immediately. The whole store seemed to be filled with workers from big cities. Runilla was the only one remotely acquainted with farm life, though her family earned their income producing straw hats and woven mats.

The entire job was busy work, nothing important, but time went fast. Joy opened her packed lunch while sitting down beside Runilla in the break room, out of sight from the customers. Runilla was having a conversation with Adeliza, a middle-aged woman who'd been in the USA for more than a decade, though she was close mouthed about where she was raised in the Philippines.

Joy opened her Tupperware container filled with leftovers. Pot roast, Bill had called it. At least it didn't have cheese on it. Americans seemed to have a fascination with beef and cheese.

The group was talking about someone's children.

"Yes her kids are very cute. Mixed blood."

"I can't wait to have kids," Runilla said, the containers in front of her mostly consumed. "I need to convince Georgie of it first."

"Trust me, you can wait." Adeliza had three teenagers. Sports, dating and drugs had worn her out.

Runilla waited until Joy's mouth was packed with luke warm beef when she fired her question at her. "When are you and Bill planning to have kids?"

"Mmm. Well, we haven't exactly planned it. We just got married, you know. There's so much other stuff going on."

"Stuff in the bedroom," Adeliza said, laughing. "Lots of practice, *na*."

Joy politely smiled along with the chuckles at the table.

"I remember what I did when I was a newlywed," Adeliza continued.

"Are you sure? That was a long time ago," Runilla quipped.

"I'm not so old. He's not blowing dust out of my *okie*, yet."

As the banter continued, Joy wondered if Adeliza had been a GRO— Guest Relations Officer, the government term for prostitute—in the Philippines. If she had not had a life in the sex industry, then she certainly had been affected by the barrage of sex in the American media.

The good natured lunch conversation soured as RoseEllen sat in a huff.

"She won't get off of my back. She's such a witch today. So bossy."

No one at the table had to ask. Only Maiza produced such statements. The woman's father owned a grocery in Makati that catered to internationals, so she naturally thought she knew how to run the Fil-Mart better than anyone else, even the real owners. Maiza had no authority over anyone, but felt a compulsion to offer unneeded advice.

"It's bad," RoseEllen lamented. "Just now she was trying to show me how to stock shelves. One bottle out of a dozen has a label that isn't facing exactly forward and..."

Joy had a sudden flashback to Merly Legadi trying to show her how to cut vegetables.

"Someone should take her down a notch," Adeliza suggested. "The managers won't do it. They like her because she comes off as an ambitious worker."

Runilla chimed in that she overheard Maiza talking to Richard, who handles the fresh fish, about the way her husband kicked her out of the house. She was eliciting information on a better place to stay than her hurriedly-found apartment. "They're getting a divorce already," Runilla explained. "But she just got her green card last month."

Everyone at the table exchanged knowing glances.

"That's disgraceful," Adeliza said. "Marry him, get here, two years to your green card and then dump him."

"Oh, that's good," RoseEllen said. "Maiza tries to treat me like I'm stupid, I'll ask her if she gives love advice too. And then I'll hit her with a comment that at least I didn't use my husband simply to get here."

Joy kept her mouth shut, eyes following each woman in turn.

"It's Filipinas like her that make it so tough for those of us in love with our husbands and trying to get out of the Philippines to live with them. I was in love, married and pregnant and the Dragon Lady at the embassy had the nerve to tell me my wedding was a con," Adeliza complained. "It took three months longer than normal to get my spouse visa. Thank God I got here in time to have my baby here and not there."

Joy bit her lip nervously and slid further into her chair, no one noticing her expression since she was at the fringe of the conversation.

"What a fake she is, so proud to show her wedding pictures. Her husband is more handsome than mine. He doesn't have a big belly."

"Addie, he has a big belly because he didn't want you to feel bad while you're belly was full of babies," someone teased.

"At least I lost my belly after they popped out," Adeliza snickered.

"I can't imagine falling into bed with a man just to keep up the appearance of a loving marriage, knowing once that letter from the government comes in the mail that you're out the door," RoseEllen said, shuddering at the thought.

"Imagine what he thinks," Runilla said. "Going through all of that trouble to get her visa, maybe even hiring a lawyer to do it, paying her ticket over here out of savings, supporting her..."

"Maybe her beat her," RoseEllen said, filling her mouth with lunch. "I know I'd like to do that. Mr. Maiza doesn't seem like a military type, I wonder how they met?"

"Maybe penpal like Joy."

Joy sat straight, suddenly feeling their eyes on her.

"At least Joy's in love. You can see it in their kissing when he drops her to work," Adeliza said, curling the edge of her lips in a teasing smile.

"I came through Singapore, it was faster than Manila embassy and there was no Dragon Lady," Joy said just to say something.

"I thought the two years green card and say goodbye scheme was just a myth," Runilla said. "Can't he get the government to kick her out?"

"Not if she catches another man first. She can get married and stay with the new guy, no worries any more about the ex-husband ... Now Richard here, he's a catch," Adeliza said as the fish man appeared. "Maybe Maiza is trying to catch you in her net."

"Oh, no, don't include me in the *chika chika*," he said, sitting down to join them.

Joy was pleased the conversation turned from Maiza and her deceptive practices. She wondered if these women would be gathered here someday talking about her in the same way.

That is, if there was anyone back home that wanted her to come back a few years from now.

"Would you look at that forlorn face," Adeliza said, interrupting Joy's thoughts. "You just got here a few hours ago and you miss your husband already?"

"Stop teasing her, Addie," Runilla said.

"It's okay, she knows I'm just teasing because I like her, not like Maiza..." Adeliza cut herself off because Richard was sitting beside her. "Break time is over already? Lighten up Joy, you'll see your man in a few hours. Hoy, what I'd give to be a horny newlywed again."

Richard groaned and commented about the filthy mouth.

"That's what you get Mr. Campos when you sit down in the middle of *chika chika.*"

Richard mumbled something that sounded relieved that the gossips were leaving.

Joy went through the rest of the day awaiting an explosion from Maiza and RoseEllen. She caught an unhappy expression from Maiza close to quitting time, but there was no opportunity to investigate the source. She was pulling a relief shift on the cash register at the time. All of them had cleared out for home by the time Joy was finished cleaning. Arrive late, leave late. It was convenient though, allowing Bill to finish his daily toil and then pick her up from work.

But it wasn't Bill today. Brother Bob was waiting outside in his Excursion with the engine running. He needed the beast of a machine to haul around the basketball team that he called his family. Climbing into the passenger seat, she got a howdy and wave from the one-year younger version of Bill.

They exchanged pleasantries. How was work. How was school. Say hi to Auntie Joy, boys. The two of the five in the back seat complied in unison.

She was happy Bob was a good natured person and open minded about Bill's fast paced leap into wedded bliss. Their mother, however, wasn't pleased with the marriage. Overhearing the woman's conversation with Bill just before she met her conferred the opposing view.

"Sounds fishy to me. A girl half your age wants to be your wife?"

"We had to get married quickly, mother, because of all the immigration," Bill had explained.

"So where is your Japanese trophy wife?"

"She's from the Philippines, mother."

"Who cares. It is all the same."

The woman killed her with fake smiles. She poured so many sugary compliments on her that it was obviously contrived. Joy didn't care to see the woman again and understood why Bill rarely spoke to her himself.

Bob, however, frequently made envious comments about Bill's relationship with her. He dropped hints about not seeing Bill this happy in years. "That divorce from Monica messed him up. I couldn't get two sentences out of him for awhile there."

The reason Bob was picking her up today instead of her husband was a last-minute revision on a project. Bill double checked some drawings by a subordinate and found an error. The subordinate was in Kansas City, forcing Bill to correct everything himself.

"Did he say when he was going to be done?"

"It was a one-page problem with the FedEx guy waiting in the lobby, so I'm assuming it was a quick fix," Bob said, pulling out into the four-lane boulevard near the shopping center where the Fil-Mart was situated.

Bob drove the normal way from Hoffman Estates to Des Plaines, allowing Joy the chance to observe the landmarks to know her way home when she finally got her license. She asked Bob's help with the highway and road designations to keep her sense of direction straight.

It was a quick fix. Bill's car was in the driveway when Bob dropped her home. She waved goodbye to one Vandemark and kissed another.

She kicked off her shoes at the door, threw her coat on the rack and sat on her usual stool at the dinette table. The kitchen was hot with supper preparation. She stared off into the nothing while Bill cooked something with large noodles and tomato sauce, peeking in the oven obsessively.

"You look exhausted. Want a drink?"

"Yes." Joy frowned. "Water, please."

"How about this?" Bill shook an empty glass, holding a wine bottle in the other.

"I don't drink alcohol."

"Sure?"

Joy shook her head.

"Romantic Italian dinner..."

"No, Bill. My father was once an alcoholic. Long ago, he was always out of work, we had no money, there was only a bit of rice to eat each day. Father was using all the money to buy gin. Wounded pride and gin made him a violent drunk."

"Sorry, dear, I didn't know."

"That's why I don't drink. And I wish you wouldn't either—or at least don't do it in front of me," she conceded.

Bill bowed his head apologetically and returned the wine to its rack on the kitchen counter and the wine glasses to the shelf above the sink.

Joy's thoughts returned to the same topic occupying her mind the entire day: what to do about her real—but illegitimate—marriage to Thomas and her fake—but legitimized—marriage to Bill?

Bill cupped Joy's cheek. "Feel okay? I didn't hurt your feelings by offering the wine, did I?"

Joy shook her head and invited a kiss for assurance. Then she buried her face into Bill's shirt and made an excuse that she was a little homesick.

"Isn't that odd? I dream of coming here all of my life and I want to go back after only a few months."

"It is just the winter gloom."

"No, my family, I think. Other than that week in Manila, I hadn't really seen them in years. We didn't go back to Abra, so that I could spend time with my friends. Ronaldo got married to a girl I never met. Jon-Jon and Car-Car had a baby. I've only seen Tam-Tam in pictures."

"Car-Car is Maricar?"

Joy bobbed her head. How the man so frequently forgot names, she couldn't guess. His response was always a grin and a response to the effect of having a rolodex for a reason.

"No one ever called you Joy-Joy?"

She laughed. "No, just Joy my joy."

Thomas' pet name wasn't easy to say. Instead of dwelling on him, she skipped back to talking about the rest of her friends.

"Reggie is nice. She is really shy around people she doesn't know. She does most of her talking with her facial expressions. She'll give you the shirt off her back, but complain the entire time she's doing it."

Bill laughed a lot at Ronaldo's girl crazy antics and frowned over Jon-Jon's chicken fighting obsession.

"Now that he's married, Car-Car probably has stopped that. He has better things to spend his money than for gambling."

Bill placed a slice of lasagna in front of her. "Here you are, Joy my joy."

Joy cringed.

"I did something wrong again?"

Joy nodded. "Mmm. Bad memories with that nickname."

"Back to honey ko it is." He sat beside her with his own plate.

"Well, if you're that homesick, maybe we can plan a vacation. My calendar clears up in late spring. Most of the projects are then in the construction phases, not planning phases anymore. I don't have to assign myself a construction manager mission, giving me some time off."

He was suggesting a vacation back to Calamba.

"After the election, please," she said. "It isn't safe for anyone while all of the politics have people worked up."

"Politics?"

"Election time. Mayor. Council. Barangay captain. It is not safe."

"Too many television commercials?"

"Elections in the Philippines are won by guns and bribes. Bribe enough supporters to show up to vote, but somehow intimidate the detractors into staying home. When the dust clears and the temperaments cool off, then it will be safer."

"Why doesn't the government do something about it?"

"It will. Something will happen and the army will roll into the rural provinces that have become hot spots."

"I thought everything happened through People Power. Overthrow governments without firing a shot."

"There's a difference between millions of people marching in the streets of Manila under the watchful eyes of the world compared to hundreds of isolated people without means to defend themselves."

Bill was about to continue the discussion, when Joy waved in the air that she wasn't in the mood to educate Bill about her political system.

There was a reason for the romantic dinner, he said.

"What's that smile? A secret?"

"We got a new job today. A big one. The University of Chicago is expanding its medical program. And I'm the one designing the new building."

Joy wasn't pretending to be happy for Bill when she kissed him. The elation was pure. He'd been working for that since before he knew Joy, it was in his first letter to her, mentioned in the first phone conversation, dotting dozens of emails.

"So you'll be very busy very soon."

"Not soon. It will take the university board a month to finish its due diligence concerning our contract, then there'll be meetings for a few months with the board members before I start drawing anything or making cardboard models," Bill explained. "We'll still have time to fly to the Philippines."

They celebrated the good news for the rest of the evening.

When Joy woke up the next morning, she had a new problem on her mind: how to foil the vacation plans.

< <> >

The dancers weren't moving to the music. The music was so loud that it bounced and jostled the building and the people on the dance floor merely had to stand still.

Joy wasn't sure a girls night out was such a good way to celebrate her first day as a legal driver. But she filled the old Chevy with Runilla, Maiza and RoseEllen, who reached an understanding after a few heated arguments and then created a friendship.

"Asians like this club," Maiza said at the entrance, "because it is like the ones back home. American ones are completely different."

Joy experienced some of the night clubs in Singapore. She loved learning how to dance. She hated the rest of the experience. She didn't touch any alcohol and everyone else got drunk, so she had to be the one to make sure they got out of the taxi to their front door.

Being tonight's driver gave her a good excuse not to drink. Being under 21 gave her insurance.

Most of the people in the club were Korean and Filipino. There was an even mix of men and women, different ages. There was a lot of activity. For the most part, the group stayed together on the dance floor, giggling at one another's moves and lack of moves. Maiza was occasionally singled out by a few men since she was the only one without a wedding ring.

Joy consumed her water and then dismissed herself from the group with the excuse that it was too hot. There was an outdoors porch on the side of the club that people were using to have enough quiet to talk on their cell phones. It was too chilly to stay out there for a long time. March was no better than December.

She fumbled with her new cell phone in her purse, along with the international calling card and the paper with Lopito's phone number. Her old cell phone didn't work in America, so Thomas couldn't call her so that she could keep up the charade that she was still in Singapore. She finally called her friend and put an end to the arrangement of sending boxes on her behalf every month. There was no sense in continuing to pretend she didn't come home to Calamba because the Songs extended her contract against her will and forced her to stay in Singapore for another year—all the while being in Chicago.

The tricks were meant to shield Thomas. He was never supposed to know what she was really doing.

There'd been no contact with Thomas after all these months. She periodically checked her web-based email account and there was never a message waiting there. No questions. No anger. No pain. Nothing.

Getting information on Thomas independent of her parents had been as fruitless. Maricar slammed down the phone when she tried to call. Ronaldo had moved to Bangued. Regina was in Manila and wasn't in a position to know anything.

"Waiting for your husband to call?" Runilla asked, breaking Joy's solace with her phone.

"No. I've been thinking about calling someone."

Runilla said it was nice outside, easy to cool off. It was doubly terrible inside because people were expending energy and the heat was turned up high. She noticed Joy's face was starting to turn red in the cold.

"Hoy ... Joy ... wake up. You've been staring at your phone since you came out here. Who are you trying to call?"

"What if he's the one that answers," Joy answered absently.

"What...?"

It was Saturday morning there. He won't answer the phone, but he'd certainly be at Lopito's house. Unless he went to Calamba to check the farm.

Or, as she feared the most, he was with Nina.

When Bill visited Joy in Singapore for the first time, she spent the night with him at the hotel. The next morning while Bill was in the shower, she had called Thomas. She really tore into him about talking to Nina. Her cousin Grace was a great spy. All during the night she'd thought about him doing the same thing that she'd just done with Bill. It was all in her head, but she was so jealous and so angry. After yelling at Thomas for nothing, she slipped into the shower with Bill and did it again. When it was over, she was showered and clean, but felt so dirty. Bill took her shopping, sight-seeing, to nice restaurants and a short round of dancing. When her day off was done, he dropped her to the Songs house, where she laid in her bed for an hour, paralyzed by conscience.

Now Thomas was with Nina. For revenge or otherwise. That explained his lack of contact.

"So just call him already," Runilla said in Tagalog.

"I can't."

The doors to the porch opened again and let the driving beat permeate the chill. When RoseEllen joined the pair, Joy put away the cell phone.

"Come on back, we convinced the DJ to play some line dancing."

CHAPTER 16

Standing in ankle high water to keep his legs cool, Thomas watched his father throw sticks toward into the sodden meadow. A blond cocker spaniel darted to retrieve it. The beloved Mack reminded his father of the dogs that were his pets as a child in Wisconsin. Mack overshot the stick and backtracked to pick it up in its mouth.

"Let me race him, Daddy."

"In English, Tommy. I can't understand you," Ted replied. He knew plenty of Ilocano, but not the quickly mumbled version that came from Thomas.

"I ... want ... to ... race ... the ... dog," Thomas said in English, though he still had the accent that annunciated every vowel sound and transformed the TH sound into just a T.

Ted gestured for his 11-year-old son to get out of the rice paddy. Thomas took long strides to his father's side, squeezing out Mack, who was bouncing in place for the next toss.

"Ready. Set. Go."

There was no chance for Thomas to beat Mack to the stick, but he laughed as the dog overshot his target again, leaving the youngster an opening to pick it up. Mack did circles around Thomas as he trotted back to his father.

It was then that Thomas saw a flash of pink in the tree line that blocked the view to the nearby river. He picked up the blur of a pink shirt and gray pants further down the river bank.

"You want to throw some, Tommy?"

Thomas shook his head, distracted by the person in pink. Mack waited at Ted's feet and tore off in a sprint as the stick arched its way to the dirt and rough grasses near the trees that marked the back yard.

"Oh, I see," Ted said as he turned his tan face to see where Thomas was looking. "Shadow is playing hide and seek with you again."

Thomas frowned. "*Ading*, not Shadow."

"Yes, yes, sister. Joy is your sister," Ted said in the parental tone that he was agreeing for the sake of avoiding an unnecessary argument.

Thomas didn't like the nickname Joy picked up from elementary school. Well, she was always following Thomas around it seemed. People in town started combined their nicknames, Little Joe and Shadow, as though they were the title of a television cartoon.

Little Joe was good natured when it came from his father, teasing, expecting of a tackle and some roughhousing. It was another thing coming from the older kids at school. Hey, Little Joe, where is your shadow today? She's always on your butt, I bet she can smell your farts really well. How come you're always playing with girls? Are you a girl too, Little Joe? Or do we call you Little Joey He's So Girly?

It hurt worse when Jon-Jon or Ronaldo picked on him like that. They were supposed to be his friends, not enemies like Aris the bully. They did it sometimes in jealousy. Sometimes to separate themselves from him to avoid getting bullied. It wasn't fun being called Fat, Ugly and White, the three amigos.

Thomas thought Joy must have seen him watching her run down the river, but wondered why she didn't wave. She just stopped, looked and then kept going.

"Go see what she wants, Tommy," Ted said. "And no army games or racing. You two will start racing after each other and splash through the water. We just fertilized everything. Your mother doesn't want your clothes full of manure water."

His mother's complaints came often enough, he could hear them in his head.

Joy was already inside the old church when he arrived. "*Hoy, 'ding*," he called into the shade.

There was rustling and sniffling. She didn't answer him.

"*Ading?*"

Thomas could feel that something was wrong. He knelt beside her in the corner. She was scared.

"*Manong* Thomas, hide me."

"Come into the light."

Hesitantly, she slid out of the darkness. The swelling around her left eye was a purple donut. Eyes were red, but not from tears. She hadn't been sleeping again. Who could sleep when your father came home in the darkness and awakened you with punches. Thomas had seen bruises on Joy's arms and legs, small burns where ashes had been flicked at her. This time he saw small bloody holes on her arm.

"Nails," she said.

"He poked you with nails?"

She nodded. Father was upset that Carmona Balao-as dismissed him from installing the addition to his house in Pulot.

"He said he lost the job because he couldn't concentrate. He didn't get enough sleep last night because I was making too much noise."

He touched one of the marks and she winched.

"I ran when he said he was going to get his hammer."

Thomas checked outside to see if Marino had come looking for his daughter. He knew he needed to clean and bandage the nail holes. His father had showed him infections. People sought the former medic for injuries since there was no doctor close to Calamba.

"Wait here."

Joy whimpered.

"I'm going to get something to help you. If you see your father before I get back, run to the cave."

Thomas ran to the house. A strong sprint, determined.

He had run like that once before. Joy was planting rice. A snake sliced through the water and bit her on the leg. It was the poisonous kind. Thomas never ran so fast in his life to get across the river to Auntie Dina's house. The aged nurse had anti-venom. He even stuck the needle in Joy to administer it.

Thomas reached the wood-walled, thatch-roofed structure they affectionately called the barn. Ted built it to house the tractor he'd just purchased from someone he knew in Baguio. He crept inside and found his father's military stores. The green painted metal case had a red cross on it. No one saw him leave with it and race back across the countryside to the old church.

At the old church, he soaked his white T-shirt in the river and then tended to Joy's wounds.

He followed the steps in his memory of Ted cleaning bloody wounds with the damp shirt, then the cotton swabbed in alcohol. He wrapped the gauze around the arm and secured it with a piece of white tape. He had no ice for the swollen eye, but made Joy hold the wet T-shirt there. At least it was a little cool.

"Where I am going to live, *manong*? I don't have a house."

"Live here. God used to live here. He'll protect you."

Joy examined the dirt floor warily. Sleep here? Alone?

"Can you stay here too?"

Thomas pursed his lips. He was thinking. Mom and dad wouldn't let him out of his chores.

"If I'm quiet, maybe dad will let me live at home again."

Thomas was angry. "No, *ading*, it wasn't your fault. Don't blame yourself for your father stabbing you with nails. You didn't do anything wrong."

Joy continued to struggle as more levels of fright stacked up in her mind.

"Don't worry, we'll figure it out. You're good at figuring out things. You're always creating good games."

Thomas' words did little good. She curled her legs close and shook. He sat beside her and hugged her to him.

"It's okay to cry now. I know it hurts."

< <> >

A banging at the door startled Thomas out of the nightmare. The wraiths of the past had gotten to him again.

Thomas sometimes chastised himself for wallowing in his own pain for so many months. No one told him anything, but he knew he was too late. After all, Elnora had gotten married two days after landing in Las Vegas. Joy had already married the American and that sent him into a depression.

People paid Thomas in food and drink, not money. When each day's work in the fields was done, he let himself become numb with *tuba* and *basi*. He knew from plenty of experimenting how much *basi* it took to get himself inebriated. He even knew how much more of it he had to drink to shut down his motor skills and pass out. He had not found the level of alcohol needed, however, to quell the dreams.

Joy always said when you have dreams about a person, it meant they were talking about you.

There were more thuds at the door.

Hard ones.

Loud ones.

Urgent ones.

He remained still. The kitchen table was his pillow. *Basi* and spittle pooled under his mouth. He was acutely aware of his hard breathing and heavy chest. The kerosene lantern was running low and did not illuminate enough of the clock to show the time.

The knocker started calling his name.

"Thomas. You're home, I can see a light." Thud. Thud. "Thomas, it is Lopito."

The dog added itself to the ruckus.

Thomas slid away from the table and willed himself to stand. Through the dim light and drunken fog, he made it to the door.

It was Lopito, standing with his back to the door. It was pitch black beyond the walls, there was nothing to see. There was no security lighting at the farm. It wasn't necessary. The dog provided any warning that a stranger was around.

"Please let me in, Ringor is after me." There was fear in the voice.

Dizziness misdirected his first attempt to turn the doorknob. Colliding with the door and hugging it helped his hand reach the knob on the second attempt.

Lopito didn't hesitate to step inside and close the door behind him. His face was flushed. There was a red streak on his chin, the result of a branch catching his face, he said, while moving through the trees in the dark.

"Ringor is after me. I hope I lost him. He has been after me for weeks now, each time getting closer. Marino wants me to go to Manila to hide until the election is over."

"But Manila is the other way." Thomas belched and clutched his stomach. Alcohol and acid churned.

"Always go in the opposite direction of where you are headed," Lopito said.

Thomas wasn't sure he could have understood that logic if he were sober. Joy wasn't alone in her odd notions, it seemed to be a Lapez trait.

"Can I hide here for a few days? I won't be much of a burden."

Weak in the knees from the *basi*, Thomas went back to one of the chairs at the kitchen table. Lopito sat beside him.

"A few days out of sight and then I can flee to Manila. Quezon City with Rowena's aunt."

He touched Thomas' shoulder, eyes pleading.

"Why should I help you? No one across the river seems interested in helping me. I wonder who the real enemy is to Marino, me or Papa Justo."

Thomas stared at Lopito and saw the resemblance to Marino. The anger swelled. "I ought to throw you out now ... Lapez," Thomas dripped venom over Lopito's surname. "Where is my money, Lopito? Marino stole my money. He stole my future."

"Please, Thomas, I didn't know..."

"Liar. You probably came up with the idea. You're his right hand and left brain."

"No, Thomas. Please."

"How am I going to live, Lopito?" He grabbed the older man by the sleeves and failed in attempting to shake him. "I understand the idea, take my money so I cannot follow Joy to America to stop her. But why did Marino take it all? How can I return to college? How do I live until the harvest? Plain rice every day? I already sold all of my livestock."

Lopito said nothing.

"At least I can make my own *basi*," Thomas spat. He shifted his position and dipped his hand into the kitchen water bucket. In a cupped hand, he splashed his face.

"You're not okay, Thomas. You shouldn't drink so much at your age. You'll get an ulcer, or worse become an alcoholic."

Thomas brushed him off.

"I'm sorry for all of this, Thomas. Politics can be a rough game. You know how it is here in the provinces. In Baguio, the candidates can fight with just words. Go to Vigan or Bangued and you need bodyguards..."

"And Marino hides behind his to keep me from strangling him."

Thomas wanted to strangle Lopito too, but it was the memory of Lopito boarding him for nothing for his months at college that prevented it.

"What Marino did to me wasn't politics. It was personal. Joy was my wife, Lopito! *Asawa ko*! Mine. Not some American with a money tree in his backyard."

In a rage, Thomas swiped an empty *basi* jar from the table, not caring that his arm was now covered in the spittle.

"Get out."

"No. Please, Thomas, let me stay one night. Just tonight," Lopito said, putting his hands together like a street beggar. "I'm not the only one in danger. I have to flee. Ringor was in Baguio, on our street corner. He might have tried to knock me off in my own house. Grace is scared. My wife is scared. I'm the talker. I campaign. I don't handle the guns. You lived with me, I don't have any guns. I couldn't defend the family if Ringor wanted to attack."

Lopito explained that Ringor also tried a few times to intercept him on the road between Calamba and Bangued. "Whenever I'm in Abra, there is always some protection. Aris walks with me, mostly Fernando, as I go door to door to talk with people for Marino. I don't have that at home. I am vulnerable there."

"Maybe he followed you here." Thomas stood and walked to the door. "He is probably taking his time, knowing that you're cornered and tired. I'll call him for you." He whistled as though he were calling a dog. "Oh, Ringor. Here, boy."

Lopito barred Thomas' from opening the door. "Okay. You have a right to be mad. You can even torture me like this. What if I pay you to let me stay? I don't have many pesos on me now, but I'll help you."

Thomas leveled his stare into Lopito's eyes. He had the upper hand and Lopito knew it. The man was scared. Scared enough to lower himself to begging and pleading.

Thomas retook his seat. His eyes became unfocused for a moment. The combination of sugar cane alcohol, anger and the up-and-down motion made him nauseated. "I don't need your money, but I let you stay tonight—and tonight only—if you give me information. Tell me about Joy. How is she? Where is she now? What is she doing?"

At hearing the conditions of the bargain, Lopito drew in a sharp breath. "I know she meant so much to you…"

Thomas brought his fist down on the table to cut off the non-answer. While Lopito was silently assessing the situation, Thomas kept his hands squeezed into fists. Lopito wiped some of the sweat from his face.

"Under the circumstances, I'm more afraid of being captured for Papa Justo than receiving reprisals from Marino. You're not going to like the news,

Thomas. She is already married to him. The wedding was as soon as she arrived. She is now Joy Vandemark in Chicago. She lives in some barangay there, because I did not recognize the city name on the return address from her letter."

The realization that Joy was married to someone else was sobering. What hope lingered that he still might stop her faded. His breathing became long and deliberate.

If Lopito did not outweigh him by half, he would have dragged the man to Papa Justo's house personally. No, he told himself, a bargain had been struck. Lopito was in his keeping until morning.

"I understand the *kano* is generous and sent some of his own money. He is an architect, you know," Lopito continued. "Joy has authorization for work privileges in USA now. Marino told me that much. She may already have a job there. The plan is working, though that is no consolation to you."

Thomas scowled. That was an understatement. He wondered if Lopito would have been so casual if he were giving the same devastating news to Grace's husband.

"I'm sorry about what happened with Joy," Lopito repeated. "I've had a few heartbreaks in my life. You will get over it eventually. A handsome guy like you, especially a bit white skin, is going to get a lot of attention from girls. You could double for Jose Dantes on TV." There was a nervous smile with the compliment. "You'll meet someone new, I'm confident."

It's Aga Muhlach, not Jose Dantes. And that Someone New treated him like a trophy and once paid people to throw shit at his face.

"Thank you, Lopito," Thomas said, though the gratitude had nothing to do with being compared to television heartthrobs.

As his mind wrestled the *basi* out of the way, Thomas saw the blessing Lopito's visit had become. He now knew where to look and the name to search when he got there.

"Don't be mad at her. There was no convincing Marino against it."

"Why would I be mad at her? She is just another victim of Marino's greed like the rest of us here in Calamba."

"He wanted *kano* money like Papa Justo. Unfortunately, he has only one daughter to send out. Be understanding, Thomas. Joy could not refuse her father's request. It is the only time I have ever seen Marino ruthless to one of his own children."

"I've seen plenty of those times," Thomas muttered.

"He even attacked her, punched her." Lopito shook his head in sadness over the memory. "Joy fought the idea. Marino told her that your life was in danger. Win or we all die, he said, including Thomas. You know what Justo could do to us if he wins."

Lopito described the concessions Joy wanted. The family was supposed to care for Thomas in her absence, as a son. All of the money she earned in

Singapore was for Thomas' education. The money from America went to Marino the election, but then everything left over in the war chest when the election was won was supposed to go to Thomas.

"Just like that, eh?" Thomas snapped his finger. "Marino wins next month and he is going to hand over a fortune? Do I also get back the college fund his mistress at the bank stole on his behalf? It was my money that sent Joy to Singapore in the first place. As compensation, can I expect to get his house in Bangued? How about the truth? Yes, that would be a refreshing reward."

"You were not supposed to find out from Ricky. You were never supposed to find out … never. She had arranged some way to fool you into thinking she was still in Singapore with a contract extension."

That explained the mystery *balikbayan* boxes. More of them had arrived, even one filled with Christmas gifts. He sold the shirts and wall hangings. The canned food in the boxes became the only food he ate for the week after they arrived.

Lopito looked at Thomas as if to ask if he had parted with enough information to earn a night's sanctuary.

"Did you bring a bag?"

The older man smiled.

"Thank you, Thomas. Thank you. No, I only have the clothes on my back. The decision to run was sudden. Ringor was in Baguio, like I said."

Thomas had some shirts, but all of them would be too small to fit Lopito. The man's chest was too big. The stomach too.

"Let me catch my wits. I can worry about clothes later. I can sleep without a shirt."

Despite the onset of an alcohol-related headache, Thomas tried to be a good host, offering food and drink, though it was only tepid river water and cold rice.

"Thomas, what happened to your kitchen? There used to be a refrigerator here. A small television there. No more electric rice cooker?"

"Except for the food people pay me when I work as their farm hand, I don't eat. All of my farm land belongs to someone else now. Remember? The rice I had today was pity from Old Masakayan."

Lopito continued to look around, cataloging the items that were missing, sold for money. There was some truth in what Thomas said, he did not eat much, he did not spend much.

The money from selling the animals was lost, but the money from selling the appliances accumulated in a box under his bed. That was Plan C. He left it there for the airline ticket. The frig went for 6,000. He got 500 for the old television, 1,000 more for the rice cooker. Masakayan paid 5,000 for the old thresher. The old man also officially owned the tractor, though he could only afford a down payment of 5,000 pesos. Thomas had 17,500 in the box. With the Botalicos in possession of the farm land, the only thing left to sell was the house. If Armando was interested in purchasing it, that would get him close to a ticket. A little shortfall could be made up. Jon-Jon or Ronaldo could loan him a few thousand.

The barrenness of Thomas' house made Lopito eat with some reverence. Between bites, Lopito explained his escape plan. Thomas couldn't blame the man for wanting to change the subject away from Joy.

"I know a way through the mountains that will get me to Tuguegarao. From there, I turn around and take the coastal road south, back to Angeles City. Aris' sister will take me in for a few days."

"I am sure your Mrs. Lapez will like that arrangement," Thomas observed.

"Lovelyn is the same age as Grace. I would not... I know that Lovelyn is a dancer there, but ... I hadn't thought about what my wife would think about it."

Lopito kept eating and talking, but Thomas found himself lost in thought.

He saw himself hop out of a taxi, knocking on the door of a snow covered house. The tall, redheaded American answers the door. Yes, you can help me. I'm Thomas Wagner and I'm here to fetch the love of my life. Oh, no, I have the correct address. You are Mr. Vandemark the architect? I knew it. We've met before. I was yelling at you and Joy at the airport. Me? Oh, I'm Joy's husband. No, this is not a mistake. Joy and I have been married for more than a year now, 15 months exactly. See the ring. She has one just like it somewhere. Oh, it was a small ceremony in the Catholic church in Calamba. Just three of us were there—her, me and God. Is she home? I am sure she'd be delighted to see me. Oh, she is at work. Yes, I imagine she would be working overtime to feed money to her corrupt father that made her marry you just for your wallet. What am I talking about? Here, I'll come inside and explain...

"It is bad this time, Thomas. The people in Calamba need a strong pep talk because Justo is so strong. The governor is on his side and that is a strong endorsement. I have to give twice the goodwill money just to get them to listen."

It was the lesser of two evils, not any strength in Papa Justo. He was just as capable of ripping out the water system as soon as he took power, all in spite because Marino had finally put it in.

"Hoy, this campaign has made my mouth dry and tired. I have to make everything the governor's fault, you know, not Marino's. Of course, the blackouts are really the governor's fault. The bad roads and the cut water pipe I have to blame on vandals. Of course, it really is the vandal's fault."

Thomas sighed.

When Lopito's tongue tired, Thomas showed him to the spare bedroom, which was actually Thomas' old room. The older man thanked him again for allowing him to hide in his house.

He didn't seem to mind sleeping on the mattress of a dead person—Emma's bed. "It is better than being dead myself."

The nervous humor had no effect on Thomas.

He left Lopito, closing the bedroom door in his wake. He shuffled into the kitchen contemplating more swigs from the jar of *basi*. He hadn't consumed enough to be rid of the dreams. He stared at it. The longer the stare, the more it seemed to call to him. A blast of acid in his stomach bent him in half. Hand over his abdomen, Thomas took a deep breath and then spit the bile into the sink. No more alcohol. Water. Yes, water to settle the stomach.

He lamented about the lack of aspirin in the house on the way to his bed. Flat on his back, he stared into the darkness. He knew he was going to dream about her again. Maybe this time the show was going to be the morning they lost their virginity in the old church. Or it could be a replay of the wedding ceremony in the other church. Let's go way back in time, so that he could play with his dead sister.

He willed Joy's voice into his mind. *Sika ti immuna ken siksikanto laeng.* My first and only. He'd always be the first, but no longer was he the only.

Joy Vandemark instead of Joy Wagner.

He touched the side of the bed that she once occupied. He tried not to think about where she was sleeping now, of what kind of exploration was happening—had happened. Was happening every day. It made his skin crawl.

He vowed to change it. The injustice would be undone. Mr. Vandemark didn't deserve to be a pawn in this feud either. All he needed was a break, a burst of good luck, like tonight with Lopito's information. Some money. Just enough for Philippine Airlines to hand him a ticket.

"Damn you, Marino," he mumbled into his pillow. "May God damn you."

The dog was barking.

Thomas opened his eyes and turned his ears to listen to the dog. It never barked like that. The sound of a thud was followed by a whelp. Then a second thud and a second whelp.

Thomas bolted upright. He whisked the sheet off his body and plowed through the mosquito netting on his way out of the room. Something metallic crashed across his chest and he went to the floor in a heap. A flashlight popped on and blinded him temporarily. The metallic object was a gun in the hand of the man standing in his hallway with the flashlight.

The man brandished the gun into Thomas' face. He could not tell who it was from the bandanna stretched across the lower half of his face.

But beyond him Thomas could see Ringor walking around in the kitchen. Moonlight streamed through the open main door. The dog was crawling away on its front paws, the back legs dragging behind it, bent in the wrong direction, all the while whining in pain.

"What are you doing in my house, Ringor?" The dog had crawled under the kitchen table and was panting heavily. "And what the hell did you do to my dog?"

"It followed us inside, so I got it off me," Ringor said. "I should have taken out my knife and popped the thing quietly outside. We could have finished our work before you noticed we were here."

"What work is that?" Thomas demanded.

The handgun got closer to his face. Thomas closed his mouth.

"Come out, Lopito. There are others watching the windows, old man, there is no way to escape," Ringor said to the closed door. "Lopito!"

Papa Justo's main lieutenant calling his name produced a frightened cry from Lopito, who opened the bedroom door and slowly emerged. The unknown man continued to hold Thomas at bay while Ringor grabbed Lopito by the arm and dragged him into the kitchen. Ringor motioned with his head for them to exit. They were intent on snatching Lopito and just leaving.

Thomas gritted his teeth against the pain in his chest and the hangover pounding in his brain.

"Not in my house," Thomas said. But no one heard over Lopito's wailing and Ringor's taunts.

A break-in. A kidnapping. Violence against his pet. The feud had already claimed Joy. Then his future. Now they dared to bring the feud into his last refuge.

Lopito was going to be killed. Or tortured and then killed.

"Not in my house," he said louder.

Thomas made a run at the Justo guard, driving his forearms into the back. The blindside blow sent the unknown man to the floor. A somersault and he crumbled into the corner.

Thomas ducked underneath Ringor's sideways swipe of the baton. He brought up his left hand and connected with Ringor's jaw.

The gunshot was deafening. The bullet careened off the ceiling.

"Stop, you damned White or I will keep shooting." Thomas understood the dialect. Itneg.

Thomas stopped his fisticuffs with Ringor and observed the man whose flashlight was again shining in his face.

"You're not taking anyone. Not from my house."

"Calm down, Thomas. We don't want you, just Lopito," Ringor said. "You're lucky to be Nina's boyfriend or I'd break every bone in your body for punching me."

Thomas returned his attention to Ringor, who no longer had a grip on Lopito. Lopito, though, was frozen in place.

Nina's boyfriend?

"Well, as Nina's boyfriend and future husband, I say get out of my house and leave us alone," Thomas said, thinking he might as well make the best of her desire to defuse the situation.

"Not so simple as that. Nina is not in charge of this." Ringor smiled. "Papa Justo wants Lopito. Just to talk."

Thomas scoffed. "This is no request to sit down and drink San Miguel and talk about the rice crop. You are kidnapping him for ransom. If you need a hostage so bad, why not wait for Aris to pop his head out of the compound and capture him."

"You would like that, huh?" Ringor chuckled. "Me too, but Mayor Lapez won't pay to get Aris back. He will pay plenty for Lopito. Maybe enough to bankrupt himself and pull out of the election."

Thomas kept up his defiance. "Lopito is my guest here. This is my house. I say what happens here."

"Why are you helping a Lapez anyway? You should be happy we are taking him away."

"Not all the Lapez have been evil to me. Uncle Lopito has been kind."

"He's helping Lapez because he is a stupid White." The unknown man was standing again.

The voice was familiar. He was speaking Itneg. He kept calling Thomas *puraw*. The body shape was long and lanky. Thomas pieced it together. Abel Botalico.

"What are you saying?" Ringor asked Abel.

"He understands me," Abel replied to Ringor in Ilocano, gesturing to Thomas with the weapon. "He needs a lesson. Let's shoot them both and burn the house to send a message to Mayor Lapez that nothing is safe."

"I give the orders," Ringor retorted sharply. "That's not the plan. Papa Justo wants Lopito. Quick in, quick out. Leave Thomas alone. Those are the orders."

"Botalico is bigger than Justo." Abel was now arguing with Ringor. "I say we shoot them both. Lapez doesn't have enough money to pay a ransom anyway. Neither does *puraw*. My grandfather built this place. Look at it now. It's old, empty shack. It has that damned mark outside, the mark of the *kano*, an insult to this Botalico house."

"My name is not *puraw*. It is Thomas. I am Thomas *Botalico* Wagner. We're family. We're the same blood."

"You've never been part of the family."

"That's your fault, not mine. I was kind to you, Abel, giving you food from my own hard work in exchange for a small amount of sugar cane. My mother was nice to you too and you still looked down on her. After all of that, you still can't bring yourself to accept us? You've spent your lives being narrow minded bigots..."

Thomas saw the gun barrel come up as the insult left him mouth.

Ringor was more swift, however, making a downward swipe with his metal baton and clipping Thomas on the shin. The bone broke and the force of the blow sent Thomas hurtling to the kitchen floor.

While falling, Thomas saw the flash from Abel's gun.

It was then that Lopito lost his nerve. Lopito was barely one step toward the hallway when Thomas saw Abel change his aim to the escapee. The gun blazed again and Lopito joined Thomas on the floor.

Ringor made a second blow to Thomas, this one to the back of his head, sharply silencing the cries of pain.

< <> >

It was the panicked whining of the dog that awakened Thomas. They were painful yelps followed by frightened squeals.

When Thomas opened his eyes, he saw the reason to be frightful.

Orange waves of flames sat above him on the ceiling.

With eyes wide, Thomas quickly scanned the rest of his surroundings.

The kitchen table was afire, growing in size with each piece of the ceiling falling upon it. Other flammable areas were also ablaze, the kitchen cabinets, the doors, the rattan bench. If not for the smoke, Thomas would have been blinded by its light.

The dog was under the kitchen table. It wanted to move because the fire was above it on the table top, but it couldn't escape. Thomas noticed the hind legs, seemingly broken, laying flat on the concrete. Front legs pushed the dog backward toward the wall whenever something flaming would fall from the ceiling and land near the table.

Thomas' instinct to escape the house rose a notch when a creaking sound emanated from the ceiling. The fire-weakened beams were giving way to the weight of the roof.

Thomas rolled to his stomach and the pain from his right leg struck. If he had screamed, he didn't know, with the roar of the fire in his ears.

It was then he finally spotted Lopito.

It took three drags on his elbows to reach the unmoving body in the hallway back to the bedrooms. What was once a white T-shirt was now pink in the torso. Darker red spots, nearly black, marked the bullet holes in Lopito's chest.

He tried to rouse the man by yelling into his ear and slapping his face. Lopito's eyes were closed. Thomas pried one open and it was dilated, looking far into the distance, not living.

There was no time for remorse. Thomas searched for an escape route.

The front door was closest, but it was engulfed by flames. Windows too.

A running start at the door? Leap through and then be in the front yard?

Thomas pushed up to try to stand. The pain was sharp and dropped him back to his previous position.

The dog gave him an idea. The dog door in the back of the house. It meant crawling into the bedroom, then to the bathroom and fumbling with the lock to open the old dog door. It also meant dragging Lopito with him the entire way to save his life. If he was still alive. Lopito's weight was a concern. Thomas closed his eyes to ask for God's help. Strength.

Thomas tugged at Lopito's shirt collar to no avail. With no ability to kneel or stand, Thomas could not get sufficient lift to slide the man's body.

With horror, Thomas watched part of the ceiling collapse. The corner over the kitchen table came crashing down. Items in the attic and the roof came with it. The kitchen table was gone, awash in orange light. The dog was dead.

No more waiting.

"Sorry, Lopito."

Thomas went to his stomach again. He found it hard to breathe and harder to move with a broken leg. His elbows propelled along the hallway into his parent's bedroom and then through the door to the bath.

The bathtub was practically unused. The toilet was just a seat over a French drain, a bucket of water to dump into the bowl when done.

Thomas pushed aside the empty bucket and began to work on the planks of wood nailed in front of the dog door. Ted's spaniel was a beloved animal. Once it died, Emma boarded up the dog's back entrance into the house, mostly as a deterrent for other dogs.

Thomas did not have to look above him to know the fire had spread into this room too. It was providing the light he needed to see the dog door. He was thankful the nails were old and rusty. Two of the planks came off quickly.

Thomas shoved the door, opening it slightly. Enough to notice the difference in air quality outside. He put his lips to the opening and took three deep breaths of less smoky air.

As more of the house cracked and fell in on itself, Thomas pushed frantically at the door. He had forgotten until then that there was wood nailed over the small doorway on the outside of the house too.

CHAPTER 17

SANGAPULO KET PITO

"A five month anniversary? There's no such thing," Joy called out from the bathroom.

Within she was trying her hand at makeup, applying a liquid base that made her face look lighter than it was. She was pleased, but consumed with impression that she'd put too much. She didn't want to look like a GRO in Angeles City who seemed to always have three pounds of makeup on their faces.

"Why did you close the bathroom door?"

"So you don't see me naked. It makes you crazy."

Bill chuckled.

"Well, I won't bother you this time or we'll be late."

There was a time Joy hid her nudity out of self-consciousness. Now it was for practicality. The presence of Bill and Joy Vandemark was required at the University of Chicago for a reception of distinguished alumni. She asked Bill if this was related to his new assignment of designing a building there. Yes, but not really was the response. Which she understood. He was an alumnus, but going this time because of the building.

So, because of the dress up involved, this was to be considered their five month wedding anniversary.

"Oh, I have a pimple. I must be in love."

"What?"

"A pimple on your face means you're in love with someone."

"Does that mean you love me?"

"Who else?"

She finished her makeup and then dressed. Backwards, but she didn't want to ruin the red dress with a mistaken dab of Avon.

"How am I going to talk to these people? I have an accent."

"So do some of them. Mike talks with his 'Canadian eh?' My friend Vlad is Croatian."

She'd feel better if Bill didn't get constant amusement from the way she spoke English. "I have to change the shits. Where are the shits?" "The what?"

156

Joy gestured to the bed. "Oh, the sheets," Bill nodded. "That's what I said. Shits."

Bill laughed. He had laughed that way before while they were lounging in Laguna Beach. "Let's go to the bitch," Joy had said. "The bitch? The beach..." "Stop teasing my accent." "Don't sing itsy bitsy spider." "Why?" "It's not itchy bitchy spider."

Her accent had improved over the months. Ps were no longer pronounced as Fs. She still couldn't find a TH to save her life.

"Don't worry, there'll be Filipino doctors crawling all over the place too."

He was right. As well as Indian and Pakistani. Joy was easily the youngest and tiniest person in the ballroom and was waiting for someone to chastise a doctor couple for bringing their daughter to the reception.

She was introduced to this Mike and Vlad and so many other people that the names ran together. They were all in some measure running their own firms, medical practices or consulting agencies. The man on a speaking tour had a lot of energy.

All of them had smiles for her when introduced by Bill. Only the Filipinos talked to her though.

The first question from Filipinos was where she was from. Ilocos. Oh, then they had to list everyone they knew from northern Luzon, as though Joy would somehow recognize them all. Most of them were from Manila or Cagayan de Oro and they tested her knowledge of Tagalog. It was learned, but just wasn't used in common speech in the Ilocano region. If it wasn't the language on the television, it wouldn't be heard at all.

Joy got conscious of the way everyone looked at her.

"Doesn't that bother you?" she asked Bill while away from people, getting something to drink.

"What?" the oblivious Bill asked.

"Don't you notice people staring at us? You can see that they're thinking is that his wife or his daughter? Why is a 38 year old man is married to a 19 year old girl?"

"Why is Celine Dion married to a man twice her age? Love."

"Everyone here graduated from this college. Aren't you ever embarrassed of me? I'm not an educated woman."

Bill shook his head and squeezed her hand.

"Stop worrying. If they have something bad on their minds when looking at us as a couple, then they're the ones with issues to address. And if your education bothers you enough, then I'll make you a college educated woman."

He said it so matter-of-factly that it took Joy by surprise.

"College? Me?"

"Sure. I can get you into U of Chicago without a problem. The dean of admissions is right over there."

Joy didn't look. She'd stare at the man and obsess about what to say if she knew what he looked like.

"It is not that I'm not happy you want me to go. It is just that ..." She sighed. "My mother always grilled me about college." And Thomas. "I never figured out what I wanted to take when I got there. I wasn't a great student in high school. I learn as I do, not from book study."

"You'll be fine. I can coach you if you hit a hard topic, so long as it isn't ancient French literature or Japanese religious scholars."

Those were college classes?

"Accounting," she suggested.

"Sure, math is my thing."

An Indian doctor approached Bill seeking to talk to him about the new wing. Joy listened absently. She wasn't sure how much of it Bill was even bothering to mentally catalog.

She always saw her future as a wife and mother with a few odd jobs. A professional woman? She wasn't so sure of that. At least thoughts of college shook off her paranoia of being stared at by the throng of people in the room.

Bill grew tired enough of the reception to say from farewells to Mike and Vlad.

"We're not staying for dinner?" Joy asked as they were exiting the ballroom.

"No, I've got reservations for somewhere else."

"Five month anniversary?"

Bill smiled.

It turned out to be down the street. Something Chinese. Bill explained that the proprietor was Singaporean and cooked the exact style of spicy fish and crab he'd eaten his second trip to Singapore.

"Oh, the night you proposed," Joy recalled.

The knee bending, ring revealing part was in private, on the balcony of the hotel with the city skyline in the background. It was a hot, whirlwind romance, just like she wanted.

They both ordered the spicy food. Joy missed the cuisine in Singapore. It was so spicy at first that she cried to eat it. Then spicy became a taste, not a sensation, and she grew to enjoy it.

Joy strived for contentment for the longest time. She got closer to that life in Singapore. It was hard there, but not as hard as in Calamba. It had people who liked her, who didn't consider her strange, who weren't forced into a friendship with her because they were equally outcast. It had bosses who weren't mean and critical.

She was on course to have what everyone else in Calamba would have, a primitive house near a farm, lucky to have a running fan during the day, spending most of the morning tending to animals, the rest of it cooking for the family, lucky to have the electricity come back in time to watch a small television with shaky reception at night. Now she wanted more than that.

If Thomas succeeded in becoming a doctor, it was likely Mrs. Dr. Joy Wagner would be living in a pleasant concrete home in a gated subdivision in Baguio or Laoag. Not Manila because Thomas hated congestion. She'd have her own maid to cook and clean, the children would be off to private school all day, she'd have a circle of friends who wanted to play mahjong with her every other night.

Even that wasn't good enough now.

In this short time in Chicago, Joy felt that she reached contentment. She had an independence she never knew before. Her own car to drive where she wanted. A pleasant job that paid more than a dollar a day. A house bigger and prettier than she ever dreamed.

When she got here, she didn't even want a green card. Now she had second thoughts about going home to Calamba as planned.

In order to settle in, there were some areas she needed to explore further.

"Why don't you ever tell me about your ex-wife?"

Bill got a stumped look and shrugged his shoulders. "Never think about her much."

"Yes, you do. I get the sense you've been making a lot of comparisons since I got here. You are surprised that I don't drink, I don't mind to do laundry, I have no interest to go shopping."

Bill had a thing with his eyebrows every time she said or did something that contrasted Monica.

"Why are you interested in Monica? There's no chance of me going back to her, so you don't have to worry about me leaving you."

"No, I am not asking because I am worried about that. But she has affected you. She is in your head. It is in the way you act around me. Isn't it odd that we never fight? Bob said you and her fought all the time."

"We didn't get along."

"Fights don't always mean you don't get along. I know people who squabble. To them, the fact that you have an argument means you care about something. That can translate into caring about the person."

"Does this mean you want to have arguments all the time?"

"No, we are what we are," Joy said. "We shouldn't change the nature of our relationship just to fit with the way other's lived."

Joy sipped at her water and kept her gaze on him.

Bill finally cleared his throat. "Monica ... right."

"You never forgave her?"

"No. There's something about finding her car parked at another man's house and then watching her take away my house after she got caught that left a sour taste in my mouth."

Joy wondered how forgiving he would be about his second wife disappearing one summer afternoon and turning up on the other side of the world.

"Did you ever forgive your father?" Bill turned the tables on her.

Monica was still too much of a sore spot. Maybe that's why he waited so many years to find someone new. Maybe starvation for love was why he grabbed that someone new so quickly. She decided to find a spot in the future to inquire about how he and Monica met. Perhaps diving in before knowing about the water was a repeat behavior.

Bill gazed at her because she hadn't answered the question. Her father...

"Not for a long time, but recently he has treated me much better. Forgiveness doesn't work like you wake up and say so, like a decision about what clothes you're going to wear today. It is something that happens over time. When I talk to my dad on the phone now, I don't remember the things he once did to me."

"Sounds like you've forgiven him then."

Joy smiled. "Must be."

The drinks arrived. The Chinese man in the tuxedo was also quick to bring a salad.

"So when should we have children?" Bill asked.

The question stunned Joy slightly. The talk of Monica struck a nerve. She felt responsible for the table talk being so serious, since she started it.

"Shouldn't we wait until all this immigration status is over. I'm not going back to Philippines with a baby inside."

"I'm not worried about that paperwork. There's no reason the government is going to send you home. The guy at work who went through this already said it will take some time for the Chicago office to get your fingerprints and then schedule an interview. Probably we won't see anyone up there until you've already been here two years, just like his wife. The government is slow. His wife got her two-year temporary green card in time to file for her permanent one."

Joy swirled her fork around in the lettuce.

"Well, since you don't want to take some classes, maybe we should start our family now. I'm not getting any younger. I want to play with my grandchildren before I end up in the old folks home."

Bill was chuckling. Joy was cringing on the inside.

"Let's get some of these other things settled first," Joy said. "Like the election, some savings in case I want to change jobs..."

"Is this one of those times we should be arguing? It is something I care about. I am eager for a family."

Joy pinched Bill's cheek. "Is it the baby you want or just the practice?"

Joy's salacious quip put an end to the subject for the rest of the meal. Bill was testing the waters about having children. Joy knew it would come up again until she made a choice about her vocational future.

Bill saw the answering machine blink. He pressed the button and heard a scratchy message in Ilocano. It seemed to go on for awhile, but he understood none of it. None of the few words that he knew were used.

Bill stopped the message before it ended and called for Joy. "It is a message for you on the answering machine. No idea who it is or what it is about."

Joy came into the bedroom, walking without shoes and still removing her earrings.

"Not again," she said, rolling her eyes. 'Come on! I sent money on Friday. It has to be there by now."

Bill pushed the button again and Joy translated as the message went along.

"It is father this time. He tried to call ... this morning our time ... but we must have gone to work ... also a few times this afternoon our time ... very late at night his time ... but no one was home yet ... going to leave a message then ... something important..."

Listening closer, Bill heard what sounded like a name. He also heard one word that he understood, the word *patay* – dead – as the message ended.

The shriek from Joy's mouth was such that Bill had never heard in his life.

"What is it? What happened?"

Joy trembled violently, eyes locked on the answering machine as it rewound the small tape inside.

"Dead. Dead," she sobbed. And then another shriek, like a mother who's baby died in her arms.

"Dead? Who is dead, dear?"

Joy could not answer honestly.

CHAPTER 18
SANGAPULO KET WALO

Bill Vandemark watched in awe.

The relentless sobbing that dominated Joy's life for the past three weeks found renewed energy after she knelt beside a fresh grave near a big tree. A grave marker, flat and flush with the ground, bore the name of Thomas Wagner.

Bill's eyes were frequently drawn over to a similarly horrid scene, the blackened heap of timber behind him. Ash and heat had discolored the short concrete wall that surrounded the dead house like a moat.

They missed the funeral. United States immigration was a slow moving process. Joy had no official status with the federal government since the papers to obtain her initial green card were filed so recently. Red tape for what they called Advance Parole delayed their departure.

Bill recalled only a few equally emotionally exhausting periods in his life: the death of his own father, his first divorce. But in none of those times did he feel as helpless as he did with Joy's tragedy. She was going through this without him. And he didn't know why.

He knew from his own personal tragedies that it was therapeutic to talk about the loss. Joy had said little about this Thomas. Questions to Joy were met with non-answers or no answer at all as she stared into space. She would mumble in the night about not seeing a light to say goodbye to the light. In later days, she rambled that she wasn't seeing the light because the spirit was trapped and God needed convincing to let him into heaven.

Bill's best guess was that Thomas was an illegitimate brother born through either Marino or Rowena. That was until he saw the last name, Wagner, and that threw his theory for a loop. He saw the stones next to the lad's grave. Emma Wagner. Theodore Wagner. Joel Wagner. Josephine Wagner. The illegitimate brother theory was still a possibility, but to be true needed a twist akin to daytime soap operas. How was Thomas Wagner so important that Joy needed to see the grave for herself, pray for his light to be released by God, and yet so unimportant that she never mentioned him?

Joy often spoke of Maricar, who was standing next to him and crying herself. In stories of her life and times in the town, she told of escapades involving these characters "Car-Car" and "Jon-Jon," a *girl* named "Reggie" and a disfigured man named "Ronaldo" who fancied himself a womanizer. Never a story about a Thomas. Not even a Tom … a Mas … a Tom-Tom … Wag-Wag or any other quirky nickname that remotely came close to a Thomas Wagner. Yet, there was Joy lying motionless on the grave of this mystery person.

Bill got some information from the Dutch priest, who spoke some English, but not all the words were understandable because his tongue shot them out with the Filipino way of accenting each and every vowel. Very tragic story. Orphan boy. Lost everything. Died in a fire. We all knew and loved him. It still didn't answer the question of Joy's emotional breakdown.

Mayor Lapez dismissed any questions about Thomas with a speech about not talking about the dead. His father-in-law seemed more interested in getting an update on someone named Lopito from the subordinates that approached him.

Maricar ducked questions about Thomas through a shy smile that Filipinos used on him when they were uncomfortable talking in broken English. Even the talkative Ricky would simply dig his toe into the dirt and shield tears of his own. Joy's mother went into fits to rival Joy when the subject came up.

Joy and Rowena now were looking up into the sky and were talking up to heaven. Some kind of list. Father Herman said the lad was a good altar boy, which got added to the list. Were they trying to convince God to take him into heaven?

Maricar and Jon-Jon left not long into this never-ending list.

"Car-Car" had calmed considerably since their jeepney ride from the Bangued bus stop to Calamba. Bill knew the Ilocano curse words. Most of that illustrious dictionary was lobbed from Maricar to Joy during their heated argument in the back of a colorful chrome elongated jeep. Bill gleaned that Maricar was upset about Joy being in America, a little about himself, but mostly about this mysterious "brother." Jon-Jon nodded agreement at each scathing remark. The little girl on his lap tried to help drive sometimes, but mostly stared in curiosity at Bill while Maricar shrilly attacked Joy in multiple languages. "Do you know how he lived the last months of his life?" Maricar had belted. "They told me he was fine and back in Baguio," Joy had retorted. Maricar pounced on Joy with Ilocano gibberish … "alcoholic, vomiting in the street in front of the sari-sari" … more Ilocano … "just sat out there for weeks" … more Ilocano … "took away his land and then burned his house down with him inside of it."

When it started to rain, Bill and Rowena peeled Joy from the small graveyard and back across a rope bridge to go home. Joy slept with her mother, who stroked her hair and murmured in an apologetic din.

Bill slept in Joy's bedroom. He saw his wife in yet another new light. There was no wall to be seen. From floor to ceiling, and even part of the ceiling, was covered in posters and pictures. The Golden Gate Bridge, St. Louis arch, Kelly Clarkson, a few boy bands that didn't exist anymore. In the spaces around the posters were pictures of Joy and her friends, the one's he'd met, and even a few he hadn't – Ronaldo was obvious, his upper lip cut in half. This other kid in all of the other pictures must have been Thomas. He looked Filipino, yet he didn't.

Bill felt claustrophobic and frustrated. He was unable to sleep because his body's clock told him it was lunch time, not midnight. A small fan blew nearby. As it swept back and forth across the room, it would sometimes send its breeze to him. He grew tired of watching Joy's white curtains flutter.

He walked outside.

No one named Lapez noticed his departure.

Mosquitoes and flies swarmed in the flood lights of the courtyard. Men sat on wooden benches and drank gin out of small clear bottles. Many of them smoked and fondled handguns, occasionally swatting away some of the insects. Tiny lizards clung to the outside walls of the home, unmoving, seemingly unalive until one of them lifted a foot or changed position.

The mosquitoes paid attention to Bill. People did not. Everyone except Aris ignored him—that one sees everything, though, Bill surmised. When Aris went back to watching the card game, Bill ducked under the arch and went into the dark street.

It was nicer in the breeze.

There were only three places in the town with any light shining onto the street, the Lapez residence, the Justo residence and the town hall had lights for the basketball court. Each house had its own inner light and gave off just enough illumination for him to keep track of his stroll.

Dead on the street, yet the town was alive. As Bill passed the houses, he was met with Euro pop, bad and good singing on karaoke machines, the cheesy music that accompanied dramatic scenes on evening soap operas. There was also the evidence that this was as much a Western nation as Eastern, hearing dialog from a Rambo movie, the theme song to Baywatch, announcers commentating on the Detroit Pistons. Stone Cold Steve Austin just did something amazing.

Bill wished he was able to come to Calamba a few months ago during his first visit to the Philippines to experience Joy's hometown under happier circumstances. This was not the tourist trap beach resort with its own knockoff version of American fast food restaurants. This was like staying on your uncle's farm. Everywhere smelled like trees and dirt and animals.

Bill noticed he was taking the path through the town that eventually led around the church to a wide wooden bridge that crossed the slow moving river. He leaned on a rough sawn rail. The river trickled under him. Roosters called after each other.

Bill turned Thomas over and over in his head and found no thread to lead to a solution. Women holding secrets about mysterious men drew butterflies into his stomach, the same sensation that ate at him before he found out his ex-wife had a new lover.

Lost in thought, Bill never noticed the other man step onto the bridge.

Moving so slowly.

So quietly.

Holding a black baton.

< <> >

Bill was only acutely aware of two things. The back of his head hurt. And wherever he was, it was loud.

Everything else was fuzzy.

He found it difficult to breathe through the cloth that pressed his tongue to the roof of his mouth and seemed to fill every gap. His legs did not move. His hands were bound together and where one went, the other followed.

The men in the distance yelled. Or was it cheered? It was like the sound of a bar at closing time. Drunk men cheering something. The foreign words went by too fast. There was a flicking sound. Cards!

But this wasn't the Lapez house. And those weren't his men playing cards.

It was Lino Justo standing over him. Smiling. The kind of smile you see in movies. The one by the villain at a time of victory.

"Head hurt, eh, *kano*?" he said, tapping the side of Bill's head with his shoe.

Bill grimaced, but did not try to answer through the gag.

"Ringor, you have redeemed your previous failure with this find," Justo said to a man holding a black baton. "A better blackmail than Lopito would have been."

He clapped Ringor on the shoulder and for once the stone faced Ringor smiled.

Justo knelt near Bill and patted his chest.

"I just may win this election now. And all you need to do to help me, *puraw*, is lounge on a floor for a week. Lapez may not have dropped out of the race to win back a brother. But for his *kano* son-in-law ..." He trailed off into laughter, matched by the rest of the room.

Bill wasn't laughing. He was a prisoner of this political war between two stubborn, corrupt men who desperately wanted to be the biggest fish in this small pond.

Papa Justo barked orders and then stood out of the way as some of his men picked Bill off the floor and sat him in a chair at the card table. His head swam in pain to be moved so forcefully.

A bodyguard grabbed an antiquated instant camera and began to photograph the bound and helpless American husband of Marino Lapez's only daughter.

Joy will cry worse than ever now, Bill thought. Her brother is dead and now this. Dammit, where was his head? Two small militia armies vying against each other and he had to go off wandering in the night.

"Have they even set off to find him?" Justo asked his immediate lieutenant.

"No, they seem to be focused on Joy grieving over Thomas," Ringor replied in Ilocano. Bill only caught the "no" and "Joy" and "Toe-mas" in the conversation.

"Karma is on my side. I thought Thomas' death was the worse thing to happen in this campaign, although there are a lot of people who now hate me for the death of that beloved boy. Instead, it turns into the circumstances that lands us the biggest prize save one of Lapez's own children," Justo said. "Rough him up! Break his nose or something. I want blood in the pictures to make Lapez nervous."

Joy saw Aris return from the search and hand an envelope to Marino. She strained through the open kitchen window to catch their conversation. She hissed at Ricky to be quiet. The guards had been gone for more than an hour to find Bill.

Joy awakened before dawn and noticed him missing. Her first thought was that he'd taken his morning walk. When the darkness lifted and he hadn't returned, she became worried. She inquired of the guards and was told that Bill left the compound last night. Aris received the hardest slap across the face. She knew he took the blow only because Marino was standing behind her, but he deserved it—and not just for letting her husband walk away into the night.

Unable to catch the conversation, Joy drifted out of the house and inched her way toward Marino, who was red-faced after reading the note.

"Who gave this to you?"

"Pedro Botalico."

A grave expression washed over Marino's face. "They killed Thomas and now they have the *kano*."

"We spotted Pedro working with Ringor. I think Papa Justo has the *kano*, not the NPA."

"The sons of the NPA work for Justo, so the NPA wants Justo. Even after my gesture to them, all that land, they still side with Papa."

"He could be anywhere then," Aris mused. "Justo might have him in his house or over at the mill. One of the Botalicos could have him in a house."

"And I no longer have favor in Pingaping," Marino said. It seemed the Botalicos took the land and then remained loyal to Justo.

"Maybe he's under guard in one of the NPA's caves."

"Hundreds of them," Marino lamented.

"Albio…"

"Won't be able to get the manpower he needs. The governor wants Justo to win. He isn't going to release a cadre of police to comb the countryside to help me. Besides, having the police or the army running around here will shut you down trying to thwart Papa Justo."

"Did you see the pictures?"

Marino nodded.

"Were there arrangements for my answer?"

"Yes."

"Then tell Pedro I don't accept the terms. I don't. I won't."

"What?" Joy's shrill reaction snapped around Marino's head. "You are going to let them keep him? You greedy bastard, you won't pay a ransom!"

"The ransom isn't money."

"I don't care. Land, jewels, a car, a house. I don't care what they want, give it to them to free Bill."

"Papa Justo and the Botalicos don't want any of that. The price for the *kano* is unacceptable. I'm not going to resign as mayor, promote Justo and then pull out of the election. The feud is being decided now and Justo thinks he has something to move me. I call this desperation. I'm going to do now what I would have done even if he captured Lopito. We don't sway. We keep up our defenses."

"What if they kill Bill?"

"I wouldn't have this problem if you had just stayed in Chicago," Marino snapped.

"Oh, so this is my fault? Aris is the one who watched him walk away and didn't think to go look for him after an hour."

"I'm not going to give up so close to the end. Justo is desperate."

"Desperate enough to kill," Joy pointed out. "They already killed Thomas. Now you want to let Bill die too? How many men do I need to sacrifice to keep you rich and powerful?"

"The ransom is too steep. Complete defeat is the price for the *kano*. It is an unacceptable bottom line. I have to be strong. I must defy Justo. Financial ruin…"

"Ruin? How long do you think you'll survive without my money?" she seethed. "I want him back."

"Get back inside the house," Marino ordered.

Joy stood her ground. The forgiveness she reluctantly admitted only weeks ago in Chicago eroded. "I won't shoulder all the blame for this. If you had kept Thomas alive, I wouldn't have come back. I agreed to do this because everyone promised me—Promised! Promised!—that Thomas would be cared for. You promised me that you'd treat him like a member of this family. You promised me that you would protect him. Instead, you took away everything he had left, alienated him and then sent a target to his house."

"I told you already that I thought Lopito would be safe there for a few days before moving on to Manila. The Wagner house became an isolated spot and I thought no one would see Lopito travel there. I knew Thomas would accept Lopito and help him."

"Bullshit!"

It was the only English word in the fray, but its impact was felt immediately.

"I'm not a silly, foolish girl. I'm a world traveler. I've been around these political games long enough to know that Thomas was watched by Justo's men. Thomas was already a political target, remember? He would suffer the same as us if you lost, remember? You used that fear to twist me into accepting this marriage plot with Bill. You broke your promise to me. You sent Lopito to hide out with a defenseless man. Aris has weapons! He has guns and knives. The rest of these idiots that I paid for have guns and knives. Thomas didn't have weapons. He had a tractor and a friendly dog. You killed him the same as those arsonists."

"Be careful with your tone to me. I'm your father and I'll remind you of that harshly no matter your age."

Marino turned to face Joy. He was coiling. She noticed it. The Joy of the past would have backed away to avoid the lash of anger. Words would have gone unsaid. She was not going to swallow them any more and let him rot her stomach.

Her mind picked the first on the list, the top complaint, one that was sure to uncoil the spring. No alcohol required.

"When have you ever been a father?"

Marino's hand was swift, brushing harshly across her face. Even Aris was fazed and backstepped. Joy had been prepared for the blow and did not cry out. Rowena whelped though, crying out "*anak*" from the kitchen window.

Joy's cheek stung. She willed her hands to stay at her sides. She did not touch it. She opened her eyes and accepted the pain.

"Do it again!"

Marino cocked his arm to strike again.

"Yes, come on. Hit me again," Joy challenged. "Do it in front of everyone. Hit me again."

His hand froze mid strike.

"Don't just slap me. Punch me here again." Joy pulled down the collar of her T-shirt. The bruise was long gone, but not its memory. "Pop me in the eye. Grab some nails. I'm not going to run away and hide and let you get away with it anymore."

Her piercing stare into Marino's eyes told him she knew she had been betrayed.

"I did this for you. Where's my thanks? You bullied me into doing this and now there's no appreciation? When there was a paycheck in my hand, you were so proud of me, but now that I'm here to demand answers, I'm a problem, I'm a disappointment again."

Marino lowered his hand.

"Despite everything you've done to me, I still did this for you. I made a sacrifice to keep you all safe. And it was for nothing, wasn't it? I lied and kept secrets for nothing. You can't even bring yourself to say thank you. I broke my promise to the love of my life for nothing. He's dead and this was all for nothing."

"If you get hysterical, I'll slap you again," Marino warned.

"Go ahead. I'm not intimidated by it. I went through it before. I can endure it again."

"Child, child, what are you doing?" Rowena trotted up to Joy's back and pulled her at the arm since Marino was coiling again.

"How long would you have lasted without my money?"

"Take her inside the house," Marino bellowed to Rowena. "And make sure she stays there."

"They work for me, not for you." Joy gestured to the throng of slack jawed guards. "I want Bill back."

It was Rowena's insistence, not Joy's willingness, that forced the retreat. Ricky was in as much awe as the rest of the compound.

"Ricky, go back to your room," Rowena said, pleasantly, as though he really didn't just see his father and sister combating.

"No, let him listen," Joy railed. "He needs to see his father for who he really is. He's old enough to understand. Let him learn. Let him see. Why protect him from the truth?"

Ricky shrank into the rattan couch.

"Leave Ricky out of this," Rowena said. "Don't let your anger over your father spill over onto him. Your father struck you because you were disrespectful. You shouldn't anger him like that. He's on edge enough as it is with the election."

"He's going to let Bill die. He isn't going to make a counter offer. He isn't going to try to pay off Papa Justo to get Bill back."

"He's doing what he thinks it right. Lopito is missing, he has to rely on his own wits."

"You're going to defend him again aren't you?" Joy threw up her hands.

"Yes, I am. The *kano* will be fine. Papa Justo has never been a cruel person. He is God fearing…"

"His name is Bill, mother. He's a person, not a thing. He has a brother and nephews. He eats thick hamburgers with extra pickles. He likes professional football. He designs hospital buildings. Don't call him *kano* like he's a thing."

Joy stomped down the hall to her room and emerged with her bags.

"No one is going to help me now. I'll do it myself. I'll get Bill back myself. The Justo house is just down the road. I have my purse, I'll write him a personal check."

Rowena was sent into a tizzy again. "Your father won't let you leave."

"Why not? He let Bill leave." Joy rummaged through the bag and produced a small oblong book.

"And if Papa Justo holds you for ransom too?" Rowena was now fearful.

"I'm not going to be a hostage, *nanang*. Even Papa Justo knows that I'm worthless to Marino."

"Sit down, Joy."

"I'm not going to sit in here for days and wait for them to kill Bill."

"*Anak*, calm down. Please. I know you're upset over Thomas … and now Bill. Trust that your father knows what he's doing. He's upset about it too. He doesn't want to see people get hurt or die."

"You *are* going to defend him again." Joy finally touched the tender spot on her cheek. "I don't deserve this. I'm *not* going to defend him anymore. I'm *not* going to cover up the bruises and go on like they never happened. I'm *not* going to shut up and sit in my room like a good little girl. And how dare you defend Marino to me. He just beat me up again in front of you. Can't you stand up to him? No, it is just like the old days. While he was beating us up, you were too busy ignoring the problem, hoping it would just go away."

"Don't turn your anger toward me," Rowena warned. "I handled it the only way I knew how. I did the best I could. You weren't the only one that suffered."

"Did your best? You never stood up to him. Ted got him to stop drinking, not you. Ted found out that Thomas was raiding his old military medical supplies to mend my wounds. Then Ted became concerned that his little boy was trying to become a surgeon to care for his beloved *ading*. Ted confronted Marino, not you. Ted got Marino to stop hitting us, not you."

"I have scars too Joy. I have real ones, from knives and cigar butts, so don't show me a red cheek and expect me to coddle you."

Joy knew the wounds. That's why Rowena never wore shirts that were revealing to her back and shoulders.

"I took the worst of it all, so that you wouldn't. And when it comes to Ted, that man was part of the problem. He and Marino drank with one another constantly. Ted confronted Marino when it got bad, but he didn't fix

Marino, he just gave him a different obsession. I was the one that held Marino's hands when he got over his alcoholism, not Ted. I took his confessions of remorse, not Ted."

Rowena stopped her finger pointing to tell Joy that Marino had gotten her out of Calamba and to a life in America, by the way. And that was supposed to make her feel grateful? She lowered herself to his level. She lied and cheated her way to Chicago.

"You're blind, mother. He didn't do that for me, he did it for himself."

Joy swung her purse over her shoulder.

"I defend him because that is my duty. I obey my vows. I told God through better or worse. Marriage is until death do us part. I know where his heart is. He wants to be successful to give you and Ricky a good future. And you're just like him. You get obsessive. I dealt with him the way I dealt with you, wait until it is out of your system. Marino with his drinking, then womanizing, then politics. You with your skin and your nose and Thomas and America."

The anger that she'd released at Marino swelled inside her again. Thomas was no obsession. He was no passing fancy like boy bands with T-shirts and posters.

"You should know better than to talk about Thomas like that to me. He raised me. He raised me more than him." Joy gestured to Marino. "I took away the innocence and happiness of Thomas' childhood to make him my protector. I followed him everywhere. I smothered him and bound him to me, no different than what you did with Auntie Emma. Emma was your shield against Marino. I made Thomas my shield. He was only a little boy, yet he did it anyway. He defended me, he mended me, he taught me. Thomas' fingerprints are all over my soul. So you can stop telling me that Marino is such a good father."

Her parents had lied to her to keep her mind at ease so that she would remain in Chicago. If she was worried enough about Thomas' well-being, she would have ended the charade with Bill too early. Marino would have missed some big paydays.

She shocked her mother again with her mouth. "Thank God he's dead. At least his suffering is over."

Joy knew her mother had lied to her as much as Marino had. Thomas had not been fine, he had not returned to college, he had not accepted the plot and was not dealing with it as best as it could hoped to be.

Rowena wrung her hands into her dress. "I did take care of him while you were gone. He's was as much my son as you were Emma's daughter."

There wasn't time to confront her mother. If that was true then why did she let him live in squalor for months?

Outside, Joy saw Marino giving orders to the men. Aris wasn't in sight, probably on his way to deliver the message to Justo's man. Pedro Botalico.

She didn't know the man. Joy heard Marino barking that no one was to enter or leave the compound without his permission or knowledge. Then he left himself, in the direction of the municipal hall, with Fernando and several others in tow. To get Albio? He wasn't going to arrest anyone and put them in the municipal jail. If he wasn't such a spineless police chief, he would have arrested someone for Thomas' murder.

She saw her chance to leave the compound and confront Papa Justo herself.

"Oh, Lord, help me get Bill out of there so we can go home and never come back."

Bill laid in his corner, back to the wall, unable to sleep, barely able to breathe through the crusted blood in his nose. He watched his guard slumbering in the dimly lit room that now smelled of urine and alcohol vomit.

It was the second night here.

The second photo shoot depicted them slugging fists into his abdomen. The bloody nose must not have been enough for Lapez to succumb to Justo's demands. Bill was scared that his father-in-law wouldn't bend. What then would be the next escalation of violence to be photographed?

There were too many more days before the election day. More thirst. More starvation. More beatings. Ringor hit the hardest. He was the meanest of the group.

Things were rustling outside. He could hear them through the mortar climbing the walls. Something fumbled with the window and it slid up. Then nothing came inside. Bill turned his head to the window above him and waited, but nothing came inside.

Then there was a bare foot creeping through. Then a leg. Then the second leg. The man sat on the ledge, and slowly moved a thick stick fashioned into a make-shift cane.

His skin was dark. Clothes were tattered and dirty. Bill did not see a face because of the lighting.

The figure dropped to the floor and slowly limped over to the guard with the aid of the cane. There was some wood lashed around the bum leg.

It wasn't one of Lapez's men, Bill knew. Someone was trying to rescue him, he hoped. He seemed to be a disheveled old man with a walking stick. Perhaps it was a bold robbery.

The old man patted the guard on the shoulder and said something to him in Ilocano. "Pedro? Pedro?"

No movement.

The hermit carefully adjusted Pedro so that his head no longer rested on the table, but hung back across the chair top. Tongue hanging out. A snore. Then the guard started to stir.

The hermit reached for the shotgun sitting on the table, but grabbed it by the open end, not the stock. He swung himself around, crashing the butt of the gun sharply into the Pedro's jaw. There was the thud of the body to the concrete floor. Then there was the thud of the broken weapon onto the table.

The blow was sharp. Bill didn't wonder how many teeth Pedro lost, he wondered whether he was still alive.

The disheveled man shuffled his way over to Bill and produced a knife out of nowhere. He cut the bonds, removed the cloth from Bill's mouth and offered a hand to help Bill to his feet.

The hermit had a strong grip for being so old. Steadied with the carved up branch cane, he was able to help Bill to stand.

Up close, Bill saw a dark face, a young face. It wasn't wrinkled and old, just dirty.

"Who are you?" Bill asked, his voice cracked, dry and unused for two days.

In the whisper, Bill heard, "Toe-mas Wag-nur."

Bill woke in a place not much more pleasant than the other two mornings, but at least he wasn't bound and gagged with guards pissing on his head to awaken him. His head rested on a mound of rags that smelled of armpit. His body was prone on a dirt floor. He rolled over and saw a backdrop of sky, trees and a steeple through a hole in the roof. From the sounds—or lack of them—he knew he was no longer in Calamba. Even from within Justo's building, he was able to hear some sounds of civilization. Here, there were no roosters, no engines, no radios. There was only the rustling of wind through trees and an occasional bird.

The night had been a blur. With the aid of a chair, the person claiming to be Thomas Wagner helped him out of Justo's room through the window. He had been weaker than he thought and almost impaled himself on a metal fence post. Calamba was asleep and quiet. Still, Bill was terrified that the sound of his own footsteps would draw the attention of Justo's bodyguards. He was too happy to be free and too tired to argue with the direction that Thomas was leading him. Bill recalled falling into a small boat when they reached the river. He lifted some of the water to his face and mouth as Thomas paddled them downstream. At some point in the journey, he passed out, not remembering how he was moved from the boat to his position on the floor of an abandoned church.

Two trees had smashed the side of the church and had evidently not moved since their toppling crumbled the block and mortar. There was another makeshift bed beside the trees, under a tent of mosquito netting. Sitting there was the hermit, chopping mangoes into pieces with a long machete that Joy had called a bolo. Bill's movement caused notice that he had roused from sleep. There was the limited movement in the hermit's right leg. The foot wasn't aligned straight. It bent inward at nearly a right angle. The foot was also discolored.

The hobbling ended near Bill and the Thomas hermit sat down in a much smoother motion than it took to stand. The deformed man deposited the slab of wood holding the fruit chunks. He pointed with his lips to the mangoes. Breakfast, evidently. They were yellow, ripe, and sweet.

"There are wounds on your wrists," Thomas noticed. "And your face."

The accent was distinctly Filipino, but he spoke perfect English. There were no broken, out-of-place words as was the case with Joy.

"Full of dirt. Don't go anywhere."

Thomas labored to stand and hobbled to a tall earthen jar filled with water. The young man returned and dabbed at Bill's face with a damp cloth that smelled of mildew.

"Don't worry. I'm an expert with cuts and bruises," Thomas sighed. "Sorry, no ice, though, for the swelling."

In better light, Bill was able to recognize the sun-darkened man as the boy in the pictures in Joy's room. The young man more resembled the Hawaiian surfers he'd seen on late night sports cable network shows than the Filipino men he'd encountered so far.

"Where are we?" Bill was barely able to choke out the question.

Thomas snorted. "That's probably not the most pressing question you want to ask me, but that's okay. We have time."

There was truth to his comment. Bill had many questions. How was a dead man walking and otherwise acting alive? Bill wanted to know when they were going back to town. Back to its safety. Back to Joy. Back behind a wall of gunmen to prevent him from becoming a hostage again. He was scared and paranoid enough that he thought even crossed his mind that he might still be a hostage.

"We are in the old Catholic church. You are an architect, so you will enjoy the nice Spanish architecture when you have a chance to see it from the outside. Destroyed and abandoned before I was born. I don't know why, something about the rebels probably. They did not rebuild out here because town is closer and safer and people don't have to cross the river to get to it."

"Far from Calamba?"

"Yes. We're half way to Pingaping."

"Ping-aah-ping?"

"A barangay of Calamba," Thomas explained. "Part of Calamba, though it is really its own town. It even has more people than Calamba town, but they all have to follow the rule of Calamba's mayor and council."

Thomas grabbed a few mango slices for himself.

"We are safe here. No one else comes here. Furniture was moved or stolen a long time ago, so there are no fortune seekers. Kids come here to prove their bravery, since there is a cemetery full of ghosts behind the church. No one is walking alone into the mountains in these days."

A broken down church in the middle of nowhere didn't feel reassuring.

"Speaking of ghosts," Bill started. "If you're Thomas Wagner, then how is it that you're alive when I saw your name on a grave marker just days ago?"

Thomas stared at him. Perplexed.

"You didn't know you had a grave?"

Thomas shook his head. "I've been here hiding from Papa Justo's men."

Thomas was silent for a moment. Bill saw the information cycle through the hermit.

"So they assumed I was dead? That's why no one came to find me. It was a big fire. They probably asked themselves who could live through all of that? I almost didn't."

So the discolorations on his skin were burn marks.

"I saw the house. I'm surprised myself."

Thomas stopped smiling and cocked his head. "You saw a grave? Where? Did they bury me with my mother and father?"

Bill nodded, unaffected by the morbidity of the question.

After a moment, Thomas seemed annoyed by the answer. "Do you know anything about the fire? Anyone say anything about a grave for Marino's cousin, Lopito Lapez?"

Bill said he did see such a grave and Thomas' annoyance grew to anger.

"So they thought Lopito was me. They found his body in my house and thought it was me. They buried a goddamned Lapez next to my mother and father. Forgive me Lord for taking your name in vain." He crossed himself and looked back to where the altar must have been, though it was void of any Christian symbols. "A goddamned Lapez...!"

Bill kept his mouth shut, quietly watching and eating, letting the tirade flow from Thomas. By virtue of his rescue, Bill concluded Thomas wasn't on Justo's side. He assumed the lad was on Marino's side, but this behavior was causing some doubts on that front.

"You know what? Being dead suits me fine then," Thomas said when he was calmer. "If I'm already dead, no one is hunting me."

Bill could not keep himself from glancing at the leg, twisted near the ankle.

"Yes, it hurts," Thomas said, breaking Bill's stare.

Bill mumbled an apology and asked how he got the deformity.

"Ringor. Just before they shot Lopito and set fire to my house. I escaped the fire, dragged me and my broken leg down to the river and floated away. I didn't know where I was for most of the trip until I saw the church silhouette in the moonlight. I ended up hiding here by chance."

Ringor's baton had made a clean break, Thomas continued. It was a horrific experience for the first two weeks to move around without painkilling medicine.

"I tried to splint it, but it didn't heal straight. Still hurts, but not so bad."

"I've been hit by that baton. I can empathize with you," Bill said.

Thomas gave a half-hearted smile. "Honestly, Ringor saved my life by knocking me down. I think Nina had given him some orders regarding my protection. Those idiots with him were too gung-ho. Gung-ho, right? Yes, they were intent on shooting and burning. He was trying to knock me down and out of the way of a gunshot. Then I woke up to the fire..." Thomas trailed off, choked up by the memory.

Though it was juicy, Bill was having trouble swallowing the mango. Thomas acted the dutiful host and went to fetch water. Bill felt sorry that he was making the kid stand and sit. He dipped a cup that was really a coconut hull into the same jar of water he'd just rinsed a rag. Bill had traveled enough to be wary of the water. He was sure to contract gastrointestinal problems by drinking it, but thirst and dehydration were immediate problems. He took the cup in big swallows.

Thomas cleared his throat and pointed to a spot near Bill's eye. "You're bleeding again. I must have brushed a scab."

Thomas grabbed the rag again.

"You've got an easy touch," Bill said while Thomas tended to his face.

"I was on course to be a medical student when God decided I needed to be closer to him here."

When Thomas finished, he returned to the water jar.

"Where are my manners? We've been talking all this time and I haven't thanked you yet for rescuing me." Bill extended his hand to Thomas. The gesture of gratitude was accepted. "You know who I am, I take it?"

Thomas nodded. "You are lucky."

Was that a new nickname?

"Yes, lucky, but still confused. You know who I am, but I don't know who you are. Beyond your name, I mean. I know all of my wife's friends, Car-Car, Jon-Jon, Ronaldo and Reggie. I even know a few of the people she hates like that Nina you just mentioned. She never mentioned a Thomas Wagner. Yet, upon word of your death, she became desperate to fly back here to attend her brother's funeral."

"Back to *manong* Thomas are we?" he muttered, eliciting a blank look from Bill. "Looks like you both raced back here for nothing."

"So you're her brother?"

"You could say that. We were raised together."

"Are you saying you're not really a brother?"

"You don't have to be blood to be family here. Ricky calls me his big brother too. My mother was very close to Rowena. When she died, the Lapez adopted me ... for awhile at least."

"Sorry, if I come off the wrong way. Joy never gave me a straight answer about you. She cried all day long and was insistent that we come back here for the funeral to see for herself that you were dead. I didn't even know your name until I saw the grave marker. She kept crying about an *ayat* and ..." Bill butchered the pronunciation and missed a word, but Thomas knew he had just said "my first and only" in Ilocano.

"Both of those are my nicknames," Thomas explained, turning away from Bill to avoid having to further explain what they meant.

"When are we getting out of here? Back to the town? Your family would be relieved to find out that you're alive."

"Maybe one or two of them would be relieved," Thomas said. "But we're not going yet. You're not in shape to be moving. Calamba is at least a 25 minute walk for the quick and healthy."

"We got here by boat..."

"In daylight? Upstream? With kidnappers searching to get you back?"

That silenced Bill for the moment. He couldn't argue against that point.

With the mangoes gone, Bill found himself talking about unimportant things with Thomas. Something to fill the silence of the countryside. Bill talked about his work, about Chicago, about the traffic, about Joy learning to drive in the traffic, about Joy's job, about the White Sox, about the Bears, a lot about the Bears.

"You and my father wouldn't have gotten along," Thomas interrupted.

"Why is that?"

"What does a big white G with yellow and green mean to you? There's one painted on my front porch."

"Packers?" Bill smiled. "So your dad was from Wisconsin? I've noticed that you don't look completely Filipino. I know a few Wagners in Wisconsin. Milwaukee. Construction company that we've contracted in the past. Packers fans in the Philippines," he chuckled. "The hottest place on earth cheering for the coldest. They beat us twice this year. I guess that makes us rivals."

"Rivals," Thomas repeated. In more ways than one.

Bill confided that he didn't know what to do over the dilemma of Joy and college. She'd said something about accounting. That made Thomas snort.

"She should be in business. She has tools to be an entrepreneur. Her mind is unconventional ... but what is the slang for it?"

"Out of the box?"

"That's it. She needs to channel her ideas into more constructive purposes."

Bill nodded that it was a good idea.

"I've been talking all morning. Nervous energy, I guess. A little reflection, like when you're life passes before your eyes just before you die." Bill pushed himself to sit. "Tell me about yourself. Your wife. You're married right? I see your wedding ring."

Thomas turned his attention away from a carving up a coconut to the dull gold band. "I don't really want to talk about her," he said tentatively. "I was betrayed. She left me for another man."

"I know how that feels. My first wife dumped me for another man. That was ... oh, three years ago now. How long ago for you?"

"I found out about it five months ago. She and I ran to the church so fast to get married. No one was around to witness it. No chance for a dress or a party. She left right away to go overseas to support me. Did a very good job of keeping the affair a secret, a newfound talent I didn't know she had. The support suddenly stopped and she never came back."

Bill whistled. "The priest was right, you are a tragedy. No parents, house burned down, wife left you."

"I'm dead too, don't leave out that part."

"And you have the wits to joke about it."

"Will crying get any of that back?"

Bill spent the rest of the morning resting. Thomas spent the time being a guard, slipping outside to watch the river, the road on the other side of the river, the hills behind the church that became the mountains in the distance. He would sometimes beat off large snakes that slithered from high grasses.

The only food available seemed to be fruit Thomas was collecting from the surrounding trees. Coconut was for lunch. Thomas apologized for the menu, but it wasn't practical to fish, he had no way to start a cooking fire. Not to mention the danger of starting a fire would draw attention to himself.

Bill noticed periods where Thomas' hands shook. But the lad didn't seem to be the nervous type. Thomas grimaced and breathed heavily through gritted teeth. He was sweating, but so was Bill. Even the walls were perspiring. The shaking spells were short lived and Thomas continued with his routine.

Bill finally climbed to his feet when nature called. Outside, the landscape was sky, mountains and trees.

"There is civilization out there?"

"In the valleys," Thomas replied.

"I see a cell phone tower. Too bad I can't call for help."

Throughout the day, Bill had heard the sounds of jeepneys and tricycles traveling on a road somewhere across the river. It piqued his paranoia at first, but his fear subsided when he saw how unaffected Thomas was by the travelers.

So close to the equator, the time of sunset and sunrise did not waver much. It was dark at 7:30 here, always. As the dusk came, so did the din of insects and animals. There was a chorus of crickets out there. Bill soon discovered he was the favorite meal of mosquitoes. He hid underneath the mosquito netting that had been Thomas' bed.

"You want to take a bath? Should be fine to go outside now. Darkness is coming. Just hop in the river."

"Water snakes."

"I said hop in the river, not swim in it long enough for them to find you."

Bill took him up on the offer. Fully clothed, he tiptoed into the water. He had thought all day long that he was strong enough to travel until he hit the current and it knocked him off his feet. He laughed at himself, taking a page from Thomas' positive attitude. He crawled to shore and waited for Thomas to finish his more dignified entrance into the water.

Bill laid on the river bank and looked to the sky. Thomas sat beside him, running the excess water out of his longish hair.

"If your father was American, how come you never moved there?"

"He chose to live here because all the Wagners back home were already gone. I'm a U.S. citizen, so I could come and go as I please, but I've been too busy with school and survival. I don't know anyone there anyway. Where would I go? I suppose I have some distant cousins in Wisconsin, but everything I know and love is here."

"You could always come back to Chicago with Joy and I. It would do her good to have some family in the same hemisphere. Then later in October, I'll take you to a Packers-Bears game." Bill glanced up to see how the invitation was received. Dusk was causing some long shadows, but he could make out the smirk. "U of Chicago has a decent medical school. I know the president."

Thomas snorted.

"Why not? You don't have anything left here."

"Save your pity."

"It's not pity. Saving my life shouldn't go unrewarded."

"You shook my hand and said thank you."

"By the way, your hand is shaking again."

"Malaria."

Another snappy answer. There was something eating at Thomas and he wasn't going to let on what it was. It was like he wanted to say something but kept deciding against it.

Well, something had been eating at Bill all day. "You look familiar." And it was more than just pictures on a wall.

"People say I could be a double for a famous Filipino TV soap opera actor," Thomas quipped.

"No, that's not it." Bill snapped his fingers. "You were the one yelling for Joy at the airport?"

Thomas hesitated and then nodded.

"I didn't think anything of that moment until now. Joy was pretty spooked. She said she didn't know the person yelling her name. She yanked me down the corridor to get away. So it was only you. You two were close for so long, she could have at least said goodbye ..."

Something about remembering an incident five months ago triggered it. Five months. Overseas. Never came back. That wailing cry when she heard the answering machine message. It was too clear to be a coincidence. Bill closed his eyes when the epiphany's anguish overcame him.

Thomas glanced over as Bill curled up on the stones. "What? You got a stomach pain also?"

The rumbling of many large engines in the twilight was so out of the ordinary that even Thomas nervously raced back inside the church to look out a window that faced the river. Visible were only the lights piercing the darkness.

"Armored personnel carriers," Thomas said toward Bill, who was slower to move. "I got to ride in them during civilian army training. Word has gotten out about Calamba. Probably in the newspapers. Now the government is clamping down. The troops will set up in town until the election to keep the peace."

"That's good." Bill's sour demeanor quickly turned to elation.

Thomas pursed his lips.

"Not really. Let me explain," Thomas said as Bill arrived at the window to peek. "Candidates' goons are in Calamba now. Military shows up, so the goons leave. Calamba is now safe. But the goons are now out here with us. Goons with guns are now going to be camped out here. Could be bad out here in our direction near Pingaping, could be good out toward Pulot instead. But we don't know. We do know that the war has only moved location."

Bill's jaw dropped and he asked what the plan was to get back to town. "I assumed we were going to sneak back there soon, maybe tonight, in the boat, now that I've recovered some strength."

Thomas regarded him as though he were crazy.

"Did you hear what I said? A bunch of trigger happy men who think they are the next Fernando Poe action movie star are going to be wandering around the countryside."

"We can make it to the troops then. They'll protect us and drive us into town," Bill suggested.

"Too late for that. You going to swim over there and run down the road to catch up?"

"The boat..."

"Okay, Mister Muscles. Calamba is upstream and you've been so full of energy that you slept most of the day."

Exasperated, Bill threw up his hands. "How long are we going to stay here? We have to get back to Calamba. We have to let the mayor know we're still alive. I need to see Joy."

Bill shuffled for a side door to leave. He mumbled to himself that it wouldn't be difficult to creep back up the river to Calamba now that it was dark. It was safe in the town now.

Thomas hissed at him to stop.

"Come on," Bill urged. "We don't have to race to catch up to the Army. You snuck into town last night with the boat. You can do it again."

Thomas spat at him in Ilocano. Bill understood *gago* and *bagtit*. Stupid and crazy.

"Do you know what you're talking yourself into? Don't you have any common sense? Why do you think I didn't take you straight to the Lapez house as soon as I got you out of Papa Justo's mill?"

Bill stopped halfway in the doorless entry. He wanted that answer.

"As scared as you are of Ringor, you should be twice as scared of Aris. He hates Americans and would kill you himself if he is in the right mood for it."

"I'm Marino's son-in-law, he isn't going to let Aris kill me. And Joy…"

"…is safe," Thomas finished. "You're not. And stop thinking that Marino is your friend. He is as much the enemy as Papa Justo. You're a liability to him now. How many days did he let Justo beat you up? He has you as a son-in-law, right? He should have plenty of money for a ransom payment right?"

"You're only saying this because you don't like him."

"You've known him for a few months. He is my godfather. I've known him all of my life. He is a misogynist greedy egomaniac," he told Bill forcefully, stifling any more protests. "I saved your life once already. If you want to keep living and ever see Joy again, you will do whatever I say and do it without question! I know it is not pleasant to be cooped up out here with me, but I'm the only person keeping her from becoming a widow."

Bill shrunk under the weight of Thomas' verbal bludgeoning.

"You are in the Wild West, cowboy. There is a big difference between me sneaking into town in that boat than trying it with the both of us. I can get *me* out of any situation because this is my home. I know everyone. What if *we* get caught? There's no disguise around here. You're not fooling anyone. The first farm hand we meet might be a Justo supporter and would recapture you himself in the hopes that Justo will pay him some favors later."

Thomas gestured for Bill to leave if he wanted to go. But Bill didn't move.

"John Wayne did some incredible things, but at least he had a gun."

The rumble of military vehicles died down and the church was again filled only with the sounds of insects, trickling water and small things running through the underbrush outside.

"I'm not going to get killed on the way home because you're too weak and clumsy to move."

When Bill had calmed down, he sat beside Thomas and shook his head, astonished that such a small town would boil over into such violence.

It was an old fight that was never settled until now.

"We're not all a bunch of savages in this province," Thomas said. "A year from now, once all the election fever is gone, you could knock on any door in town and become their honored guest. They'd go out of their way to impress you with a feast of roast pig and *pancit, sinagang, adobo*. They will drink beer with you and sing karaoke. We Filipinos are a warm people, solid in Christian beliefs. Unfortunately, the combination of ignorance, poverty and politics makes some of us crazy."

"I hope I don't have to live in this rundown church for a year to see it."

"A joke. See, you're getting better."

"Are we going to get out of here?"

"Yes. Smartly. Patiently." Thomas said with confidence.

Bill watched Thomas stand, hobble to the water for a drink, hobble to the other end of the church, in and out of the moonlight. The humidity was as heavy as his confusion.

Bill imagined walking down Calamba's main road, with Thomas leaning on his walking stick beside him, Joy running out of her house and into his own arms. He wanted to believe that's what would happen.

Was Joy desperate to come home to see the grave of a brotherly figure? Or was Joy desperate to come home to see if her first husband was really dead? If Joy was the wife that abandoned Thomas, she had done a good job of concealing her past. There was no hint of someone else. Bill didn't want to ask Thomas point blank.

Bill went over to the water vase and wiped his face with a wet hand. Mosquitoes started to find him. The slaps echoed.

"There's room for two under the mosquito netting," came Thomas' invitation.

When there wasn't an immediate answer, Thomas continued, "Fine. But don't expect me to help you get well from malaria."

CHAPTER 20

The compound was empty when Joy emerged from the house. Everyone seemed to be in the street admiring armored vehicles and uniformed men.

Joy dipped her feet into her *sapatos* and strode toward the street, coffee mug in tow.

Aris was standing just outside the arch. The mayor was meeting with the captain of the army attachment, he told her.

"Where is everyone?" Joy asked, gesturing to the empty compound.

"Hiding from the military. No guns allowed in town. Mayor Lapez wants no trouble with the captain," Aris answered. Yet Joy noticed his knife clipped at his belt.

"Hiding where?" Joy asked, taking sips of coffee.

Aris seemed reluctant to talk. Joy asked again.

"You won't like the answer," Aris said, again not answering the question.

His evasiveness won him an exasperated sigh. Aris chewed on the butt of his fully smoked cigarette and saw she wasn't going to stop staring without an answer. "Mr. Lapez sent them to stash weapons at the Wagner house."

Joy didn't like the answer, but she swallowed hard and said nothing.

Joy gestured with her chin down the street toward the town hall. "You're not with father?"

"New orders," Aris replied, pointing his finger at Joy. "Your actions yesterday worried Mr. Lapez and he wants you watched and safe. I can keep up with you if you start having more ideas of walking over to the opposition."

Shadow with her own shadow. It was worse that her shadow was going to be Aris. He always made her uneasy. It was the way he watched her. Seemingly undressing her with his eyes. And now he would be able to do it all day long.

Aris spit out the cigarette butt.

"I can get your *kano* husband back," he said slyly. "Justo's compound is as empty as ours. Maybe he is there. Maybe one or two guards there. Church is tomorrow, so Papa Justo and his family, and Ringor, will all be gone for a time."

Joy made a rude noise. "And people have the nerve to talk about my notions. Who's going to guard us if you go over there and get yourself killed? Anyone competent among that band of goons?"

Joy secretly wished he would go over there and get himself killed tomorrow.

"Yes, pretty big risk for me. Reward should be just as big," Aris felt Joy's sleeve. "Maybe I should get a down payment."

Joy slapped the hand away. "You're lucky father isn't here, you snake. I'll not give you my body in exchange for a rescue attempt."

"Well, if I die trying, I die satisfied."

Aris caught her arms before her blows landed.

"Why not, Joy? Don't you think I'm as good as your *kano* lovers? Filipino not good for you? Maybe if I put powder on my skin to look whiter then I'll be more attractive to you."

Joy tried to yank her arms from his grip without success.

"There are no secrets in Calamba. People here know why you went to the States. You have a car now. You have a big house in the world famous Chicago. All you needed to do to get it all was smile and open your legs to an old man *kano*," Aris continued.

Joy's mind swam with fright and anger. Anger at the suggestion she was a dirty whore like his sisters. Fright at what the stronger Aris might do to her with everyone gone to the town hall. Aris had always been lecherous, but Joy never thought him capable of rape until now.

"I am not a dirty prostitute!" Joy screeched—loud enough, hopefully, to attract some help. "I love my husband!"

"Oh, really? Which one?"

The question froze Joy.

"You are not so clean. You cheated on Thomas. You sneaked away to Singapore to hide your quest to find another man. This other man made you a rich woman. What's it to you to cheat on this rich, white man? Maybe it will save his life and you can stay a rich Filipina in America."

"Never. You have been a goddamn bastard your whole life. I'd rather shove Ringor's baton up my *okie* than to feel you there."

Aris released her arms rough enough to upset her balance and force her to the ground.

"Your choice to let your husband die," he sneered. "Mr. Lapez is not going to pay Justo's ransom. Papa Justo may get desperate and order death if Mr. Lapez doesn't give up the election."

Joy returned to her feet and rubbed feeling back into her forearms. Aris gestured for her to go back inside the compound and she complied. He just stood there again at the entrance and started his next cigarette.

Joy could not dispute how things appeared to Aris, and evidently the town. The phrase cheated on Thomas burned in her head.

"I'm not Bill's concubine. I love him," she whispered to herself.

Yet she could not lie to herself. Married only these few months, her love for Bill did not approach the feelings she once had for Thomas. With him dead, it didn't matter which loved her the most. She was aware the death freed her of the burden of having to choose between the two men once this scheme reached its conclusion.

"I could have said no," she said softly. "I could have stayed faithful to Thomas. I could have spared him so much anguish in the last months of his life. I could have ..." her voice faltered. Died in that fire too.

Joy recalled the scene as if it were yesterday, being told by Marino that she was the family's only hope of survival. Losing to Justo would have preceded ruin. The family would have to flee Calamba. Flee from Justo's men in pursuit. No more home. No more money. No more future. Even she and Thomas would have been ruined in the aftermath, he told her. The money of a housemaid's salary wasn't going to be enough, father complained. It wasn't this violent seven years ago. Money wasn't this crucial. That's when he told her that her Singaporean maid's salary would not be enough. "Find a rich man, Joy," Marino had said. "A man who will think nothing of helping a poor Filipina's family back home. Make it a *kano* or Australian. Or make it a rich Chinese, it doesn't matter."

Joy left the memory and returned her attention to Aris' frame standing just inside the gate.

Sipping her coffee, she decided her new life wasn't going to go wasted. There was a chance to get mother and Ricky away from Marino. Two years and then a green card. Another year after that and she would be able to file for American citizenship. As a citizen, she could petition her mother and brother as immigrants. Marino would have his power, his mistress, his houses. Everyone else would be safe.

It wasn't possible if Bill died.

And only Aris had the plan and the means to get Bill out of there.

< <> >

Bill Vandemark wasn't sleeping on the other side of the church when Thomas awoke with the first rays of dawn.

He fought the urge to curse aloud and began scanning the immediate vicinity. He better be pissing out there in those trees.

He saw no one and heard no movement.

In a patch of dirt where Bill had been sleeping he spotted some handwriting. Inscribed in the dirt, likely by a stick, was "I can't wait 2 more days."

The election was in two days. Thomas suggested they might be the safest if they waited until the morning of election day to return to Calamba. Security would be the thickest then. There would be more squads of soldiers rolling through the province, not to mention the dozens of federal elections overseers.

"Stupid. Impatient," Thomas mumbled and climbed to his feet. He tied the brace branches to his leg.

The boat was still in its hiding spot. Bill was going to walk it then, probably along the river. He wouldn't know any other way to get back.

Thomas knew he wouldn't catch up. Bill would be slow, scared and cautious, but still had two good legs, long legs, to carry him along the shore. Thomas pulled the flat boat into the river, close to the shore and crept upstream.

The beads of sweat on his forehead had begun their move down into his eyes. He took off his shirt and wrapped it around his head. He paused often to catch his breath, holding on to a low tree limb or paddle jammed into the muck to hold his position. Daily subsistence over the last weeks was primarily fruit from wild trees, bananas, mangos and coconuts. He was happy it wasn't the rainy season with a raging river and rapids to deal with. He was 15 minutes or more away from the church and had no luck. He was also pleased that he'd not seen anyone else either.

He was tired of looking for Bill. He looked for the redhead and Joy for nearly two days at the airport and now he was stuck searching for him in the mountains.

He was just as eager to see Joy again, but he'd no idea of how to handle it. Bill thought he was Joy's brother. As much as he wanted to fly to Chicago and ruin the plan, he didn't have the strength to spill everything to Bill yesterday. It seemed Joy was no longer on a mission to satisfy her father's greed. She had a life there. Friends. Driving. A job. A husband. Perhaps something that should be preserved.

There were no voices, no rustling underbrush, no cracking of limbs. No white face peeking out from the trees, no red hair dancing in the distance.

Thomas knew another few minutes of paddling and he would start to see houses and nipa huts in rice fields. Up further would be the big bridge. Around a bend would be the rope bridge. Then the screen of trees obscuring his house.

Perhaps Bill made it.

He stopped the boat suddenly when he encountered yelling. He spotted the back of a soaking wet man crouched near a tree. Thomas quietly parked the boat, hugged the nearest tree and observed the huddled Filipino. He didn't recognize him. Was he Lapez? Justo? Someone else's bodyguard?

The man turned, changing the view from the back of his head into a profile. Fernando Cabasan? One of Marino's workers. He clutched at a handgun resting on his knee.

Thomas parked the boat on the river bank and crept slowly on foot. Following Fernando's gaze, Thomas saw others in drab clothing hiding down the river. All were watching something off to the left.

Thomas wondered if he had stumbled onto an ambush attempt. The yelling was mysterious. The other group had found something, but it didn't seem to be this squad of bodyguards.

Bill.

Thomas' heart raced and it took force of will to move slowly toward the yells. From tree to tree, Thomas slid to the left until he could see down the incline to a clearing. Bill was surrounded by men armed with handguns and M16s.

Bill looked scared, hunched down in preparation to dodge any shooting, though few of the men were pointing their weapons at the American. Regardless of who they were, Bill wasn't interested in surrendering.

One of the men approached Bill, tapping a black baton into the palm of the opposite hand.

Thomas closed his eyes and cursed.

"Stand up, *kano*," he heard Ringor order.

Bill shook his head in defiance. "I'm not going back with you! I'd rather die than go back with you!"

Bill was scared, a trapped animal not knowing what else to say.

Thomas assessed the odds. At best, Bill would become a hostage again. This time beaten longer and harder than he'd been previously. At worst, they would just kill him now and dangle the carcass from a nearby tree as a symbol of what happens to the defiant.

"Killing you won't be so hard," Ringor said. "Lapez don't have to know you are dead until after he steps down. Couple of pictures and a note saying we got you back and the mayor will give up. Did you know your wife came to Papa's house to demand your release? She offered money of her own for you. We kicked her out."

Ringor stopped his approach at arm's length.

"If money is what you want, then I can add some of my own," Bill pleaded.

"No amount of money from you or Joy is enough. The only terms for you is the mayor's surrender," Ringor said, kneeling to match eye level with Bill.

Pointing at Bill with his baton, Ringor told him he and his fellow bodyguards would likely die if they let him free for just money.

"But ... But ... Why? This is a little town. There's nothing here. The mountains are full of trees and wild animals, there's no gold there, no oil. What's so important about Calamba that people have got to die over a damn election?"

Bill was getting more frantic. There was no more time to dawdle. Thomas knew he had to act before Bill went to the last resort and tried to fight his way out of the trap.

Thomas wished he had time to make a plan. Outnumbered. No weapons. Possibly walking between an ambush.

The other group's intent was unknown, though Thomas assumed Marino would want Bill back as much as Papa Justo. He doesn't have to pay a ransom for a free man.

Gambling again, he thought. This time there's no eating balut or fish eyes if he lost.

Thomas said a prayer and limped down the incline toward the ring of Justo men. One of them turned at the sound of a heavy foot moving in their direction. It was Abel Botalico, with a machete in one hand and a handgun in the other. He blinked and shook his head in disbelief.

Thomas nodded and walked past Abel.

Ringor turned his head and his eyes grew wide.

"Haunted ground out here," Thomas said.

"Ghosts don't walk with canes," Ringor said. "How? We left you both bleeding on the floor."

"Not bloody enough," Thomas answered. He stopped close enough to form a triangle with Ringor and Bill. "Maybe I should break both of your legs like you did to my dog."

Ringor laughed. "Boasting while outnumbered? You're Jesus now, eh? Returning from the dead?" Ringor gestured to the rest of the guards to join him in laughter.

Thomas turned his head and looked in the direction of the hiding Fernando. He assessed the angle and took a step backward, all the while staring in the direction of Marino's men.

"Let me have him, Ringor," Abel said. "Maybe he's the one that broke Pedro's neck with the shotgun."

Thomas held in his verbal jabs. He was waiting for Fernando. He was hoping they would spring their ambush and help him out of this mess.

"No, Abel. Two hostages. Two reasons for Lapez to give up. Maybe we'll get a raise," Ringor laughed again. "We'll kill them both after Lapez loses the election. We'll get to have fun then, mopping up, making sure the Lapez family can't ever vie for power again."

Bill looked at Thomas and mouthed that he was sorry.

Ringor ordered Abel and the others to grab Thomas. Ringor reached for Bill's arm.

Thomas flipped up the tip of his staff and deflected Ringor's arm. Bill took advantage of the brief distraction to grab both of Ringor's wrists and begin to wrestle with the younger man.

Thomas lunged and slipped the baton out of Ringor's hand.

Instead of bludgeoning Ringor, Thomas spun on his good leg and brought the baton against the skull of the charging Abel. The blow bloodied his cousin and nearly sent him to the ground. Abel recovered, using an arm to stop his fall, and came back upright.

Subordinates aimed their weapons but were hesitant to shoot with Abel and Ringor locked in hand-to-hand combat.

It was then that Thomas heard the bullet whiz past his ear and make an impact with the other side of Abel's head. The recoil forced Abel's head backwards and sent him hurtling to the ground.

The ambush had started. A series of three-shot bursts erupted from the trees.

Thomas slid to his right, intending to tackle Bill and put him to the ground where it was safer, certain that bullets would soon be exchanged. He wasn't fast enough. A few bullets put Bill on the ground for him.

The firefight took less time than Thomas thought. Marino's men were not only able to hit Abel and Ringor, but a few of the others in the first salvo. Morale broke quickly. The remaining Justo men returned fire into the trees while they were backing up into cover of their own. Out of the corner of his eye, Thomas could see two of them in a dead sprint from the clearing.

Ringor was rolling on the ground nearby. Bill wasn't moving at all. Thomas did not have an angle of sight to see where Bill was wounded.

Seconds. It only took seconds.

"Keep shooting. Keep shooting. Make them run," came an order from the trees.

Several of Marino's men entered the clearing, firing indiscriminately in the direction of the fleeing Justo bodyguards. One of them with boots kicked Thomas in the side as he passed over top.

"Ringor is the one with the baton right?"

"No, this is Ringor," Aris said, standing over his rival. "I don't know what that is," he said, referring to Thomas.

Aris stared menacingly at Ringor, waving the gun in front of the prone man's nose.

"Shame we didn't get to fight man-to-man, Ringor. But I did have fun shooting Abel in the head."

Bleeding from his shoulder and chest, Ringor could only curse up at Aris.

"What you're mad about? Not my fault you lost the *kano* to us."

Aris laughed. Done with his fun, he leveled his silenced handgun at Ringor's head a shot twice.

Fernando had been checking Bill's condition and reported unconsciousness and a loss of blood.

"Stop the bleeding. There. Use the shirt on that Justo pig's head to wrap the arm," Aris commanded. "I'm not going to lose him now. Girls are going to line up just to give the hero a blow job. Ha! Too bad you're alive *kano*. I could have gotten some more attention from your wife."

Fernando crawled to Thomas and grabbed the dirty, sweaty shirt off his head. Aris was yelling orders to the others to stop shooting.

"This one is still alive, Aris."

Fernando took the shirt to attend to Bill's arm, tearing the rest of its tatters to make uneven strips. As the strips were being wrapped around Bill's arm, Aris grabbed Thomas by the hair to lift him off the ground.

Thomas grimaced at the rough treatment.

"Going to be no more Justo pigs running around when I get done today." Aris maintained a firm grip of Thomas' hair and gave his head a shake. "Eh, pig?"

"Get off me, Aris!"

Aris stopped jostling Thomas' head and stared at the dirty, hairy face. Sweat had made streaks in the dirt on his skin. The moustache and beard were white with the dust from the ground. Long hair in tangles fell into his eyes. The shape of the face was familiar, as was the nose. The voice. Before Aris could get *puraw* out of his mouth, Thomas shouted again.

"Get off me, Aris!" Thomas wielded Ringor's weighted baton, smashing upward into Aris' arm, releasing the grip. "I'm not a Justo pig."

Thomas hopped backward two steps on his good leg. Aris examined the way Thomas was standing. "Leg problem?"

He kicked Thomas' bad leg in revenge. The blow was perfectly placed. Face frozen in agony, Thomas returned to the ground.

"Attack me again and I'll kill you." Aris rubbed the spot on his arm where Thomas had struck him. "You smell like a pig, Little Joe. How do I know you're not with Justo either. Found you out here with Justo men and the *kano*. Maybe you're part of the kidnapping. You get rid of Joy's husband to get her back for yourself..."

"I'm not a killer like you," Thomas said.

Fernando had finished bandaging Bill's arm. "Are you sick, Aris? Quit playing so we can get this guy out of here, back to the house," he said. "We're not safe yet. What if they come back?"

Aris asked Fernando if he were scared. "Dying isn't permanent. You could come back to life like Little Joe here, Fernando." And then he dismissed the notion of Justo men returning with a wave of his gun.

Fernando remained hunched near Bill's body, scanning the distance, seeing a few of his own men wandering back toward the clearing. Fernando directed them to stay at the edge of the clearing, stay down and protect their departure.

"We're not leaving yet," Aris said. "There's the matter of this Justo sympathizer."

Aris stood over Thomas in the same manner he'd just done to Ringor.

"I'm not Justo, you know that Fernando. I'm the one that helped the American get out of Justo's hands," Thomas said.

"Leave me out of this, Thomas. You haven't exactly been with us either," Fernando replied.

"You're not Lapez. You've been interfering with the mayor's plans ... trying to stop Joy at the airport, trying to fly to America, getting Lopito killed..."

Thomas was enraged enough at that charge that he tried to stand, returned to his back by a stomp from Aris onto his chest.

"Pedro killed Lopito, not me!"

"Then how is it that you lived through that fire?"

Aris wasn't toying with him. These seemed to be real accusations.

"What is this, some cheap excuse for murder? Justo's men burned my house and forced me to hide in the mountains. And you have the guts to stand there and act like I'm working for those people. If it weren't for this damned feud, I'd still have my house. I'd still have my wife. Children!"

Aris smirked, apparently pleased at getting Thomas riled up.

"Well, well. If you had any money, Little Joe, I'd kill the *kano* for you. Then you would have Joy to yourself again." He put the butt of the silencer to his lips as though he were thinking. "Or I could wake up the *kano* and ask if he wants to pay me to kill you. He was willing to give money to Ringor for his freedom. Maybe he'll give me money to be free of you."

Thomas was beginning to feel the way Bill must have felt confronted by Ringor just moments ago. Trapped. On his back. Barely able to move. Overpowered by Aris, waving his gun around. Fernando wasn't going to help. Thomas didn't know any of the others in the Lapez squad to play on their sense of right and wrong. There was no conscience in Aris to play with.

Thomas wasn't going to die here. Not with Joy right over there. Not thousands of miles away. Right there where he could see her again.

"I just had another thought," Aris continued, "How about this? If you're dead and the *kano* is dead, then Joy's free to be mine..." He licked his lips and kissed the air.

"You've always been jealous of my relationship with Joy."

"No. Disgusted by it. Trying to dilute the Filipino with a half-breed *puraw* like you. Now worse, with him." Aris pointed to Bill's unmoving body. "I loved beating you, Thomas. You deserved it. You are the product of a *kano* dick. Your mother wasn't a clerk in Subic, she was a whore in Olongapo and got pregnant prostituting herself to sailors and marines."

"My mother wasn't like your sisters," Thomas replied, eye's focused on the handgun. "My creation may have been a mistake, but my parent's love wasn't."

Thomas knew he couldn't get out of this scrap through Aris' conscience. He needed to use the machismo and arrogance to his advantage.

"If you love beating me, Aris, why don't you try it now. You could never bully me. I never slinked away from fighting you, no matter how many times I lost. As a matter of fact, I think I won the last fight," Thomas said. "Are you going to pump me full of bullets like a coward or fight me like a man?"

Aris sneered. He stepped away from Thomas and jammed the gun into his pants.

"This is not time for a fist fight, Aris. Come on! Let's get out of here," Fernando pleaded.

Thomas slowly climbed to his feet, not taking his eyes of Aris, wary of a cheap shot.

"What did you tell me once? It wouldn't be fair to beat up a one-legged man? How about killing a one-legged man, Thomas? Is that fair?"

There was shooting in the distance. Not shotguns and handguns. Large guns. With explosions. Grenades.

Aris reacted to the sound of combat by turning his head. Thomas dove, driving his weight into the knee that he'd struck before. The impact hurt his shoulder, but it produced the same result. It chopped Aris to the ground on top of him.

Aris rolled to his back and reached for the handgun. Thomas clasped Aris' hands and tried to force the man's arms above his head so he could not aim the weapon. It went off twice, sending silent shells hurling into tree branches.

Gunfire near and far sent Fernando scrambling for cover, leaving Bill's body unattended.

Thomas saw the knife in Aris' belt sheath. With Aris' attention so focused on the handgun, Thomas reached the knife with his free hand and removed it.

The gun was above Aris' head. With his arms extended, Aris had left open his ribcage. It was a simple task for Thomas to jab the tip of the knife between two of the exposed ribs.

There was hesitation after the whelp.

Thomas withdrew his other hand from the gun and added it to the knife grip. He twisted the knife. The width of the blade spread and then cracked the ribs.

Aris hunched over that side and roared. Thomas braced himself on one knee and yanked out the knife, taking with it tissue and bone. The gash in Aris' side began to gather blood.

Thomas scooted on hands and knees to the gun, tossing it and the knife from the clearing. He retrieved Ringor's baton and returned his attention to Aris.

Aris had rolled several times to the edge of the clearing and was using a tree to help him stand, the other arm clutched tightly to the wound.

"How does it feel to lose, Aris?" Thomas prodded. "How does it feel to lose to a *puraw*?"

"I didn't lose anything yet." Still hunched to one side, Aris stood and waited for Thomas' slow approach. "I'm going to be one of the big winners of this fight. You had Lapez upbringing. You had mayor's food, mayor's money, mayor's clothes ... mayor's daughter."

Aris laughed a lot for a man who couldn't use the left side of his body and was already down a pint of blood.

"Now I've got mayor's food, mayor's money ... mayor's daughter."

Thomas' eyes narrowed. He knew this was Aris trying to psyche him out to find an opening, just a tactic to get an edge and regain the advantage. Even so, Thomas didn't like Aris' insinuation.

"I got her, Thomas," Aris said slyly. "I got Joy. I got her in my bed. She cheated on the *kano* to convince me to rescue him from Justo. Ah, he escaped before I could help. Too bad for Joy. But not too bad for me, I still got to taste her *okie*."

Aris tried to laugh, but the loss of one lung made it difficult and painful.

"Don't believe me, Thomas? Why not? Joy spread her legs for the *kano* to get her life in USA. Why don't you believe Joy would spread her legs for me to keep that life in USA?"

Thomas was unmoved. He stopped at arms reach.

Aris brandished a fist.

"Come on, Aris, do it."

He did.

Hunched over the injured side, Aris jabbed with his good arm. Missed. Then he tried a hook punch with the same result.

Thomas feigned a swing of the baton to Aris' knee. When Aris moved the arm to block, Thomas redirected the baton and used it as a ram, jamming the weapon under the chin and crushing the voice box. Aris lost his balance and back-flopped onto the ground. He rolled a few times clutching his throat.

Thomas knelt over the prone body. He knew he had won, but he wasn't even. The baton crashed down into Aris' injured side.

"Sex with Joy, eh?"

Slam.

"Who was she thinking about when she did it?"

Slam.

"Did she bury her face into your chest when it was over?"

Slam.

"Did she drag you into a church to pretend to marry you?"

Slam.

"Did she ignore you at the airport when you called her name?"

Slam.

"Did she marry another man and leave you when you needed her the most?"

It was then that Thomas stopped, arm raised for another baton blow.

"Just like what Elnora did to you?"

Thomas found his wits and realized he was punishing Aris for Joy's actions. Aris had stopped reacting to the strikes. He also seemed to have trouble breathing.

"Get off him!" Fernando demanded.

Thomas did not hear the cocking of the handgun, but he felt the bullet pass through the calf muscle on his bad leg. It wasn't until the second shot hit the other leg that he dropped the baton and rolled off Aris' body, wrapping his hands around the new wounds.

It was Fernando's gun, an unsilenced gun. The gunshot was so close to Thomas' ears that they only rang. He did not hear himself yell. Nor did he hear the final approach of the military vehicles. Nor did he hear the orders of uniformed men for everyone to drop their weapons.

CHAPTER 21
DUAPULO KET MAYSA

The ride to La Paz District Hospital was a tense one.

For several minutes the military medics hovered over Ringor, who was prone and unmoving on a stretcher next to Thomas on the floor of the armored personnel carrier. When their efforts to revive Ringor failed, they pulled the blanket over his face. Too much blood loss, they said to one another.

Thomas had a corporal from Dagupan sitting next to him. Thomas' bullet holes were suitably bandaged. From time to time, the corporal asked Thomas how he was feeling. Eventually, the morphine shot began its work and the pain subsided.

Aris' body, covered by a sheet, was lying at Thomas' feet. Another two barely injured militia men sat and had watched intently the frantic CPR performed on Ringor.

Thomas did not know where Bill was. He could only assume the American was in one of the other troop carriers headed for La Paz.

Probably La Paz, Thomas thought, since that was the closest hospital.

The corporal started to ask Thomas questions.

What's your name? Thomas. Thomas what? Wagner. You *kano*? Half. What happened out there in the mountains?

"They were fighting over me and the kidnapped American," he answered. "Lapez faction and Justo faction."

Thomas pointed to the dead bodies to indicate which of them belonged to the mayoral candidates.

"Which faction are you?" the corporal asked.

"I don't work for either," Thomas replied. "I'm from Calamba. I rescued the *kano* from Justo and hid him until you military showed up. We were trying to get back into town when both militias jumped us."

The two men sitting in the carrier were Justo men and confirmed Thomas did not work for Papa Justo when they were pressed by the corporal.

"Okay, we're at the Calamba hall. I'm getting out to report to the captain," the corporal said to the other troops.

At some point during the corporal's departure, Thomas fell unconscious from the morphine.

< <> >

"Joy is here," Father Herman yelled to people outside the church, interrupting Joy's solace in the front pew.

She reacted to Herman's frantic waving and the commotion outside.

"He's been found," Herman announced.

"Found? Bill? They found Bill?"

"Yes, yes," the priest answered, sweating and out of breath. "You've got to hurry. The Paculdar jeepney is loading in front of the town hall. The Army is on its way to La Paz, to the hospital. All that shooting just now was them."

Bill. Hospital. Shooting. Those were the only words that registered in Joy's mind as she jogged past the bewildered priest and out to the street. Joy propelled herself down the concrete road, past a few blocks of houses to the center of town.

Her mother met her there with a complaint that people had been hunting for her for 15 minutes.

"Only one of the vehicles stopped. One of the soldiers jumped out and reported to the captain that they had found a bunch of injured or dead Filipinos and two *puraw* ... assuming Ameri*kano*s."

Rowena said the other vehicles didn't stop, continuing down the road to La Paz. The captain then left to follow.

"We're only assuming they mean Bill," Rowena said.

"He's talking nonsense," Ricky said. "Two *kano*s? Except for Father Herman, Joy's *asawa* is the only white guy in town now."

People were climbing on top of Jon-Jon's dad's jeepney. Another full one was already leaving ahead of his, people nearly falling off its roof.

"Where's father? Why don't we just take the red jeep?" Joy asked.

Rowena shrugged. "He drove off with it when the shooting started. He didn't tell me where he was going."

"He abandoned us?"

"I don't think so." Rowena pushed Joy toward some empty spaces in the back of the jeepney. "He went off in the direction of the shooting with Albio."

Before Mr. Paculdar could leave, vice mayor Ramirez walked out the hall and strode quickly to the driver's door. He had been able to call the La Paz mayor, who looked outside his window and saw the commotion when it arrived at the hospital. Several people were whisked inside when the military vehicles parked, he could not tell if there was a redhead *kano* in that group. He also said there was a group of people taken inside with sheets over their bodies.

The dead.

< <> >

"Is your name Thomas?"

He nodded, or at least thought he was nodding. His head was swimming with drowsiness. Fuzzy yellowish light fell into his eyes. Standing over him was the outline of a person in a nurse's uniform with the triangular hat atop her head. She was speaking Tagalog to him, telling him he had just come out of surgery.

"The doctors took out the bullets," she said. "We could not straighten your leg, though, we do not have an orthopedic surgeon on staff to reset it."

Thomas nodded again.

"Thomas, there's an army captain here to see you. It is important or we wouldn't have awakened you so soon after surgery," she explained.

The questions were about the rescue of Bill Vandemark.

You are sure it was Lino Justo's place? A back room near the wall at the mill? Where did you hide after that? Where are you from? Some people from Calamba are here at the hospital, are any of them likely to be your parents? Orphan? I'm sorry. Married? Not anymore? I'm sorry, again. You've got an American last name, you *kano*? Yes, I can see you look half. Get some rest now. We'll talk later and get the rest of your story. You are safe now. Lino Justo will be under arrest soon. Some of my men are here to guard you and the redhead American.

Yes, he's alive.

With that news, Thomas felt relief, succumbed to the drugs and fell back into oblivion.

< <> >

Thomas was battling many things, not the least of which was a staph infection. That accompanied fatigue, anemia and continued depression.

He already spent two days in a coma.

There was a note from Nina at the corner of his pillow when he first awoke. It was too dangerous for her to wait until he was awake to say her goodbye. She cried so hard when she found out he died. She was so happy that he was still alive. She was headed for Manila with Bennie and her mother Imelda. She'll come back for him when it is safer. With love, Nina.

Despite his fondness for Nina, it wasn't the note he wanted to read.

In the hallway, he heard Lara's command, "Luis, get back here."

"Luis can't walk," the boy wailed after being caught doing something that displeased him mother. "Luis can't walk."

"You and me both, Luis," Thomas quipped to the ceiling.

Luis was instantly quiet, so Lara must have picked him up into her arms to spare the hospital the effects of his all-too-frequent temper tantrum.

"There is a woman outside the hospital, a reporter from GMA, I think. She keeps asking about you. We keep telling her that you are still in a coma," Maricar said as she entered the room with Tammy on her shoulder.

"She is always asking us because the nurses are tired of her and won't talk to her at all," Lara said.

Auntie Betty was the one carrying Luis. In her other arm was a plastic bag with *bibingka* and *halo halo*. She handed them to Thomas with a smile. He nibbled politely at them, though a beer sounded more appealing.

The day was looking to be a repeat of yesterday. They brought him a collection from the church. Father Herman was able to supply him a wardrobe better than his tattered and blood stained hermit attire. It was waiting for him in a suitcase at the foot of the bed.

Thomas stayed in hospital dress and under a sheet as the visitors came. His friends surrounded him for most of the day. Maricar stood along the wall and carried Tammy. Ronaldo and Jon-Jon resumed their tradition of trading barbs, ending once with Jon-Jon saying Ronaldo's kids were going to be ugly and blind, Ronaldo retaliating by saying the Paculdars will eventually need a forklift to get their children into bed in the loft at night. Thomas suspected it was a show for his amusement, but the frown never left his face.

No one dared mention Joy.

Auntie Betty said Father Herman had arranged for Lopito to be exhumed from the tiny Wagner graveyard and get his own proper burial.

"Keep the grave marker with your name on it, Thomas, you'll need it someday," Ronaldo said.

Those gathered chastised him thoroughly for his lack of tact, but Ronaldo was able to coax a weak smile from Thomas.

"It is true. We're all going to die eventually. Thomas will be able to save some money, he already has his. Just chisel away the date."

The visitors spared him the onslaught of questions they asked yesterday. They knew Thomas would answer them when he was ready.

The fire, he could talk about.

Hiding in the church, he could talk about.

Rescuing Bill, he could talk about.

He kept to himself the fact that he was going to Calamba that night to break into Valera's store for bottles of gin. It was luck that he overheard people talking about Joy's husband.

He kept to himself the fact that his leg was twisted at the ankle because his alcoholic shakes had been so violent for two days that he couldn't adjust his makeshift brace during the critical time that the bone was healing.

He kept to himself the fact that it was too late when he investigated parts of the old church that he'd not seen in years and found the small stash of *basi*. For a time, it quelled the pangs.

"Can you find a fan?" Maricar asked a nurse. "Thomas is sweating so bad."

He felt the shakes coming back so he faked a nap to evacuate the room. They weren't as violent as before. He tucked his arms under his body to conceal his condition from the nurses.

In the quiet, he tried to make sense of the hand God had dealt him. There was so much to absorb.

Joy's absence spoke volumes. The loss did not take long to accept. Most of the mourning, denial and bargaining with God for her return had happened before the house burned.

But acceptance did not stem the despair. *"You have a wife, Joy, who can't imagine another day without you. What is important is that you know you are never going to be alone again."* Words that had given him so much hope now provided a new anguish.

The real war was with hate. There was plenty to pass around, but he fought the urge to include Joy on that list. Real hate was only possible with an emotional bond. The weight of his love for Joy would make her the most despised person in his life if he let that weight spill over.

Joy cowered from her father all the years of her life and now she was too scared to face Thomas to own up to her decision. Distasteful. Gutless. Joy had not changed in Singapore. That was an illusion. She was the same Joy who was incapable of courage. Running away to Singapore to marry Bill behind his back. Not acknowledging his presence at the airport. Only returning to the Philippines to talk to a grave marker. She was getting worse, taking on the qualities of her father. Sacrificing relationships for personal gain. Turning to dishonesty and deception to accomplish goals.

Yet, that wasn't a version of Joy that he'd ever known. Lifelong emotions could not be squandered so easily. Perhaps she was just caught in circumstances that were inescapable. Perhaps she felt duty bound to stand by her husband, to honor the vows she took in public, to make the best of where life had taken her. Given those circumstances, perhaps there was an unborn Vandemark child to consider.

Confusion rocked him again. Chase her. Wait until nighttime and then escape. Father Herman had given him some money to go along with the clothes. Use it to hire a trike to Bangued, then hop on a bus to Manila, get off at the Cubao bus station and hire a taxi to St. Luke's Hospital in Ermita...

No. Joy didn't want the future with the orphaned farm boy. She never did. It was fine to dream of a life in Baguio with Thomas The Doctor with a big air conditioned house and vacations in America. But personal tragedies soured that dream to a reality of a hard life stuck in the province with a poor farmer—whom she married only because she knew no other man.

Or worse, she married him out of pity and then jumped at the chance to marry someone else to erase the mistake in judgment.

In that moment of inadequacy, Ronaldo's words resonated oddly. Someday manifested into someday soon. His thoughts surprised him. He had never wanted to die.

CHAPTER 22
DUAPULO KET DUA

Quezon City is the largest city in Metro Manila. It has a subdivision named Commonwealth, so named for the avenue that runs through it. Aunt Rosella was four streets removed in a middle class neighborhood. Among the houses behind a guarded street entrance is a white two story with a car port and a Subaru parked there. Despite the guards, black bars covered every window.

For two refugees, Aunt Rosella carved some space out of an upstairs bedroom. Sisters separated in age by nearly two decades finally got to sleep in the same room together, with Ricky pressed between them in the small bed. Regina shared some of her wardrobe with sister Rowena, they were the same height and weight. Ricky lived out of a small gym bag with a few changes of clothes. It was all they could grab in the chaos. All authority in Calamba disappeared with Marino. Papa Justo was whisked away by provincial police. Ringor and Aris were dead, so there was no one to keep the thugs in line. And the thugs found the Lapez residence. They looted it and pelted it with rocks. Fleeing became a priority when one of those rocks smashed through and struck Ricky in the shoulder.

Rowena and Ricky escaped through the grove and made it in stages through the mountains to Lopito's house in Baguio. Lopito's wife wouldn't take them in since Marino had gotten her husband killed and she didn't want to be next. The only place left was Aunt Rosella in Quezon City.

Joy was unsure who would find them first, a cheap Justo hitman or government agents. News agencies reported the disappearance of former mayor Marino Lapez, who was being sought by the governor for the theft of the town's money. His houses in Calamba and Bangued had been seized. There was no home to go back home.

Joy lived out of her suitcase in Bill's recovery room at St. Luke's Hospital, a few blocks away from the American embassy. She bathed in a public bathroom sink at the end of the hallway. She slept in a short slippery plastic chair in the corner. When word of Bill's captivity and injuries reached upward in the chain of command, the answer came down to move him out of Abra. He was transferred to an Army ambulance. The soldiers grabbed Joy and threw her in the back with him.

Since arriving in Ermita, Bill came in and out of surgery, in and out of consciousness, in and out of conversations with authorities. He was fine.

It was Thomas she worried about. She couldn't shake the sight of him on the gurney. Dirt crusted skin. Thin in the face. Ratty long hair. Blood everywhere. It wasn't the smell of urine, dirt and blood that bothered her the most. It was the odor underneath them. For just a moment, her mind concluded Thomas smelled of decay. Death. She yelled and shook him, but he didn't awaken. The nurses physically removed her from the hospital room to keep her from harming Thomas more.

Joy kept thinking that she did, indeed, get back in time for his funeral.

While Bill was in surgery at the hospital in Ermita, Joy used a public pay phone to call the Calamba municipal hall in an attempt to get word on Thomas. The old woman there hung up on her twice, rejection for being the daughter of Lapez, she supposed. She had forgotten the numbers for Jon-Jon's or Maricar's cell phones.

Bill's kidnapping had brought to bear the brunt of the media. First the Philippine's national papers and ABS-CBN television news. Then the Associated Press' foreign desk. Rumor had it that Bill's ordeal had made it onto the front page of the Chicago papers too.

Joy read and watched Calamba become the scorn of the country for its election violence. There had been election-related incidents in other parts of the Philippines. A grenade exploded in Zamboanga del Sur. Someone in a barangay near General Santos City grabbed a ballot box and tossed it into a stream. A victorious mayor on Leyte was assassinated. Nothing compared to Calamba and its body count.

The election results had come in as anticipated. Lino Justo defeated Marino Lapez, making Papa mayor, but only on a sheet of paper. Papa Justo lounged in jail while government lawyers prepared a case for the kidnapping and beating of an American architect. There was no chance of bribing himself out of the situation and it was likely he would still be in prison by the time the next election came around. Thus, Justo had been immediately replaced by vice mayor Ramirez.

When ABS-CBN ran Bill's story, they reported nothing from La Paz on the man who had saved the American. They were crediting the Army troops on patrol for stumbling on the gunfight and saving Bill. It was as though Thomas didn't exist.

However, a groggy Bill, just out of surgery, credited Thomas with his rescue. He chronicled his kidnapping. He described the way Justo and his men had beaten him, demanding Marino declare defeat as the only terms for his release. He described the rescue and hide out in the old church. He described the walk home and the ambush, encircled by Justo's men, rescued again by Thomas, only to be shot in the back while wrestling with Ringor.

In a fit of desperation, Joy tried to return to Abra to get Thomas' condition. Ricky pleaded to got with her—she noticed that he'd asked more about Thomas than his own father. Aunt Rosella told Joy she'd probably be safe staying with her grandmother Flora in Calamba. Rowena went into a tizzy over the trip, not over Joy's safety, but for leaving Bill unattended for the day the trip would use up.

"Then go visit him yourself. You speak English," Joy told her mother. "If he asks about me, then tell him I'm being question by the NBI about *tatang's* disappearance. Teach him how to play mahjong."

Ricky then said he'd go see Bill. He was bored. He'd been cooped up in his own house for his own protection and now he was cooped up in Rosella's house for his own protection. Kids were playing basketball outside. It was probably maddening.

"Ask him what he and Thomas discussed for the day they were hiding in the old church," Joy said to her mother, ignoring Ricky.

"Maybe the *kano* doesn't know." Rowena was in desperate denial to believe that.

Regina interjected that Jon-Jon and Ronaldo told her about Thomas trying to sell everything he owned in order to chase Joy to America so that he could stop her. "I can't imagine Thomas not discussing everything he knew with the *kano.*"

Rowena didn't want to hear that.

"The more reason you need to be in that hospital room with him. That *kano* is our only hope for survival. Auntie can't support us all."

"That's right," the old woman said. "My pension isn't going to feed all of you."

Joy wanted to tell her mother to get a job. No, they were in hiding.

"We don't have a home to go back to, Joy. The grove is gone. Marino has all the money with him, wherever he is. You're our only chance for survival. You have a job in the States. You need to convince the *kano* to keep you."

"How? Kiss him a hundred times and hope he forgets everything Thomas probably told him."

"Thomas was the past," Rowena reasoned, hoping Joy would catch the hint. "Be at his side. Comfort him. Wait on his needs. Be affectionate. Tell him you forgot Thomas the moment you met him. Tell him he's the one you love. You told me that you loved him."

"I do have feelings for him, mother, and that's why I'm not going to throw myself at him like that. And you can stop throwing guilt trips at me. Sacrifice myself for the good of the family. I heard that before."

Joy finished stocking her purse for the trip. When Ricky rose to follow her, she pointed to the wall for him to return to his perch at the window.

"We'll find some other way to find out about Thomas. I can send Reggie there instead."

Regina perked up and momentarily stopped feeding Aunt Rosella. Her expression told Rowena to leave her out of this.

"This is not about finding out if Thomas is fine. It's about moving him here. I want him out of Abra. I want him where I can see him."

That sent Rowena into a worse spin.

"Reggie, go get Bong Bong. We're going to drag Joy back to the *kano*'s hospital room even if we have to stuff her in Bong Bong's trunk to get her there."

"Listen to your mother, Joy. The most important thing to anyone is their own family," Rosella said.

"Thomas is our family," she told her great-aunt.

Ricky reiterated that he wanted to go with Joy to see Thomas.

"What makes you think Thomas even wants to see you again?" Regina asked. Otherwise, he could have run over to the house as soon as he rescued Bill. That struck a blow to Joy's confidence. "I think you should leave him alone. You've done enough to hurt him."

The phone rang before Joy could explain to Regina that betraying Thomas was her brother-in-law's idea and was backed by her dear older sister.

It was Bill on the phone. He wanted to speak to Joy.

Rowena waved her hands excitedly in the air. He's wondering where Joy went, she announced nervously. She asked Regina to awaken her taxi driver boyfriend, who was napping upstairs. They were going to Ermita. She told Ricky to be on his best behavior so Joy can keep her husband and go back to the States with him.

"I'm going alone," Joy said when put the phone down.

Bill was getting visitors.

Joy played the dutiful wife when she got to the hospital. She smiled at the doctors and nurses. She smiled at the American ambassador. She smiled at the Filipino officials who came with the American ambassador. She smiled at the reporters who came with the Filipino officials and the American ambassador. She listened to them all apologize to Bill on behalf of the country for the ordeal.

They were clueless that his time in captivity was the least painful aspect of the ordeal. The more difficult apology had to come from Joy.

Papa Justo confessed so there was no reason to ask Bill to stay in order to attend to legal matters. Bill's demeanor improved at the chance to go home as soon as the doctors cleared him for travel.

Joy politely escorted the entourage of dignitaries out of the room.

Bill was quietly staring at the ceiling when she returned to the room. She stopped in the doorway. This would be the first time they'd been alone and able to talk since the kidnapping.

Joy didn't try to fool herself. Thomas and Bill spent the day together, she was sure they talked about her. Bill knew he'd been used and deceived. She was saddened about the possibility—no, the probability—that she would lose her tall, handsome, redheaded Old Man. This could be the last time she saw his face and heard his voice. The fright of losing him to Papa Justo had broken through the grief of Thomas' death. The mental and emotional barriers of "being in the plan" were not standing. She was battling her father and then Aris. She was vulnerable and alone. In that moment, she conceded that Bill Vandemark truly had a voice singing in her heart.

Bill's chest rose and fell. He blinked a few times. There was a knot growing in her stomach. Was Bill carefully gathering his words? Or was he so disgusted with her that there was nothing to say? Joy realized she'd never seen Bill angry before. Was this it? Silent stewing? She didn't know how to combat silence as a weapon.

Joy went to the side of the bed and kissed him on the cheek.

It broke the ice.

"You are some kind of pro," Bill said in false admiration. "I never saw it coming. Not a hint. I don't know how you managed to sleep so soundly every night. Must be something in the water up there that erases a person's conscience."

Joy bowed her head. This was going to deteriorate quickly.

"There were all kinds and hints and warnings with Monica. She tossed and turned at night, gave me frowns whenever I wanted sex, a drawer full of clothing mysteriously disappeared. Nope, not you, Joy my joy. I was completely blindsided."

"I'm sorry, Bill."

His eyes told her it wasn't believed. There was no combination of apologetic words that would adequately convey her remorse, but it was a start.

"I thought I had found this cute, young, innocent woman. You never had a boyfriend before me. You had strict parents that never let you date. They were overly protective and that was why you were a virgin."

"I remember what I told you after our first time in bed, Bill." Joy didn't need her words recited back to her. "I'm not going to start denying…"

"And all along I was having sex with a married woman?"

Married in every way that was important, she wanted to say, but that would be interpreted as skirting the issue. Bill was seeking clearly drawn answers, no gray, no smudges. He wanted the drawings in perfect order.

His question was the confirmation that he and Thomas had talked about her. Anyway, she was well past that realization that it was useless to be deceptive now.

"Then Thomas told you everything."

"No. I figured it out on my own." Bill surprised her. "His story to me was that he's an adopted brother. I asked him about his wedding ring and the story of him losing his wife is clearly you."

Joy stiffened, waiting for Bill to ask where the companion ring was located. He won't believe that she'd misplaced it. At some point in the traveling from Singapore to Manila to Chicago, the ring went from hidden to lost.

"What does aye-yaht mean?" Bill asked in an even voice.

"*Ayat* means love."

"And that other nickname you have for him?" Bill again butchered the pronunciation of *sika ti immuna ken siksikanto laeng.* Joy corrected him and then answered, "my first and only."

"Jesus," he said again. "You're a real pro."

Bill's sneer made her face hot. It had too many traces of Aris' insinuations in it. She'd been a good wife to him in Chicago. She'd been faithful to him since the day they'd met. Even Aris' offer to save Bill's life wasn't enough for her to cheat on him.

"Before you finish painting me as a heartless bitch, just remember that I walked into Papa Justo's house and offered him every peso and dollar that I had in exchange for your freedom. He could have tied me up and thrown me next to you."

"Yes, you're a real hero..."

"And we don't have to play question and answer to dance around everything. I know I betrayed you. I know I betrayed Thomas. I knew from the moment that I wrote the Asian Love Connection ad that I was going to hurt someone eventually. I acted sweet and innocent and it made you crazy in bed. I know I was cheating on Thomas every day I was with you. I know I committed a mortal sin. I alienated my friends. I gave my enemies ammunition to use against me for the rest of my life. I made this situation that I'm in now and I have to find a way to live with it."

"Why are you yelling at me? You're the one..."

"...That married you for the color of your passport. Yes, I'm guilty. I set you up from the first letter. My father forced me to marry for money. He beat me up one afternoon and threw a guilt trip at me that I would be responsible for the family's downfall—and probably death—if I didn't help him win re-election to keep power. I kept Thomas a secret from you so you wouldn't have any doubts about marrying me. I wanted to get married as soon as I got to Chicago so I could get work privileges. I wanted a job right away so I could send money home."

Bill's frown deepened with each of her validations.

She wanted to tell him, at the bottom of it all, that money wasn't the reason she did it, but she knew he wouldn't believe it.

"Since you're suddenly so open about these plans, tell me the rest. Don't stop now. What was supposed to happen after election day when your father didn't need money anymore?"

Joy hunched her shoulders. "When Thomas died, I didn't have to think about that day anymore."

"He's not dead…"

Joy clamped her eyes shut. It was a test of will to prevent herself from bawling. She turned her back to Bill so that he wouldn't see the few tears that disobeyed. Thomas kept coming and going, living and dying in the blink of an eye.

"What? You didn't know? I thought you'd have already planned your reunion. I thought you'd be anxious to see him again. Mission accomplished, after all. Ditch the white guy and go back to the old days."

Joy wished she could go to him now. She wished she didn't have responsibilities in Manila. She wished she didn't have to sleep in a chair every night and bathe in a sink every morning. She wished she didn't need to visit Aunt Rosella's house twice a day to see if what was left of her family was still alive.

"So…"

Joy didn't turn around for her explanation of the rest of the plan to Bill. "If things were going perfectly and Thomas had no idea I was really in America and father had won the election, I was going to work long enough to pay cash for my plane ticket home and then disappear one day. I was going to hop off a bus in Baguio, go to my uncle Lopito's house and surprise Thomas with my return."

A nurse broke up the conversation. Bill's accelerated heart rate had shown on the monitors.

Joy was glad for that. Her voice was cracking. The fact that Thomas was alive was pouring from her eyes. She left the bed while the nurse tended to Bill. The nurse refilled the pain medication that was dripping into Bill's intravenous solution. She asked his well-being and left when Bill told her that he was fine.

Joy was cross legged on the floor with her head against the wall when the nurse walked out.

"Where were we? Oh, yes, here's your chance to hop on a bus and return to Thomas."

Bill was sitting now. His comment was laced with anger, pain, disappointment. Uncertainty? Yes. He was fishing for an answer Joy wasn't certain she had.

"How can I even face him again?" she sniffled.

Bill laughed, but not because the comment was funny. "You have no problem facing me. You're not so ashamed to be in my presence."

"Would you trade places with him? What I did to him was far worse than anything I've done to you."

Thomas gave and gave. She took and took. When it was her turn to give, she left.

Bill cast the line. "What are you going to do, Joy? You can't have us both."

Joy stared at her left hand. The wedding band—Bill's ring for her— glistened as much as it could in the fluorescent lighting. The Ring Of Fraud.

Not having spoken to Thomas, there may not even be a choice to be made. Regina might be right. He didn't want to see her again. He saved Bill to satisfy his code of honor, to see justice done to Marino and Papa Justo.

Overcoming the violation of Thomas' trust would be formidable. She had been sacred ground to him. Fixing that relationship would be more difficult than with Bill. Maybe it was impossible. So was it better to just leave Thomas alone now? Let Nina have him, wherever she was now.

The needs of her family washed over her again. She was the only provider left. Marino was gone. The house in Calamba was gone. The grove was gone. Her job was in Chicago. It was the only way she was going to be able to support Ricky and Rowena. They needed to start a new life. Abra was too dangerous for them to return.

She knew reconciliation with either man wasn't possible so long as a betrayal continued. So she had to pick. She had to pick soon. Once Bill got out of the hospital, he was leaving the Philippines.

Joy threw in her own fishing line. "Does it matter what I want? Is there still a place for me in Chicago?"

"That depends on why you would want to go back there."

Joy was looking for answers, not more riddles. But then, she wasn't making herself very decisive either.

She positioned herself at the edge of the bed to peer into his eyes, swimming with conflict. Rowena's instructions echoed in her mind. Comfort. Attention. Emotion.

"I do have feeling for you, Bill."

"I love you, Joy."

"You can accept me even after this?"

Bill was leaving the path for her to choose. It was so much easier in the past when all she had to do was follow the direction of her father and mother and Auntie Emma. And life as Shadow involved little choice, it was simply following Thomas through the years of her life. She wondered many times if she was with Thomas only because she knew nothing else. Now she knew another man, another life. Yet she was no closer to that answer.

Joy stared at her wedding ring again.

The decision was there.

In the vows.

For most of the evening, Thomas sat in a corner of Calamba's Catholic church.

In the corner.

His mother had often threatened that she would cripple him and sit him in a corner for the rest of his life if he did something shameful.

When the last of the people performing their evening novena had left, Thomas crept to the front pew.

His eyes traced the cross again and again. The outline of Jesus' body being crucified. The ring of thorns around his head. His eyes closed and face pointing down and to the right.

"You remember the day the snake bit Joy's ankle?" he asked the wooden cross. "It raced through the water while she was trying to plant rice. It was too fast for me to even warn her. And then I ran to Auntie Annie because she had anti-venom. I never ran so fast in my life. I made it in time to save her life."

Thomas was proud. He took a sip from the square bottle that had been sitting beside him for most of the evening. It was the second pint of gin for the day. It was nice of the Valeras to extend him a bit of credit given his circumstances. The gin worked fast on an empty stomach. Even so, it wasn't until he started the second one that he felt it numb him.

"You want to know more about Joy? She never caught a dragonfly in her life. She pinches her nose on breezy days because she doesn't want the wind to make it flat. Her favorite game was to stand tip-toed on the back of a carabao to see how long it takes her to lose her balance and fall off."

He stood from the front pew and stalked his way toward the cross, the half-empty bottle dangling between two fingers.

"Whenever she's sick, she insists that her breakfast be one *longaniza* with two scoops rice with mint leaves. She is scared of owls. She was a terrible softball pitcher. She thinks all romance novels are true stories. For some reason, she asked *me* what to do when she got her first period. That damn American doesn't know any of this, but he's got her anyway."

The bottle sailed at the cross.

It missed, but not by much, and shattered against the wall. Glass fell to the marble and clear liquid trickled down the face and body of Christ's likeness.

"What was that noise?" came a startled inquiry with a Dutch accent. "Thomas? It sounds like your voice. Thomas is that you? What is going on out there?"

Before he left the hospital this morning, he saw a story on the television news that the kidnapped American would be released soon from the hospital and then fly home.

"I waited for nothing," Thomas roared. "I knelt right here and took her as my wife. So why is she in Ermita making plans to get on that jet to fly back to Chicago with someone else?"

The old priest did not move very fast, but he was as fleet of foot that he could be, emerging from his office to the side of the altar.

"I know why she's going back to America. I'm wicked. I get it now," he testified to the echoes of his voice. "I'm wicked. I was such a poison that I ruined my mother's womb on the way out. I'm another Aris. I'm another drunken murderer walking around Calamba."

Wobbling, Thomas pointed to Jesus.

"You are the all-knowing. You knew what I really was. I thought I was honorable, good and faithful. I must not be, huh? Everyone is gone. I don't deserve a family. My mother and my wife left me within weeks of one another."

The priest shuffled up to Thomas' side. "What are you doing? You desecrated the altar. How dare you."

Herman protested as though he'd just seen a dog defecating inside the church. He walked to the cross and picked up the larger pieces of glass on the floor and the ones lodged behind the symbol. He used the cuff of his sleeve to try to wipe off the wooden face.

"Forgive me, Father, for I have sinned. It has been two years since my last confession."

"You're drunk. How did you get this? Who gave this to you? You just got out of the hospital."

"God has forsaken me for a reason, Father. There is a reason for everything and I figured out the reason."

"What are you babbling about?" Herman rose to his feet and deposited the glass pieces on the altar.

"They're all dead except me. All of the good ones. The good die young, right? My brothers and sisters were so good they died before they got out. Not me! I made it into the world. I made my father duty bound to stay here instead of going home to Wisconsin. I got my mother outcast from her family."

"This is nonsense. You're not to blame for their fate."

"I cannot die, Father. How is that? How do I survive fires and gunfights? How do I survive three weeks of starvation? My mother can die from a simple case of pneumonia, but I can walk in and out of the shadow of the valley of death. I'm still young, but I cannot die. Why? Am I suffering for my sins? I'm a murderer after all."

"Thomas, please sit down. Please, calm down. Where's your cane? You shouldn't be walking around without assistance. You need to protect that leg until we can get it properly re-set."

"Aris lives on through me." Thomas thumped his chest. "I should go break into Papa Justo's house and steal something. Something I can sell in Bangued for a lot of pesos. I'll use the money for a bus ride to Angeles City. I'll sit in a go-go bar and barfine a girl. Hell, I'll make it Lovelyn Lucero. Roll in your grave in anger over that one, Aris! *Puraw* pumping away at your sister the way you wanted to do to Joy."

That thought produced a wry smile.

"She can teach me how to do things like a bold star. Nina said Marites Galope couldn't get out of her panties fast enough for me. Let's find out! I'll get a stop watch and time her. Then I'll use my new sexual styles to dazzle her. When I get bored of her body, I can announce 'next' to all of Abra and pick a new girl for the weekend..."

"You don't mean that. It is the disappointment talking. It is the gin."

Thomas picked up a Bible and reared back to throw it.

Herman slapped down Thomas' hand.

"No, I will not let you do that here. Enough of this blasphemy," Herman exploded.

Herman, half a head taller than Thomas and much wider in the shoulder, bear hugged the young man and used leverage to lift him off his feet. The priest only needed a few steps to deposit Thomas into a pew, more harshly than intended, but his aged legs could not conjure a more gentle landing.

Thomas rolled in a fetal position on the long flat bench.

"I'm already going to hell, what's a little blasphemy going to do to me? I'm going to hell for murder," Thomas sobbed, "and God started punishing me for it before I actually killed Aris."

Herman watched Thomas wilt emotionally. He moaned of being the next Aris, of being wicked, of going to hell after a long painful life.

"Thomas, you are not to blame for all the tragedies that have befallen you."

The priest sat beside Thomas' head and patted it sympathetically.

"God has harder tests for those that are closer to him. I don't know why these things have happened to you, perhaps God is giving you the tools to meet challenges later in your life. What I do know is that you are not the next incarnation of Aris Lucero. Your mother and father instilled in you a sense of honor and justice that Aris never possessed."

"Honor? There was nothing honorable in killing him."

Herman sighed. "Do you believe Aris would have killed you if you had not fought back?"

"But I had already won the fight. Aris was down and out..."

"God forgive me for saying this, but you rid this town of an evil that day. Aris would have killed you as he was killing other men, as he killed Gloria Casao, as he killed Ringor Fillion and Abel Botalico, as he killed who knows whom else. More probable atrocities pop up every day since his death. Fernando Cabasan confessed that Aris repeatedly shot and maimed Lazy Velasquez. Aris was twisted up with a rage that never went away. His mother prayed over him a lot and told me he was trying to drink it away and it never worked. Then it was the alcohol that drove him. I know you think you are like Aris, but you are not, but I'm afraid you will become him if you keep drinking like this." Herman pointed angrily at the glass shards. "The frustration of your life is turning into a rage."

"I'm sorry, Father, I cannot stop. I have to drink. I couldn't turn down Mr. Valera's gift. I have to drink just to feel normal. Just to get through a day. It stops the shakes. I had the shakes out there at the old church. A broken leg and the shakes. I screamed into the dirt for hours. I couldn't stop it. I couldn't set the leg straight in the splint. I was shaking too hard."

Thomas told Herman of the stash of *basi* he'd found. It was the only thing that would stop the shakes long enough to collect mango and coconut that had fallen to the ground in order to survive. Saving Bill was an accident. He'd run out of booze and was hunting for more. He decided to save Bill because the man was an innocent. How hypocritical. Do the honorable thing, yet enjoy breaking Pedro's jaw with the butt of the man's own gun.

Herman was quiet with Thomas, letting the lad compose himself.

"Although I'm not properly dressed to make this a formal confessional, I can administer the sacrament of penance and return you to God's communion."

Still shaking from his grief, Thomas regarded the old priest.

"No, don't try to kneel. Your leg." Herman barred him from moving. "I'll think about a proper penance for you later. Tossing alcohol and the Holy word at the cross is not something I've ever had in my church. I think you have several relationships to work out. One of them is with the Almighty. He understands that this was a moment of weakness and He loves you no matter what you've done today. Before we can heal this shattered soul of yours, we need to do something about the demon on your back."

Herman stood and hooked his arm under Thomas' arm pits to help him stand.

"It was kind of Mr. Paculdar and Mr. Ramirez to invite you to stay with them in your first few days back in Calamba, but I'm insisting that you stay here in the church where I can keep my eyes on you. Come sleep in the back. There is a mattress I can put on the floor."

Herman rested in his desk chair throughout the night. He had found an old fan to blow air through the room.

Listening to it helped Thomas more than its cool air. The ambiguous noise was calming. A better sound than his own labored breathing. It was nearly dawn before the alcohol had left Thomas' system and his body started asking for more.

His mind knew that going through this experience the first time should have been enough to not want to go through it again. His body screamed to the mind to get a drink. The mantra would drone on as relentlessly as one of Luis' temper tantrums. He chastised himself for returning to the bottle. He knew the shakes would come back eventually this day.

"Did you sleep at all?" he asked the priest when Herman started to stretch and fidget in the chair.

"As much as I ever do when I sit in this chair."

"So, you've done this before?"

"Sit through the night with an alcoholic? Yes." Herman yawned.

"Anyone I know? At this point, there isn't a twist I don't expect."

"No, no, although that would satisfy my sense for the melodramatic. You know how much I enjoy watching soap operas every night. Esperanza. Hiram." The priest rocked forward and offered Thomas a glass. "Drink water. You're overly sweating."

Running water, it was nice, Herman said, as was having electricity all day long.

"There is lemonade to be made from any lemon. Who knew six months ago that a war between would-be mayors would not only improve the town, but then rid the town of them in the aftermath?"

"You're welcome."

The comment wasn't lost on Herman's wit. "Yes, you had a big part in its ending, didn't you? Bearing the brunt of both men."

"I'm sorry I tried to hit the cross with a bottle."

"I forgive you. He forgives you."

"Have you figured out my penance?"

"Yes, though it may be out of the ordinary. This morning, you'll clean the altar. After a proper breakfast, you'll help me with Mass. After 100 Hail Marys, you'll help me write a letter to the dean of St. Louis University to explain the circumstances of your absence. You're the miracle of Calamba, after all. Perhaps the bishop and I will have a discussion with the dean at St. Louis regarding a scholarship, using your sacrifice and valor as reasons to ask for the university's good will."

"Father, I..."

Herman held up his hands. "I know. I don't mean to get your hopes up."

"No. That's not it. I don't want any pity."

"Not all charity is pity," Herman said, dismissing the concern with a clasp on the shoulder. "I'm trying to give you options. I don't want you to lose track of what you were trying to accomplish with your life. Few people from the provinces ever get through college. I want you to realize that you're not as defeated as you think you are. The problem, Thomas, is that you have been under so many obligations for so much of your life that you don't know what to do without them. You're not beholden to anyone other than yourself right now. God has not forsaken you. He has put you in a position to choose your own path. You only have to decide what it is that you want and set yourself in that direction."

"Thanks for the pep talk."

"I meant it." Herman leaned back in his chair. "You have me to help you. You have close friends. And I want you to understand that even though you may not have any relatives left, you are not an orphan. You are not alone."

"Father, you're the second person to sit with me in this church and tell me that."

This time, he didn't believe it.

< <> >

Thomas looked out across the fields. The crop of weeds was doing well. The rice was stunted and would be unyielding. He should tell old Masakayan to let his goats and carabao loose on it. Green fodder for animals was all it's good for now. Thomas took a deep breath, relishing the sweetish smell of the green. Butterflies and crickets dotted the landscape above the waist-high mass of stalks and leaves.

They were Botalico fields still, but Mayor Ramirez was promising to do anything in his power to reverse Marino's ruling.

Thomas wasn't sure he wanted it back.

He held his cane as a scythe and knocked down the nearest row of tall weeds. "Goats and carabao," he threatened upon them.

The first step was always his good leg, propelling him forward and helping the bad leg get into motion. The motion was toward the house. He liked his new cane, but in many ways missed the taller stick he'd used all those weeks. The leg was repairable only by surgery and if it was done immediately. The bone ends had been compacted into one another and fused in their current position.

Slow was his only speed. Laying in a hospital bed, there was no strain on the broken leg. Walking around the church, the town, out to the farm, it became painful. Favoring the other leg was no good, it was still trying to heal from a gunshot wound.

The house was now only a square patch of black dirt inside a crumbled protective wall. What was salvageable, the bathroom fixtures, the tin roof, a metal bed frame, had been taken away. There was no sense in rebuilding it. Pictures, letters, wall hangings didn't survive the inferno and were relegated to the fate of memory. And there was no Joy to live in it with him.

A clean slate to do as he liked, Father Herman told him.

He didn't finish his Hail Marys. The number of them didn't matter, it was something to keep him occupied and his mind off alcohol. Herman left him in the church after the morning Mass to attend to his duties in Danglas and La Paz.

Auntie Annie had attended. The Baby Lady approached Thomas after the service. She touched him on the arm as dozens of others had. The more superstitious people in town saw him as a miracle and touched his arm or cheek in order to rub off some of his karma to themselves.

"You were a lot of work," she said softly. "Emma was in labor a long time. You didn't want to come out." Thomas opened his mouth to apologize about Aris, but Annie placed her hand over it. "This town has been suffering since Ted Wagner and Dina Casao left us. We three were the doctors and nurses for everyone. My daughter and I can't do it alone. This town needs a doctor again."

Her words told him that there was nothing clean on his slate. His parents' expectations remained with him. There were hundreds of others with expectations of him. He then came to the farm to think, seeing his home for the first time since the fire.

Thomas picked up empty beer and gin bottles that littered the area from when Marino's men camped to avoid the military. He launched the bottles, letting them smash into blackened trees. He also found their cigarettes and matches.

Aris haunted him. Auntie Annie let him say nothing. Herman was right. An evil was gone. She understood that. But there needed to be some good from the death. Calamba needed a new generation of healer.

The house wouldn't be rebuilt here. A new one would need to be erected on the other side of the river to be connected to the water system. Something bigger than the old house in order to see patients that wanted to come to him.

Thomas sighed. He'd tolerated enough unreasonable ideas and notions. He wasn't going to rely on Father Herman's.

He was tired from the lack of sleep. The vehicle bridge across the river was further from the house, but closer to the church once he crossed over. The mattress waited for him on the floor.

His nap was interrupted by a ruckus outside the church. Obscenities rang out from several voices. Someone had the nerve to show up in Calamba. The sunlight was blinding, but he saw a ring of people in front of the sari-sari store. A few boys were kicking dust and pebbles at the person standing there. Amelie Valera was yelling at the person in front of her store, calling her a pig, a bitch, a shit. The identity of the person who sparked this much animosity intrigued Thomas.

Sadly, the person near the store wasn't large enough to be Marino.

As Thomas neared, he saw that is was a woman. Her long hair was white with the dust from the road.

The loud boys were Bennie Justo's sons. They were luckier than their father, who didn't escape Calamba in time and found himself in a jail for helping his brother beat up Bill Vandemark.

Amelie and the Justo boys were running out of pebbles and dust, so one of the boys whipped a shiny piece of metal, likely a lighter, at the girl, who was shielding her head with her arms.

The girl screamed. She cursed them. She reared up and caught Amelie across the face with a slap. One of Bennie's boy got kicked her in the shin.

Amelie returned with her broom and reared back for a strike to the woman's head. A whelp of surprise. Then the woman's face was visible. Thomas recognized her as the bank teller from Bangued. Marino's mistress was being beaten in the middle of town by the Justos.

As Bennie's eldest son went to retrieve the lighter for a second toss, Thomas made his presence known by slamming his cane tip onto the road. The sharp echo brought everyone's attention to him. Amelie was in the wind up with her broom and froze.

The only sound in the middle of town was Thomas' cane tapping each of his steps toward the throng of people.

His face hardened and his eyes targeted Amelie. She lowered her gaze and backed away reverently, mumbling *manong, manong.*

Bennie's youngest teenager was backpedaling before Thomas' eyes found him. "Thomas," he said respectfully. "*Pagsasao dagiti.* Sorry, *po.*"

Others in the crowd were beginning to put some distance between themselves and Thomas, some pressed their hands together in a beggar's prayer.

Thomas held the eldest son in his gaze. When the lad didn't make his intentions clear, he lifted the cane off the pavement and held in a manner that would make it a weapon.

"The feud is over. I ended it." No one hearing Thomas' voice had to venture far to understand that he would keep ending the Lapez-Justo feud if someone forced him to do so.

Eyes convey a lot of emotions. Eyes open a soul for viewing. What the eldest son saw in Thomas' eyes made him drop the lighter into a pants pocket.

A friend of the Justo sons, someone Thomas had seen a few times in Pulot, asked why people were backing off of a crippled man. It was three against one.

"He has the spirit of The Botalico. Nothing can stop him," someone hissed at the Pulot boy.

The boy was ready to try his hand when the younger Justo pulled him back by the shirt. Thomas overheard something about Aris going into the boy's ear and his eagerness to fight Thomas evaporated.

Yes, this was the man who did that…

The new police chief Rogelio Timbengan arrived with the resident Army corporal. Mayor Ramirez trotted behind them. The crowd was disbursing back to their places and their Sunday afternoon routine before a command was needed.

Timbengan checked out the bank woman while Thomas made sure Amelie went back inside the sari-sari and Bennie's sons were at a sufficient distance.

"The feud is over."

The cane slid down to his side and tapped the road. Thomas pivoted on it and started his trek toward the church to continue his nap.

"Wait, Thomas, she's cut up," Mayor Ramirez called.

Thomas started to deflect the request to Auntie Annie. Timbengan threw out his rhetorical question that Thomas was the doctor.

Was he kidding? Help this woman who helped Marino steal his money?

He sighed. No, she was a pawn like everyone else.

"Bring her into the church out of the sun," Thomas said. "And someone get me a medical kit."

The resident Army corporal went to fetch one. Timbengan and Ramirez assisted the Bangued woman to her feet. They escorted her a step behind Thomas.

"I don't know how you can walk so fast with your leg like that," Timbengan commented.

The corporal didn't take long. He was beside them in the back row of pews as soon as they deposited the woman. She said her name was Mary May.

The only things wrong with Mary May were abrasions and contusions. Clean out the road dirt. Small bandages.

The chief talked to Mary May while Thomas fitted the white strips. She said she was hunting for Marino. Her house had been seized, her job had been taken away because of her association with Marino.

They told her Marino had disappeared and they'd likely never see him again.

It was plain to see the woman was pregnant. There was another Ricky inside her. Or another Joy.

"I hope you have a boy," Thomas muttered.

She smiled shyly.

Timbengan and Ramirez talked about punishing Bennie's boys for beating up a pregnant woman. Then Thomas told them that most of the cuts had come from Amelie's broom. The bruises were from the rocks and the lighter.

Timbengan said he'd warn them, with the corporal standing beside him, to make sure they understand not to do that again. Ramirez said staying in Doctor Wagner's good graces should improve their behavior.

The bandaging was simple and not time consuming. He was thirsty and felt the bile build in his stomach. He told his hands that he'd chop them off if they started shaking while he tried to finish this simple mending.

"You're very gentle. I don't feel any pain when you're doing that," Mary May said to Thomas. "I have nothing to give you for this."

"No charge."

She said a blessing to him and made the sign of the cross.

Thomas glanced up at Ramirez and Chief Timbengan when he was done. They took Mary May to Paculdar's jeepney so she could return to Bangued. Homeless, jobless, but at least she would be safe there.

In his awkward gait, Thomas made his way down the length of the church to Father Herman's office and the mattress where he would finish his nap. He had no idea what he would eat today, but there was time to think about that when he awoke.

As he passed the altar, he peered at the cross symbol he'd desecrated last night.

He swore Christ was smiling at him now.

CHAPTER 24
DUAPULO KET UPPAT

Three men were unloading sacks of rice from an ox driven carriage, carting them into a short pile near a motor driven mill. The men asked Thomas to grind some rice in Papa Justo's mill for them. The rice flour was needed for the *bibingka* their wives wanted to cook for an upcoming wedding in Sappaac, a hamlet of Calamba in the direction of Danglas. No one was going to complain about Thomas' presence in the mill since he once ran it.

They couldn't pay him in rice flour, so they handed him 40 pesos. That was enough for two pork skewers at the Flora's grill near the jeepney stop. One of Joy's cousins, a little 12 year old girl, had an admiring smile for the town hero. She didn't charge him for the skewers, so being the town hero had a benefit.

Thomas settled on the ground in front of the sari-sari. When Amelie saw him there, her face disappeared from the black metal bars. The Valeras had been heavily chastised. First by Father Herman for giving gin to a recovering alcoholic. Second by Mayor Ramirez for having a skirmish in the middle of town.

The little Flora girl kept smiling at him. Then she would glance toward her grandmother's house near the square. And then back again to Thomas.

Partially obscured by laundry lines was a white car with Air Con decals on the doors. A Manila taxi parked at the Flora house? Of course, Regina's boyfriend was a taxi driver, Jon-Jon had told him that while he was in the hospital.

Then Regina was back in Calamba.

Thomas finished his pork skewers. With practiced ease, he came to his feet through the use of the cane. He shuffled his way toward the Flora girl.

"Is she inside?" Thomas asked.

The girl shook her head and pointed with her lips down another road.

"She's looking for me at the church?"

The girl said yes with her eyebrows. She was one hundred percent Flora, this one, he thought.

Thomas was a few steps down the road when he wished he grabbed some more to eat. Food was trying to take the spot in his stomach once held by alcohol. Maybe it was a sign of recovery that there was a new pang in his stomach.

His soul screamed when he saw her come out of the church. Long straight hair flowed freely instead of being pulled back in a pony tail. A pink blouse instead of a T-shirt. Jeans instead of shorts. Tennis shoes instead of flip-flops.

Regina never wore pink in her life.

It was unmistakably Joy.

Thomas stopped in his tracks to watch her slowly approach. Everything he planned to say and do when – if – he ever saw her again evaporated.

The face was more mature than the last time he'd seen it. As was her frame. She'd grown a more womanly shape. She had hips and breasts. There were other subtle changes to her face that he tried to catalog as she came closer, things that the pictures from Singapore hadn't adequately showed.

Joy walked into him. She'd grown no taller as Thomas was able to fit her under his chin. She gripped the sides of Thomas' shirt and buried her face into his chest. She said nothing for several minutes, merely sobbing violently into the shirt.

Joy relinquished her grip on the shirt. Red eyes peered up into his face. She was cataloging him too. Long hair. Whisker chin. The Ilocano word for handsome silently passed her lips.

The euphoria ended when he saw what was on her ring finger. How quickly the pang in his stomach changed. He felt the bile build in his mouth and heard the scream for gin.

"Hello, Thomas," she said shakily.

"Oh, so you know me now." He made his face stern.

"I couldn't turn around in the airport, you know that. It would have been over before it started."

"Yes, that would have been too bad. I would have missed out on being jailed, being impoverished, being maimed. And everything you had to endure … which was?"

There were lots of faces watching them in the street. "Lets not talk out here." She grabbed a hand and tried to pull him toward the church.

"Dragging me in there again isn't going to do any good."

She tugged hard. It upset his balance and he hopped on his good leg twice before catching himself with the cane. He cursed and told her to stop.

"What happened to your leg? It isn't straight!" Her cataloging of his changes hadn't reached his legs. She knelt to see examine it closer.

"Sorry, *ading*. I didn't mean to disturb you with my deformity. Maybe some day I'll be able to get it fixed in Manila. There are no orthopedic surgeons in Abra."

"Some day?" Joy remained horrified.

"Don't worry, *ading*. It will only take me a few years to save up enough pesos to pay for it. Or maybe I'll keep it. My good looks were starting to put a wedge between me and my friends. Being half-white was making me a heart throb, a sex symbol around here. Now I'm back in the crab bucket with Jon-Jon and Ronaldo. Our trio has a new name now. Fat, Ugly and Crippled, the three amigos. How does that sound to you, *ading?*"

"Keep it? Are you crazy? We need to get you to Manila." Joy was now interested in dragging Thomas in the other direction, toward Bong Bong's taxi. "We need to fix it now."

"We ... *ading?*"

"Stop calling me *ading,*" she said in frustration.

"What am I supposed to call you? *Asawa?*"

Her face twisted back into grief. She closed her eyes and angled to bury her face into his shirt again. This time he held her back.

"Why don't you just say it and then leave."

"Say what?"

"The rehearsed speech that starts with thanks for all of the wonderful childhood memories and ends with you will always be like a brother to me. In the middle there is something about both of us going in different directions. You wanted the adventurous big city American life and I wanted the simple and quiet Philippines life. But, we had a beautiful relationship while it lasted. Am I right? Sure, I am. I still have it. I can still unravel your mind and know what you are going to say before you say it. You don't even need to explain everything that happened because I figured that out a long time ago. There, *ading,* everything is settled. Now you can go back to Chicago."

He smirked and opened his arms for a nice brotherly goodbye hug.

"I'm not going anywhere."

"Sure, I understand. You probably want to say goodbye to your father too before you go. Well, he's not here. He's in Angeles City. He drove his jeep through the mountains to Tuguegarao, turned south and took the road to the south through Isabella until he reached Angeles. Lovelyn Lucero is hiding him there somewhere. That was Lopito's escape route, so Marino probably used the same one."

"I'm not going anywhere."

"Sure you are." Thomas spun around and gestured to the taxi she just crawled out of less than an hour ago. "You're getting out of here. Bill's waiting with your bags. He has the airline tickets. The green passport is in your purse. You made it out of the bucket of crabs, Joy. Be practical. You have a better life in front of you. Go back there. Go back to your job and your house."

"You're coming with me."

"Great idea," Thomas said without feeling. "I can bounce little Vandemark babies on my knee while you both work. So sorry, *ading,* but my passport burned up, so I'll just stay here."

Joy couldn't believe this unemotional man was Thomas.

Thomas never gave up.

He never conceded.

He never lost hope.

"What happened to the boy who couldn't imagine a life without me?"

"I didn't have to imagine it. You forced me to live it."

Joy reached to cup his face. He again stopped her attempt at intimacy.

"I'm not leaving here without you," Joy said forcefully. "I'm not going to let you live in squalor. I'm not going to leave you here crippled, *ayat*. I already did that once. You were an emotional cripple, but I gave you a family and then they abandoned you when I turned my back."

"You can leave, *ading*. You're not turning your back on me this time. At least I finally got the dignity of a goodbye."

"It wasn't supposed to be goodbye, *ayat*."

"Don't call me *ayat*," Thomas was becoming perturbed.

"Can't stomach your own ploy ... *ayat*."

"I'm not your *ayat*."

"You are my *ayat*. You will always be my *ayat*," Joy insisted.

"My days as *ayat* ended the moment you and Bill..." He couldn't say it. He'd seen enough of those imagined moments crawl through his mind at night like worms devouring his sanity.

"You were never supposed to know. You were never supposed to get hurt. Bill was going to be my secret shame, my burden."

Thomas couldn't stand it anymore. The childish squabbling had to come to an end. It was time to really confront the truth. "You picked him over me!"

"Bill was just..."

"I'm not talking about Bill!"

Thomas lifted his cane above his head and brought it down with all his might.

He knew the bottom of it all.

Joy was still. There was a tinge of fear in her. For the first time she was wary of Thomas. This was the man who killed Aris. Now his outburst just smashed a cane into shards. Even so, she prepared to catch him when he toppled.

"You scarified your mortal soul for a piece of candy from your father's pocket, a shiny trinket you thought was praise, meaningless words from his mouth."

"They weren't meaningless to me! I waited my whole life for him to approve of me. I was the stupid one in his house. Ricky screwed up and father didn't touch him, but I had to work twice as hard just to prevent a scolding. He beat me and threatened me and scared me in order to get me on that jet, but the day I called to say I was getting letters from Americans, he said 'good girl.'"

Joy stopped to let that soak through Thomas' rage. She hated having this fight out in the open, but there was no way she could carry Thomas out of the street and away from the slack jaws and uneasy smiles from the people in the square.

"He praised me and it all changed. I thought father was finally proud of me. He finally praised me. With every call … every 'good job' … every 'good girl' … I thought I was getting closer to 'I love you.' I was so jealous of you when we were younger. Ted would play with us in the fields. He rubbed your hair and kissed your head and told you he loved you. Even after all my sacrifices, my father never uttered those words to me."

"Because he never loved you," Thomas replied in a more even voice.

"I had to try! If someone gave you a way to bring your father back to life, tell me that you wouldn't try it. Even if it meant cheating the most important person in your life, tell me you wouldn't try it."

Thomas didn't answer.

"Oh, you're too sweet and innocent? You don't know how to lie and cheat? Not even to get your father back? Or your mother? It isn't worth a few years of hell to be able to see their smiling faces again?"

Joy knew Thomas would figure it out. It had nothing to do with finding her long-dreamed life in America. It had nothing to do with money. Not the air conditioned house.

"I knew what I was doing to you, but I felt that I was finally winning a father. I told myself that you would be mad, you would be hurt, but you would always be there. I could do this and you would still be waiting for me. When it comes to me, you have always been unconditional."

"I guess you were wrong about that too."

Joy whimpered. The color left her face. It was inconceivable.

Thomas tugged hard at his finger until the golden band cleared his knuckle and became free. He held the ring in front of Joy's face. "We made promises to God in there … until death do us part."

He threw the ring down the road. It settled into dirt, a small cloud marking its landing.

"So I died. There was a funeral, a burial and now you're free, Joy. Free of your vows to me. You came here to say goodbye to my grave. Well, I'm dead to you now. Go back to your life in America and forget me."

Thomas gestured back to the car parked in front of her grandmother's house.

Without a can to aid him he, hopped to the side of the road, where people had protective walls that he could use for balance. He felt Joy's hand on his arm. He pushed it away.

"I don't need your help," he said, venomously. "You don't have to help me through bad times anymore. I don't need anyone to take care of me. I can take care of myself."

When Thomas reached the church, he went inside. He didn't even turn his head to see if Joy moved. He didn't see her search the dirt for the ring he'd discarded.

Amelia yelled out of the sari-sari that Joy had better leave. Thomas wasn't going to protect her if Bennie's sons came into town today.

Regina and Bong Bong came out of the Lola Flora's house and removed Joy from the middle of the road.

"I told you so," Regina poked.

Joy was too shaken to battle it out with her too. She sat in the house for a few hours. There was no sign of Thomas. She wanted to race down to the church and crawl inside him, to feel like it was before she left, to feel normal again, to have her worries evaporate as they always did when she was in his embrace. He could never take it when she cried. She plotted to cry him into submission.

Or she could pick a fight with Bennie's sons and he would come running to her rescue – hobbling to her rescue – and she would know that he still cared for her.

No, none of it would work. The last thing she needed to do with Thomas now was assault him with another wild idea. Leaving him money would be insulting. Offering to rebuild his house or buy back his land would be similarly received.

"Thomas is done with you. Come on, Joy, it is time to go. Bong Bong already lost a day's worth of fares by being up here in the province. Having a car isn't cheap."

"I'm coming, Reggie," Joy said reluctantly. "I have a final request."

Regina rolled her eyes.

"Can you ask Bong Bong to stop in Danglas on the way back? I want to talk to Father Herman. My hands are itchy. It's telling me that something is wrong with Thomas."

Itchy hands? Regina cryptically said there was something wrong with Joy.

Joy used the last of her petty cash paying Bong Bong for his trouble of driving her to Abra and then coming home after only a few hours there.

While Joy was back in the province to see Thomas, Bill had moved quarters from St. Luke's Hospital down the street to a hotel across from the American Embassy. The front desk had a key card waiting for her. Bill was asleep when she entered the room. She laid next to him, but didn't sleep. Her mind prevented it. Herman had been very frank. He confirmed all of her suspicions and backed up what Maricar had said weeks ago while she was on her way to Thomas' grave. Was is that long ago already?

Joy was convinced she'd made the right choice. She only had to find the will to follow through with it. During the ride to Manila, she wrote a letter explaining it all. The intended recipient really wouldn't need any further explanation though.

It was bright in the hotel room when she awoke. Darkness outside but all the lights were on. Her nose was assaulted by the smell of *longaniza*, the sweet garlic in it was powerful. Bill was cooking in the room's kitchenette. Scrambled eggs sizzled next to the sausage. Bill pointed toward a mug that must be coffee. Hot water and Nestle instant. There were places for two people to eat set up on a small round table. The furniture was too small for large amount of floor space in the room. The place looked barren.

He looked over from the electric stove. "It is settled then?"

Joy nodded. Before Bill could request details, she got out of the bed and headed for the bathroom. Joy's luggage had come with Bill. It remained packed. Joy slipped in and out of the shower, discarding her dirty clothes in the space opened by the clean ones she adorned.

"Your aunt called here. Your mother and brother are on their way over to talk to you before we leave."

"Reggie called?"

"Yes. She's younger than you, yet she's your aunt. I still can't get used to it."

"Poor Bong Bong," Joy muttered. Judging by the clock, Ricky and Rowena were probably waiting for them when they got to Quezon City. The driver hadn't slept yet. Regina must be special to this man for him to put up with this.

"How long ago?"

"An hour ago."

"Then they'll almost be here. There's barely any traffic. Good. Good timing."

"Yes, good timing. We have some time to kill before going to the airport. Eat ... say goodbye ... go."

The same route as last time. It would be leaving in a few hours. Northwest Airlines 71 from Manila to Osaka to Los Angeles to Chicago.

The breakfast was ready. Bill served two plates.

Joy wasn't hungry. She got air sick, so she wasn't going to eat even if she intended to get on the jet with him.

While Bill was cutting into the sausage, Joy tugged at her wedding ring. It budged some. Twisted, it slid over the knuckle. She heaved in a deep breath.

"Bill, can you put down that food, please, and come here?"

He cast her a sideways glance.

"Please, Bill, this is important and we only have a few moments alone to do this. I'm not going to do this in front of *nanang* and Ricky. Or in a busy airport."

Bill, confused and concerned, rose from the table and circled it to confront her. She placed her wedding ring in his palm. "Someday. Somehow. I'll make this up to you."

His eyes flared and asked her what was happening.

"I'm staying."

"This doesn't make any sense. Dammit, I thought you were coming back with me. I asked you to come back with me. You told me you wanted to come back with me."

Bill fumbled the ring in his hand and held it accusingly in front of Joy's face.

"What really happened in Calamba?"

"What kind of question is that? What do you think happened? Oh, we rolled around naked in the rice fields for a few hours and then had a laugh at your expense. No, we had a fight. A big, soap opera fight in the middle of the road. He was pissed that I sacrificed his love to earn my father's affections. He threw his wedding ring into the dirt and told me he was dead to me. He told me to get my butt on that jet to Chicago and not to worry about him ever again. That's why he didn't tell you everything at the church, he wanted me to have a chance to go back to the States with you."

"See. Even he told you to go back with me. So naturally you decide to stay? What you did to him was far worse than what you did to me so he doesn't want you anymore."

"It was all a show, Bill, can't you see that? He didn't give up on me, he thinks he's sending me to a better life. He's wrong. My purse will be happy in Chicago, but not my heart. It would be so easy to leave with you now."

"Easy? I'm the easy one?"

"Thomas will be the hardest thing I've ever done. I've had a crushed spirit before. I know how much energy he put into me to turn that around," she explained.

Their roles were now reversed. She broke him, she was obligated to fix him. The Thomas she knew would have rebuilt his house, starting the day after the fire. The man she knew never hid from anyone. The Thomas she met yesterday was a man who'd lost his hope and direction.

Thomas collected ghosts. His stillborn siblings never left him. The only way Joel and Josephine would go away was for him to hold them as his own children. His parents would haunt him until he fulfilled their wishes. How many other ghosts had he collected? Lopito and Aris. One he failed to save. One he somehow killed. Joy knew she was Thomas' biggest ghost.

"There will be stories told of me behind my back for the rest of my life. I'm going to hurt someone. I'm going to be heartless to someone. Knowing what has happened to Thomas, answer this. What will be worse? ... what you'll think of me if I stay or what you'll think of me if I go?"

Joy held his gaze. He was starting to come to grips that this was the end of their relationship, that what she was saying was true.

"You were a good husband to me. Under other circumstances, I would have stayed with you and made myself the best wife I could be. With Thomas alive, I cannot with a clean conscience ever be your wife – especially give you a family. I cannot give another man the one thing that Thomas wants the most."

The guilt of it would ruin her and drag him down with her.

There was a knock on the door.

Bill walked into the bathroom to hide his face, his anger, his despair.

Everyone was in the hallway. "Let's go," she said to them when she finally opened the door, shifting her suitcases outside with her.

"Bong Bong, can you put these in the trunk?" Joy gestured to her bags. The short, thin 20-something looped his fingers into the handles and hoisted them down the hallway toward the elevator.

When Billnor Bill's bags became visible, only a door held ajar by Joy's foot, Rowena started making her inquiries.

"You're not going to be able to say goodbye to Bill," she told them.

Ricky still wore the frown that he picked up when Joy told him he couldn't accompany her to see Thomas.

"I don't get to see him either?" Ricky bleated. "This isn't fair. You don't let me do anything. First, I didn't get to go with you to see *manong* Thomas and now I can't go inside and see *manong* Bill."

That's when Rowena started lobbing her accusations. Going to see Thomas was against her better judgment. She wanted to see Bill to smooth things out.

"No, mother, this was my choice."

Joy produced the plain gold ring from her pants pocket and slipped it into position. It fit well since she and Thomas had the same ring size.

Rowena was aghast. "Where did that come from?"

"It is Thomas' wedding ring. He gave me one just like it the day I left for Singapore. We've been married since Auntie Emma died."

Rowena could have suffered a real heart attack and been no less convincing. With Aris guessing correctly, it was hard to believe that it remained such a well-kept secret.

Joy cut off her mother's verbal onslaught before it began. She didn't need to hear it again, certainly not broadcast loud enough for Bill to hear it. The mantra had gone stale. Bill so that we can live, Bill so that we can eat. The man had been through enough, he didn't need his soon-to-be former mother-in-law to pile on about him like he was a walking, talking money tree.

Joy waggled her finger under her mother's nose. "You stood by father no matter what. I need to stand by my husband no matter what."

No matter what happens to you and Ricky, she meant.

"Thomas never stopped being my husband. I think it is time I started being his wife."

As her family walked away from the door, Joy waited for Bill to come out of the bathroom so that she could finish her goodbye. The elevator arrived down the hall and she didn't move. Ricky impatiently called for Joy from within the elevator.

Bill wasn't coming out. He wasn't going to share his face with her.

Joy fished out a letter that she'd written for Bill on the car ride from Calamba to Metro Manila. She put it on the kitchenette counter and left the hotel room. Their relationship was going to end as it had begun, with a letter.

< <> >

Joy knew she found him when she saw a new cane propped up at the entrance of the Hideout.

A noon nap? Just like when they were teenagers. Of course, the simple times, when there was nothing to care about except each other. Joy needed a nap from all the traveling. It was a long arduous bus ride from Manila to Bangued, then a bouncy ride to Calamba on Big Man.

Joy peeked inside. Thomas was lying near the fallen trees on a leaf-woven mat underneath a mosquito net. He stared through the hole in the old church roof at the swaying trees, lost in himself, oblivious to her.

"You are so handsome with that long hair. Like a rock star."

Thomas blinked. His eyes shifted to her.

"My God, look at that face," she said softly. "My earliest memory is of that face. Mouth open, eyes closed, tiny face sleeping in my bed. We were barely walking. I pulled your ear, you woke up, that face crinkled up into a pout and I laughed at you. How many faces have I seen since? I've seen that face proud while walking across the graduation stage. The mischievous face about to push Reggie into the river. The concerned face when your dad was sick. The smiling face when I got you a fishing net for your birthday. And now there's this face," she cracked, "this broken face that I made."

Joy tied her hair into a single ponytail. She worked her way under the netting so that she was positioned above him, straddling his waist and staring down into his eyes. She put her hand on his chin and lifted his sullen head, forcing them to lock eyes. He didn't protest or push her away.

"All that drama and posturing. You didn't fool me." Joy showed him the ring on her finger and mustered a smile. "I found something you dropped yesterday."

"You're only here because I'm pitiful and you feel guilty about it."

"I've done a lot of things to feel guilty, but that's not why I decided to stay."

"There's nothing here for you. Everything you've ever wanted for your life isn't in Calamba."

"Not for you either," Joy retorted.

She was really asking a question, she was searching for the one answer that hadn't been offered yet. Under the circumstances, it was insulting to suggest it, that he had done what she had done.

"Nina?" she asked tentatively.

"I couldn't do it," he admitted in a whisper. "Delusions of stardom. Treated me like a trophy. But she also dangled the chance for everything I ever wanted in front of my nose and I couldn't..."

His eyes drew her inside of him. There were months of anguish still there. Here was a man sewn to her at birth who was being suspended over the cliff by those threads, knowing they wouldn't break and let him fall to his death, yet wishing they would so that the pain would stop.

He was still burning in that fire.

He was still trying to survive starvation in this old church.

He was still calling her name in the airport.

"I'm sorry that I broke you, but I had to grow up. And I had to do that without you. You understand that. You were a better parent to me than my own. Thank you for raising me, for being my example of a good person. Thank you for your unconditional love. There was nothing right in honoring my vows one day and not another, but thank you for letting me have my adventure and forgiving me now that it is done."

One of Thomas' hands started to shake. Joy grabbed it to make it stop. It still twitched in her grasp.

"I meant it. I'm staying. I'm not going to leave you here to kill yourself with alcohol."

For as much as she'd leaned on Thomas in her life, she knew he needed her more. She filled a lot of gaps in his soul. Without her, he was trying to fill the holes with something that would eventually kill him.

"I can unravel your head as easily as you can mine," she boasted. "I'm angry with you about this alcoholism. So I'm changing the rules. You're not drinking in front of me *and* you're not drinking if I'm not around. I find out that you had any *basi* or gin, I'll ... I'll cripple the rest of you and sit you in a corner."

He averted his eyes. His hand still shook. The high emotions were driving a need even now.

"I can out match that stubborn Botalico blood. They didn't call me Shadow for no reason. I can follow you everywhere. I'm good at it," she said, smugly. "I'll even sleep out here if I must."

"What about your husband?" Thomas croaked.

"I'm looking at him."

Joy tapped the ring.

"The promises I made to Bill were witnessed by a faceless official in a government building. The promises I made to you were from my heart, a prayer straight to God ... By the way, I'm still waiting for my dress and my party."

Thomas should be laughing now. He was holding everything back. It was all dammed up inside him.

"I know I'm still in here." She touched his chest over his heart. "I'm never going to go away. First love cuts so deep. It cut us early in our lives. Mother always wished she never put us in the same bassinet. That is when God sewed us together. We can't cut God's string no matter how hard we try. I tested that string. I hacked at it with a bolo until I had my answer."

She stroked his cheek. He was relishing her touch. It had been absent from his everyday for more than a year. He didn't speak, but his mouth trembled like a mute trying to talk.

They were no longer going to be together because they knew nothing else. Each had made a choice. They would be together now by choice.

She lowered herself on top of him and nestled her head onto his chest. Slowly, she drew each of his arms around her.

"God blessed me with Mr. Right. Then he doubly blessed me by giving him to me at the beginning of my life so I could spend it all with him."

For a moment, the feel of him brought her back in time to the hug she'd gotten when she came to the Hideout as a frightened child. The day they ceased to be simply *manong* Thomas and *ading* Joy. The day she had unknowingly bent him into a role that would knock him from the innocence of youth. The time she first tested the weight of God's string.

"It is okay to cry now, Thomas. *Ading* is here. I know it hurts." Her own tears dropped onto his white shirt. She nuzzled her nose into his chest. "I know unconditional hurts so bad."

She felt his squeeze.

"Joy, my joy?"

She braced herself.

"*Ayat.*"

His chest heaved.

And then it came out.

CHAPTER 25
DUAPULO KET LIMA

Thomas supervised the construction of the makeshift camp. Ricky was helping an older woman, a clerk at St. Louis University, assemble the folding tables and chairs. A nurse from the Baguio hospital was dragging clipboards and medical kits out of the back of the white jeep.

The nurse knew the routine. As a condition of his university scholarship, he was required to conduct a daily clinic once a month somewhere in an isolated barangay in the Cordillera region. It was the first time Thomas had set foot in Pingaping in years. He'd been in other parts of Abra with his roaming clinic, Langalinang, Penarubbia, Danglas and La Paz, even a poor section of Bangued.

With the size of Pingaping, the clinic wouldn't last all day, but a few hours at the most.

Ricky didn't normally come, but he would be useful this time. He had long teenaged legs to carry him through the barangay to announce free medical care. Even growing up in Calamba, Ricky never learned Itneg, so Thomas had to tell him the word for doctor to announce.

Thomas donned his white coat and stethoscope. Time to go to work.

People with sick children were the first to venture to the end of town near the *sabong* pit. There were already places for people to sit down to wait.

Ricky brought his basketball, which made him instantly famous. His obsession had made him good, though the dreams of playing professionally would need to be curtailed to the national league.

The first patient was a little boy with a rash, followed by others with jaundice, a broken tooth and arthritis.

The old woman would talk to the people to catalog their concern before Thomas and the nurse attended them.

Thomas thought about continuing his tours even after completing his residency later in the year.

"Doctor, your phone. I heard it beep."

Thomas thanked the nurse. No one bothered him on trips unless it was something important. Four months ago, it was the onset of labor with Josephine. Last month, Joy vented her insanity over Josephine's colic.

He walked to the jeep. It was a text message from Joy: *I have an idea.*

Thomas rolled his eyes, some things never change. He punched in a querying reply.

In the time it took to finish a drink of water, the texted answer returned: *Reggie took Little Jo to QC to see Lola Ro. Empty bedroom tonight.*

Thomas chuckled. "Oh, Joy, my joy."

He returned the message that said he was going back to his patients now.

"Was it something important? Your daughter is fine?"

"Thank you, Josephine is fine," Thomas said, still smiling.

Joy was supposed to be studying for exams, hence the reason grandmother Rowena was caring for Little Jo for a few days.

"You're lucky to have your mother-in-law willing to babysit. I wasn't so lucky," the nurse said.

"It keeps her busy worrying about my daughter instead of worrying about her husband."

"That's right. You told me he was in prison. Why doesn't she just visit him?"

"No one will see him except Ricky." And he left the explanation at that.

The NBI caught up with Marino, and his small fortune, in Angeles City. From that, Thomas was able to get enough of his money back to buy Lopito's house in Baguio. Cousin Grace took her mother along when she got a job in Makati, leaving it available for Thomas to start his family there.

Rowena took over the care of Aunt Rosella when Regina got married to Bong Bong the taxi driver.

"Damn, it's going to rain."

The nurse looked skyward. "How do you know that? No clouds."

"My built in barometer," Thomas replied, tapping the ankle with the metal plate and screws.

His repaired leg had given him fits while in Chicago. Bill Vandemark had insisted that his gratitude—paying for the orthopedic surgeon—be reciprocated by a trip to Chicago to see the Packers play the Bears. A temperature at zero Fahrenheit had been previously inconceivable. Thomas came away from the experience with a renewed appreciation for the human ability to adapt and survive. The shirtless fans were particularly impressive.

As awkward as the trip was in its conception, there was no reunion of former spouses. Joy was unable to accompany Thomas due to the expiration of her immigrant status. Outside of seeing Runilla and Maiza again, she didn't regret staying in the Philippines for Thomas' week overseas.

Near the end of the day, a young woman pushed an aged man down the street. The fact he had a wheelchair placed him in a more elite status than the other Pingaping elders that he had treated. But it wasn't that aspect that made Thomas stare as they approached. It wasn't his wrinkled arms of dark, leathery skin. It wasn't the thinned white hair. What made him stare was the shape of the man's face, the sense of familiarity regarding the countenance.

Thomas thought of his mother.

It was his grandfather in the wheelchair – The Botalico, so named because no one knew his given name.

As a reflex, Thomas scanned the area behind the old man and saw no signs of any aunts or uncles. Abel was dead, but Pedro would have recovered from the broken neck and might still be alive.

Thomas did not have to ask the young woman pushing the wheelchair of the old man's complaint, he heard the deep, rumbling cough as they approached. The woman gave Thomas and the nurse some pleasantries and described the illness. The nurse went through her routine.

"How old is he now?" Thomas asked the young woman, probably a cousin since he noticed family traits in her too.

She pursed her lips. "We don't know. Maybe 90s."

The nurse's notes only confirmed Thomas initial suspicion.

"You have pneumonia," he told his grandfather. Thomas knew his Itneg was getting rusty, but the old man didn't seem to understand.

"He doesn't hear well," the cousin explained.

"He has pneumonia. It is serious. He could die from it. I know that from experience. My mother died of pneumonia. It is important that he take his medicines for it."

The nurse handed him a white box.

"Antibiotics. Six days," Thomas explained to the cousin. "No cough suppressant because I want the phlegm to be loose and come out. Tylenol if there is pain. Lucky, this is only the start, not an advanced case."

The old man watched the boxes pile up in the young woman's hands.

"You are a good boy," the toothless old man said to Thomas. "So young to be a doctor. You must smart."

"*Oh-oh, po.* Yes, sir," Thomas replied, bringing the old man's hand to his forehead in respect.

"And respectful. Smart and nice and a doctor. I wished to see one of my own flesh and blood do that someday."

Thomas signaled Ricky to bring a jug of water and a small sack of rice.

"Oh, I see that you're married," the old man continued his rambling. "Too bad. My granddaughter here isn't married yet."

"*Lolo!*" The young woman turned red faced with embarrassment.

"Eh? What's wrong with you being married to a handsome doctor?"

Ricky returned with the rice and water.

"You need to take your antibiotics," Thomas said in Itneg close to The Botalico's ear. "The church gives me rice to distribute to those who need it.

Take this sack of rice. Eat it. Eat well. Drink this clean water. Medicine and eat healthy and maybe you will live long enough to see a relative become a doctor."

The man nodded and coughed heavily.

Thomas looked back to the young woman. "Make sure he eats even if he doesn't feel like it. He is probably a bull head."

The woman smiled politely, as if to affirm what Thomas suspected.

The cousin wheeled him away. All the kids that had stopped playing while The Botalico was around went back to their noise.

He was the last patient. It was time to tear down.

"Do you know who that old man was?"

"Yes," Thomas said, putting away supplies.

"Hoy, The Botalico. There have been stories about him. Fighting the Japanese and then the Americans and then Marcos."

"And then the Americans again," Thomas muttered.

The nurse's eyes got bigger. "You helped a powerful man, maybe he will return the favor and invite you to eat with him sometime. You're born to this area and speak the mountain language."

"I doubt it." Thomas placed a box in the back of the jeep.

"Come back and check up on him in a week. Introduce yourself," the nurse insisted.

"He's just an old man now. Only stories, no real influence. There's nothing he can do for my life. Let's get back to Baguio. A couple hours on the road ahead of us. Joy will be home from classes and ..." Thomas trailed off and climbed into the driver's seat.

Ricky sat beside him, leaving the two women to endure the cramped back seat.

As Thomas backed the jeep into the road, he looked through the rear view mirror to where The Botalico had gone home.

The nurse turned her head. "Having second thoughts?"

"No. Let me hold onto the thought that he might still have said those nice things to me even if he knew who I really was."

ABOUT THE AUTHOR

Tim Paul has been an award winning newspaper reporter and columnist for two decades. He and his wife, a native of the Philippines, have three sons. He has resided throughout the Midwest and South, occasionally in Asia, but presently in eastern Georgia.